I0676672

Child of Shadows
Volume One in the Shadow God Trilogy
By Kathe Todd

Chapter 1

Morning sunlight came streaming in through the narrow window in their tiny bedroom, and Leila awoke. After blinking once she closed her eyes again, snuggling closer into Mama's embrace, feeling warm and sleepy and safe. This was her favorite part of the day, when it was just her and Mama together and everything seemed to be right with the world.

Soon though, she knew, she would have to get up and be about her chores. After they had eaten the bread, jam, and tea that Momma Droma provided to her girls for breakfast, Leila would be set to doing anything and everything that a six-year-old girl could manage – from emptying chamberpots to helping in the kitchens. Meanwhile Mama, Miriam as she was known to her friends at the House of the Golden Fish and Luci as she was called by her customers, would begin preparing herself for her day's work by primping in front of the mirror in the house's dressing room.

Leila didn't understand why Mama needed to do this. Mama was already the most beautiful woman in the whole wide world, with her long straight golden hair, blue eyes, and creamy skin. That was why the house's patrons had dubbed her Luci, after Lucia: the Goddess of Light and chief of the Seven who were worshipped (under one set of names or another) throughout the known world.

Mama would be busy working, earning their keep at the House of the Golden Fish, from early afternoon until long after Leila had gone to bed. Momma Droma, owner of the house, was a tall and stout woman who was far older than Mama but not what Leila imagined a grandmother should be. Not from the stories Mama had read to her during the time they were able to spend together in the late mornings.

Leila was one of five children at the House of the Golden Fish, and Momma Droma made sure all of her girls knew what a big concession, what a kindness it was for her to let their children live there with them instead of sending them away to a workhouse. She expected the kids to earn their keep of course – just as their mothers did – but the work was not all that hard and there was time for quiet play in the carriage house out behind Momma Droma's establishment in the afternoons. Leila had never known any other life, and she was content. But sometimes Mama seemed so sad.

Chapter 2

Miriam and Leila were shopping in the waterfront marketplace, their arms full of parcels. Her earnings had been excellent this past week, and Droma had given her some extra money and told her to go ahead and buy something nice for herself and the girl. The older woman liked to think of herself as kindly, a surrogate mother to the young women in her employ; but Miriam knew the old harridan had a mind as sharp as an awl and a heart that never seemed to take precedence over it. With what her efforts brought in at the House of the Golden Fish, petting and flattering and bedding the wealthy old fools who made up its clientele, she and Leila should have been living like queens.

Still, this was a treat – a couple of hours away from the house, a stroll along Marsine's colorful and bustling waterfront, lunch at one of the tea rooms located inland a few blocks, and a few little items to brighten their lives. Among other things she had bought a beautiful new comb, carved from the shell of a sea turtle, with teeth far enough spaced that she might be able to get it through her little one's curly raven locks without the usual squirming and complaints.

Now Miriam was searching the stands on the side of the market where used goods were sold, looking for books she could read with her daughter. She had begun teaching Leila to read, wanting her to have as good an education as she had enjoyed before her disgrace. Somehow, she must find a way for Leila to have a better life than what had befallen her.

Marsine was one of the Gaspari Dominion's foremost port cities, drawing a big share of the sea commerce that flourished throughout the Center Sea and the lands bordering it. Even goods from the realms of the Hando, thousands of miles to the east beyond the nearly-impassible Killtop Mountains, reached Marsine after first coming overland through its rival city Miradil.

Miriam found the stall she was looking for, greeting its elderly proprietor with a smile. She had been buying books from him for years now, and he was always happy to see her. As she bent over the titles on display, she felt Leila stiffen at her side.

"Mama!" the girl cried in an undertone, pulling at her skirt, "Look at that man! He has dark skin like me!" This was only the second time since Leila had begun walking that Miriam had taken her to the marketplace, and she must not have remembered the previous visit.

While the people of the sprawling Gaspari Dominion were mostly fair-skinned and light eyed like she was, there were dark-skinned people here aplenty. Sailors, tradesmen, and other travelers from the enormous kingdom of Palambo, which occupied most of the continent's land south of the Center Sea, could be seen here along the waterfront at any season. And the Nima, clannish nomads who roamed throughout the Dominion, were as dusky and dark-haired as her daughter. Quite a few of her fellow "girls" at the House of the Golden Fish had mistaken Leila for Nima, and asked if she had been a foundling.

"Hush!" Miriam hissed, drawing her daughter under an arm. "It's rude to stare!" Leila looked up at her with her enormous, deep green eyes set in a delicately pretty face the color of bur-root tea with cream.

"But Mama! Why do I have dark skin when you and all the ladies at Momma Droma's house are pale? Who was my father?"

She must have been talking to some of the other children, Miriam realized – probably Esme's daughter Dina. The subject of fathers had never been mentioned before, and Miriam had been hoping it would never come up. She hastily paid the vendor for a couple of slim volumes that she and Leila could enjoy together, then hurried her off up the nearest street leading away from the harbor.

In a few blocks they came to a respectable café where unaccompanied ladies or families with children could enjoy a light meal without fear of being accosted by drunks – the place did not serve alcohol. She took a small, private booth near the back and asked the serving girl to bring them an assortment of cold pickled shellfish with crackers and dipping sauce. It was early summer, and the weather was beginning to turn hot despite Marsine's year-round sea breezes.

Leila had remained silent on the walk here, sure that she had said something wrong. Mama had never seemed this upset before, at least not with her. Now as they sat looking at each other across the table, Leila barely tall enough to get her arms up onto the tabletop, Miriam took her hands and smiled into her eyes with love. There was a tinge of regret there, too.

"I'm sorry lovey," she said and squeezed her daughter's hands gently. "You took me by surprise, and I didn't want to talk about that out there in front of everybody."

"About my father, you mean?" Leila asked hesitantly.

Her mother nodded. "What made you ask about that?" she asked.

"Dina and I were talking," Leila explained. "She said her mama told her that her father was one of Momma Droma's customers, and that's where she got her red hair. I didn't even know what a father was! I've never met any men besides old Durgan." Durgan, now in his late forties, was the only male employee of the House of the Golden Fish. He cared for Droma's carriage and horses, performed handyman chores, and stood ready to deal with any customers that became unruly. As the proprietress of one of Marsine's most refined pleasure houses, Droma felt she had a position to uphold. It would not do for her to be seen going about town on foot.

Miriam sighed. "I suppose it is time for you to learn, then. I haven't wanted to talk about it because it's a painful subject for me. First of all, you need to know that everybody had a father. It takes a man and a woman to make a baby, and that baby will take some of its looks from each of them. In your case, I think you got a bigger part of your looks from your father than you did from me. But his hair was curlier than yours, and his eyes were much darker – almost black. He was a very beautiful man." She sighed again.

Leila's deep green eyes were huge, but just then the serving maid arrived with their food and a pot of tea. As soon as she'd left again, dropping the curtain on the booth, Leila gasped, "Who was he? Was he one of your customers? Is he dead?"

Miriam flinched, covering it with a grab for some pickled scallops. She dipped one into a bowl of a fiery red sauce that sent heat soaring up her pink cheeks. Finally, after a deep drink of tea, she spoke again. "Your father was a prince of Palambo, and I loved him more than I had ever loved anyone before you came along. I gave up my whole life for him, and he left me."

Chapter 3

Another year had passed, and Leila was coming to understand some things that she had not realized as a small child. For one thing, she now knew what went on between Droma's "girls" and the men who came to socialize with them nightly. She and her best friend Dina, a few months older, had taken to escaping in the afternoons to run with the other children to be found along the harbor, and these urchins (many of them thieves and beggars, orphaned or cast off as unwanted by their families) had provided the girls with an education that Miriam had never dreamed of.

But Miriam *had* taught her much: reading and writing, how to do sums and more complicated mathematics, the history and geography of the Gaspari Dominion that was their home. She had even learned about other lands, of the strange people and cultures beyond the Killtops in the realms of the Hando, of the myriad dark-skinned peoples who inhabited the hot lands beyond the Center Sea, many of them now united within the kingdom of Palambo.

But why was a woman so beautiful and cultured, so intelligent and well-educated, consigned to a life that was scarcely any better than slavery – entertaining wealthy customers in a brothel? Other than her mother's pained revelation that the man she loved had left her, Leila had never been able to get her to say any more on the subject. It was driving her crazy.

Finally, she approached Dina's mother. Esme was a pretty young woman only a little older than Miriam, and the two of them had little in common beyond their daughters and their lot in life – but they had been fast friends since Miriam had first come to the House of the Golden Fish.

One day in late morning, after the girls had finished with their chores, Leila accompanied Dina to the little room the girl and her mother shared. The "girls" each had a room to themselves, personal quarters where they might keep a few treasures of their own and relax, off-duty. The rooms where they entertained their clients were more opulent by far.

Where Miriam was serious, thoughtful, and haunted by her personal tragedy Esme was happy, carefree, and shallow. She seldom bothered to apply her mind to anything and drifted through life, content enough with her lot. It was better than the life she had come from, at least. Leila judged it might be possible to get her to tell what she knew... assuming Mama had ever told *her* anything.

Leila had begun trying to teach Dina to read, a skill Esme didn't possess but that seemed to Leila to be of immense value. She had fetched one of Mama's many books from their room and handed it over to her friend. "See if you can read this, Dina," she said. "It's a really good story. But try not to move your lips this time, okay?" Dina nodded. Aside from her mop of flaming red hair and the swath of freckles across her nose, she was very much her mother's child and as good-natured as anyone you could hope to meet.

They had brought a basket of clean laundry with them, and Esme had emptied it out onto the bed and was now sorting through the clothes, preparatory to putting them away. It was mostly stockings, underwear, and some of Dina's clothing. The "girls" at the House of the Golden Fish wore fancy outfits of silk and lace while on duty, dresses that were the property of the House and never laundered – only spot cleaned.

Leila stood on the opposite side of the bed and began helping, it being easy enough to tell the difference between Esme's underwear and that of her daughter. "Esme," she said casually, "did my mom ever tell you anything about my father, and how she came here?" An expression of delighted concern came over the young woman's face, and she set down the pair of linen underdrawers she'd been folding.

"Oh, yes!" she exclaimed, eyes widening to indicate what a grand tale it had been. "It was very dramatic, very sad." Leila gave the woman her best big-eyed look.

"Really?" she said innocently. "I'd love to hear the way *you* tell it." Esme colored a little, then smiled. She was not as beautiful as Miriam, but despite now being well past twenty years of age she had a certain innocent charm that made her nearly as popular with the House's clientele.

Caught up in the drama of her tale, Esme began: "Your mother is from one of the wealthiest families in Marsine. Her father Josef made a very big fortune in the shipping business, but he did not marry until late in life. Then when Miriam was a little girl, her poor mother died trying to give birth to a son. He would have been the heir, of course – but the baby died as well. Josef was very unhappy, and he did not marry again."

One of the wealthiest families in Marsine! For a moment Leila's mind drifted, imagining a world in which she had grown up in a respectable family, surrounded by every luxury. It was very hard to do, and she soon returned her attention to Esme's tale. Across the room, Dina had set aside the book and was listening in.

Esme went on, "Josef was very hard hearted, and Miriam grew up in a wealthy home but without love. Then when she was sixteen, she went to a ball thrown by the Count of Marsine – that very fellow who rules this region on behalf of our emperor – may he live forever." Leila blinked. This was beginning to sound like a children's tale. Would a fairy godmother and three ruthless stepsisters be next to make an appearance?

She sensed that Esme had interpreted the story as something of a fairy tale herself. But one in which the princess ends up as a whore, while her daughter grows up half-starved and in bondage to a fat, mercenary madam. The street kids had already relieved her of a lot of her innocence. "Then what happened?" Leila prompted.

"She met a dazzlingly handsome prince, of course!" Esme giggled, before sobering. "He was the third son of King Faraj of Palambo, a boy only a couple of years older than your mother. In Palambo the kings have lots of wives and lots of children. Then when the old king dies the Council of Eight, sort of a panel of priests, picks one of the heirs to be the new king. Anyway, being a prince of Palambo doesn't mean all that much, I guess, and Vandao – that's your father – figured he didn't have much chance of becoming king and he'd better learn a trade. So he came with his uncle to the Dominion on a trading ship, hoping to see some of the world and learn what it was like to be a trader."

Leila pondered this. It sounded like an ideal start to a romance, but there obviously was a catch. "And then?..."

"Josef had the same attitude a lot of people in the Gaspari Dominion have, and he didn't like people from Palambo. Thought they were all devil worshipers, which I wouldn't be surprised considering how dark they all are…" Esme tailed off as she considered her audience. The idea among light-skinned Gasparis that people of a darker hue were tainted by the forbidden worship of Betsalel, the Shadow God whose cult had been utterly destroyed some two hundred years ago by Emperor Fernand IV, was fairly prevalent.

"Sorry, Leila," Esme said. "It's just something people say. Anyway," she went on, happy to get back to the story and assuming no offense had been taken, "Josef was completely opposed to the idea of Vandao courting your mother. The prince had talked to his uncle and tried to open negotiations for a marriage contract, because it was love at first sight for both of them. But Josef forbade her to see him again."

Both girls were gazing at her, riveted, and Esme continued her tale with a great deal of relish. It was the best real-life romance she'd ever heard, even if the ending did kind of suck. "Of course, they would not give up just because Josef opposed their alliance. Miriam had a friend, sort of, who worked as a serving maid at a café where she and her friends from other wealthy families often lunched. She was able to get a message to Vandao, and after that he would go to the café every afternoon to get or leave notes while they plotted to meet."

Esme rolled her eyes happily. "Naturally," she went on, "their love became ever more passionate despite her father's resistance. And eventually, she discovered that she was pregnant. With you," she added, as if this weren't obvious. Leila now knew quite well where babies came from. At the House of the Golden Fish they had certain herbs that were usually effective at preventing that from happening. Her friend Dina was the result of a rare failure of those herbs, and Esme (who had been employed there since the age of fourteen) was grateful to Droma for letting her stay in spite of that mishap.

"So he learned of her pregnancy and ran?" Leila asked, the hurt and resentment plain in her voice. Esme looked troubled.

"It wasn't quite like that," she admitted. "Miriam thought that Josef would change his mind and let them marry, once her pregnancy was revealed. Among the rich folk, such weddings are common. She wrote a note and passed it to her friend at the café, telling Vandao that she had great news and she must talk with him as soon as possible. But he never got the note. He simply disappeared."

Leila was surprised. She had assumed since first learning of her father's betrayal of her mother that he had lied to her about loving her, and just skipped out on his responsibilities. But might there have been more to the story? "Completely gone?" she asked, hardly believing that could be the end of it.

"His uncle disappeared from Marsine too, and their ship weighed anchor and returned to Palambo," Esme explained. "Not long after that the news came to Marsine that King Faraj had died, killed by assassins. I guess that's a pretty common way for one of their kings to die. Miriam thought that Vandao had gone back to Palambo without telling her, to see if he could join the contest to be picked as the next king. But she never knew what had really happened."

"I guess Josef must have been pretty mad when he found out she was expecting a child?" Leila asked diffidently. She had never met this grandfather of hers, but he sounded like a character she would *not* like.

Esme's face broke into a brilliant grin. "Furious!" she crowed. "But your mama informed him that she was going to have you anyway." There were other herbs that might put a stop to a pregnancy, even one well underway. And it was rumored that mages had abilities even beyond what herb wives could achieve. Leila imagined that Josef might have been able to afford their services.

"Did he throw her out right then?" she asked.

"Nope," Esme said with a hint of a smile. "He still didn't have a male heir, see? So he hoped that even though Miriam had disgraced herself and gotten pregnant by a black boy, that he might get a grandson out of it." Leila was perplexed. Surely, people must come up lacking male descendants all the time. It wasn't like you got to pick the sex of your offspring. Why wouldn't he just leave his fortune to Mama? She was his only living child.

"So then I was born..." Leila began.

"Exactly!" Esme said, wrapping up the story. "Josef was completely disgusted. While she was holding her newborn daughter in her arms, he informed her that he was disowning her and she had twenty-four hours to leave the house 'and take that black brat with you' or he would call the constables and have them dragged out. Can you believe it?"

No, Leila could not. What kind of people had she sprung from? A young man who would tell a girl he loved her and then dump her without a word in a quest to further his political ambitions, and an old man so racked with bitterness that he would consign his only child, and his only grandchild, to a life of poverty just because she had disobeyed his orders? Tears stung her eyes, and she shook them away angrily. She vowed then, that if ever she encountered Josef or Vandao, they would rue what they had done to her and her mother.

Chapter 4

Leila awoke later than usual. Winter had come to Marsine, and the light was slow to arrive at their ground floor window. Now she was bigger she usually did not sleep snuggled up with Mama, as she had when she was little; but the warmth and familiarity of another body in the bed was comforting, these foggy nights. It never really got cold this far south (Mama had told her that further north, water froze in the skies and fell as ice crystals, blanketing the land in white!), but the winter nights could be chill and damp.

She rubbed her eyes and rolled over, expecting to see Mama waking up too. If they were too late in the dining room they would miss breakfast, and there would be no other meal until late in the day. Instead, Leila's heart clutched in anxiety as she beheld her mother breathing hoarsely, face unusually pale and covered in red blotches. Her eyes looked sunken.

"Mama, wake up!" she said quietly, shaking her by the shoulder. Miriam moaned, but did not open her eyes. Leila put a hand to her forehead, and found it dry and hot. Her mother was burning up with fever! She jumped out of bed and threw on a robe over her nightgown, then ran barefoot over the cold stones to the dining room at the end of the corridor. There were elegant dining areas upstairs, where gentlemen clients might partake of a meal during the evening if they wished; but the staff, unless they were invited to share in these repasts, ate much simpler fare in a stone-lined room on the ground floor.

Leila skidded to a halt and stood in the doorway, scanning the room. Droma was there enjoying some pastries and tea while several of her "girls," including Esme, were eating bread with jam. Leila ran to the young woman's side. "Esme, something's wrong with Mama!" she cried in anguish. Esme jumped to her feet, her face turning pale, and hurried with the dark little girl from the room. Droma, a frown painted on her face, hastily stuffed the last of the pastry she was eating into her mouth and washed it down with a gulp of tea. Then she rose to her feet and stalked after them.

When she entered the little room, scarcely eight by ten feet, that one her most popular girls shared with her daughter, she was alarmed to see Miriam was seemingly unconscious – her friend holding her hand and trying to get her to awaken. Droma didn't believe in paying good money for the services of a healer. She herself had a good fund of herb knowledge, most of it specific to the trade she'd chosen, and that was very nearly as much as any professional healer had to offer. The Gaspari Dominion was advanced and enlightened by the standards of the day, but no one in their world had any real idea what caused diseases, or how to treat them.

"Get out of the way, girl!" she snapped at Esme, pushing her aside. She pulled down the coverlet and lifted Miriam's nightdress, examining her skin below the waist. Like her face and arms, it was covered with many small red blotches. Letting the nightdress fall down again, she pried open the young woman's mouth. There too, the pustules could be seen forming. And her breath was rank, though her teeth were good.

She stepped hastily away from the bed, a look of anger with a hint of fear on her face. "Who was she with, a week ago?" Droma demanded of Esme. As the two were such close friends, she was most likely to remember.

Esme looked confused. "A... week ago?" she stammered, "Why?"

Droma's face turned red and she spat out, "Because she has the Ascari Pox, that's why! Did she service any Palambans?" Esme shrank away from her, horrified at the diagnosis as much as at the madam's fury.

"There was that one gentleman, I think he was the guest of the ambassador from Andarria, the one I served. They were just here the one night."

"Well, that's something anyhow," Droma sighed. The girl had made her a lot of money over the eight years she had been here, but she'd been reaching the end of her career anyhow. The clients, most of whom were in their forties or older, still liked them young and fresh. Esme was no younger, but she had a sort of innocence about her despite having spent nearly half her life as a whore.

"Can't you give her some herbs, Droma?" Leila asked, worry in her voice.

"No point in it," the madam replied. "There's not much that herbs can do for the Ascari Pox. Only a mage might be able to save her, but they charge a fortune for their services and even if she survives, she'll always be a carrier and pass the disease on to anybody she lies with. Not going to do me much good to have a whore who can't fuck, is it? I run a nice clean establishment."

Leila stared at her, feeling as if she'd been slapped. She'd known for years that Droma was far shrewder and colder than she wanted everyone to think, but how could she just dismiss Mama like that, after acting as if she was a mother to her all these years? Leila had lived at Droma's house her whole life, but she suddenly felt as if she'd been living with a stranger.

As tears flooded her eyes, Droma chucked her under the chin. "There there," she said reassuringly. "Maybe she'll pull through on her own. Some do, you know – that's how that rascal who gave it to her came to be walking around spreading his filthy contagion." Another thought suddenly crossed Leila's mind.

"I.. I've been sleeping with Mama every night," she said sorrowfully. "Am I going to get it, too?"

Droma grinned evilly. "Not unless you've been a lot closer to her than most daughters get to their mothers," she leered. "It doesn't work like that. You have to mix your body fluids. Blood, saliva, you know…" Leila shuddered in revulsion, pulling in on herself.

"I'll stay with Miriam and try to give her some comfort," Esme declared. Droma glared at her. "At least until it's time to go to work," she amended. "Leila, could you bring me some clean cloths and a basin of cool water?"

Leila nodded eagerly and darted from the room. When she returned with the requested items, no one was in their room but Mama and Esme. Esme soaked one of the cloths in water and began sponging Miriam's face and limbs, trying to bring down the fever.

After about an hour Miriam stirred and opened her eyes, looking blearily around the room. Esme got her to take some broth, and she dropped back off into unconsciousness without saying anything intelligible. "Leila, I think you should go and talk with Meister Klingt. See if you can get him to come and look at your mother."

"The mage doctor?" the girl replied. "But how can we afford to pay him?"

The amazingly complex spells involved in performing magic took years of study, and most mages charged a fortune for their services – be it a cure, a love spell, the finding of a lost item, or the sudden and inexplicable death of an enemy. Most could not afford their services at all, but they were universally respected and feared.

Meister Klingt's fondness for the bottle and an unfortunate incident that had ended his post as court mage for the Count of Britburg had led to him, many years before, setting up for business in a tiny shop in one of the unsavory alleys along Marsine's waterfront. His clientele were mostly poor, and his prices therefore quite reasonable by comparison with those of his more respectable peers.

But though Droma's "girls" earned money by the cartload for the House of the Golden Fish, very little of that cash actually filtered down to the girls themselves. They had beautiful clothing, hot baths, room and board, and many luxuries that few working-class women in the Dominion had access to. But other than that, they usually received only a small amount of spending money. This assured that they were not likely to just pick up and leave before Droma wanted them to.

"We'll think of something!" Esme said. She didn't care whether Miriam was able to continue working as a whore or not, she just wanted to save her friend's life. Knowing Droma as she did, she half expected the madam to have Durgan carry the ailing woman out onto the sidewalk and leave here there in order to free up the room for the House's next new recruit. They needed to act fast!

"Run, go talk to him," Esme urged the child. "I have to get ready for work soon, but Dina will be finished with her chores by then and I'll have her take over for me. It's very important that we get her to drink and keep her cool." Buoyed by Esme's seeming to know what to do, Leila gave her a quick, tense smile and hurried into her clothing before dashing away again.

Chapter 5

Leila's feet took wing as she exited via the tradesmen's entrance at the rear of the House of the Golden Fish, out through the gates of the carriage yard, and down the hill toward the waterfront. In the past year or so she'd explored most of the harbor area, drawn by its bustling life and the many things there were to see and experience. And like all the children of this section of Marsine, she knew where Meister Klingt's shop was to be found.

It was little wider than the door, sandwiched in between a tailor shop and a chandlery. There was a narrow, dusty window beside the door, which also had a window in its top half, and a wooden sign was hung out front with the symbol of the Mystic Eye on it. She had passed it in company with Dina and/or some of their street urchin friends on many occasions, and all of them had felt a delightful shudder run through them as they considered what arcane doings must take place inside.

Now, for the first time, she was opening that door and walking into the shop. A little bell mounted on the inside of the door tinkled gaily as she went in, at odds with the feelings of dread that were sweeping through her. A few paces inside the door the way was blocked by a counter that had a gate in it, and beyond that was a small space with wooden shelves lining the walls.

The shelves contained dusty and mysterious items barely discernible in the dim light coming in through the door and window at the front of the shop. Was that a baby in a jar? And what was that mysterious creature, presumably stuffed, that was shaped like a very small man but covered in mangy black fur?

Beyond the counter at the back of the space was another narrow door, this one of solid pine. After waiting a moment, Leila called "Hello? Meister Klingt? Is anybody there?" A muffled voice came from the far side of the closed door at the back.

"Chust a minute, I'm comink!" Leila had been told that the meister had come to Marsine from Britburg, a county of the Dominion far to the north and east of here. Everyone in the Gaspari Dominion of course spoke Gasparto, but different regions had their own accents.

As Leila waited, quivering with anxiety and impatience, she heard footsteps approaching and the door was thrust open. The man who stood there was not what she had expected. She had assumed that mages would be enormously tall, lean and commanding. They were all old, of course, because it took so many years to learn how to cast spells without killing yourself or those around you. But those same spells would of course enable one to live far beyond the lifespans of ordinary men – so though, perhaps, the mage would have a mane of silver-gray hair, his face would be unlined – his eyes alight with power.

That had always been the mental picture she'd formed when she thought about mages, at least. The reality of Meister Klingt was a sharp disappointment. He was taller than Leila, but then nearly everyone she knew was taller than she was. He was shorter, by an inch or two, than Madam Droma and nearly half a foot shorter than the only adult man she had ever known well, the brothel's handyman Durgan.

Meister Klingt certainly did look old, though not as old as some people Leila had seen on the streets of Marsine. His hair, what there was of it, was dark brown streaked with gray. And he was pudgy, a pot belly protruding from his ill-buttoned shirt and chins piling up above his collar. His eyes were puffy and bloodshot, and he was looking at her as if she were a mouse he'd just found in his pantry gnawing on the cheese.

"Yes?" he said, glaring down at her. "Vat do you vant?"

Leila screwed up her courage. "Meister Klingt?" He nodded. "I need your help," she said. "It's my mama, she's one of the girls at the House of the Golden Fish and she's bad sick. Madam Droma says herbs won't save her. You've got to come!"

The old reprobate looked her over with surprise. A whore's daughter, eh? Marsine was a busy port and the ladies of negotiable virtue made good money, most of them. Prostitution was legal (if not respectable) throughout the Dominion. Venereal infections were rampant, and he made a halfway decent living curing them – the more common ones, at least. But most of them were not life-threatening unless left untreated for years.

Leaning over the counter to peer at her more closely, he said "What are her symptoms?" Cute little thing, he thought, touch of the tar brush there. She almost looked like one of the Nima, with that dusky skin and curly black hair. But the Nima had their own culture, and it was unlikely one of their women would turn to whoring. More likely, this child was the offspring of a Gaspari girl and some Palamban customer.

Leila looked back at him, eyes huge in the dim light. "She wouldn't wake up this morning, and she's got red spots all over her body. Madam Droma said it's the Ascari Pox and she's going to die, probably." With that she couldn't contain her tears, and they began running freely down her cheeks as she gazed piteously up at the toad-like magician.

"The Ascari Pox!" he hissed. "That's not so easy a spell, that one." He drew back at little as if afraid she was somehow contagious. "To perform that spell, I'll need a hundred florins. And I need it up front." Leila stared at him in disbelief, tears still welling up in her reddened eyes. A hundred florins? Why not a thousand, or a million?

The most money she had ever seen in her life was no more than a hundred silver shillings. That had been on the occasion when Mama, around lunchtime on a feast day in honor of Deline, the goddess of learning and the cultured arts, had taken Leila with her to the Temple of the Seven and made an offering. The bowl had been heaped with the coins left by previous worshipers.

"Deline is the most important of the Seven to women who want more from life," Miriam had told her daughter. "Without education, without using your mind, you are nothing but a plaything for men to use as they like and toss away. Don't forget that." Leila had taken the message to heart, even if she didn't fully understand it. But that was before she had learned the full story of how she had come to be, and had come to be living in a brothel.

Leila had no idea how she was to obtain one hundred florins, but she was determined to get it if that was what it took to save her mama. She bit her quivering lip, tears drying, and drew herself up to her full height of around four feet. "I'll get your money!" she declared. "Don't go anywhere in the meantime!" With that she turned and ran from the shop, leaving the disheveled mage looking after her with a hint of regret in his bloodshot eyes. He felt a twinge of sadness for her plight, but soon turned it aside and returned through the door to his shabby living quarters in the back. He could really use a drink.

Chapter 6

Leila returned through the back entrance of the House of the Golden Fish breathing hard, and dashed through the kitchen (deserted at this hour, as no midday meal was served to the staff) and down the corridor to the room she had shared with her mother since shortly after she was born.

Dina looked up as she came in, her normally placid and cheerful features a mask of concern. "Leila!" she exclaimed. "Did you talk to Meister Klingt?" Trying to get her breath back after having run all the way from the waterfront, Leila nodded. Her face looked grim.

"How is Mama?" she asked, looking worriedly at her mother lying in the bed. She looked far older than her twenty-four years, her eyes sunken and cheeks pale except for the red blotches.

"I think the fever is down a little," Dina said unsurely. "That's good, right? What did Meister Klingt say?" An expression of fury crossed Leila's dark face.

"He wasn't what I expected," she said. "He was short and fat and looked like he had a hangover." She'd seen her share of hangovers, as the House's girls often encouraged customers to buy large amounts of overpriced spirits by drinking along with them. Madam Droma hadn't yet come up with an herbal remedy for that, at least not one that worked in a hurry. Leila had vowed that she herself would never touch alcohol. Just as she planned never, ever, to have sex.

"But will he come and look at your mama?" Dina asked. She was getting worried. Would she be losing her best friend?

"Not until we pay him a hundred florins," Leila replied bitterly. "Is your mama on the job yet? I need to talk to her."

"She's just getting ready, I think," the red-haired girl replied. "There probably won't be any customers for a while, because it's Luzday."

More than just the structure of the Dominion's organized religion had been changed when Fernand had eradicated the worship of Betsalel. The calendars had changed as well, with eight-day weeks going to seven. Each of the remaining seven deities had their own day, with Lucia, as the first among them, starting the week. This had made the calculation of dates from before Fernand's crusade a nightmare, causing great consternation among modern day historians. But did it matter, really, on what day of the week some historical event hundreds of years ago had happened? Most people gave it no thought.

On Luzday many people rested from their labors, and many families spent the day in devotions – to the Seven in general, and to Lucia in particular. A holy day, one on which most customers of House of the Golden Fish did not make it in for their ration of debauchery until somewhat later in the afternoon or early evening.

"Thanks, Dina!" Leila said, patting her friend's arm as she darted out of the room again. She had not had her breakfast, worry about her mother constricting her stomach so that she had not even noticed the lack. But as midday was sliding past, she was beginning to feel weak from hunger. She was compact, quick, and slightly built – and she did not have a lot of reserves. Before going to the dressing room she sneaked into the kitchen again. Marta, who had been the House's cook for as long as she could remember, was off duty at the moment. She was a devout adherent of Mulia, the goddess of hearth, home, and the womanly arts – so she was probably now at the Temple of the Seven making her devotions.

The pantry was locked, but Leila (who had been in servitude here since she was big enough to be trusted with a knife for chopping vegetables) knew where Marta hid the key. In moments she'd liberated a slightly stale bread roll, sliced it in half and piled it high with slices of cold cooked beef and cheese, then locked the pantry again and returned the key to its hiding place.

Munching the sandwich, feeling the pangs in her stomach subside, Leila continued on her way to the dressing room. The staff usually gathered here around midday, selecting their outfits for the afternoon and evening and applying their makeup – and chattering like a flock of sparrows as they discussed the concerns of their lives, the current crop of customers, and whatever rumors were circulating in the town. Miriam, well-educated and from a wealthy and respected family, had never really fit in with them.

Leila hastily stuffed the last of the sandwich into her mouth as she entered the room, half-choking as she struggled to chew it up and swallow it. Meanwhile her eyes roamed the area, searching for Esme. Ah, there she was – in front of one of the mirrors down near the far end of the room.

There was an overall subdued air this afternoon, for though Miriam had not been close with most of the girls they were all too aware that what had befallen her could have happened to any of them. They had Droma's herbs to protect them from unwanted pregnancies, and most of the infections you might pick up were no big deal. But the Ascari Pox was a killer – and there were no signs to tell that *this* customer might be the one to give it to you.

"Esme!" Leila hissed, gripping the woman by the elbow. Esme downed her cosmetics, giving a last pat to her hair, and swiveled on the stool to look the girl in the eyes.

"Did you find him?" she asked. "Is he coming?"

Leila grimaced, and Esme got the message even before she spoke, saying "He wants a hundred florins. How can we get that kind of money?"

Esme paled, but an expression of determination crossed her face. "Your mama once told me that she had been putting money by, a secret nest egg. She hoped that someday she could get out of the life, and if not that then at least there would be something for you. She was determined that you weren't going to be entertaining customers at the House of the Golden Fish when you grew up."

A thrill of hope ran through Leila at the words. Of *course* she wasn't going to be entertaining customers here, she'd rather die first. But money – there was money? "Will it be enough?" she demanded, clutching Esme's arm. The woman looked flustered.

"I don't know," she said, "Maybe. That was a long time ago, and Miriam has been one of the Madam Droma's highest-earning girls for years. But I don't know where she kept it."

Leila was surprised that she had not been let in on this secret. Maybe Mama thought she was too young, couldn't be trusted with the knowledge. But a lot of good that money was going to do her if she didn't even know it existed, let alone how to lay her hands on it! She gave Esme a look of mute pleading. Fix this, please.

Esme smiled kindly. "I have to get ready for work," she said. "We're supposed to be on display by two in the afternoon no matter what. But go back and help Dina, try to get your mama to drink some more broth. If we can bring down her fever, maybe she'll wake up and tell us where to find the money."

Leila nodded silently, then said "Thanks, Esme!" and dashed off. It seemed as if she had been running the entire day. In the room she'd lived in her whole life she found Dina wringing out a cloth and applying it to Mama's brow. The girl started up as she came in.

"What did Mama say? Can we get the money?" she asked. Leila looked troubled, but determined.

"Maybe we can," she said quietly. "Has my mama said anything while I've been gone?" Dina shook her head slightly.

"Not really," she reported. "Her eyes have opened a couple of times and I got her to drink some more broth. But she only moaned a little."

Leila felt a wave of helplessness sweep over her for a moment. Her world was crashing down around her, and it hadn't even been that great a world to start with. What would she do if Mama died? But no, that couldn't happen. She would find that money, somehow. Where would Mama hide it?

She put her hand on her mother's forehead. It seemed cooler than it had been this morning, but still far too warm. "Keep wringing out the cloths with cold water, Dina," she instructed her friend. "We need to try to get her to wake up and talk to us." Big-eyed, Dina nodded. Though she was somewhat older than Leila, she had always let the slighter, darker girl take the lead.

Meanwhile, Leila began searching the room. There was nothing under the bed but dust bunnies, no hidden compartments in the floorboards that she could see. Aside from the small double bed she'd shared with her mother since infancy, the room contained a single chair, a stand with a washbasin, and a small bookcase filled with the volumes that Miriam had bought over the years. She'd charmed Durgan into building it for her, out of scrap lumber that had been lying out behind the carriage house. There were also some hooks mounted on the walls on which their robes and nightgowns hung during the day.

Evening came, and Miriam had still not regained consciousness. Her fever was up again, face flushing darker, and she was moaning and thrashing around in a fever dream. The broth was long since cooled, and Leila got Dina to help her pull her mother up into a sitting position, then hold her still while they forced a little more of the fluid between her lips. She choked a little at first, swallowing convulsively – then seemed to actively seek more, gulping down the entire remainder of the broth in the tall earthenware mug. After that she lay back against the pillows they'd propped her on, panting, and a while later seemed to subside into something like sleep.

Dina went to the dining room and, after getting something to eat herself, returned with a plate of food for Leila. "I had to sneak this while Marta wasn't looking," she said softly. "She says you can't eat unless you work, and she was really put out that you weren't there to help her with the kitchen chores this morning."

Leila gave her friend a grim smile of thanks, and Dina took over the application of cool cloths while Leila hastily plowed through the food on the plate. "You couldn't get any more broth?" she asked, when she'd finished chewing.

"No," Dina replied. "But there's plenty of water." Like most large houses in this city of frequent gentle rains, the House of the Golden Fish had a cistern on the roof. Water from it was piped to every floor. Leila took the mug down the hall to the downstairs bathroom and filled it from the tap. It was going to be a long night.

Chapter 7

Sometime after two in the morning, the last of the House's clients having departed (an entire night with one of the girls was an item on the menu; but few people, especially on a Luzday, were willing to pay the coin for such a delight) a tired and frazzled Esme changed out of the lacy number she'd been wearing and put on her plain robe. Then she went looking for her daughter.

Dina was not, as she'd half hoped, sleeping in the bed they shared. She made her way hastily to Miriam and Leila's room, just a few doors down the hall, and found both her daughter and Miriam's asleep – flanking the ailing woman on the small bed. It seemed as though Miriam might be truly sleeping, or at least she was quiet for now. And touching her forehead, Esme found that the fever was not raging as fiercely as it had been earlier.

Leila must not have been able to find the money, she guessed, or surely the mage would have been here and Miriam would have been cured, her old smiling self again, by now. Unless maybe the girl had found the money, but it had not been enough. A hundred florins was a princely sum. There were small houses in the poorer quarters of Marsine that could be bought for no more.

Esme felt exhausted, but she didn't want to leave her friend. So she took a seat on the chair at the bedside and slumped down to keep watch. Before long her head was drooping, and she too fell asleep. Dawn was approaching when she was awakened by a load moan, and started up.

Both Leila and Dina were awakened too, as Miriam's fever rose again and seized her in a nightmare. She began thrashing on the bed, body contorted and arms flailing, as she cried out in anguish, "Nooo! Not my daughter! Leila, must tell Leila…" She subsided as Leila got to her feet.

Seeing Esme in the room she cried, "Help me! We need to get her sitting up so she can drink!"

Esme bolted up out of the chair and helped Leila lift her mother into a sitting position, as she continued to moan and thrash. Miriam had always been slighter and more delicate than her robust and cheerful friend, but now it seemed as though the fever had burned the flesh from her bones – as if she weighed no more than a child. Esme's face was pale and set in a mask of concern as she applied a cold towel to Miriam's forehead.

The sick woman's eyes fluttered, but she didn't wake. Rather, she seemed to be caught in some ghastly fever dream wherein she was being pursued by all the demons of hell. Esme tried to wake her, calling "Miri! Wake up, it's me! Esme!" To Leila she added, "Give me that mug!" and took it, trying to get her friend to drink.

Miriam sputtered as the water trickled into her mouth, coughed, and then drank. Her eyes fluttered open, glazed and wandering, as if she was not seeing what was before her. "Esme?" she croaked. "Esme? Where are you?" After Miriam had drained the mug Esme handed it back to Leila and took her friend by the shoulders. She was burning up, hot to the touch even through her winter nightgown.

Miriam closed her eyes again and a relieved smile came across her features. The bones of her skull were visible beneath the taut skin. "Esme, good. You must tell Leila, tell her…"

"About the money, Miri? Where is it? We can save you, if you'll just tell us where you hid the money!"

"Yes, the money…" Miriam sighed. For a moment they thought she had lapsed into unconsciousness again.

The girls and Esme all stared as Miriam stirred again, struggling to finish her thought. "Not for me, I'm dying," she murmured. "Out of the life for good," she added with a wry smile. "But for Leila, tell Leila…" Again the audience was spellbound, praying silently to all of the Seven that she would speak again. Finally she did. "Tell Leila, read *The Life of Dobbin…*" With that Miriam fell back against the pillows, seemingly too exhausted to say more.

Esme, who could not read at all, and Dina, who could read only the little bit that Leila had been able to teach her in the past year or so, looked at Leila questioningly. "The life of Dobbin?" Esme asked. "Leila, do you know what she was talking about?"

Leila's face, grim and haggard for most of the past day, took on an expression of joy. "Yes!" she crowed, and came around the bed to the room's small bookcase. After rummaging among the volumes on the shelves she pulled one out, its worn cloth binding frayed and the title stamped on the spine nearly unreadable. This had been a favorite of hers, one she'd demanded Mama read to her over and over again before she'd become able to read it herself.

It was the story of the trials of a cart horse, raised in happiness and peace on a stud farm in the countryside of Andarria but worn down by time until she had become the rawboned and abused property of a cruel carter – who beat her until she could no longer pull a load and then sold her to a rendering plant. She had been saved by a former owner and put out to pasture for the rest of her days in the same province where she'd lived as a foal.

Four-year-old Leila had been thrilled, outraged at the cruelty of the masters who had abused Dobbin or forsaken her, joyful at the happy ending. That the rendering plant would likely get her corpse anyway after she'd died of old age was not something Miriam had mentioned to her horse-obsessed little daughter. From that time on, they had paid frequent visits to the carriage horses housed behind the House of the Golden Fish, sometimes able to bring them apples from the kitchen.

The carriage, and the horses that pulled it whenever Madam Droma went out, were nothing but status symbols to her. She had not bothered to give the horses names, and never interacted with them. But Durgan had said that it was alright if Leila wanted to call the mare Dobbin. He was a dour fellow, but he seemed to have a soft spot for the lovely Miriam and her dusky but still-cute daughter.

Leila had been moving out of her horsey phase during the past year, and she hadn't had occasion to pull this book from the shelf. Now she seated herself on the room's one chair with the book in her lap and began looking through its pages. Was there a note tucked in there? No sign of one.

The book, like their entire library, had been purchased second hand. On the flyleaf of this one, in a faded hand, was an inscription that might have been fifty years old. It read "To Anna, beloved daughter, Happy 7th Birthday." When Leila was younger and just beginning to read on her own she'd been fascinated by this, imagining that Anna was now an old lady somewhere. Perhaps even living on a farm, with horses!

Now, after flipping through all the pages of the book and finding nothing Leila looked once again at the flyleaf. The old inscription was still there, but it had now been joined by a much newer postscript – in her mother's hand! "Take care of Dobbin, and Dobbin will take care of you," was all it said. No name, no details. Ah, Mama was so smart! Nobody but Leila would have been able to take any meaning from this!

Chapter 8

Lovingly replacing the book on its shelf, Leila told Esme and Dina, "Look after Mama, and please try to get her to drink some more water. I think I know where to look!" With that she dashed off. Marta was in the kitchen getting breakfast ready, but Leila darted past her before she could begin giving her grief for shirking her duties this past day – out the tradesmen's entrance, and into the carriage yard.

Durgan was up and about, forking hay into the small paddock where the horses usually spend their time when they were neither harnessed to the carriage nor resting in their stalls. The stalls needed to be mucked out daily, of course, the manure and dirty straw carried to a compost heap in the far corner of the yard. Marta used the compost as fertilizer for the small kitchen garden she kept.

The old man peered down at the rumpled gamin as she came hurrying up. He'd heard, of course, about the girl's mother. She had been such a lovely thing, and he was saddened. But this was the kind of thing you had to expect if you chose the life of a whore, he figured. Educated girl like that, why couldn't she have gotten a job as a governess or something?

"Good morning, Durgan," Leila said with an attempt at a smile. He nodded, wondering what was going on. She and her mother had often come down to visit with the horses, but never at *this* hour of the morning. "I was wondering," she went on, "if you would like some help with the horses. I could clean out Dobbin's stall, if you like."

He stared at her, perplexed. He'd been cleaning out the horses' stalls every day for years, and he certainly needed no help doing it. But perhaps she was trying to escape her sadness and anxiety over her mother by throwing herself into some useful work? No point in passing up the offer. Perhaps, in the time he saved, he could get Marta to give him a cup of tea and one of those pastries she got in for the madam.

"There's an apron hanging on the wall," he told her, pointing. "Shovel and the wheelbarrow are over in the corner, and you can pitch in some fresh straw after you're done. Give me a hand leading them out, will you?" Durgan took the unnamed gelding's headstall and led him out of the carriage house and over to the paddock, as Leila did the same with Dobbin.

The mare looked a little disappointed, and she murmured "Sorry old girl, no treats today."

Glancing at Leila again, Durgan washed his hands in the paddock's trough and then made his way across the yard toward the back door of the house. He's going to hang out with Marta, Leila thought. Good! Throwing the oversized apron over her clothes, which were already a disaster but at least not covered in horse muck, she brought the wheelbarrow over to Dobbin's stall.

The floor of it was covered with straw, dirtied now after the horse had spent the night standing on it. Leila had a pretty good idea that there was only one place Mama could have hidden her money here where it would not have been discovered by Durgan.

Wielding the broad-bladed shovel, Leila began scraping the fouled straw and manure up off the wooden floor of the stall and dumping it into the wheelbarrow. She was small and wispy-looking, but she had been doing physical work from a young age and she had a wiry strength.

In a few minutes she had scraped the much-abused wooden floor clean, and began scanning it with her eyes. There must be a catch somewhere, a patch of floor that would open to reveal the cache where Mama had been hiding her money! But she could see nothing. She tried tapping the floor all over with the shovel, but it was hollow everywhere. There was a crawl space below, no more than a foot in height.

But it had to be here! Where... Leila began scanning the walls of the stall. They were around four feet in height on three sides, with the back wall being the wall of the building itself. The carriage house boasted two additional stalls, having been set up for a wealthy family with a coach and four at the time the house was built. But those were unoccupied now – full of dusty cast-off tools, old buckets, tack awaiting repair, and similar detritus.

Leila's eye fell on the back wall. As she stood only four feet high herself, a rusty nail in that wall caught her eye more than it would have that of someone taller. Just a nail, hammered in so you could hang a bridle on it, perhaps? But tack was stored elsewhere.

And why, with all of the unblemished wood on the wall, had someone chosen to hammer this nail into the center of a large knot?

Leila had tried using hammers and nails, "helping" Durgan when he was building their bookcase. Knots were much harder than regular wood, and not easy to get a nail into. She walked into the stall and grasped the nail, and the knot pulled right out of the hole as if the nail were its handle.

Which it *was,* she realized! The knothole was at least half again as large as any coin in use throughout the Gaspari Dominion. There was a space perhaps four inches deep between the wooden inner walls of the carriage house and the masonry outer walls – it helped to make the building more weatherproof. Could Mama have been slipping into Dobbin's stall for years, dropping coins into this hole whenever she had a few to spare? It would certainly have helped to strengthen her resolve not to spend the money, for once it was there how was it to be gotten out again?

Elation soared as Leila became convinced that she'd found the solution. Now, if only that entire space was full up with coins! Durgan was still dallying in the kitchen. Neither he nor Marta had ever married that she knew about, and while the idea of the two of them setting up housekeeping together (or worse, doing the deed she and Dina had watched one of the "girls" doing with one of the customers through a hidden peephole a few months ago) was ludicrous, she supposed they might enjoy each other's company.

Leila knew where Durgan kept his tools, and she soon had a pry bar in her hand and was attacking the board the knothole was in with a will. The board ran from the floor up another foot past the knothole, more than four feet in length, and the carriage house had been sturdily built. But it was more than a century old, and the frequently damp climate had begun to warp the boards. Leila was finally able to get the end of the pry bar into a crack, and begin levering it up.

With the shriek of tortured nails the board at last pulled free from the wall, and a shower of coins cascaded down and across the floor of the stall. It's a good thing I cleaned it first, Leila thought, her eyes as big as saucers. That looked like a *lot* of money! But was it enough?

A feed wagon came once a month, delivering bales of hay and straw and also burlap sacks of oats. When the horses were working, usually a few days per week, they got oats with their hay to give them extra energy and keep them in good condition. Durgan stored the emptied sacks in a pile in one of the disused stalls, to be returned to the feed company when the wagon came again. In moments, Leila had seized one of these and began shoveling up the coins, stuffing them into the sack.

When she had gathered every one of the coins, the sack was nearly full and weighed so much she could barely lift it. How was she to carry the money to Meister Klingt? She could not get in through the House's front door to go get help, as it was locked at this hour. But if she went in through the tradesmen's entrance Durgan and Marta would see her, and want to know why she was not out there finishing the job she'd volunteered to do.

The wheelbarrow! Hastily, Leila picked up the barrow and wheeled it out to dump its contents onto the compost heap. Then she wheeled it back, heaved the heavy sack into it, and began pushing it out the gates to the street. Thank the Seven, it was all downhill from there!

Chapter 9

The door was locked. "Meister Klingt! Meister Klingt!" Leila screamed, pounding on it to no avail. She had worked so hard, and as fast as she could – and that old sot was sleeping in? How dare he? In desperation, Leila lifted the heavy sack of coins out of the wheelbarrow and heaved it through the dusty window beside the door. It fell inward under the onslaught, its small panes shattering on the floor inside while its mullions lay broken amidst the debris.

Leila crawled over the sill, careful not to cut herself, and leaving the sack on the floor she vaulted over the counter and began pounding on the inner door. "Meister Klingt!" she shouted, "Wake up! I have your money!" There was a faintly-heard groan on the far side of the door, then the sound of shuffling as the old mage crawled from his bed.

Leila backed off a little, and in about a minute Meister Klingt opened the door, dressed in a nightshirt and a robe and looking far worse even than he had the previous day. "You again?" he said in disbelief, glaring blearily at her. "Do you haff any idea vat time it is?"

She stared at him furiously, all respect for his fearful mage powers swept aside in her desperation. "Time for you to get out of bed and come save my mother!" she said. "I brought your money, a whole sack of it. So let's *go*!" He looked around him, confused.

"How did you get in?" he asked, still refusing to respond to her demands.

"Uh, your window was broken. So I just threw my sack of money inside and then climbed in." It was more or less the truth. The old man stepped forward and peered over the counter. At this time of the morning, little enough light was coming in from outside. He took an oil lamp down off one of the dusty wooden shelves and, with a muttered string of incomprehensible words and a complex hand gesture, caused it to flare into light. Leila's eyes got big, and she backed away from him a little.

"P-p-please," she said, softer now, "my mother is dying. I need you to come and cure her now before it's too late." The old mage sighed. He wasn't a hard-hearted monster, just a pragmatic man

36

struggling to make his way in the world after the brilliant career he'd planned had taken a wrong turn.

"Wait while I put on some clothing," he told the girl, and went back inside. In only another minute or so he returned. In the meantime Leila had climbed back over the counter and gingerly picked up the sack of money, carefully brushing off shards of broken glass, then leaned it up against the wall.

Meister Klingt unlocked the gate in the counter and stepped through, then gazed in dismay at the mess on the floor inside the shop's entryway. "I zink perhaps I may need a bit more than one hundred florins after paying to repair zis vindow," he said with asperity. Gesturing to the sack he said, "Dat's your payment? I'm going to need to count it."

Becoming hysterical with anxiety at the delay, Leila couldn't stand it. "No please," she begged, "there's no time! I brought it here in a wheelbarrow and there are hundreds and hundreds of coins in there – silver, gold, copper, and some jewelry. I'm sure it's enough, but can we please just take it back to the House of the Golden Fish? You can count it there after curing my mama!"

If the woman did indeed have the Ascari Pox, Klingt realized through the pain in his throbbing head, the girl had a point. He opened up the drawstring on the sack and looked inside. It was, as she'd said, full up to the top with coins – and most of them were not coppers. Likely this would be more than enough to cover his fee for the spell, and pay for the repair of his window as well.

He cast a somewhat complicated spell, creating a magical ward that would incline anyone passing by not to notice the missing window. Not that there was a lot to steal in the front of the shop, in any case. The inner door and the gate through the counter were both locked, and he picked up the heavy sack of coins and unlocked the shop's front door.

As the girl had said, there was a wheelbarrow out there. From its smell and appearance, it was regularly employed in the mucking out of stables. Ugh. A wave of nausea passed over him, but Meister Klingt took it in stride. Nausea and headaches were his regular companions, of a morning.

The mage tossed the heavy sack back into the wheelbarrow and locked the door behind him. Money was money, however besmirched. He glanced down at his minute client. "I zuppose you expect *me* to push dis back up the hill?" he asked in wounded tones. She looked up at him with innocent appeal.

"It would certainly help us get back faster than if I push it by myself," she said. "But you could run ahead, if you'd rather."

Running was not something Meister Klingt had done much of, the past forty years. Nor was pushing manure-smeared wheelbarrows, for that matter. But needs must, he supposed. "Dat's all right," he told the girl. "Lead the vay." He knew where the House of the Golden Fish was, generally speaking, but had never been among its clientele.

Chapter 10

Puffing and panting, the elderly and overweight mage and the scrawny, underfed girl between them pushed the heavily laden wheelbarrow up the steep streets leading away from the harbor district. He would as soon have gone to the front door, which was somewhat closer; but Leila led him around the back to the carriage entrance.

They found Durgan in the yard, angrily looking around and calling for her. "Where have you been?" he demanded angrily. "The gelding's stall hasn't even been cleaned out yet… and that's my wheelbarrow! What are you doing with it?" Leila quailed, half hiding behind the portly mage.

"I'm sorry, Durgan, really I am! I promise I'll finish cleaning the stalls, but first we need to see to Mama! This is Meister Klingt, the mage healer!" The old handyman's anger bled away as he recognized the mage. Klingt might not have been much as mages go, but everyone in this part of Marsine knew of him – and who knew what powers he might use on you, if crossed? Besides, Durgan was fond of Miriam and hoped that her life might yet be saved.

"All right Miss Leila, you and the mage go on inside," he told them, his hat in his hands. Meister Klingt found an inner reserve of strength and hefted the heavy, none-too-clean sack full of coins out of the wheelbarrow and carried it with him as the child led him to the House's back door.

Hastening through the kitchen and into the dining room they found that breakfast was now being served. But the group eating their bread and jam seemed subdued, and neither Esme, Dina, nor Madam Droma herself was in evidence. "Hurry!" Leila cried, trying to pull Meister Klingt along by a sleeve as he lugged the sack in both arms and waddled along the hallway behind her.

They arrived at the door to Miriam's room and found a tableau that sent a sharp pain like a knife blow through Leila's heart. Miriam lay flat on the bed, pale and unmoving. Esme sat on the bed, her face a mask of grief with tears running down her cheeks, and Dina – standing on the far side of the room – looked the same. Just inside the door, to one side of the doorway, stood Madam Droma. Her mouth was set in a scowl, a look of fury in her eyes.

The occupants of the room turned to stare at the newcomers, as Leila looked at each of them. "Mama...?" she said, and grief flooded her as she saw the look on Esme's face. Bursting into fresh tears, the woman rose and fell to her knees in front of the girl, hugging her tight.

"I'm so sorry, Leila! So sorry..."

Meister Klingt let the heavy bag down onto the floor with a sigh. One look at the woman in the bed and he knew he was not going to be getting his fee. No spell known to White Magic would bring this one back. His headache, which had begun to fade during their urgent journey, returned in force. He squeezed his eyes shut and pinched the bridge of his nose, wishing he had never gotten up this morning.

Dina had come around the bed, squeezing past Madam Droma, and was now hugging the sobbing Leila from the other side. She and her mother were both crying as well, while the madam continued to look annoyed. She let the mourning go on for another minute, then began trying to break it up.

"Esme, may I have a word with you?" she said, and the young woman rose to her feet wiping a hand across her nose. Her face was red and swollen, her robe sodden from the tears that had fallen on it. Dina and Leila continued to cling together, crying inconsolably.

"I am so sorry, so very sorry really," Madam Droma went on, "that we were not able to save young Miriam. And it was so close! I assume, sir, that you are the mage doctor I've heard about?" This last question shook Meister Klingt out of his misery, and he nodded.

"And what's this?" she asked, nudging the sack of coins with her foot. "Ah, that was to have been my payment for performing the spell to cure the Ascari Pox," the mage said. And added hastily, "and an additional sum for damages to my shop window. I believe that this young girl broke in because of her anxiety about her mother, when I had not yet opened shop."

Madam Droma put a hand on Dina's shoulder, and said curtly "Go clean yourself up girl, and get dressed. I believe you are late for performing your kitchen duties?" Dina stared at her in incomprehension. Miriam had just *died*! And Madam wanted her to go mop the floors? Droma turned her flinty gaze on Esme, and she gathered her wits and shooed her daughter off to do as bidden. Without this job, their little family had nothing.

With a stifled sob, Dina turned and fled. Bereft of her comforters, Leila looked around in confusion. How could the Seven be so cruel? Everything she had gone through, and it was *too late*? Then and there, she vowed that forever more, those useless and faithless deities could do without *her* worship, at least.

Turning back to the matter at hand, Droma dragged the sack over for a closer look. There was a lot of money in there! "Where did you get this money, Leila?" she asked, with a look that suggested she didn't doubt it had been stolen.

"It was Miriam's!" Esme broke in, seeing where this was likely going. "She had been putting money away for years, ever since she got here I think. It was for Leila, for the girl's future."

"Was it, now?" Droma said thoughtfully. "And where did *she* get it, I wonder?" She usually let her girls have only enough cash to fritter away on trifles, keeping them content with their lot. In a few years they'd be used up and turned out, with nothing to show for their years here, and was it her fault if they spent their money on fripperies?

"Perhaps she was stealing money from the purses of the clients as they lay exhausted," Droma mused. "Or perhaps taking in tips that she did not turn over to me?" Esme and Leila looked at her aghast, even Meister Klingt (who was still hoping he might have some small compensation for the morning's efforts) looking at her in growing apprehension. This avaricious old harridan appeared as though she might be unwilling to part with any coin that was not pried from her cold, dead fingers.

Droma pulled herself up to her full height, well above that of anyone else in the room. "Perhaps Leila is indeed entitled to some of this," she said reluctantly, "but I think I had better hold onto it for the time being until an investigation can be made. In the meantime, we have… arrangements… to be made."

She turned to the mage. "You're primarily focused on the healing arts?" she asked. He nodded, as fascinated as if he were watching some loathsome serpent from the darkest jungles of

Palambo in the process of swallowing a pig. "Might you be in the market for that…" she gestured toward the corpse on the bed, "for your anatomical studies?"

Meister Klingt drew back, shuddering slightly. "Common physicians may resort to such things, Madam," he said coldly, "but we mages have no need of such crude methods."

"Well then, I see no reason why you should linger in my establishment," Droma said dismissively. "I have a man who will find a buyer. Certainly there are many such here in Marsine, and there is no need to spend money on a grave."

All in the room stared at her in horror. Leila had never heard of such a thing, the selling of corpses to medical students for study. Esme knew well that this trade went on, but she couldn't believe that the woman she had halfway regarded as a surrogate mother for more than half her life would treat Miriam in this way.

"But my window, Madam…" Klingt reminded her. Droma looked at him with irritation, but then considered that he *was*, after all, a mage. Better not make an enemy of him. She bent to the sack, which was standing open and upright on the floor, and removed a handful of coins. Paper money had not yet come to the Dominion.

She sorted through the coins in her hand and handed some over to the mage. "I believe four shillings ought to be adequate – *more* than adequate," she said with a glare, "to cover any damages to your shop." She handed them over, and he nodded helplessly. It would probably cost no more than half that to replace the window. "Good day to you, then," Droma said. She stood there with her arms crossed, waiting for him to leave.

After Meister Klingt had crept out, shaking his head, Droma returned her attention to Leila. She was staring after the departed mage in a daze, scarcely able to believe everything that had happened during the morning. "Now then, Leila," she said, her voice oozing the false kindness that she employed when she wished to appear motherly, "It is a tragedy that you have lost your mother. And now, how will you live?"

"My money…" Leila said, but Droma pulled the drawstring on the sack and stood as if defending it.

"The House's money, until I have determined otherwise," she said firmly.

Leila's face was bleak. Everything was being taken away from her, and she was only a helpless child! There was nothing she could do. She might as well lie down beside her mother and die, so that Droma could have another corpse to sell! But a wave of resistance rose in her at that thought, and she stood up straighter.

Seeing that the girl had some grit, Droma continued with her planned speech. "You could, of course, continue to live here as you have since you were an infant," she said. "Right here in this room, with your room and board covered…" Leila looked at her in disbelief, with a hint of hope. She had been working for her keep here since she was barely past toddlerhood. Could she keep doing that, stay here with the people that she knew and loved?

"Yes, Momma Droma!" she said, using the term of endearment the madam had urged on her when she was much younger. "I'll work ever so hard! I can help Marta in the kitchen, do the laundry, even help Durgan with mucking out the stables…" Droma smiled, an expression like you might see on a wolf admiring the cute little lambs at play.

"Ah Leila, you are such a good worker. I've always thought that about you." Droma took a step closer and put an arm around the girl. Dark, but she was a beautiful and exotic little thing. They could bill her as one of the Nima, an almost unobtainable rarity.

Leila, her tears drying, looked up at Droma with a shy smile trying to find its way onto her face. "What I have in mind for you Leila," the madam went on, "is something much cleaner, and less strenuous." Leila looked blank, while an expression of horror was growing on the tear-streaked face of Esme. "I was thinking that you could just take your mother's place as one of my girls," Droma said, as casually as if she were suggesting a visit to the greengrocer's.

Esme stood bolt upright, her face white with fury. "She's *eight years old*!" she gasped. Droma gave her a look, and she unconsciously stepped back a pace. "And customers will pay a lot of money for that," the madam said smoothly, "don't you see? Our Leila's maidenhead will go for a fortune! And after that, she will

43

have years in which to cater to the tastes of our customers who think *you*, Esme, are an old hag!"

The barb was duly noted, and Esme withered under the attack. At nearly twenty-five, she had not many years left before she would be seeking employment at a less prestigious house – or worse, out in the alleyways trying to lure less well-heeled customers to some shabby room.

Leila was staring at Madam Droma in shock, but with an edge of disdain. Oh, what had ever made her think for even a moment that the milk of human kindness flowed in this woman's breast? She was despicable, a monster who should be destroyed for the benefit of mankind.

In her young life Leila had already sworn off alcohol, sex; and just recently, worship of the Seven. To this list of personal vows she now added Madam Droma. The woman would die by her hand, though today would not be the day. She drew herself up to her full height, and said "I would rather die than ever work for you another day in my life, Droma. You have no hold on me, and I will be leaving now. Goodbye."

With that Leila turned and went to the bed, where her mama lay so pale and cold. And now, forever free from the burdens that had haunted her life since love – the one thing that had been missing in her life since the death of her own mother – had brought her low. She kissed her mother's brow, now cool, and then turned to Esme. "Thank you for all your help, Esme," she said sadly. "I will always love you."

Tears were running down the young woman's cheeks again, as they had been almost continually since she had woken up today. "We'll help you, Leila, I'll make sure you have some food and some money," she promised.

"You do, and you and that red-haired brat of yours are out on the street with the black girl," Droma snarled. Esme looked at her with consternation. She was not bright, not educated as Miriam had been – and she'd been living here since she was only a few years older than Leila was now.

"It's all right Esme," Leila said. Her tears had dried, and she didn't know whether they would ever be able to fall again. She hugged her, then turned to take her leave.

"Wait," Esme said softly, and pressed something into her hand as if she just wanted to prolong the touch. She bent close as if giving the girl one last hug, and murmured in to her ear, "This is yours now. It was your mother's and she told me to make sure you had it if anything ever happened to her. Your father gave it to her as a token of their love, of his pledge that they would be wed."

Leila hugged her back, and with her hands hanging seemingly empty at her sides she shuffled from the room. As she went down the hallway she thrust the object, a ring from the feel of it, into a pocket of her smock.

Chapter 11

The maid eyed her with suspicion. "And whom may I say is calling?" she asked, far snootier than seemed appropriate for her station.

"His only living descendant, tell him that," Leila replied. Her stomach growled, and she grimaced. She had done what she could, washing her outer garments and her body as much as possible in one of Marsine's public fountains (all of them fed by aqueducts piping water from the River Marse some fifty miles to the north, where the stream ran clear and the water was safe to drink); but she was still a mess.

Without soap, which she could scarcely use in a fountain people where drawing their drinking water, it had been impossible to remove the grime that had accumulated after a week of living mostly outdoors. Leila had connected with Tomas that first morning, one of the harbor-district street urchins with whom she and Dina had played on those golden mornings (what seemed like a lifetime ago) when they'd been freed from their chores and able to do some exploring.

For them it had been just play, for Tomas and his fellow orphans a deadly earnest quest for survival. Now she was one of them, an orphan in fact – even if perhaps her father still lived, somewhere. The boy had been sympathetic to her plight and had welcomed her into his gang.

They slept nights under small fishing boats turned upside down on the gravel beach south of the harbor, and spent their days hunting for whatever they could find that would let them live another day: cast-off "trash fish" that could be toasted on sticks over a fire, unwatched clotheslines that would yield used clothing to be sold for cash, apples fallen from a cart or unwary travelers with purses that could be cut.

After a week of this, Leila had decided that it was time to break down and meet her grandfather for the first time. There was a certain joy and freedom to be found in the life of a penniless orphan, each day you survived another triumph; but it was winter in Marsine. If only Mama had arranged to die in summer, she thought – her resolve never to cry again working well for her so far.

So here she was on the doorstep of the imposing mansion, high up in the hills overlooking the harbor, where Josef Sampson made his home. He had a shipping office near the waterfront, where customers booked passage for themselves or their freight on his dozens of fine ships. But the secretary there had said he was most often to be found at home these days. He was, after all, an old man.

Leila had been waiting at the door for so long that she was nearly ready to give up and go on her way, when the maid appeared again. "Come in please," she said. She did not go so far as to curtsy (an affectation of the upper classes Mama had told Leila about, but not actually shown her how to do), but there was no longer the suggestion that the maid thought Leila might be carrying an infectious disease.

The maid deposited her in a downstairs parlor, an opulent chamber perhaps three times the size of the room at the House of the Golden Fish where Leila had lived the first eight years of her life. It had a rich, deep woolen carpet on the floor and beautiful works of art on the walls, with windows looking out on two sides to the fine houses of other wealthy merchants that filled this area of Marsine.

A magnificently polished wooden table stood along one wall, far grander than anything Leila had ever seen – even in the upstairs areas of the brothel. Madam Droma was quite wealthy, and pretended to be a member of the upper crust; but her tastes were common, and her kind was not welcome in polite society.

"The master will be with you shortly," the maid said, and departed. Leila immediately rose from the comfortable upholstered chair she'd been seated in, and made a beeline for a bowl of fruit sitting on that table. Where on earth had Josef gotten such exotic delicacies at this season? There were some familiar apples and oranges, both grown in the regions a little to the west and north of Marsine; but what were these, long, curving yellow fruits? And these little round, pale orange ones?

Any fussiness Leila might have had about what she ate had gone right out the window when she'd left the only home she had ever known. She began gnawing on an apple immediately, and stuffed her pockets with as much of the other fruit as would fit without showing. On her second day Silvia, one of the other gang members, had shown her how to use scrap cloth to create what amounted to enormous sacks concealed inside her tunic. With these, she could carry off huge amounts of whatever loot was available without being too obvious about it.

She heard footsteps, and was back in her chair in an instant. The half-eaten apple was hastily shoved into a pocket atop the cornucopia of other fruits already residing there. An old man came into the room, and Leila rose to her feet as a gesture of respect. She was here to win the old bastard over, though she'd as soon have spat on him.

He looked to be old indeed, probably in his seventies she judged by the thinning white hair, heavily wrinkled face, and slightly stooped posture. And someone who had known very little joy in his life, if his expression was any indication. He glared at her in the manner of a man seeing something he knew existed but strongly disapproved of.

Leila's courage failed her for a moment, but she swiftly rallied. She was on her own now, and she had nothing but her own skills, her boldness, her refusal to lie down and die to carry her through. "You must be my grandfather," she said, and sketched what she hoped might be a curtsy. She was still wearing the coarse skirt, tunic, and heavy leather shoes that she'd had on the day that she had gone to seek help from Meister Klingt – the day her mother died, and everything she had known up to that point in her life had been taken from her forever.

He stood as if transfixed for a moment, then motioned for her to sit. He took a comfortable chair opposite her, and sat down as if taking an immense load from his feet. "So," he said, after studying her for a while (and noticing that she did not squirm under his gaze). "You're the child. The get of that black 'prince'."

She eyed him coolly, her deep green stare seeming to discomfit him. She was unmistakably Miriam's daughter, though so dark. "So I've been told," Leila said. "By my mother, Miriam, who also told me that you were her father." The old man sighed.

"Yes," he admitted, "that girl was once my daughter. But she betrayed the honor of our family when she gave herself to that perfidious black bastard."

"And you disowned her, your only child?" Leila asked, though she knew the answer.

"Yes, yes, I did," he replied drily. "What, does she seek to return to my favor, and hope that an appealing child will turn aside my anger?" He fixed her with a gimlet gaze.

Leila was horrified to see resemblances between this unrelenting old reprobate and her mama. It was there around the jaw, in the eyes and nose. Though Josef Sampson was not what anyone would call a handsome man, still he had clearly contributed to the beauty that Mama had possessed.

"Not at all," she replied coldly. "She's dead."

The finality of that statement penetrated to Leila's core. She'd told it to herself every day for the past week, and it was beginning to lose a little of its sting. But it still threatened to open the abyss, the pit of despair into which she might fall and be utterly lost.

The effect on Josef was less profound, but still noticeable. He grew still paler for a moment, and his expression became more fixed. "Dead?" he asked. "How?"

"Does it matter?" Leila asked. "When you disowned her you consigned her to a life that was filled with danger. A more forgiving man might have kept his only child safe." She didn't want to tell him, would not reveal, that mama had died of an infection that was one of the many hazards of the life she had chosen for them. Why, indeed, had she not sought a post as a governess?

The old man's shoulders slumped, as if he was only now acknowledging something he had known for years would come. "Well," he said, "she made her bed. And now I suppose she'll be lying in it for all eternity. What is it *you* want, then?"

Josef's callous dismissal of his daughter's demise brought Leila up short for a moment. She had hoped that there might be some rapprochement, or at least some remorse that he had sent his young daughter away and it had resulted in her death. But there was no sign.

She gathered herself. For most of the past week she had been rehearsing this meeting in her mind, running over her lines, imagining what it would be like when she finally met the grandfather who had seemed little short of a monster since she had first learned of him. But he was not a monster, just a tired and crabbed old man trapped by his notions of propriety and unable to accept love. She suspected she had known more love, in her eight years of life, than he had known in all his decades.

"I wanted," Leila finally said, "to meet with you and see who you were. You're my only living relative, and I presume I am also yours. And I thought I had a duty to let you know that your only child was dead." She waited for his response, but it was a long time coming.

Finally he spoke. "Yes, well, thank you for that. There is a little bit of her, and a little bit of her mother in you. And I am glad to see that. But there is no escaping the taint of your father on you. He was a devil-worshipping black Palamban, and though you probably have never even heard of Betsalel you cannot escape the darkness there. I am sorry for what happened, but I have moved on."

Leila looked at him uncertainly. "Moved on?"

"Yes," Josef replied, a self-satisfied smile beginning to suffuse his features, "I am now in negotiations with the Count of Sturia, and shortly I'll be wedding his daughter. I may look old, but I am still a capable man. She will give me sons aplenty before I follow your mother into the afterlife. And I won't have to look to the offspring of black devil-worshipers for heirs."

She stifled a gasp. The old goat! This Count's daughter, if she were fertile, must surely be young enough to be his granddaughter. Leila felt a momentary burst of gratitude that she was *not* highborn, and didn't have to have her destiny controlled by her nonexistent father.

Well, *technically* she was at least half-royal – and perhaps if things had gone differently she would have grown up in a harem with her mother just the first of her father's several wives and her troth already plighted, at age eight, to some boy she'd never met living on the other side of the continent. Maybe life on the streets of Marsine wasn't as bad as all that.

The old man seemed ready to dismiss her, demand that she leave his home. But he hesitated, asking "How are you living now? Does the brothel still provide for you?" Leila stifled the anger that rose up in her at that remark. She truly would rather have died with her mother than to have spent another day under Droma's roof.

"I chose not to live there anymore, so I am living on the streets of Marsine," she told her grandfather. At his look of surprise, she assured him "It's far more common than you might know. You should try spending a little more time in the harbor district, and open your eyes. No one cares if we live or die, but for the most part we get by."

A look almost of guilt passed across Josef's features. With his money, he could easily have funded an orphan's home or at least a soup kitchen that would provide Marsine's homeless children with a meal once a day. That half-eaten apple was the first food that Leila had consumed since midday yesterday.

He got to his feet, reached into a pocket, and came out with a handful of coins. "Here," he said gruffly, "take some money and get yourself a meal. It's the least I can do." Rising as well, Leila looked at the money in his palm and then up into his face.

"You're right," she said, "it *is* the least you can do. No thank you." With that she strode past him and let herself out the front door. Damn, she thought, I wish I could have taken that money. But she didn't want to do anything that would let Josef Sampson feel any less guilty than he already did – already far less than he should have.

Though Vandao's betrayal and Madam Droma's avarice had contributed to her mother's death, it was Josef's attitudes and actions that were the primary cause of Miriam's sad, short life and what it had come to. Yet Leila had been willing to come here, prepared to let him take her to his bosom and provide for her if he'd been so inclined. As she walked down the street, returning down the winding ways to the harbor district, she finished her apple and considered her actions. It was worth a try, she thought. But I'll never go to him again.

Chapter 12

Leila shared her stolen cache of fruit with her fellow gang members. There were six of them in all, with Silvia the eldest at twelve and little Ricard, only six, the youngest. Being invited into their fellowship by eleven-year-old Tomas, the group's leader, had been a great privilege – and without them and their knowledge she might well have died that winter.

Besides stealing and scrounging the gang members sometimes begged, usually on Luzdays when more respectable citizens might be doing their shopping in the harbor district marketplace. Ricard was an appealing child, his wan babyish features earning him sympathy and more than a few coins as he stood there in his rags, hat in hand while his big eyes made a wordless appeal.

But Leila soon found that begging would not work for her. The Gaspari prejudice against the "black devil worshipers" from Palambo meant that her appeals for alms were met with suspicion, or outright hostility. She had tried begging coins from some of the wealthier looking Palambans she'd seen on the waterfront, but soon learned that their culture looked on begging with grave disfavor. She was able-bodied, why did she not work for a living? They would be happy to give her a job scrubbing decks, but she declined.

Instead, from early in her time with Tomas' gang, Leila began perfecting her skills as a thief. Tomas himself taught her to pick pockets and cut purses, and even gave her one of his daggers. The boy's dark brown eyes and curly hair suggested that he, too, might have a little Palamban ancestry – though his skin was only a light tan and paler still in winter. Perhaps he felt she was akin to him, somehow, for he mentored her and helped her whenever he could.

It was at Leila's suggestion that the gang began targeting customers at the House of the Golden Fish. Some of the House's wealthy patrons arrived alone and departed, hours later, well into their cups. Leila recognized a few of them from her time as a resident there, though she knew none of their names or what they did for a living that made them so wealthy. And some, she knew from talking to Droma's girls, were mean bastards.

At one in the morning on a Belanday, a work night, Leila was hidden near the House's front entrance in among the shrubbery that grew on the east side of the front steps. Twin lampposts fronted the establishment, each of them with a collar of red glass encircling the flame at the bottom to indicate that this was a pleasure house. The top parts of the lamps were clear, casting enough white light that tipsy customers might descend the steps in safety.

A pair of customers exited the house arm in arm, and made their way down the steps before turning to the left. Then, happily bellowing the lyrics to "The Carter's Daughter" in no particular tune, they staggered off down the street. Leila remained hidden. Another came out, this one alone – but he seemed to be relatively young and vigorous, was armed with a cane that she knew to be a swordstick, and did not seem to be particularly the worse for drink.

He passed unmolested as well. Then another lone customer emerged, humming a tune and negotiating the stairs with some difficulty. Luckily for him, there were handrails on either side. On the walk at the bottom of the steps he paused, weaving, and looked about him muzzily for a moment before recalling in which direction his home lay. Then he set off walking.

Leila darted from her hiding place and followed him, stopping when she got to the circle of light cast by the right side lamppost. She pulled a mirror from her pocket to signal Tomas, lurking in the shadows near the mouth of an alleyway in the street ahead. Two flashes, for right. He and the rest of the gang moved off down the alleyway, running to intercept the mark as he staggered along.

As soon as Leila's signal had been acknowledged she turned and followed the customer, a portly man in his fifties, running silently behind him. Her head and shoulders were swathed in a black scarf stolen from a market stall, hiding her hair and most of her face as well.

Her sharp eyes picked out movement at the next intersection. The rest of the gang had run down the alleys and were now in place ahead of them. Closing the gap, Leila spoke just loudly enough for their target to hear, "Sir! Oh please, kind sir!" He halted his progress, swaying slightly, and turned to see who had spoken to him. He was surprised to see a little figure covered from head to foot in dark cloth.

"Wha… whatta you want?" he asked. Though not at his best at this moment, he was a respected man in Marsine, and was not used to being addressed by strange persons in the wee hours of the morning.

"I am so hungry," Leila said, her words muffled by the scarf. They meant for him to be unable to identify any of his assailants, when the police were called. She suspected, though, that many of their victims never reported the assaults.

"Can you please spare a coin?" Leila asked piteously, moving closer. The man stared at her in disbelief. Accosted by a begging street urchin, at this hour? Weren't they all supposed to be asleep in the gutter by now, or wherever it was they went?

"I don't think so," he said coldly. "Go away."

Before he could turn again to continue on his way Leila threw herself at his feet, wrapping her arms around his lower legs. "Oh *please* sir! I'm so hungry!" Flummoxed, the drunk struggled vainly – trying to extricate himself from her grasp. At this juncture Tomas and three other members of the gang (little Ricard, judged too small for this action, was standing lookout) leaped on the man's back and he toppled over onto his face, tripping over Leila.

She squirmed out from under his lower legs at once, avoiding a kick, and as the other three sat on him to hold him down Leila began quickly and expertly going through his clothing. In moments she'd relieved him of a goodly handful of change, a gold watch, a diamond stick-pin, and a pinky ring with a large red stone in it. Then she cut through his belt at the back of his pants, slicing down far enough that she could pull them down while he remained face down on the stone pavement of the street. With his pants around his ankles, he would be slow to arise.

"Done?" Tomas hissed, and Leila replied "Done!" Then all six gang members, Ricard leading them, dashed to the nearby alley mouth and began running at full speed through the maze of streets – soon lost to sight. Their victim lay struggling face down on the filthy cobbles for another moment before managing to get to his feet. He reached for his ruined pants to pull them up, but found he must clutch them with both hands to keep them from falling down around

his ankles again. He looked around dazedly, but of his assailants
there was no sign.

Chapter 13

Summer had passed, and it had been one of the happiest times of Leila's life. She was nine now, and not since she'd been too young to understand what her circumstances truly were had she enjoyed such a carefree existence. In Marsine's warm climate they had not suffered from cold or exposure, and food had been plentiful.

So much produce came into the markets of Marsine from the surrounding countryside that shopkeepers would toss away the less perfect fruits and vegetables, those with a moldy spot (that could easily be cut out) or those too deformed by insect depredations to be appealing to paying customers. Tomas' gang ate well, and they all thrived.

They'd continued rolling customers at Madam Droma's a night or two per week, until the activity began to hurt business at the House of the Golden Fish and Madam had hired a guard to stand watch outside the place. Durgan was getting too old for such work, and Leila could only take satisfaction at the thought of how pained Droma must have been to spend money to hire the guard.

In the meantime, they'd acquired a lot of money and had spent it on some things that were less easy to steal – like good shoes and clothing that fit them, and some bedrolls that would make sleeping out more comfortable when cold weather came along again.

Sleeping out under boats on the beach as they had been doing, they had had to carry all their worldly possessions with them wherever they went or leave gang members behind on guard. But on one nighttime prowl through the harbor district in late spring, Tomas and Leila had discovered a top-floor window ajar in one of the many warehouses where goods from all over the world were stored awaiting buyers.

An adult could probably not have reached it; but for an agile, underfed child like Leila it was no problem at all. She went up a drainpipe until she was above the window, which was hinged at the top, and pulled out the bottom edge until there was an opening big enough to pass her body. Then she slipped over the sill and inside, moving as silently as possible.

Moments later, her feet on the dusty wooden floor, she jumped up and grasped the bottom sill to peer down at Tomas where he stood on the street below. He knew she was better at this sort of thing than he was, and it hadn't taken much argument for her to convince him to let her be the one to make the climb. "It's completely deserted!" she called down softly to him, "There's cobwebs everywhere. I don't think this place is in use – come on up!"

At nearly twelve Tomas was beginning to grow faster, helped along by the better rations the gang had enjoyed since Leila had come on board. But with the extra size and weight had come more muscle, and he had no trouble swarming up the drainpipe and in through the now fully-opened window. He pulled it closed behind him.

The number of streetlamps in the harbor district was far smaller than could be found in the more prestigious residential districts on the slopes above. The Count of Marsine believed in public works, and much of the city slept each night under the soft glow of oil lamps on tall bronze stanchions (lit as dusk approached by a cadre of lamplighters).

But the extent of these public works was limited by the funds provided by the people they served – and the warehouse owners along the docks mostly preferred to spend their money on guards and night watchmen, frequently accompanied by dogs.

No watchman patrolled here, however. The top floor of the warehouse was ringed with windows like the one they had come in by, and a dim illumination came through them though the floor of the space was well above the height of the tallest streetlamp.

Though it was clear no one was here, Leila and Tomas spoke in hushed tones. He looked around, his sharp eyes taking in the nearly empty room and assessing it. "It looks like nobody's been here for years!" he said. The room was festooned with cobwebs and heavy with dust. "Did you check the door?"

Leila gestured toward the far end of the room. "There isn't a regular door, just a trap door in the floor. I think this must be the attic, maybe, like extra storage that's not needed very often." The two of them walked very quietly down the length of the room to the far wall (those guards and dogs, for all they knew, might be right beneath their feet), and examined a trap door some four feet by six feet that was set into the floor near it. Above them in the dim light, they could just see a pulley attached to the ceiling, ropes from it trailing off to a cleat on the wall.

"I think you're right, Leila," Tomas murmured. He had liked the child from their first meeting, a bright little spark despite her dark coloring. When she'd showed up submerged in grief, fresh from the tragedy of her mother's death, he'd leapt at the chance to include her in his gang. And he hadn't been wrong. As young as she was, Leila was an asset.

Without any discussion, both of them dropped to the floor and put their ears to the trap door, listening for any sounds coming from below. They stayed thus, motionless and without any talking, for more than ten minutes. Then Leila whispered, "Nobody down there. Shall we try the door?" This empty space held potential, but both of them would be much more interested in the opportunity to drop down from it and raid an unattended warehouse full of goods.

Tomas considered, then decided to go for it. "Okay," he said, rising to his feet. The door was hinged near the wall, with a large U-shaped metal handle mounted on the side opposite. On the wall where the pulley ropes were attached to the cleat, they could see a couple of hooks that were apparently designed to hold the trap door in its open position when cargo was to be lifted up. He and Leila walked over to stand on the floor on the side of the trap door where the handle was, and he heaved on it with all his might.

A wooden door as thick as a floor designed to hold tons of palleted cargo, and four by six feet in size, would be heavy. Tomas wasn't sure whether he would be able to lift it. He did manage to get it to budge slightly, but then all his tugging failed to move it any further.

"Too heavy?" Leila asked. Tomas nodded unsurely. Could it be barred from the other side? "Let's use the ropes!" his companion suggested, and he slapped his forehead. Of course, that would work – though clearly this trap door had been designed to be opened from below. He wondered what system they had in place down there – a lift of some kind?

The cleat was too high for Leila to reach, but Tomas had soon gotten the rope ends down and tied one end to the trap door's handle. Then he and Leila tugged on the other. The door rose smoothly, less than half an inch – and then stopped. No matter how they pulled, it would rise no higher.

"It has to be barred from below," Tomas pronounced. "And nobody has been up here for a really long time, I think." They untied the ropes and Tomas put them back onto the cleat. Now that the possibility of getting into the lower floors of the warehouse and stealing its contents had been ruled out, they needed to consider what other benefits this find might offer them.

Leila knew what she wanted from it. "This place could be a shelter for us!" she exclaimed. "We could sleep here when the weather's bad, and stash our stuff here so we don't have to carry it around with us always!" Tomas nodded, liking the idea.

The gang's numbers had dropped from six to five and he was now the oldest member, as Silvia had abandoned them for a chance at a job as a kitchen maid in one of the houses up the hill. The remaining gang members should all have no trouble climbing up the drainpipe and in through the window, though clearly that was something that could only be done at night.

"What if they get in extra cargo and decide to open up the door and store it up here?" Tomas pointed out. Leila looked around the room. Other than cobwebs and dust it was *not* completely empty. There were a few crates scattered here and there, broken for the most part. What was in them?

The two of them went around the room exploring. The crates contained an assortment of what looked like junk: broken crockery, wooden boxes of nails that had probably been invaded by seawater judging from the rusted mess to be found within – it all looked as though it might be sea cargo that had been the subject of some long-forgotten insurance claim.

They were now pretty sure that nobody was wandering the floor below. If there had been anyone, they would surely have noticed their attempts to open the trap door. So they began pushing the crates across the floor, manhandling them into position atop the door. "Put them near the handle," Leila told Tomas. Mama had explained leverage to her. "It'll make it harder to move."

Soon all of the accumulated junk in the room was weighing down the trap door. If as Tomas had assumed they had some fancy mechanical device down there to push it open, the extra weight might not delay opening the door by much. But the noise of such an attempt might buy the gang the time they needed to gather their possessions and flee out the window.

The gang took to their new quarters with glee. There were drawbacks, of course. You had to keep a sharp eye out for passersby before climbing up. Tomas had rigged the window, the latch of which had broken off, so that you could close it all the way with only a small piece of twine protruding. Pull the twine, and it came right open so you could climb in.

Plus of course they could not light any candles while they were in there – such lights might be seen from the street, if anybody was watching. But at least, over the course of weeks, they gradually added more weight to the top of the trap door. Loose cobbles stolen from the street, an entire pile of broken bricks left sitting after a burnt-down house had been demolished… Slowly, the weight atop the trap door increased until it was questionable whether it would really be possible to open it again from below.

When it rained, and rain was frequent in Marsine winter or summer, the kids had a dry place to lay their heads. And the more valuable or useful items they acquired in their daily foraging expeditions ("foraging" in this case also including stealing, of course) could be safely stored there. Life was good!

Chapter 14

Leila watched silently from hiding as the carriage pulled away from the curb. As she'd read in the society section of a newspaper scooped from a stack destined as fish wrappers, tonight's charity ball in aid of the Marsine Ladies' Society for the Preservation of Art was starting soon. And as she'd assumed, the Beauvoir family – father, mother, and marriageable daughter – would be in attendance.

Darkness had already descended, though it was no more than six in the evening. In the family's absence, Leila expected, the servants would be relaxing in the kitchen – perhaps opening a bottle from the wine cellar for a little celebration. She knew what it was like to be on the back side of the glittering wall society's wealthy erected to make themselves feel as though the world was a perfect place.

She was dressed in her darkest clothing, skirts hanging down over long knit underwear and a scarf tied around her head and shoulders. At her waist hung a sack, and she had a dagger in her belt. Another rode in a makeshift scabbard along her left calf, below the knee.

All was dark on the floor above, and Leila approached the house and began her climb. The skirt was an annoyance, but she had learned to work with it. She had never worn anything but skirts her entire life. The massive mansion was three full storeys, and she'd been studying it for more than a week.

At the ball tonight Madam Beauvoir would surely be wearing her famous sapphire necklace, known throughout the southern reaches of the Dominion; but she had dozens of other pieces nearly as valuable, and Leila meant to obtain some of them. She was getting tired of petty thievery, her restless intellect demanding a greater challenge. And now she had found it.

Leila climbed the drainpipe that ran from the roof to the ground at the northeast corner of the building, then began moving laterally. The architecture of the Beauvoir mansion was boxy, a style that had been popular a generation ago (in fact it had been built by M. Beauvoir's father after he'd made a fortune developing a new metal alloy that was as strong as steel but never rusted). There were windows galore, with protruding stone sills on each of them, and it was no problem for someone as light and agile as she was to work her way across from window to window.

She knew which window gave on Madam Beauvoir's personal dressing room, where (as far as Leila had been able to learn) she kept her jewelry. The treasure was said to be locked up in a chest of cunning manufacture, with a lock that was impenetrable to even the cleverest of thieves.

Leila had been practicing with lockpicks for several months now, and she was getting good enough at it that most ordinary locks fell to her ministrations in no more than a few minutes. But she was not relying on her skills in lockpicking for this mission – she'd brought along some cruder instruments that she expected would have the chest open even faster.

Ah, this was the window. Leila scanned back to her left through the darkness and counted the sills to make sure. This would be her first challenge, but she didn't think it would be much of a problem. With the household staff gathered below getting jolly with the spirits, she should simply be able to break the glass with the small hammer she'd brought along, then pop the latch.

Except, the latch was already open. Had Madam Beauvoir had the window open earlier for some reason, and forgotten to latch it? As it was the middle of winter, this didn't seem feasible. But Leila could think of no other explanation. The glass was intact. Clinging to the window sill, the toes of her boots pressed into the spaces between bricks in the masonry wall below, Leila pulled the casement window open and crawled inside.

After putting her feet quietly on the floor, Leila stood there silently catching her breath, all senses alert. To her right was Madam Beauvoir's dressing table, an affair of carved wood painted white with gold-leaf accents and a mirror far larger, and far fancier, than any the dressing room at the House of the Golden Fish had to boast.

Light from the streetlights outside was caught by that mirror, giving a little light to the room. The glass surface of the dressing table was cluttered with pots of cosmetics and delicate cut-crystal bottles of perfume, which Leila favored with a bemused glance. She supposed it was possible some of those perfumes were worth more than some of the jewelry; but she hadn't learned enough yet about these things and didn't want to burden herself with a bunch of smelly stuff.

Further in, the narrow room was dark. This entire room was just an adjunct to Madam Beauvoir's bedroom, after all –sort of an enormous walk-in closet. At the far end was storage space for her many gowns, cedar chests for woolen items and lingerie. And over to the left, that notorious jewelry chest.

Leila froze as she heard a sound coming from the far end of the room. In addition to the door on the side, that led to the bedroom, there was a door opening on the hall so that the maids could come and go, bringing in clothing that had been cleaned and replacing supplies on the dressing table. Might one of the staff be skipping the party, and about the work for which she was paid?

But no, the door at the far end remained closed. There it was again, a sort of "tink" noise. Not coming from the area of the door, but over to the left. Where the jewelry chest sat on its four carven legs. Leila's heart froze, and her eyes got wide as she strained to make out what she was seeing. Was there a dark shape there, breaking into the chest… just as she had intended to do?

The Seven curse it, there was! Damn him to all the available hells in the afterlife, what did this oaf of a man think he was doing, after she had spent more than a week casing this job? He must be twice her size, but Leila's fury drove her beyond sense.

Pulling a dagger, she approached on silent feet as the figure (surely a man, by his size) carefully worked at the chest standing in the far left corner of the room. Leila felt a frisson of pleasure as she realized he had not become aware of her, not even when she had come in through the window. Her stealthiness was supreme!

She thrust the point of the razor-sharp dagger forward, just enough to barely pierce the skin but not enough to provoke an involuntary reaction that might knock her to the floor. "Hold it right there, or I'll run this dagger into your kidney," Leila murmured as gruffly as possible. The man flinched a little, then stiffened into immobility.

He was clad head to toe in close-fitting clothing, not black but a deep gray. In a city, at least, there was always so much ambient light that black would stand out. The man remained stiffened, and she could sense his shock. He had been utterly confident that he was alone, free to work his will with the famous jewelry chest without fear of interruption. Leila could scent his fear.

"You've got me," he said, in a young-sounding voice. Likely this sneak thief was no more than a few years older than herself. He made as if to turn, and Leila pushed the knife in another quarter of an inch.

"I told you to stay still!" she croaked, trying to make her voice sound deeper. It was beginning to occur to her that she'd been insane to try to handle this person twice her size, all by herself. The man froze into immobility once more, and Leila could almost hear his mind ticking over. Who was it that had somehow crept into the room without his noticing? They could not have come from either of the room's two doors, or he would have seen. So they must have come in the window, and that meant...

Before Leila could react, the man had whirled in place and seized her wrist, the knife wrenched to the side before she could thrust it anywhere useful. Damn! Not for the first time, she cursed the fact that her powerful mind was residing in the frail body of an undernourished nine-year-old girl.

Her fellow thief had barely managed to find her in the darkness. He'd been expecting a larger opponent. He dug his fingers into her wrist, and her own fingers went limp. The dagger clattered to the floor. Before she could consider reaching beneath her skirt for the backup weapon strapped to her lower leg, he ran his free hand down her body from her head to the floor and found it – taking it out of its scabbard and pointing it at her.

"What have we here?" the young man said, amusement replacing the terror that had gripped him but moments before. "A little girl?" Leila glared up at him, shaking with fury. And perhaps a bit of terror, as well. This was apparently a professional thief, a member of Marsine's criminal classes. The fact that she and her fellow gang members robbed and stole all the time didn't really register with her in that regard. They were just penniless orphans, trying to survive. Would he simply dispatch her with her own dagger, then complete his interrupted burglary before stealing off into the night with Madame Beauvoir's jewels?

But now that he no longer feared imminent harm to his kidney, this burglar didn't seem to be all that hostile. "What's your name, little one?" he asked. His air of profound amusement infuriated Leila. Dark of appearance and keeping mostly to the shadows, she had come to identify with them. And Mama had taught her a two-florin word that meant the same thing.

"I'm called Penumbra," she said hoarsely.

"Penumbra!" her antagonist laughed quietly. "Good one. What are you doing here?" Sensing that he didn't plan to run her through, Leila felt her confidence returning.

"The same thing you are," she said. "But apparently you didn't bother to wait until the Beauvoirs left for the ball. When did you get in?" She thought she had been watching continually since before it got dark. How had he managed to sneak inside?

"Oh," he said, revealing his youth again with his casual air of braggadocio, "I've been here all day."

"But..." Leila began.

"But Madam Beauvoir was in here not half an hour ago, getting ready for the ball?" he asked. Leila glared up at him in the dimness. There was little enough to see, just a tall shape swathed in dark clothing with a slight reflection off the eyes.

Leila's adversary chuckled softly, though he still held the dagger pointed at her face. "I came with a message at the back door," he said casually, "and told the cook I'd be leaving by the front after delivering it. She thought I was bringing a message to Madam B. from her lover, but once I was upstairs I let myself into one of the unused bedrooms. Can you believe these people have a dozen bedrooms, though there are but three of them living here?"

Leila gaped at him in the darkness. Clearly, there was more to be known about people like the Beauvoirs than she had been able to discover in her few days of research. "Why was the window unlatched, then?" she asked.

He hesitated a moment, then said "I was preparing my exit, of course. The servants are all gathered downstairs, and I didn't want to have to steal past them laden with my ill-gotten gains."

All right, then. "What next?" Leila asked. "Do you plan to leave the bloody corpse of a nine-year-old girl lying on the floor for Madam to find in place of her jewels?" He flinched a little.

"Nine? I thought you were seven."

"I haven't been getting fed regularly," she growled. "Well?"

The hand with the dagger in it fell to his side and the shadowy figure convulsed with laughter. "I'm sorry," he gasped. "I'm just having trouble accepting that I was very nearly skewered through the kidney by a *nine-year-old girl!*"

Grrr. "Get to the point!" Leila snapped. "Did you get the cabinet open yet?" The figure took a deep breath and his laughter subsided. Her dagger vanished among his clothing.

"Not quite yet," he admitted. "I had just broken my third lock pick when you stuck your dagger in my back."

"Lock picks?" Leila asked, incredulous. "Why are you messing with lock picks?" The figure seemed taken aback.

"Uh, they're traditional," he said. "I've been using them since I was your age, and that was six years ago." Aha, she thought, a stripling. That he was two-thirds again her own age didn't really bother her. She felt as if she were laboring under a handicap, her extreme youth; and what little experience she owned had already shown her that *that* was a very temporary thing.

Leila brushed past her dimly-seen assailant, saying "Allow me." She bent and, in a complicated maneuver, extracted a large pry bar from somewhere under her skirt. Then she attacked one of the narrow cracks between the door of the fabulous jewelry chest and its frame.

This pry bar, which had started life as a perfectly ordinary one identical to the one she'd used to open her mother's secret stash in the stables behind the House of the Golden Fish, had been carefully honed until its leading edge could be used to shave with. Leila inserted it into the crack, pounding it softly deeper in with the heel of her hand. Then she leaned back against the long end of the bar, and with a splintering sound the door of the cabinet shattered raggedly – leaving its cunning and hard-to-pick lock still in place.

"But!" the thief cried, outraged at the crudity of her attack. "They'll know in a moment that a theft has occurred!" Leila, busy applying the bar deeper within the cabinet to complete the destruction of the door, turned her head to the side.

"And when Madam comes home and tries to put her sapphire necklace away, she's not going to notice that all the rest of her jewelry is missing?"

The figure sighed. "You're right," he said. He stood watching for a moment or two as Leila began grabbing jewelry right and left and stuffing it into hidden pockets in her tunic. Then he roused himself.

"Wait!" he hissed. "I'm not going to let you just take all this stuff."

She spun on him. The balance of power seemed to have tipped, and she was rushing to salvage what she could from this job before it tipped again. "Why not?" Leila asked. "I spent more than a week planning this job. Why shouldn't I have the loot?" The boy hesitated, then sighed.

"Because," he said, "this job is one of Fandal's. And you don't cross Fandal in this town if you hope to live here afterward."

The jewelry case was empty. Leila whirled around to face the boy. "What's your name?" she demanded. "I can't keep talking to you without knowing who you are."

"Ed.. Eddal," he stammered. "I'm one of Fandal's crew – the Night Guild. They've had this place under surveillance for months, and I was tasked with getting in and doing the job. It was my chance to move up in the organization."

Leila blinked. For nearly a year she had been part of Marsine's underworld, running with Tomas' gang and stealing whatever they needed to get by. How had she not heard about this Night Guild? Trade guilds flourished throughout the Dominion, and held a tight rein on its economy. But that there might be a guild just for thieves had not crossed her mind. Wasn't the nature of crime supposed to be anarchic? Perhaps it was just the gang's name.

"What's up with this Fandal and his 'Night Guild'?" Leila demanded. She was envisioning a gang along the lines of the street urchin gangs, as many as a dozen members and none of them older than this boy Eddal. But she was not stupid. It wasn't just half-starved orphan kids who turned to crime. She suddenly realized what an idiot she had been, operating in the world of the kids' gangs and completely discounting the fact that there must be at least one, maybe dozens, of *adult* gangs out there. What was she thinking?

Though Eddal was feeling at a disadvantage, her question made him stifle a laugh. They were trying to be *quiet*, here! "It's *the* gang in town if you want to operate as a thief," he murmured to his juvenile "assistant." "But there's more than a dozen gangs in Marsine," Leila pointed out quietly.

"Yeah," Eddal said dismissively, "like the one you belong to. Packs of ragamuffin children, robbing market stands and rolling drunks. Fandal mostly just ignores those gangs. Nobody is ever a member for long. If they live, they move on. But he keeps an eye out, always looking for new talent. He's going to want to talk with *you*."

A wave of uneasiness passed over Leila. She'd enjoyed her freedom this past year, beholden to no one but her fellow gang members and all of them just kids like herself. Was this Fandal a male version of Droma, exploiting the thieves under his control and taking the lion's share of the proceeds from their work while sitting around on his fat ass doing pretty much nothing?

"What if I don't *want* to talk with him?" she asked.

"Not an option," Eddal assured her. Leila realized that she was now unarmed, and if Eddal was not yet a full-grown man he was more than capable of trussing her up like a chicken for market and hauling her off whether she wanted to go or not.

"Okay," she said, with more cheer than she felt. Let him think she was just delighted by his invitation. "But I want my cut of this job." Eddal grunted. Damn, all his work was going to be blown on this one. No way he was getting full credit. But the kid deserved something for her efforts, he supposed. He liked her audacity. She reminded him a little of himself at that age, but he suspected she had a lot more talent than he had ever had. His mother was a member of the Guild, else he might never have been given the chance to join.

"Sure, Penumbra, no problem. But I'll hold the loot for now, if you don't mind. Just until we get back to the Guild's headquarters." He held out a sack, and Leila had no choice but to reach into her pockets and transfer their contents into it. She held back a small ring, one she hoped would not be noticed, just in case. Together, they made their way over to the window and slipped outside.

Chapter 15

Eddal and Penumbra moved through the quiet streets of Marsine's hilltop district like a pair of ghosts, and made their way downhill toward the harbor. He led her to a crowded tavern, a rough-seeming place, some three blocks inland from the waterfront. In the meantime each of them had had a chance to see the other in better light, what there was to see. Eddal had removed the dark gray hood he'd been wearing inside the Beauvoir mansion, and thrown a medium green cloak over his burglar gear so that he looked like any young man out and about the streets of an evening. His hair was a rusty medium brown, and he had a wealth of spots on his face.

There wasn't the loud carousing and fighting Leila had seen spilling out of the taverns in the harbor area. Those places' customers were mostly sailors, eager to cut loose after weeks or months at sea with little or no alcohol to be had. Here, there was the clink of mugs and the murmur of conversation – which ceased, briefly, as the two of them came inside and all eyes turned to see who it was.

Moments later everything was back to normal. An enormous, ominous-looking fellow dressed in heavily woven trousers and a leather vest, muscles bulging beneath scarred flesh, was sitting on a bar stool facing into the room, eyeing everyone who came into the place.

"Evening, Oliphant," Eddal said shortly as they came up to him.

The man nodded, and replied "Eddal…" Meanwhile their fingers were flying in what Leila realized must be some kind of secret hand talk. Amazing! After the two men's silent conversation had been concluded, Oliphant stretched his massive right hand down beside him and pulled a lever. A section of the bar opened up and Eddal led her through and down a corridor at the rear to where another thuggish-looking fellow sat on a chair beside a door, incongruously reading a book.

He glanced up at Eddal, and produced a set of keys with which he opened the door's three locks. Soon the two of them were descending a series of staircases, going back and forth and carrying them down to a level that surely must be dozens of feet below the street outside. Leila was doing her best to remain unimpressed, but it was not easy.

The tavern above had been built of wood, as were most of the buildings in Marsine's less prestigious districts. But below all was stone, finely shaped blocks of the granite that was quarried in the mountains to the north and east. This place must be ancient, Leila realized. Mama had told her that there had been a city on this spot for thousands of years, its harbor one of the best on the Center Sea.

At the bottom of the stairs was a heavily built ironwork door like you might expect to see on a jail cell. Leila had never actually been inside a jail (and she certainly hoped that situation would continue!), but there had been descriptions of them in a couple of the stories she'd read. Tales of heroes wrongfully imprisoned were a popular theme. Some six feet down the stone-lined corridor, beyond the door, a corridor gave off to the left.

Intriguingly, a mirror sat at an angle in the bend, giving them a view of the room beyond that corridor – and the guard in that room a view of them. Yet it would be impossible for an armed force coming down those stairs, and finding them blocked by this door, to attack the guard with weapons. Maybe a battle mage (and there were rumors that such existed) could get past this point; but it was unlikely a team of thugs from a rival gang, or a squad of constables, would be able to go any further into the Guild's lair. Very clever, Leila thought.

In the mirror, Eddal signed another one of those silent conversations – this time, it seemed, with the gestures reversed. Then the guard in the room beyond came forward and pulled a lever on the wall of the corridor hidden around the bend, and the gate swung open. There was no lock to pick.

Eddal grinned boyishly at the guard in the next room – a tall, gangling dark-haired boy who looked little older than he was though his skin was clearer at least. The boy (he must just be a lookout, Leila guessed, set to call for serious help in case of an attempted invasion) grinned back. "I hadn't realized Madam Beauvoir's famous jewel chest was quite so capacious, Eddal!" he said with amusement. "Are you sure you should have gone to the trouble to carry this piece off, though? It doesn't look all that valuable."

Leila glared at him, but with a twinkle in her deep green eyes. She knew he was just teasing. Eddal smiled ruefully. "I didn't really have a choice in the matter, Diego," he said. "She brought herself along." Considering Leila would have preferred taking her loot and returning to her gang's hideaway without getting anywhere near Fandal, that was a bald-faced lie. But she decided to play along. She needed to see what this "Night Guild" had to offer – and what the consequences might be if she declined that offer.

"He's waiting to see you," Diego said, and ushered them to a massive door, one of three set into the walls of the anteroom. He executed what sounded to Leila like a secret knock, and the sound of numerous bars being thrown could be heard before the door finally swung open. On the far side of it was a good sized room with two doors leading out of it at the rear.

A large guard stood before each door, and in the center was the most massive and elaborately-carved wood desk Leila had ever seen. Behind it sat a small, middle-aged man with twinkling blue eyes and a neatly-trimmed sandy beard, strands of gray beginning to pepper it. He was scarcely half the size of Oliphant, standing guard in the tavern above.

There were three comfortable-looking chairs sitting atop what must be a fabulously valuable Hando carpet on this side of the desk, and the man Leila presumed to be Fandal gestured to them to sit. He had not stood up when they came in. Turning first to her companion he said, "Eddal, it seems you have found us a new recruit? She seems a little young." Irritated, Leila spoke up.

"I'm nine, not that young. I'm just small for my age." Fandal turned to her and smiled at her avuncularly.

"No offense meant, my dear," he said reassuringly. "I took you for no more than seven, but your small stature is an asset in… our line of work."

To her astonishment he got to his feet and reached across the desk to offer her his hand. "I am Fandal," he said politely, "the master of the Night Guild. And might I ask your name?"

Taken aback, Leila blurted out "Leila… But I prefer to be known as Penumbra," she added hastily. Fandal chuckled, shaking her hand.

"Very well, Penumbra. Might you remove your scarf so that I can get a look at you?" Leila had remained swathed in the long, dark strip of cloth that she wore while she was working. Her dark skin and curly black hair were a little too distinctive among the permanent residents of Marsine.

He certainly had a nicer manner than did Madam Droma, she thought. And her instincts told her that it was not entirely an act. The much-feared leader of Marsine's foremost criminal organization appeared to be... kindly. She unwound the scarf from her head and shoulders and then gave him a slight curtsy, grinning impishly at him. "I very nearly skewered your Eddal this evening," she said disarmingly, "and for that I apologize. I had not even heard of your organization until tonight, and had no idea any other thieves were planning to steal Madam Beauvoir's jewels."

Fandal sat again and gestured for her to do the same. "Remarkable," he said, shaking his head. "I assume you're a member of one of the urchin gangs that work the waterfront?" Leila nodded.

"Tomas is our leader," she said, "and we do alright for ourselves. We've been eating pretty well since I joined the gang."

The diminutive guildmaster put his hands on the desktop and touched the fingertips together. They were long, nimble-looking fingers and Leila would be willing to bet that he could get through any lock in a fraction of the time it would take her. He eyed her speculatively. "I'll bet you have," he mused.

"It's not many nine-year-old street urchins who would take the time to case a mansion for a jewel robbery," he said almost as if talking to himself. "And you speak quite correctly for an urchin as well. I suppose you can read?" Leila nodded.

"My mom was an educated woman," she explained, "and even though she'd fallen on hard times she tried to teach me what she knew."

"Aha, that makes you even more valuable. What I would like to propose," Fandal went on, "is that you join my organization as an apprentice. We will house you in our comfortable headquarters, feed and clothe you, and teach you everything you need to know to become a master of our trade – including self-defense, so that next time you're holding someone at knife point you won't get it taken away from you."

Leila smarted at that. Being so easily disarmed by Eddal had been a blow to her ego. Fandal seemed to have learned far more about what went on this evening than seemed possible, she mused. But who knew what information was passed in those silent conversations, or what ways such information could have found its way to the guildmaster's ears before they arrived?

"What about my share of the loot?" Leila asked, gesturing toward the sack of jewelry that Eddal was holding on his lap.

Fandal raised an eyebrow, and explained "Every member of the Guild has a share in the profits it generates. Even the lowliest apprentice begins with one share, and as you rise in the organization and your efforts produce more income for us, the number of shares you hold increase. My top lieutenants and I are wealthy men, but nobody ever goes hungry."

Leila considered this. Why should her efforts, her risk go to support some layabout apprentice with no talent? Wouldn't she be better off on her own, with nobody but Tomas and the rest of their little gang to worry about? Fandal seemed to be reading her thoughts, and went on, "There are many advantages to working within the Guild. We have numerous contacts throughout the city, and with similar organizations in other cities. If you are caught stealing, what is likely to happen to you?"

It hadn't happened to Leila yet, but it had happened to a few people she knew among the harbor district urchin gangs. "If you're under twelve it's a workhouse," she replied, "Or if you're older it's prison or maybe even hanging, if anybody got hurt or what you stole was worth a lot. And prison's likely a death sentence anyway, from what I've heard."

"That's right," Fandal said. "But with our contacts among the constables there's a good chance that you would find yourself being released from custody before you got to the jailhouse. And if you should be thrown into jail, we have learned masters of the law on retainer who will do everything they can to get you off or reduce your sentence. Even should you be sent to prison, the organization will make sure that you have more food and better living conditions than your fellow inmates."

Huh, Leila thought. Full of confidence in her own skills, she'd been blithely going about her life of crime with little thought of the consequences. But that did seem like a big benefit. "And another thing," Fandal said. "When you steal items of value that you can't use yourself, how have you been disposing of them?"

Leila colored. The one fence they knew about in the harbor district took advantage of the child thieves, she knew, giving scarcely five coppers on the shilling of their actual market value. Selling Madam Beauvoir's cache of jewelry to him would have netted her a pittance. "Old Faroud is the only fence we can find who will buy our goods," she admitted.

"And he cheats you, does he not?" asked Fandal. She nodded.

"Our Guild has access to a network of fences, and they will bid against each other for the opportunity to move some of our more valuable pieces. The money we make from the sale of tonight's haul" – he gestured at the sack in Eddal's lap – "will pay you, as a one-share member of the organization, almost as much as you would have made keeping it and selling it yourself. Especially after you'd shared the take with the members of your own gang. Plus, you receive a share of the take from every other thief's loot, as well."

There was no refuting his arguments, Leila realized. Safe and secure housing, food and clothing, and invaluable training in her chosen profession – on top of what sounded like it might be a pretty good income? How could she refuse? But she had one more question. "You've convinced me, Fandal," she said, "but what about my gang? Without me, those kids aren't going to be eating so well."

Eddal gave her a friendly glance. This dark little creature was a fireball, but it seemed her heart was in the right place. Fandal, too, seemed to give her credit for her loyalty. He sat lost in thought for a few moments, trying to come up with a plan. Finally he spoke again.

"As a starting apprentice, you will mostly be involved in learning your trade and won't be doing much actual stealing during the first year or so. We prefer not to send untrained children out where they could be killed by a watchman or suffer some other unpleasant fate. So you will have some free time to yourself, and you are welcome to use this time to help out your gang if you like."

"I could pull jobs?" she asked, scarcely believing this could be true.

"Not jobs like the one tonight, nothing that conflicts with Guild business. But the sorts of thievery that most of the urchin gangs are involved in, that's no problem. We don't allow independent adult thieves to operate in Marsine," Fandal explained, "but we encourage our home-grown urchin gangs to flourish. It's from among the more enterprising orphans that we get most of our new recruits. Did I mention there's also a retirement plan?" He grinned.

Leila grinned back. She suspected this neat little man was something of a charlatan, but she also had the feeling that his kindness was real. It was time for her to move on in life.

Chapter 16

Life in the Night Guild was not what Leila had expected. It ran less like a traditional trade guild and more like a large company – employing not only thieves and blackguards, and the counselors whose job it was to keep them out of jail, but seamstresses, cooks and kitchen helpers, an armorer, and other perfectly legitimate workers. She suspected some of them did not even know the nature of the organization that paid them.

She had a comfortable bed in a dormitory with five other girls, most of them years older. Three times daily they gathered in the dining hall for meals, which were plentiful and delicious. Fandal aimed to keep his people happy, as the damage a disgruntled member could do to his organization was profound.

Leila continued to visit with her friends in Tomas' gang whenever she had time free from her training, but she found that they were doing better without her than she had feared they might. They'd learned from her ideas, and with their reasonably secure lair in the warehouse attic they were warm and comfortable through the winter.

The gang had been her family, just as in her early life the whores and their children at Madam Droma's had been. But now she was coming to find friends and a new sense of family among the thieves working with the Guild. She liked Eddal and his friend Diego, who were cheerful and fun-loving despite the seriousness of their work.

And Oliphant, as forbidding a figure as anyone she had ever met, proved to be a big sweetie at heart. He seemed to have adopted her as a mascot, and sometimes when he was on duty in the tavern (the Laughing Ass, which sported a wooden sign showing a donkey rolling with laughter) she would come and keep him company. They talked for hours, about nothing in particular.

With many young people of both sexes in his organization, Fandal thought it best to ride herd on their interactions. This helped to prevent things like pregnancies and lovers' quarrels that could disrupt the smooth conduct of business. So the girls in Leila's dorm were watched over by Julia, a woman who looked to be a few years older than Miriam would have been now, had she lived.

Leila could hardly remember, now, what her mama had looked like. She rejected memories of those last troubled days, instead painting an image in her mind of a golden, blue-eyed angel. Though Julia had assumed the role of mother in the young apprentice thief's life, there was little resemblance. Her hair was dark, nearly black, and her eyes the same though her skin was much paler than Leila's. And where Mama had been sweet, and sad, and scholarly, Julia was merely grumpy a good deal of the time.

She was not only a surrogate mother to her young female charges, but also an instructress in the arts of lockpicking and knife work. "Again, Penumbra!" she demanded, and Leila ran to retrieve her daggers (there were now four of them, a matched set perfectly balanced for throwing) and repeat the exercise. Assassination was not part of the usual work of the Night Guild, but they had been known to take on such jobs from time to time. At the very least, every member beyond the level of senior apprentice was expected to know how to extricate themselves from dicey situations with blades, crossbows, garrotes, and unarmed combat.

Leila tucked the knives back into their hiding places in the well-fitted dark gray outfit that was standard issue when working: soft leather boots, trousers of a soft material snugged at the ankles and flowing loosely to the waist, a similarly tailored long-sleeved blouse, leather gloves, and a hood that obscured all but the eyes.

The assumption was that she had been discovered in the act of cleaning out some rich man's money cache, and must quickly immobilize whoever had found her before making her escape. While the Guild paid for legal expenses, they greatly preferred that their members should avoid discovery and capture in the first place.

Her daggers once more in their hiding places (one up each sleeve, one in her left boot top and one down her back), Leila turned her back on Julia and relaxed, as if she had no expectation of trouble. Julia rearranged the targets spread around the room, as the rest of the class (standing well off to the side, out of the action) watched.

Julia joined them, then called "Aha!" That was Leila's signal, and as quick as a striking snake she whirled and began throwing her daggers into the targets that had been exposed. One, two, three! But the last knife, from her boot, was thrown wrong and clattered to the floor after bouncing off the target, handle first. Damn!

The other girls gasped and murmured, astonished that this girl more than two years younger than the youngest of them had been able to hit all but one of the targets. Julia was not impressed. She sighed heavily. "Perhaps someday, Penumbra, you will learn how to handle your daggers. Go get them and stand aside. Michelle, you're up next. Show 'er how it's done."

Stifling a similar sigh, Leila darted over and collected the knives. She was cursing herself for her failure, though she had only been practicing with them for a few months. So much had come easily to her, with her natural talent, that she had once thought she was the Seven's own thief. Now after spending time in the company of people with as much talent as she had plus years of experience, she sometimes wondered if she would ever succeed at all.

Since Tomas' gang appeared not to need her after all, and Leila burned to show Julia what she could do, she spent many of her free hours in practice. Julia was not unkindly, but winning praise from her was like squeezing pomegranate nectar from a stone. You did exactly what she asked of you, and if you did it less than perfectly she would take you to task, or shake her head as if she wondered why she bothered to try teaching such a ham-handed idiot. Do it perfectly, and she would nod curtly – and move on to the next lesson you hadn't mastered yet.

Michelle, the eldest of the girls in Leila's dormitory, completed her Final Test and moved on to journeyman status. As a journeyman she was considered to be an independent adult, free to take one of the individual rooms the Guild offered its members or go out into the city and take lodgings on her own. With her journeyman's share of the gang's profits, either was an option.

She'd been seeing one of the older boys in the gang, who had made his journeyman notch a few weeks before, and the two of them went out into Marsine and found rooms together. They would become a team, assigned to jobs where two were needed. Another girl, ten like Leila, took her place – and Penumbra rose slightly in the rankings. She was no longer "the new girl."

Sometimes Leila looked back on her old life and she could hardly believe that had been her. She'd been so young, so innocent then – and so limited by her situation. Most of the women working at the House of the Golden Fish had felt they had no other choices in life. Yet now, as a girl of ten (she didn't think of herself as a child, and had not for some time now), she had room and board superior to what they'd enjoyed, and a cash income far in excess of theirs. She amused herself fantasizing that the whores at Droma's would arise and imprison the old bitch in the cellars, taking over the place and splitting the profits among themselves as Fandal's crew did. If only they all had a little more backbone!

Her mama had loved her, Leila knew, and so had Esme and Dina and perhaps a few of the other women at Droma's. But now, for the first time in her life, she was in the hands of adults who valued her for who she uniquely was – who nurtured her and were helping her to develop valuable skills. Plus, she had the comradeship of her fellow apprentice thieves. She threw herself into her studies with a will.

Chapter 17

Penumbra took one last look at herself in the dormitory's full-length mirror, using the image to focus her mind on anything she might have missed. Tonight was her first attempt at the Final Test, and she was determined not to fail. She had chosen the target herself, and it meant a lot to her to succeed. Plus there was that whole thing about failure probably meaning she'd either been killed by a guard or taken into custody by the constables.

The person looking back at her from the mirror wasn't much to see. Penumbra knew she was never going to be tall, but she *had* grown nearly a foot since joining the Night Guild four years before. At thirteen she stood just about five feet high, and there wasn't an ounce of spare flesh on her whipcord frame. Though the food here at the crew's headquarters was nourishing and plentiful, she'd burned it all off pushing herself to ever-greater feats of speed and agility.

Only her deep green eyes and a little of the dark skin around them was visible through the eye slit of her burglar's hood. She now had six daggers secreted about her person, a garrote, and (something she'd bought with her own money) a cunningly-wrought little spring-loaded bolt gun.

It was a little shorter than her forearm, and mounted along it in a specially-crafted leather holster. With a twist of the wrist she could drop it down so that the barrel was in her palm, release the safety catches, and fire it with the click of a button. Cocking it again required inserting a new bolt and pressing it down against the floor with her full weight (all ninety-five pounds of it), while holding the safety catches open at the same time.

It was definitely a short-range weapon, a little surprise for when a thrown dagger wouldn't do. But the cleverness of its design, and the beauty of the filigree work on the barrel, had captured her desire. She'd saved for months to buy it. It was steel blued to a matte black color, non-reflective. This was much the same color as her habitual dress, and it suited her.

Penumbra turned from side to side. She might have been an eleven-year-old boy for all of her figure you could see in her working garb, and she sighed. She had already had her first moon blood, but so far she had little going on up top. Mama had had quite bountiful breasts, as she dimly recalled. Though big ones would be a disadvantage, in her daughter's chosen career.

Julia came into the room behind her and very nearly smiled, a look of something like affectionate pride in her eyes as she beheld her star pupil. Never had such a young apprentice risen so far so fast, and while it was clear the girl had natural talent most of the credit had to go to the hard work Penumbra had put in over the years. Julia expected that in years to come, when she'd grown old and fat and was long since retired, she'd be able to boast "I was the one that trained Penumbra!"

"About ready, Pen?" she asked softly. She hadn't made a sound coming in, but part of the training Penumbra had received made her alert to everything that was going on around her. Though seemingly unaware of Julia's approach, she had not flinched at all.

Penumbra grinned nervously, unseen beneath her hood. The girl Leila had gradually receded into the past, until she now felt that she truly was Penumbra. It wasn't a bad thing for a thief, especially one who intended to become a master thief, to adopt an alias by which they would be known. Sort of a public-versus-private identity.

"I suppose I'd better be about it," she told her mentor. Julia pulled out a pocket watch and Penumbra did the same, making sure they were both showing the same time. It was now nearly midnight on a foggy Belanday in early winter, and it was likely there would be few people out and about on the streets of Marsine. The technology behind the pocket watch had come to the Gaspari Dominion from the realms of the Hando less than twenty years earlier, and a good watch was fabulously expensive. Yet the thieves of the Night Guild never had to want for high quality equipment.

"Off you go, then," Julia said. "You must be back here by three, with the loot, in order to receive your journeyman's notch." A thrill of excitement ran through Penumbra at the words. She was ready, she knew she was! And when she considered her target, her anticipation rose. She was going to obtain the greatest of satisfaction from the completion of this task.

Penumbra left out the back way, heading for the warren of tunnels that ran below Marsine. Centuries ago, foresightful rulers had built enormous storm sewers to carry the runoff from the city's frequent rains down under the cobbled streets to drain into the bay. In later generations many homes had also made connections to these sewers, for the venting of household waste. So the smell down there was none too pleasant.

Fandal was only the latest in a long line of guildmasters to take advantage of the headquarters beneath the Laughing Ass. In fact, Penumbra had learned, the Night Guild had been active for centuries. Some but by no means all of the Guild's leaders had been descended from those who came before. And this particular one, she gathered, had been one of the most able and best-liked in living memory.

Penumbra let herself out through a guarded door that could only be opened from the inside, and stepped out onto the walkway of a large, stone-lined tube. The ceiling was arched, the bottom flat, and there was a stone walkway several feet above the usual water level. She threw a reversible cloak she carried in her pack over herself, covering her from head to ankles. The waterproof side was out, and it would help to prevent the stink of the sewers from penetrating her clothing.

As she made her way quickly through the labyrinth of tunnels, meeting no one at this hour (though there *were* some wretched souls who got a small living scavenging among the wrack that flowed through them), Penumbra held her small glowstone close to her body and low, illuminating the path. These tunnels were ancient, and in some places bits of the walkway had crumbled – requiring a careful leap over the damaged area. Fall into that and she'd have failed her test before she even got started!

When Penumbra had first been shown a glowstone, her eyes had gotten wide. Surely, this must be some kind of magic! Though she was happy enough with her life since, she would regret forever that she and Meister Klingt had not gotten back to the House of the Golden Fish in time to save her mother. Not only would her beloved mother have lived, but she would have been forced to get out of prostitution – and Leila (as she was then) would have been able to see real magic in action.

But Meister Klingt never cast that spell, and had since died of liver failure – unable to heal himself, at the last. And Penumbra learned that the glowstones' ability to cast a pale blue light for several hours at a time was a natural property of the mineral. You left them out in the daylight for a few hours, and got back several hours of light later on. Was there no real magic in the world?

Part of Penumbra's apprentice training had included exploring these sewers until she knew them as thoroughly as she did the streets above. To the casual eye they seemed an impenetrable labyrinth, but there were distinguishing marks at each intersection, if you knew what you were looking for.

She climbed out at a manhole set into a cobbled street in the upper reaches of the city; not the Palace District, wherein the Count of Marsine and his ilk made their homes, but in a wealthy area where bankers, merchants, and others who'd made their fortunes in trade had built mansions to rival anything their "betters" might have.

There were street lamps here, ones that would burn all night. The Night Watch patrolled this district too, though they were spread thin and it would be the worst sort of bad luck should Penumbra encounter any. Still, she peered carefully out of a slight crack and listened hard for any sounds before opening the manhole fully enough to emerge onto the street.

The manhole cover was solid brass and heavy, but she was far stronger than she looked. She closed it again silently, and quickly made her way into a patch of shadow. Penumbra was now only about a block and a half from the mansion that was her intended target. She removed the cloak and laid it flat under a large bush gracing the lawn of a nearby house. Then she carefully made her way along the deserted street, moving without a sound.

Another block further on, with her target in sight, Penumbra again took shelter in a pool of shadow and waited for a few minutes though the clock was ticking. She wanted to be sure she had cleared her nostrils of the sewer stench, and could make an accurate assessment. Then she began sniffing herself. Yes, no traces of the scent had penetrated her clothing. A little embarrassing, it would be, to be silently rifling the jewelry chest and have the lady of the house sit bolt upright in bed crying *"What* is that awful smell?"!

Satisfied that she was ready to proceed, Penumbra made her way quickly but silently to the looming three-story mansion and crept around to the rear of it. The household kept no dogs, she knew, for the owner despised such animals and would not have their noise and mess around his home.

Penumbra had been casing the place off and on for the past month, building up a thorough picture of the house's strong and weak points, and the routines of its inhabitants. But she had been here before that, long before – when she had come here, figurative hat in hand, some five years ago.

Josef Sampson had indeed married the Count's daughter, Catarina of Sturia, just as he'd said he would. In her voracious reading of Marsine's broadsheets, Leila had seen the wedding notice. And over the years since, the couple were occasionally mentioned in the society pages as guests of this or that notable personage. But there had never been any birth announcements.

Penumbra smiled grimly to herself as she considered that her grandfather's lovely blonde bride appeared to be barren. She was unlikely to be producing any sons to inherit the family fortune. Besides, the old man must be pushing eighty now; and while she'd heard rumors of men who could still perform in the bedroom at that age and older she thought it pretty unlikely. Any year now, she thought, she would read one of those broadsheets and see the old curmudgeon's obituary. Might he rot in one of the purgatories of the afterlife for a few hundred years!

Hmm, Penumbra mused as she climbed the wall leading to the rear garden as easily as if it were a ladder, neatly avoiding the spikes at the top. That would probably make Catarina heir to Josef's fortune, unless maybe the laws wouldn't let a woman inherit. Then it would probably go to her nearest male relative, her father the count or perhaps one of her brothers. Certain aspects of the legal system had been part of the Guild's curriculum, but inheritance law had not been among them.

The enormous house was mostly dark. Likely the cook or her helpers would be arising around three to begin the day's baking, but Penumbra would be long gone by then unless something went terribly wrong. A faint light shone on the second story, from a window that Penumbra knew gave on a hallway lined with bedrooms. Likely it was a night light, in case someone wanted to make their way to the privy in the middle of the night.

Penumbra darted across the yard by the ambient light filtering in from nearby streetlamps, and mounted a large cast-iron drainpipe that ran from the roof three stories above to the ground below. It had a lightning rod mounted atop it, but there were no thunderstorms tonight – just a swirling fog that obscured details. Perfect weather for a thief, and this thief's small size and light weight were ideal for climbing up the side of the building without making a sound.

The house had more than a dozen bedrooms in addition to numerous parlors, servants' quarters, and a small ballroom – though only Josef and Catarina lived there, along with four maidservants, the cook and her two helpers, a scullery boy, and a groom/coachman who lived above the stables. As she had taken in the absurd size of the place, Penumbra wondered why the couple didn't just sell the enormous old pile and move into a nice townhouse in one of Marsine's more fashionable districts.

The casement window nearest the corner gave onto an unused bedroom, and the climbing thief had soon jimmied the latch and crawled inside. The bed and other furnishings in the room were draped in white dust covers, giving the place an eerie, ghostly look in the dim illumination from the window.

Penumbra crept silently across the room, mindful of squeaking floorboards in a house this old, and stood listening at the door for two full minutes. There were no sounds beyond the slight creaking an old house makes as it adjusts to the atmospheric conditions surrounding it.

An occupant of this bedroom could have latched the door from the inside for privacy, but there was no lock. Penumbra inspected the hinges to make sure they would not shriek, then silently opened the door and went out into the corridor. She was pleased to find the floor covered in soft Hando carpet, making it that much easier to move quietly.

She took a moment to orient herself, then went down the hallway to the furthest door on the right. This, Penumbra knew from her research, was the lady of the house's dressing room. As was often the case with the upper classes, Catarina and her husband slept in separate but adjoining bedrooms.

The door to the dressing room was locked. Her ears tuned for any sounds that might suggest someone in the house was stirring, Penumbra knelt beside the keyhole. The faint light of an oil lamp in the hallway provided enough illumination for her to see what type of lock it was, and she set to work with her lockpicks. Julia was justifiably proud of her star student when it came to picking locks – Penumbra had an almost supernatural skill with them.

With the faintest of snicks, the lock yielded and the latch opened – the door swinging inward. Penumbra remained crouched for another moment, muscles tensed and all senses alert, as she assured herself that the house remained still and quiet. Then she rose to her feet in a silent, fluid motion and went inside before gently closing the door behind her and locking it again.

The teenage thief breathed a silent sigh of relief. So far, so good. Facing into the corner on the far side of the room, away from the door to the hall and also the door halfway down the room's length that connected it to Catarina's bedchamber, she cupped her glowstone close to her body and used it to read her pocket watch. Nearly one! She had plenty of time yet, but also lots to do and she had better get to it.

A certain amount of light was coming in through the room's narrow window. This was a similar setup to the dressing room of Madam Beauvoir, that highborn lady whose misappropriated jewels had led to Penumbra's induction into the ranks of the Night Guild all those years ago. But while the mistress Beauvoir's jewel chest had been large and famous, Penumbra saw in the dim illumination that Catarina Sampson had a rather more modest repository for her personal valuables – a door perhaps three feet in height gave onto what she assumed was a recessed cabinet.

The door's lock yielded to Penumbra's lockpicks in less time than it would have taken her to locate the key, which Catarina kept hidden beneath a powder jar on her glass-topped dressing table. Within, she found the cabinet deeper than expected. The wall on this side must be thicker than usual. There was a series of rotating arms with indentations on them designed to hold necklaces suspended, and a collection of deep, velvet-lined drawers containing bracelets, rings, and earrings.

Though four years' training with the Night Guild had begun to develop in Penumbra a fine ability to appraise the value of loot, in this dim light she could not see any of the jewelry well enough to be certain whether it was genuine or merely very good fakes. The ultimate value of her score on this job, her test for journeyman, was secondary to her execution of the heist. But for her pride's sake, she hoped grandfather Josef had not been miserly with his bride.

Penumbra worked fast and silently from top to bottom, stripping the necklaces off of their hangers and onto the surface of a length of black velvet she'd brought in her pack. When those were done she folded the cloth over them, then again for extra cushioning, and began dumping the drawers one at a time onto the velvet as soundlessly as possible.

Between drawers she folded the cloth over again, minimizing the possibility of any clinking sounds; and listened for a few moments for any sounds of alarm from the next room. Suppose Madam was a light sleeper? But there were no interruptions. Within five minutes the contents of Catarina Sampson's jewelry chest were swathed in a pile of soft black cloth, and Penumbra tucked it into her pack. Then she closed the door and re-locked the cabinet.

Part one of her plan, completed! But part two was riskier, and likely would take longer. Her heart pounding, Penumbra crept to the door and listened, ear pressed against it, for a long moment. No sounds at all, and she unlocked the door again and stepped out into the hallway. She locked it again behind her. As an exercise in professionalism, she wanted the evidence to be as puzzling as possible. "We must have been robbed by a ghost!" she imagined Catarina saying, with Josef unable to refute the statement.

Beyond the hallway was a staircase leading down to the ground floor. Below that there was a basement level with the servants' quarters, a cold room for foodstuffs, and a medium-sized wine cellar. From her research Penumbra had learned that her grandfather was an abstemious man (something she very nearly applauded, though she could not find it in her heart to award him anything but spite), but she supposed that maintaining a decent cellar was as much a required part of the wealthy lifestyle as decking one's women in jewels.

Perhaps there were bottles down there from ancient and rare vintages, bottles that would sell for more than the price of a modest house to the right customer. But Penumbra had no intention of lugging around heavy (and presumably delicate) bottles of rare wine. She was going for Josef's ground floor study, where she had reason to believe he had a secret cache of valuables. To rob him of what he most held dear would please her immensely. Had not his callous actions robbed her of an entire life of comfort and ease that might otherwise have been hers?

She crept down the carpeted stairs with the utmost caution. Windows along the front entry hall, where she'd been admitted five years before, provided Penumbra plenty of light to see by now that her eyes were almost completely dark-adjusted.

On reaching the bottom of the stairs she looked around her, ears straining for any signs of life. Unless the house had suffered a recent robbery (and as such a thing had not been reported in the press, Penumbra believed it had not), it seemed unlikely that penny-pinching Josef would spend the money for an overnight guard. The neighborhood was a safe one, the Night Watch on duty patrolling the streets. Who would dare to breach his sanctuary?

On the far side of the room in which the front door sat, Penumbra bypassed the entry to the sitting room where she'd been interviewed by her grandfather five years ago and found a hallway leading down. This floor included the kitchen and pantry, a large formal dining room, a privy chamber, the house's small ballroom, a couple of drawing rooms… and Josef's private study.

This room, large by the standards Penumbra had been raised in but compact in comparison with most of the house's other rooms, was where Josef conducted what little business he still engaged in for the shipping company that had made his fortune. In his late seventies he still kept his hand in; but the day-to-day business had long since been given over into the hands of subordinates. She thought with satisfaction that there was probably not a day that went by without him regretting he had no son to train up and carry on the business for him. Tough break, old man.

He also kept his personal papers there, and while Penumbra had not been able to obtain details she had a belief based on strong rumor that this room also held a secret cache of treasure – one she meant to penetrate, if she could find it. The door was locked not with one lock but three, which she greeted with delight. What stronger sign could there be that she was right? No way the old bugger would bother with three keys to lock up a room with nothing more important in it than some business correspondence!

These locks were far superior to the one on Catarina's dressing room, which gave Penumbra a qualm as it reinforced the notion that Josef wasn't worried about the "valuable" jewelry contained within. They might all be worthless fakes, after all. But eh, so what? In the nearly-dark hallway she set to work with her picks.

These were constructed out of the finest spring steel, the sort used in watch mechanisms, and were very nearly unbreakable. The complete set had been awarded to Penumbra as a prize after she had come in at the top of her class in lockpicking, and she treasured them. With these, every lock in the world would open at her command. Or so she thought.

No doubt there might be a few highly advanced locks, perhaps in the realms of the Hando or in darkest Palambo, that would not have yielded to Penumbra's touch. But the locks on the door to Josef Sampson's study didn't stand a chance. Click, click, click, and the door swung silently open.

Checking around her once again before moving inside, Penumbra closed the door behind her but didn't take the trouble to lock it again. The room had no windows, and if she heard anyone coming she wanted to be able to get out in a hurry.

The room was pitch black inside, not even a faint glow coming in from beneath the door. Penumbra pulled out her glowstone and held it up, looking around. Josef's study was perhaps fifteen feet wide and twenty long, lavishly furnished in deep-pile Hando carpets and polished bloodwood furniture. Several comfortable-looking, well stuffed sofas and easy chairs were spotted along the far wall, suggesting that Josef might entertain some of his cronies here with a pipe of asash after an enjoyable dinner. Though she found it hard to imagine the dried-up old stick taking enjoyment from much of anything, let alone a convivial evening with friends. Did he even *have* friends?

Her grandfather's social life, or more likely lack thereof, was of little concern at the moment. Penumbra gravitated on instinct toward the enormous bloodwood desk that took up most of the end of the room to the right of the door as she had come in. *There* was the room's center of power, there where the old spider sat in his web.

By the Seven, there were more drawers on the front of the thing than she could imagine things to keep in them. Penumbra had gone from whore's brat to street urchin to professional thief, and while she'd had a considerable education along the way none of it had addressed what went on at a clerical level within a large and prosperous business concern. What could you possibly need to run a business, she thought? Some paper, some ink, a few quills or maybe one of those new-fangled fountain pens?

Therefore, Penumbra's exploration of Josef's desk was something of a revelation. All of the drawers were locked, but she discovered on picking the lock in the central drawer, and the ones on either side of it, that all of them now opened freely.

Anxious about the passage of time, she began a hurried search. The top drawer seemed to be full of pens, nibs, extra bottles of ink, miscellaneous receipts, and a little kit containing sealing wax, a candle, Lucifer matches (another recent innovation in the Dominion), and Josef's personal seal. Penumbra stuffed it into her pack, grinning.

Other drawers mostly contained paperwork, in which she had no interest. She had no desire to bring down the Sampson Shipping Company, since she doubted that Josef had another ten years left on earth before his time would be up. Penumbra bore Catarina no malice, feeling only pity for the young woman who had been sold off by her father to this horrible old man. Perhaps as a wealthy widow, she could find a happier life.

One of the drawers contained a cache of gold coins, and Penumbra took those as well. But where was the real trove? She felt time slipping away, and if she failed to find what she was looking for within another forty minutes she was going to have to ditch and leave. Catarina's jewelry, even if it proved to be fake, would be enough to win her her journeyman's notch. But she really, *really* wanted to hit Josef where it hurt.

Now Penumbra turned her eyes to the room itself, from the perspective of the desk's well-padded and opulent leather-upholstered chair. If I were a greedy old fuck with the compassion of a stone, she thought, where would I hide my stash? The various room furnishings seemed unlikely, and she turned her attention to the walls. Clearly the cache would need to be accessible enough that he could get into it quickly in case a sudden contingency arose, so it was probably not buried under the floor.

Fine paintings lined the walls. Might they not be a cover for some kind of vault? Coming around the desk, Penumbra started on the side the door was on and began moving around the room, checking each painting where it hung. Josef had not been a tremendous amount taller than she was now when they'd met five years ago, and she was willing to bet that wherever the cache was, he wasn't going to have to use a ladder to get at it; so she only tried the paintings that were in reach.

A picture rail ran around all four sides of the room at a height of around ten feet, a couple of feet below the height of the ceiling. Each picture Penumbra checked had been hung from it on a wire from that rail, and moved easily when she touched it. None of them had anything behind them but bare wall.

Until, that is, she got to the large one at the far end of the room. That one refused to budge, as if it were screwed to the wall instead of suspended from the picture rail. She held up her glowstone and could see no sign of screws or nail heads in the frame. No wire came down from above. How was it being held up? Oh, if only the light in here were better! Penumbra considered lighting a couple of the room's wall-mounted oil lamps, but thought better of it. A bar of light showing under the door would be a dead giveaway to any member of the household wandering this floor late at night.

Penumbra returned to the desk to think for a moment, then began pulling the drawers out again. This time, she removed them completely from their slots and examined the entire drawer by the dim light of her glowstone: sides, bottom, back. She started with the narrower drawers on each side, returning each one to its slot after inspection. Under one of the bottom ones she found an envelope taped in place, and eagerly retrieved it. The contents appeared to be an IOU from one of Marsine's prominent citizens. She tucked it into her pack.

Finally Penumbra reached the broad top drawer, pulling it up onto the shining, uncluttered desktop to examine it in detail. Nothing on the sides, nothing on the bottom, nothing on the back. She leaned down beneath the desktop, her glowstone in hand, and peered up at it from below. What was that?

Mounted on the bottom of the desktop, quite unseen from above or from below if the drawer was in place, was a sturdy looking lever that seemed to be attached to a steel cable. Penumbra reached up, pulling the lever toward her as far as it would go, and she heard a "snick" from the far end of the room as a catch was released and the hitherto immobile painting rotated out into the room on unseen hinges!

That cable must have run through pulleys down inside the desk, through the floor, and up into the wall, Penumbra realized. Amazing! She hurried over to the wall eagerly to see what was behind the painting. It had been mounted with a series of brackets attached to the frame, and to a wooden panel set into the wall several inches inside the frame. All that had been completely invisible, though if she'd used one of her daggers to cut the canvas out of the frame it would have been obvious, should she not have managed to find the lever. She filed that revelation away for future reference.

Within the recess revealed by the now-opened panel, a heavy-looking steel safe was embedded in the wall. All that was visible was the door and its frame, of course – and it had the most complicated-looking lock Penumbra had ever seen! She set the glowstone on the lip of the recess and pulled out her watch. Only another half an hour until she must flee, or miss her deadline.

Penumbra cared little or nothing for the supposed fabulous riches on the other side of that steel door. And she already had her journeyman's notch sewn up – all she had to do was saunter out the front door, leaving all of its locks and bars undone, and hurry home. But she wanted, she craved, she *must have* the satisfaction of adding insult to injury and leaving Josef Samson devastated by his loss. She needed to have him know a little taste of the loss she had endured, when her mother had died thanks to his refusal to forgive what she had done in giving birth to a dark-skinned daughter out of wedlock.

So, she attacked the door's lock with all the skills at her command. Oh Andros, how many tumblers did this thing *have*? Working as quickly as she could, Penumbra freed one row after another for what seemed like forever and was probably not more than five minutes. Then with a click that seemed troublingly loud in the silence of the darkened room, the latch yielded and the safe door opened.

As Penumbra was gasping in relief, there was suddenly a brief, loud, high-pitched shriek from the door in front of her. An alarm of some sort? Unless you were willing to pay for magical wards and had access to a mage who could cast them, their world offered little in the way of that type of protection. Most people relied on organic means (guards, dogs) to protect their goods.

Oh, it was some kind of a small rubber bladder, like the inflatable balls children played with. Rubber was one of the kingdom of Palambo's major exports, and it was widely in use throughout the Dominion. Some people were even using it as tyres on their carriages, creating a ride (so it was claimed) as smooth and comfortable as river travel.

This bladder had been squeezed between the safe's door and a lip inset around its frame, and when the door had opened it had begun to inflate – pulling air in through a thin reed set in its narrow orifice, and producing the momentary sound. Her heart pounding, Penumbra pushed the thing aside. What were the chances, in this sleeping house at well past one in the morning, that anybody would have heard that thin shriek? Even had it awakened one of the sleepers above or below, they would have immediately concluded it had been a dream and gone back to sleep.

Or so she was willing to tell herself. Grinning from ear to ear now, Penumbra began shoveling the safe's contents out through the door and into the pack that already contained the velvet cloth with Catarina's jewels swaddled within it. Seeing exactly what riches she was gathering could wait until she was home safe and had a good light to see by – all she cared about now was robbing Josef Sampson of everything he held dear.

Penumbra was so engrossed in her task, racing for the finish line now, that she failed to notice the soft footsteps coming down the hall. There was a scrabbling at the door, and she turned just as it opened to reveal a tall figure holding a lit candle in one hand.

Fortunately the Sampson household's coachman Bergen, for it was he (raiding the kitchen for a late snack after a session with the cutest of the housemaids, and only by a freakish chance having heard the noise made by the safe's bladder alarm), was so astonished at the sight of the dark-clad, diminutive figure raiding the safe that he failed to immediately shout for help.

Penumbra whirled in dismay, finding the man already halfway through the door and brightly illuminated by the candle he held. In a heartbeat her left-sleeve dagger was out and on its way, thunking into the wood of the doorframe and pinning the man there by his shirt. It had nicked his arm on the way through, and blood began to soak the sleeve within seconds.

Oh, she didn't want to kill him! Through a year on the mean streets of Marsine's harbor district, and another four living fairly comfortably in the bosom of that city's foremost organized criminal enterprise, Penumbra had never taken the life of a human being. And though she harbored a great deal of enmity for Josef, and perhaps even more for Droma, there was nobody she really wanted to kill any more. Her vow to put the madam in her grave had faded over the years.

But if she didn't do something before this man started screaming, Penumbra was doomed! Thinking fast, she rushed to the man's side. He was where he should not be, in the middle of the night, but had investigated a noise. Now he was bleeding, and was caught between his desire to thwart what looked like a crime in progress and the wish not to be questioned about what he'd been doing creeping around the house at this hour.

"Oh, are you hurt?" Penumbra murmured as she approached him. He looked at her in disbelief. Was this a child? The person clad all in dark gray scarcely came up to his shoulder and the voice was soft, feminine. "I'm so sorry," she went on, as if she were a lady whose carriage had inadvertently splashed a bystander with mud, "I thought you were someone else!"

Penumbra produced a small vial from an inner pocket of her tunic. Her burglar garb had many such. "Here," she said, overrunning any objections before they could be formulated, "drink this! It will stop the bleeding, and prevent infection. Then I can take that nasty knife out of there and we'll see about getting you patched up!"

Still coping with an adrenaline rush, Bergen felt dazed and confused. But these words of tenderness and mercy coming from a small figure who might easily be a woman seemed to soothe him somehow; and without thinking about it, as she held the vial to his lips, he drank.

Moments later he sagged to the floor, tearing the sleeve by which he was pinned, as the sleeping draught did its work. Herbal lore and the apothecaries' art was another study in the curriculum of an apprentice for the Night Guild, and Penumbra had learned those lessons well. The man was enormous, more than six feet tall, and it was all her wiry strength could do to drag him into the room and lay him out on the floor so the door could be closed.

The wound was nothing, the kind of small cut you might get chopping turnips in the kitchen. Penumbra retrieved her dagger from the doorframe, wiping it on Bergen's shirt, and returned it to its hiding place in her left sleeve. Then she closed the door gently, and resumed her emptying of the safe at the far end of the room.

In another minute the space was bare, not so much as a crumb to tempt a mouse left behind. Penumbra examined her victim resting quietly on the floor. The bleeding had already stopped, and likely the carpet would not even be stained. She stifled the impulse to leave a taunting note behind and lock the safe up tight. Too much trouble.

From the size of the man on floor, he would be sleeping for only another couple of hours. Unless the cook or her staff came in and discovered him when they started work making bread dough, he would probably wake before anyone else in the house and might be able to get away unnoticed. Penumbra, her heavy pack balanced on her shoulders, left the door to Josef's study unlocked to facilitate that and made her way to the front door.

Before opening it she peered out the window to the left. The street, fairly well lit by streetlamps, appeared to be deserted. Penumbra threw the door's several bolts and then used her lockpicks to open the lock. Evidently someone with a key must come through here nightly to lock up. Then, leaving the door wide open, she strolled out onto the stoop and down the front steps. Come one, come all, she shouted in her mind. Help yourselves!

Chapter 18

Penumbra returned to the Guild's headquarters through the front door, passing Oliphant with a triumphant grin and working her way on through the layers of sentries to Fandal's office. It was 2:45 in the morning, but no one seemed asleep on their feet. For thieves, this time of day was the middle of their work shift.

By now Penumbra knew that there were speaking tubes running throughout the building, and one of them led directly from Oliphant's station in the Laughing Ass to Fandal's office. So she wasn't surprised to see not only the guildmaster and his two lieutenants there, but Julia and the other five girls from her dormitory as well. All of them were smiling broadly, their eyes alight with joy. The home team had won!

As soon as Penumbra had gotten a fair distance away from the district of fine homes where Josef Sampson and his wife lived, she'd removed her hood and thrown her cloak, now suitably aired out, over her dark clothing with its pale blue side out. It covered her from head to toe, not inappropriate in this season, and should anyone have stopped her she was only a young girl hurrying to call for the midwife, her mother in bad labor. No one had.

Happiness swelled in Penumbra's breast. She had triumphed, wreaking vengeance on her tightfisted old grandfather, and she had a pack full of treasure to show for it as well. Life was good! Fandal rose and they all crowded around the desk as Penumbra tossed her cloak over a chair and removed her heavy pack. All that paperwork was weighing her down unnecessarily, but she thought it best to examine it carefully before consigning it to the fire. Perhaps there would be opportunities for blackmail here, or something incriminating about Josef that could be anonymously relayed to the constables.

Eyes shone around the table as Penumbra began pulling items out of the pack. There were sacks of cut gems, purses of gold, stacks of what looked like bank notes. While governments had not yet discovered paper money, people transferring large sums could furnish their creditors with signed notes, authorizing the bank where their money was held to pay the bearer what was owed. It was far more practical than lugging around tons of gold and silver coinage.

The various papers could wait for later. The Night Guild employed some clerical and accountant-types, who kept track of the organization's assets and would be able to look those over with a knowledgeable eye. With a certain amount of showmanship Penumbra extracted the wad of black velvet fabric from the bottom of the pack – as anxious to inspect its contents, herself, as her audience was. Would the jewels prove to be glittering fakes?

They were not. Fandal's eyes glittered as brightly as the jewels themselves, as they were unwrapped layer by layer and spread in a pool across the soft, night-black fabric. Diamonds, rubies, emeralds, gleaming gold, and luminous pearls from the seas beyond the kingdom of Palambo glowed and sparkled on the desktop. A rich haul, indeed! Penumbra had won her journeyman's notch beyond a doubt; but it was hard to imagine what she would be able to do to top this, when it came time for her to graduate to master.

Smiling broadly, Fandal reached across the desk and took her hands. "Congratulations, Penumbra! You have utterly surpassed my expectations! May I have your medallion?" The Guild called it a medallion, but it was really no more than a small, polished bronze disk hung like a pendant from a neck cord.

Each member of the Night Guild, from the cooks and accountants to the strong-arm robbers, was given one of these. It had a molded design that resembled a pie cut into slices, and a notch was made in the edge for each share you owned. The public was largely ignorant of this, and of the Guild itself as well.

But the constables tasked by the count with keeping the peace were all too aware of it, and they dreaded taking a thief and finding them with a notched pendant around their necks. Sometimes they just let them go with a warning (and the removal of any stolen goods in their possession, along with a fine equal to the contents of their pockets) rather than get involved with the legal muscle the Guild could and would bring to bear.

The Guild had more than a hundred members, making it one of the largest companies in Marsine (though some, especially banks and shipping companies, had branches in other cities that made them larger overall). Only Fandal himself and his top lieutenants had personally met every single one of them; and to assure the medallions weren't misused he alone made notches when an additional share was earned.

You could earn notches through completion of special assignments like the Final Test for journeyman or master, or simply by providing satisfactory service over a period of years – like moving to a new pay grade. Guild members who failed at a task, as by getting caught by the constables, were not demoted; but those who betrayed the organization or stole from a fellow Guild member were given a trial and then, usually, never seen or heard from again. Their medallions were melted down, to be used in casting new ones as new recruits came on.

Fandal had a specially designed instrument for cutting the notches, one that he kept locked in his top desk drawer. Its hardened steel blade had a unique shape, producing a notch that resembled a teardrop curling over to the left side at the tip. Now, with great ceremony, he unlocked the drawer and removed the tool. It had a circular platform on which the medallion sat, and a long handle providing leverage so that almost no effort was needed to cut the neat hole through the rim of the medallion.

He placed Penumbra's second notch in the rim of the pie slice beside the first, and a spontaneous cheer went up among the spectators. Ceremoniously, Fandal handed the medallion back to her. "This calls for a celebration," he said smilingly, "but I think it would be better to wait until we've all had some rest. It's been a long night, eh?" Looking around the room, he got no arguments. Despite her excitement and the elation singing in Penumbra's veins, she realized that she was nearly ready to drop.

Placing the medallion's neck cord back over her head, she smiled sleepily and said, "Tomorrow!"

Chapter 19

Penumbra planned to sleep only one more night in the dorm bed that had been hers for the past four years. It felt like home as much as any place ever had for her, but she was looking forward to moving on and up. In her imagination she pictured Penumbra, the dark shadowy figure of legend who came in the night, passing locked doors without so much as a whisper of sound, and vanished along with the possessions of the wealthy – never raising an alarm, never leaving any clues. She would be rich, and famous, and she'd get revenge on everybody who had ever crossed her.

Before falling asleep she fingered the other item that rested on a cord around her neck – her father's ring. It was a curious-looking thing, a rich deep matte-finished gold with intricate black designs incised into it and a tiny, blood-red ruby in the center. Mama had never worn it that she could remember, but she must have kept it well-hidden during all the years when she was working at Madam Droma's. Leila had never, that she could recall, set eyes on it before Esme had transferred it to her possession.

That it had come from Palambo Penumbra didn't doubt. From its size, it was probably a man's ring – belonging to Vandao himself and given to Miriam to lure her into believing his intentions were honorable. Maybe someday, when she had risen to the top of her profession, she would travel to Palambo and track him down. What surprise he would feel to meet the daughter he had never known he had – right before she ran her dagger into his heart. With a sweet little smile on her lips, Penumbra dropped off to sleep.

Having gone to bed at well past three, the residents of Penumbra's dormitory slept until nearly noon. Then there was a rush to the bathhouse, where enormous pools of hot water were available for communal bathing along with cool showers. The latter were more popular in the summer.

When everyone was clean and dressed, they met with Julia and learned that they'd been given the day off. A party celebrating Penumbra's rise to journeyman status (the youngest Guild member to achieve this accolade in more than a generation), was to take place in the Laughing Ass starting at five this evening – free food and drink for everyone. While occasionally strangers to town accidentally wandered into the Ass thinking it was just another tavern, those poor souls were soon shown the error of their ways and asked to leave. Coming from Oliphant, these requests were usually honored.

Julia, who seemed to be in a happier mood than Penumbra had ever seen her in before, gave them all a little extra spending money and suggested they might want to go into Marsine's garment district and buy themselves new dresses for the occasion. It wasn't often that young female thieves-in-training got a chance to dress up.

The six of them were jubilant as, dressed in everyday shifts that would attract no attention, they set off in a party to walk a half mile to the section of the city where clothiers and seamstresses had their shops. Most of these entrepreneurs sewed a range of popular designs in the most usual sizes, for purchase "off the rack" – and then altered them to better fit the buyer before the customer left the store.

After they had arrived in the area lined with clothing shops, the party spread out. The four older girls (aged fourteen to seventeen) went off in pairs to some of the shops specializing in clothing for bourgeois matrons and their marriageable daughters. They could scarcely afford the sort of party dresses one would see at the count's ball, after all. But anything remotely pretty and feminine would be a huge improvement over their working garb.

Penumbra and Anita, at thirteen, went looking for a store offering apparel for children from infancy to early adolescence. Penumbra, at least, had no interest in boys. Her vow to remain virginal forever precluded the kinds of adolescent flirtation many girls her age were beginning to enjoy. She'd stay single all her life, single and sober. And rich and famous, of course. Men would throw themselves at her feet, and she would spurn them all. Her personal experience had her convinced that all men were cads.

Anita was the daughter of two members of the Guild, which accounted for her presence in the girls' apprenticeship program though Penumbra doubted she really had any talent for it. She was of medium height and pretty, with wavy ash blonde hair and big blue eyes. She'd been a bit on the plump side when she'd arrived in their dorm at age ten, and was not enthusiastic about the physical training; but those disciplines had taken the baby fat off of her and given her some muscle in spite of herself. Lately she'd begun hanging around with some of the teenage sentries when she had some time off, convincing Penumbra she ought to just sign up as a cook and forget about a career as a cat burglar.

Finding what they sought, the two of them went in through the shop's door and began browsing the dresses displayed on the racks. Though they were thieves, neither of them would have been inclined to steal clothing – the stuff wasn't worth enough to be worth the trouble of fencing it. And you needed to try things on to make sure that they fit if you wanted them for yourself, thereafter making them harder to steal.

As a team, they could probably have tried on clothing until they found what they were looking for, and then distracted the proprietress of the shop while one of them made away with the goods. But they had money to pay for what they wanted, and neither of them really felt right robbing a small shopkeeper who worked hard for her scanty living. Much better to relieve the rich of items they didn't really need anyhow!

Anita soon spotted a dress that suited her to a tee, and snatched it off the rack to hold up in front of her, spinning around. It was a demure little number, with a high waist and a lacy bodice. The skirt fell to the floor in a long, slender curve but was split up the back to the knee so that movement at a speed above a crawl would be possible. The color was perfect for her, a blue that almost precisely matched her eyes. "Oh, Pen!" she cried, "I love it! Find something and we'll go try them on!"

Penumbra avoided rolling her eyes, though she certainly felt like doing so. Anita's enthusiasms were so shallow, and now that she was a journeyman thief she felt as if a gulf had opened up between them. They might be nearly the same age, but they were not at the same place in life. Yet they'd been friends for three years now, and were part of the same big family. So she glanced around the rack and selected something that didn't look awful. The styles these days seemed awfully frivolous – how was a girl supposed to run in these, or climb stairs even?

Madam Broussard, the lady who owned the shop and also sewed most of its wares with the assistance of her two grown daughters, smilingly ushered them back through a curtain at the rear of the establishment. Inside there were three expensive full length mirrors, her greatest investment, allowing multiple customers at once to see how the clothing looked on them. She granted them the privacy provided by the curtain, but hovered nearby.

The two girls removed their outer garments and hung them on hooks that had been provided. Then they stood there looking at themselves in the mirrors, turning this way and that as they assessed their appearance in their underwear. Both were wearing linen camisole tops and bloomers, standard undergarments for females from six to sixty.

"Hey Pen," Anita teased, you're busting out of your top a little there." Penumbra realized that her breasts *were* becoming a little larger.

"Nothing compared to you, though, Nita," she replied. Anita had more padding over her muscles than her friend did, and looked likely to be developing an hourglass figure by the time she was finished growing. Another reason "cat burglar" was probably not her best career choice. Anita dimpled, then reached up and slipped the dress she'd chosen down over her head.

Penumbra helped her pull it down, and fastened the hooks that ran up the back. The dress seemed a little snug, but Anita didn't seem to mind. The bodice gave her some significant cleavage. Penumbra had to admit that her friend was, pretty much, a vision of feminine loveliness. She was sure whichever young sentry Nita had her eye on (or was it, perhaps, all of them?) would be drawn to her like a moth to a flame. A small, nearly silent sigh escaped her lips.

"Oh!" the girl exclaimed, admiring her reflection then whirling around. "This is *wonderful*!" She turned to Penumbra. "Go ahead, try yours on!" she urged, and her reluctant friend lifted it over her head. This one too had a low-cut, snug-fitting bodice – but at least the skirt had some fullness to it. In a pinch she could hike it up above her knees and run.

The color was a muted green, a good match for her own eyes though red might have gone better with her dark complexion. As if a journeyman thief would go around dressed in red! Penumbra was all about stealth, and she shied away from anything that would draw attention to herself. Though, within the tightly-knit circle of the Night Guild, she didn't mind the accolades of her fellows.

Anita fastened the dress up the back for her. It had lacings all the way up the bodice to ensure a snug fit, and Penumbra was surprised, looking at herself in the mirror, to see that even *she* had a little bit of cleavage. Standing at her shoulder, Anita surveyed the image. "Not bad," she mused. "but you need to let your hair down, Pen!"

Penumbra had considered just cutting off her unruly locks to an inch or so in length, to save the trouble of constantly fussing with her hair and keep it out of her face when she was working. But that carried its own trouble: the need to keep cutting it every month or so to maintain the short length. So instead she braided it into a queue that hung down her back, and rarely ever took it out. She even left it braided when she washed it, more often than not.

She looked at her friend in the mirror, and reluctantly told her "Okay, I guess. Do you have a comb?" Anita grinned at her.

"I have just the thing!" she declared, and her nimble fingers began untying Penumbra's braid. "Wow," she remarked as she worked, "your hair's gotten really long…"

When the mass of curly black hair had been freed, Anita pulled a flat object like a 4-tined, short-handled serving fork out of her bag. It was around six inches long overall, the tines spaced broadly. "Even my hair gets tangled when I wash it," she explained to her friend as she began gently running it through the raven curls. "This doesn't pull nearly as much."

In moments Penumbra was standing there looking into the mirror at a young woman she had never seen before. She was small, inches shorter than her companion, but noticeably a woman in her green dress that hugged her tightly around the torso and then fell in loose folds to the floor. Her head was surrounded by a mass of glistening black curls that spilled out over her shoulders and fell nearly to her waist. The effect was startling!

Watching her friend's expression in the mirror, an expression of delighted startlement was coming over Anita's face as well. Wow! Pen was nice, and a staunch friend when the chips were down, but she could be so intense and serious sometimes. It filled Anita's heart with joy to see her looking like she was heading for a party and planning to have some fun when she got there – and not the kind of fun you got from stealing the jewels off the ladies when they weren't looking.

Speaking of jewels... "Pen, this is perfect!" Anita declared. "You have to get it. And there's an emerald necklace in the vault that would go great with it, too!" Among the Guild's many assets was a vault where they kept certain items that were either awaiting a buyer with the right price or were considered useful for their operations. In addition to stealing rich people's valuables by stealth in the middle of the night, some of the Guild's operations involved con games in which certain items might be used as bait for a mark, or to convince their victims (most of these were team efforts) that the Guild members were part of the aristocracy. The Dominion was so huge and sprawling, it wasn't all that difficult to pass oneself off as a count of some minor region a thousand miles away.

Penumbra grinned, completing the pretty picture. "Do you really think Julia will let me borrow it?" she asked. The jewelry in the vault included some fakes, but there were many genuine pieces as well. Anita shared her grin. "Are you kidding? Julia is so proud of you right now, she'll deny you nothing!"

Chapter 20

Five o'clock came, and the girls of the apprentice dorm were gathered in the Laughing Ass in their new finery. Only five of them were dorm residents now, for a couple of hours earlier Penumbra had selected a room of her own within the headquarters complex. It was nearly as big as the dorm where she'd lived the past four years, and she had it all to herself! Not counting the warehouse loft she'd shared with her fellow street urchins in Tomas' old crew, this was the biggest living space she had ever known.

It had a comfortable double bed with a wool-stuffed mattress, some decent carpets over the stone floor, and a sitting area with a couple of upholstered chairs and a table. It even had a reading lamp! Penumbra had acquired a few books of her own since joining the Night Guild, and she planned to buy many more now that she had a bookcase in which to keep them.

There was also a handsome carved wood wardrobe with a mirror on the front of it, so that she could inspect her appearance before going out. Someday, Penumbra thought, she would like to have a suite of rooms overlooking the city, perhaps with a view of the harbor and the ships coming and going in the bay; but for now, this was heaven.

Though she was only thirteen, Penumbra's journeyman notch granted her adult status. She could still take meals in the dining hall with the girls who'd been her fellow apprentices, but Julia would no longer be supervising her movements. The door to her room even had a key, which she hung on the same neck cord that held her father's ring. The penalties for stealing from a fellow Guild member were so severe that locks were scarcely needed, but it was nice to know that she had privacy. Tonight would be the first time she'd ever slept in a room by herself though, and she was wondering if she was going to like it. I'll find out soon enough, she thought with a thrill of excitement.

Two of the tavern's tables had been pushed together so that Penumbra and her five friends, along with Julia, could all sit together. The place had been closed to the public for the evening, and branches of rosemary (in bloom at this season) had been hung around the room to fill the air with its spicy scent. Gaspari lore associated the plant, which grew all around the northern shore of the Center Sea, with memory – and Penumbra planned to remember this celebration for the rest of her life. It marked the first of what she planned to be a long series of triumphs.

Remy, the smiling barman who was on duty this evening, came over to their table with an enormous tray laden with food and drink. There was an assortment of bite-size seafood batter-dipped and fried, salted nuts, and plenty of fresh bread with butter. Fresh vegetables were scarce at this season, but he'd included a bowl of oranges. Also on the tray were seven fine crystal glasses and a bowl of ice in which nestled three green bottles.

"Spumi! You didn't!" gasped Julia. Penumbra had never seen the usually grim and businesslike woman so… jolly. It made her feel odd to consider that it was her successful performance of her Final Test that had produced this effect. Did Julia really care for her so much?

The tray was unloaded, and the girls began eagerly helping themselves to the snacks. They'd treated themselves to tea and cakes at one of the garment district's cafes after their shopping expedition, but none of them had had a real meal all day.

Grinning broadly, Julia set the glasses out around the table and pulled one of the bottles from the bowl of ice. Its cork appeared to be secured in place with fine wire, which she began to unwind. Penumbra watched her curiously, devouring bits of succulent fried shrimp as she did. Mmm, that was so *good*!

Julia freed the cork and then, with what seemed unusual caution, drew it slowly from the bottle. There was a slight "pop" and a small amount of foam rose up from the bottle and spilled down the side. Then Julia poured its contents equally into the seven glasses, set the empty bottle down on the table, and declared "Here's to Penumbra, our star! Congratulations!"

She raised her glass in the air, and several of the older girls did as well. Penumbra gathered this was a ritual of some sort, and she and Anita lifted theirs as well. What was this stuff, anyhow? She had never seen its like. Her vow to eschew all alcohol momentarily forgotten, Penumbra clinked her glass with her comrades' glasses and then, like them, lifted it to her lips and took a hesitant sip.

Ooh, it was bubbly! The nearly clear fluid had a wealth of tiny bubbles rising in it, tickling her nose as she lifted the glass. The flavor was slightly tart, slightly sweet, and it went down easily. Hey, that wasn't bad! A cheer went up at the table as everyone downed their glasses of the Spumi, and Julia immediately set about opening a second bottle.

As she was working at that, Penumbra asked her "What is this, Julia?"

The woman who'd been a sort of bad-tempered (but caring) surrogate mother to her for the past four years smiled and said, "Spumi. It's a kind of wine produced in the county of Piedra, way east of here. You like it?"

Wine, huh? Peer pressure overwhelmed the conviction Penumbra had held since long before she'd been Penumbra. Surely, wine wasn't that bad. It was hardly even alcoholic, was it? Not like brandy at least. She'd had a whole glass of it, and she felt just fine. Not even remotely drunk. So, she raised no objections. "It's pretty good," Penumbra admitted, and let Julia pour her another glass.

The revelry was soon underway. The hard-working members of the Night Guild were a surprisingly sober lot, given that their trade was quite illegal; but they loved the chance for a party and it wasn't often that Fandal cut loose with such an extravagant affair. A trio of musicians had been hired for the evening, and before long space had been cleared and people were beginning to dance. Anita was out on the floor with Jacques, a boy a couple of years older than she and Penumbra were, within moments after the music had started.

The physical training provided to the apprentice thieves made them all agile and graceful. Any who were not soon washed out of the program and found other niches to fill. So good dancers were the rule, not the exception. Penumbra, on her third glass of Spumi, was surprised to be asked to dance by Staeven, one of Fandal's chief lieutenants.

He was good-looking enough, a well-set-up young man. Though he was usually to be found on duty in Fandal's office whenever Penumbra had occasion to speak with the guildmaster, she had rare spoken with him alone. A rumor widely regarded to be truth in the Guild had it that Staeven was Fandal's son by an unknown woman (a serving maid, or was it perhaps a countess?) with whom he'd had an affair decades before. She'd handed the bastard boy over to him to raise, and he was grooming Staeven to become the next guildmaster.

He was in his early twenties, far too old to be of interest to Penumbra; but she was feeling no pain and flattered by the attention as well. Perhaps he was just making nice with her by way of welcoming her into the adult ranks of the Guild? She happily accompanied him to the dance floor and they whirled and spun, having a great time. Then she was stolen away by Oliphant, who insisted on having a dance with his "little sablet" (a small, black-furred member of the weasel family, familiar throughout the Dominion).

As the huge man cut in and wafted Penumbra away, grinning jovially while he lifted her high in his tree-trunk arms and spun her off into the crowd, Staeven glared after him with a look of pure poison. Nobody noticed. Food and drink flowed unstintingly for hours, and everyone Penumbra met was jubilant and congratulatory. Never in her short and insignificant life had she ever felt so welcomed, so much a happily accepted part of a group. It lifted her higher than the sparkling wine had done.

When she nearly fell on her ass on the dance floor, twirling with one of the young male apprentices, Penumbra realized blearily "oh crap, I'm drunk!" That wasn't supposed to happen. She began passing up any further drinks, and after about half an hour she began to feel as though she was in full control of her limbs – at least. A good thing the stuff wore off so quickly!

Even Fandal took her onto the floor for a sprightly jig. Oh my, how the man could dance! Penumbra didn't precisely think of him as a father; she scarcely had any idea what a father was supposed to be. The closest she'd had to one in childhood was old Durgan, and he'd been gruff most of the time. Were there fathers who loved their children and showed them affection? She couldn't say, but if the rumors were true clearly Fandal had cared enough for his bastard son to bring him into the Guild and raise him far higher than most men his age could ever hope to achieve.

Speaking of Staeven, there he was again. In the whirling, chaotic crowd he'd been watching her, a smile on his face and a look of barely-suppressed hunger in his eyes. Why was he not off getting into the pants of some of the young female journeymen, or perhaps the assistant cooks? There were plenty of unattached young women in the guild, in their late teens and early twenties – no doubt any of them eager to tumble the handsome young lieutenant who rumors had it would someday be guildmaster. So why was he bothering her?

At around one in the morning things were beginning to wind down. The party had begun early for a reason, and already many of the Guild members had stopped by one more time to squeeze Penumbra's hand and offer their congratulations before going on their way. Only about half the Guild's complement lived at headquarters, and some of them were married and had children. It was permissible for a Guild member to marry someone not in the Guild, provided they swore never to reveal any details to their spouse.

Now fewer than two dozen were left in the Laughing Ass, and the musicians were about to call it quits. They'd been playing lively, fast-beat dance tunes all evening, with occasional breaks; but for their final number they would wrap it with a traditional Largo. In this dance, the man and woman stood close, arms around each other, and swayed to the music while executing a series of gliding steps. It was a dance for lovers or would-be lovers, and not many made their way onto the floor. Most of the couples had already departed.

Penumbra had been drunk, then sobered up, then got tipsy again, before sobering up once more. Now she was feeling tired and sleepy and happy, content to watch the last dance before calling it a night. A shame, really, she thought, that her long-held vow of lifetime celibacy meant she'd probably never get to participate in such a thing.

Julia had shepherded the apprentices off to their dorm an hour ago, to many complaints, so Penumbra was now sitting alone at the table they'd occupied through the evening. Then Staeven appeared. He was moving carefully, as though he might have had too much to drink. But she found his expression alarming. He looked like a fox that had arrived at the farmyard at midnight to discover the chicken coop standing wide open.

He leaned across the table in a sort of courtly bow, still grinning, and took her hand. "Lady Penumbra," he said – slurring his speech slightly – "You must allow me this last dance." She eyed him warily. His persistent attention was beginning to give her the creeps. Back when her mother had died, Madam Droma had alluded to the existence of men who were more aroused by children, or by girls barely flowered, than they were by full-grown women. Was Staeven one such?

A cutting answer was at the tip of her tongue, but Penumbra thought better of it. Staeven was a highly-placed member of the Guild, and regardless of the truth of the rumors it was clear he had Fandal's favor. Better not to piss him off! She looked at him with lowered lids, then stretched and yawned. "Oh, I beg your pardon!" she said. "I thank you for your favor, but it has been such a very long evening and I've never had Spumi before. I'm afraid that I'm asleep on my feet, and must be taking my leave."

With that, leaving no room for argument, she rose from her seat and made her way, with firm lithe strides, over to where Oliphant sat. It had been a long day for him, too, for though he'd been more or less off duty this evening he had needed to keep at least a minimal watch on the entryway through to headquarters from the tavern.

Penumbra squeezed him around the middle, some two feet shorter than he was, then bid him good night and he passed her on through. The portals in to headquarters were manned at every hour of every day, but the ones watching them tonight seemed a bit below their usual level of alertness. Had the Chief of Constables had spies to alert him of this event, he might have staged a raid and successfully penetrated to the Guild's inner sanctum. For all the good it would have done him...

Chapter 21

Penumbra had not been lying – she truly felt as if she were about to fall asleep while traversing the maze of corridors that led to her new lodgings. Having held the room for less than a full day, and in her impaired condition, she got lost on the way and had to retrace her steps before finding the right corridor. Living in the female apprentices' dorm for the entire time she'd been here, there'd really been no occasion for her to come to this section of the Night Guild's underground labyrinth.

Few people were stirring now. Today's holiday had extended through the night for some of the thieves, putting a hold on jobs that would normally have been conducted at around two in the morning; and presumably those people had all now gone to bed. The thought that she was now just about to spend the very first night in her life alone in her very own room, in her very own bed, washed over Penumbra like a cold wave of seawater – and she suddenly felt a lot more sober.

Oh, I was bad, she thought, as she fumbled around her neck to pull off the cord on which her room key and her father's ring hung. I should never have had that Spumi... But now that she'd actually tried alcohol for the first time, she had an insight into the appeal it held. She was no longer so quick to condemn the men and women she'd seen suffering from its effects.

Penumbra slid the key into the lock. She knew full well how this lock, or any lock she'd yet encountered, could be breached in a matter of moments by a skilled practitioner – such as herself – with a good set of lockpicks. But here in the Night Guild's headquarters, these locks were symbolic. And woe betide any thief who failed to honor them! Besides, she was not carrying any lockpicks. For form's sake, she'd kept a couple of her half dozen daggers on her in places where they were unlikely to be seen while she was dancing. She now felt naked without them.

As the key turned in the latch and Penumbra opened the door, about to step inside, she suddenly heard heavy footsteps moving at speed down the corridor. Quickly hanging the cord back around her neck, she peered out to see what was going on – and was astonished to see Staeven bearing down on her. Of course, he lived here in the headquarters complex just as she did. There would be no reason for Oliphant or any of the other guards not to pass him through.

She didn't actually know where his room was – perhaps here, on this very same corridor? That would be awkward. She turned hurriedly, intent on getting inside and closing the door behind her. And was brought up short by a broad forearm pressed up against her throat.

"Penumbra," he purred in her ear, "don't run away! I was just coming to see you!" She had been caught unawares, and the grip he had on her combined with the fact he was nearly a foot taller and almost twice as heavy prevented her from throwing him over her shoulder as she'd been taught to do in her unarmed combat classes. They really ought to have brought Oliphant in for us to practice with, she thought irrelevantly.

"Let me go!" Penumbra squalled, and Staeven released her. But at the same moment he flung her forward so that she went sprawling, stepped into the room and slammed the door shut behind him. On this side, the door had a thumb latch and a bar – which he quickly fastened. Then he stood, hands on hips, that foxy grin in place as she rose to her feet in a quick, sinuous motion.

Penumbra glared at him, but inside she was quivering. He was the boss' son! How was she supposed to repel his advances without utterly screwing up her intended career? "I'm thirteen years old!" she raged. "I only flowered three months ago! Why don't you find somebody closer to your own age?"

Staeven's grin didn't lessen by a notch. "Oh, perfect," he said smoothly. "I assume you're still a maiden?"

"Of *course* I'm still a maiden, you idiot!" she screamed at him. "I plan on staying that way, permanently!" His face fell for a moment, then the oily smile returned.

"Oh, what a sad waste that would be," he said in mock despair. "If you only knew what joys are to be found in the joining between a man and woman…"

Penumbra goggled at him. Was this man insane? Speaking carefully and enunciating clearly, as if talking to a deaf person or an imbecile, she said. "I do not wish to experience the 'joys of joining between a man and a woman' at this time. Get out of my room, Staeven, or you will regret it."

He just grinned, and stepped closer. "Oh, I don't think so," he said. "I think I will enjoy having your maidenhead a great deal. It's a specialty of mine, don't you know..." Oh, shit.

"I'm the golden girl of the Guild," Penumbra pointed out. "Everybody loves me here. How are they going to react when they learn that you forced yourself on me, eh?"

Staeven stopped his slow advance and laughed. "They all saw you out there, skirts in the air, dancing with every man in the Guild!" he crowed. "It's your first day of adult freedom! Who's going to think you didn't just have a bit too much to drink and decide to fall into bed with the handsome lieutenant, then maybe got some second thoughts afterward? It's your word against mine, and nobody's going to believe I forced you!" With that he closed the distance between them and tried to seize her, but she dodged away and pulled the dagger that had been resting in a sheath on her left thigh. She was feeling more sober and alert by the second.

Staeven's eyes glittered at the sight of the blade, but it only seemed to excite him more. Penumbra took him in from head to toe, and she could see a significant bulge in the crotch of his snug-fitting trousers. This was turning him on! Oh shit, oh shit...

Despite Julia's disparaging remarks early in her training Penumbra had gotten good with her blades – very good. But Staeven was ten years her senior, and had surely been in training with the Guild for at least that long. The two of them crouched, maneuvering, on the carpet that stood between the bed and the room's small fireplace. As far underground as they were, it rarely got cold enough in Marsine even in wintertime to want to light a fire – and while wood had been placed there, it was not lit.

Staeven lunged toward Penumbra and she swung at him underhand with the dagger. She expected him to dodge back from the blow, but instead he came on – then jigged to the side and kicked at her elbow. With a cry of pain, she dropped the dagger and he swept it up almost before it had hit the stone floor.

In another moment he was on her, and for the first time Penumbra feared for her life. The look in Staeven's eyes suggested that taking her maidenhead might be fun, but taking everything she had, slowly, might be even more enjoyable. The man was not right in the head. Now he had her own dagger, just as Eddal had had all those years ago. But while Eddal had been a sweet, pimply-faced kid without a trace of harm in him, she was coming to realize that Staeven was some kind of monster.

He seized her in an iron grip with his left hand, his right holding the dagger, and ever so carefully pressed the sharp blade into the bodice of her dress. "Ow!" she said, trying to shrink away from him.

"How does this open?" Staeven asked with a leer.

"The back, the back!" Penumbra squealed, eager he should not attempt to slit it open from the front and her along with it.

His amazingly powerful left hand yanked her around so that she now had her back to him, and he set the point of the dagger at the bottom of the lacings and began cutting upward. That dagger was sharp, as Penumbra well knew – she sharpened it herself, daily. In seconds the dress fell open at the back and Staeven spun her around again. This time the point of the dagger went in at the front of the bodice, and pulled it away until her breasts were exposed.

Staeven admired her maturing body greedily, taking in the look of terror in her eyes with satisfaction. Then he released her shoulder, transferring the dagger to his left hand, as he used his right hand to seize what remained of the dress and rip it away. It fell onto the floor in a pool of green cloth, as Penumbra stood there naked except for her bloomers.

"Oh yes," Staeven murmured, tossing the dagger aside now that he judged her helpless, "let's have some of that, shall we?" He stepped close and began passionately kissing her neck (bare except for the emerald necklace), while his hands ran down her body and he untied the drawstring on her bloomers. Soon she would be his, her body subject to his command and her mind forever under his sway after he'd shown that he could take her whenever he wanted to.

Thus occupied, Staeven completely failed to notice the point at which the fear in Penumbra's eyes turned to incandescent hatred. As his hands lingered on her hips, squeezing, she pulled her second dagger from the cloth sheath she'd devised for it, sewn into the waistband at the rear of her bloomers, and brought it around to ram into his chest, up under the rib cage on a sure course for the heart.

With a grunt of pain Staeven lurched away, eyes wild with disbelief, and then fell backward as his life's blood began gushing down out of the wound inflicted by Penumbra's dagger. Her dark face was ashen with shock, a voice at the back of her mind screaming "No, I didn't mean it, take it back!" Blood spattered her bare torso and the bloomers below, as the heir-apparent to the Night Guild fell back, gurgling, and expired at her feet.

Chapter 22

Penumbra fell to her knees and then bent over, retching, as she emptied the contents of her stomach over Staeven's feet. The corpse had stopped twitching, life quickly fled as the enormous pool of blood spread over the stones. What had she done? She was doomed!

Tears poured down her cheeks, and for a minute or more she knelt there sobbing, unable to accept the enormity of the catastrophe that had befallen her. She had been so happy, warm in the bosom of the family that had embraced her – and now, all was in ruins!

It wasn't my fault, the thought came to her after thoughts had begun to form once again. But Staeven was right – who was going to take her word as she tried to explain the murder of Fandal's chief lieutenant? Even if she somehow managed to avoid being done away with, her brilliant career was over even as it had barely begun.

Shuddering and gasping, Penumbra rose to her feet and stood listening. The walls were of thick stone, and no sounds reached her ears. Likely no one had noticed Staeven invading her room, no one had heard her screams. And no one would be looking for him before morning…

Augh, the blood – it was everywhere! Penumbra was horrified by what she had had to do, but there was no remorse for snuffing out the life of Staeven. The bastard had deserved to be killed. She wondered how many innocent young girls on the cusp of womanhood he had ruined, in his career.

Well *she* was not ruined. She'd already decided half her life ago to stay a maiden forever, so it wasn't like he'd put her off sex. Just made her a hell of a lot more careful of whom she flirted with… But what now? The fine mind that had served her in good stead through her time as a street urchin came to the fore, and she began planning her escape.

An hour later, it must have been three in the morning, Penumbra was ready to move. She'd used the basin of water in her room to wash the blood from her body, then mopped up most of the pool of it around the corpse of Staeven with the remains of her ruined dress. That had gone into the fireplace, lit with a Lucifer match from the packet of them that was part of her usual kit. The chimney pipes in this place must be cunningly routed indeed, she realized, for the smoke to rise from this underground labyrinth and be vented in such a way that it went unnoticed.

With considerable effort, Penumbra had managed to stuff the body into her wardrobe. It was no longer leaking much blood, so much of it having poured out before the heart stopped beating. She used another spare garment, wetted with the remaining water from the basin, to wipe up the smears. Then she'd rearranged the floor coverings in the room so that the biggest bloodstain was covered by a clean rug. The one Staeven had fallen onto was rolled up in the wardrobe with the body.

Penumbra had gathered everything she thought she would need, and could carry with her, either on her person or inside her pack. She was dressed head to toe in her night-work gear, nearly anonymous under the hood, with all six of her daggers and her other weapons as well secreted about her person. She was short of cash, so seldom needed here where all her immediate needs had been provided for; and she'd stashed the emerald necklace at the bottom of the pack. The Guild's penalty for thievery from her fellows wasn't likely any more severe than the penalty for knifing one of them.

Penumbra stood at the door, looking back at the room and trying to spot any anomalies that would immediately alert the casual observer to something wrong. Everything looked alright. The likelihood that Staeven would soon begin to stink was something she could not avoid (ah, if only she could just drag that piece of shit down to the sewers and let it make its way to the bay), but she thought she ought to have as much as half a day before anyone would begin to get suspicious.

With a stab of regret, Penumbra stepped out through the door and locked it behind her. Then she broke the key off in the lock. She wished there were some way to throw the inside bar from out here, but if she had those kinds of powers she probably wouldn't have gotten into this fix in the first place.

Lamps burned twenty-four hours a day in the labyrinth, there being no daylight down here. The corridor in which Penumbra stood was deserted, and she made her way hastily to the back door. That door, which could only be opened from the inside, was supposed to be guarded at all times. But she had a plan.

She met no one along the way. The normal operating hours here in the Guild headquarters had been disrupted by the celebration. But as she approached the back door, down at the end of a dimly lit, deserted corridor, Penumbra spotted a figure seated in a chair beside the door. It was leaning up against the wall, two legs of the chair in the air, and it appeared to be asleep.

Penumbra moved silently forward. It was Eddal, nearly twenty but he still pulled sentry duty now and again. He had gotten his journeyman's notch a couple of years ago, but lacked the brilliance he would need to rise much further. He'd been having a high old time at the party a few hours before, and she wasn't surprised to see him snoozing at his post.

She considered just slipping out past him without waking him and going on her way. But as with the door of her room, there was no way to bar the door here after she'd gone; and Penumbra came up with another scheme. She pulled her hood down, exposing her face, and nudged Eddal in the shoulder.

He started, nearly falling out of his chair as he wobbled in it before coming fully to consciousness. "Wha...?"

"Eddal!" Penumbra hissed, "Wake up!" Soon he had all four chair legs on the stone floor and was looking a little more alert.

"Pen?" he asked in disbelief. "What are *you* up to?" He'd expected her to be still carousing, or else enjoying the wonderful bed that had come with her new status.

She grinned at him, not a shadow of the past hours' trauma showing in her face. The Guild's apprentice program included a full course in con games and deception, after all. "I've got a score on the line!" she confided in hushed tones, "Something to top the haul from Sampson's!" Eddal's tired-looking eyes widened slightly. The robbery that Penumbra had pulled off for her Final Test was something few Guild thieves could ever aspire to. And she planned to beat it, only two days later?"

"But... now?" he asked, scarcely willing to believe that anyone who'd been enjoying herself as Penumbra had a few hours ago would be feeling up to any kind of a heist.

"I'd sooner sleep," she admitted. "But tonight's the night the family is away from the mansion. They're taking their guards with them too, so it's now or never. I should be back by breakfast time. If I'm not, have Fandal call out the legal department and seek me at the jail."

Eddal pulled the bar and keyed the lock that opened the door into the sewers. He looked at Penumbra worriedly. She was just a kid, but she was taking on so much. He hoped she was up to it. "Be careful," was all he said as she donned her hood and stepped out into the darkness.

Chapter 23

Penumbra moved quickly through the warren of sewer channels, not up the hill toward the wealthy parts of town but down toward the harbor. When she had gone a goodly distance and around a couple of bends, she halted at a wide spot and set her pack down on the stones. Time for a complete alteration of her appearance.

She stripped off her burglar gear and tucked it into the pack, then pulled out some old clothing that she'd kept for grubbing around in. It consisted of a simple pair of drawstring trousers and a loose shirt. After assessing the look of her chest, Penumbra brought out a long scarf. It was similar to the one she'd used years ago to wrap her head and shoulders, hiding her face from the victims of Tomas' gang.

This didn't go around her head, however. She took off the shirt again and wrapped the scarf tightly around her torso, holding down and diminishing the appearance of her breasts. Then she put the shirt back on over it. It might be uncomfortable in warm weather, but it was all right for this season. And the shirt's fabric was coarse and opaque. The scarf wouldn't show through.

The footwear was a problem. The soft boots she wore when working would look totally incongruous, so they had to go into the bottom of the pack and stay there. She put on a pair of crude leather sandals instead, ones she kept as slippers. They were hard to move quietly or quickly in, and a little inappropriate for winter, but they'd do until she could lay hands on something better. Even as a street urchin, she had not been accustomed to going barefoot.

Sighing, stifling the urge to break into sobs again when she considered all she'd lost, Penumbra reached into a side compartment of the pack and came up with a pair of scissors. They were finely made, part of her burglar tool kit. A bit at a time, she began hacking at her long, curly hair. As she severed each lock, she tossed it into the flowing sewer below her and watched as it drifted, gradually sinking, downstream.

In minutes, where the mysterious-looking figure in dark gray had stood, was now a perfectly ordinary looking boy of perhaps ten or eleven. He was short and slight and quite beardless, rather pretty with those black curls and green eyes. Penumbra had brought along a small hand mirror, another part of her kit (useful for signaling accomplices or seeing around corners), and inspected the results with a clinical eye. Not bad, she thought. But too pretty.

Her first thought, as her panic was subsiding and she was making ready to go, was that she would transform herself into a boy and head for the harbor, try to get a berth as a cabin boy on one of the many ships that were always coming and going in the port of Marsine. But now that stage one of the plan had been executed, she was having second thoughts about the rest of it.

For one thing, though she had been born in a major seaport and lived here all her life, Penumbra had never been on the water. Nor did she know anything about ships. She would have to admit that, as to lie about her knowledge and abilities might see her thrown over the side as soon as the lie was discovered. And on the close confines of a ship, how would she be able to maintain the pretense of being a boy?

Then there was that other thing. During her year as a street urchin, Leila had spent much of her time in the harbor district and talked with sailors and ships' boys. A penchant for sex with other men or pretty boys was common, she'd heard. What if she had thrown away all of her prospects with the Night Guild to avoid being raped, only to voluntarily put herself in a position where rape would be unavoidable?

Picking up her pack, Penumbra shouldered it and retraced her steps – heading north, up the hill. There was most of an entire subcontinent out there, with plenty of places to hide in. She could connect with the main road to the north, east, or west and soon be lost in the vast reaches of the Gaspari Dominion, even if she had to walk the whole way.

Glowstone held out in front of her, Penumbra picked up the pace – jogging along in her sandals (about the quickest she was able to move in them) and heading for a sewer exit she knew that would drop here near Marsine's west gate. Well, they called it a gate. In ancient times, Mama had told her, Marsine had been a walled city like most cities of any size in the vast region that had later become the Gaspari Dominion. But it had been a thousand years since

Emperor Ostden the First had united the subcontinent – his native kingdom of Gaspar having been absorbing its neighbors, one by one, for nearly five hundred years before that.

With the natural barriers of the Killtops to the east and the Center Sea to the south, most of the Dominion had seen little in the way of war in the last millennium. And humans are a practical species. If you're not going to need that stone wall to keep out your enemies, why not just borrow a little of the stone for this house you're putting up now – or to build, say, storm sewers?

So Marsine's west gate was just a couple of pillars with an arch across them, straddling the main road that led up the coast and eventually, to places like Sturia and Catal. There were hundreds of counties in the Dominion, and every one of them had a pair of representatives in the Grand Assembly in Parat (once capital of Gaspar, and now of the entire Dominion).

There, so Penumbra had been told (back when she was Leila, that is), the Grand Assembly met four times yearly to discuss and vote on the affairs of the Dominion, and advise the Emperor. The vast, domed chamber where they met sat two thousand people, and had special acoustical properties that were said to be magical in origin. Now that would be something to see. Should she, perhaps, journey all the way to Parat?

As she hurried along, it occurred to Penumbra that she could no longer go by the name she'd used for the last four years of her life. Her mother had named her Leila, which she said meant "dark beauty" in the language of the desert people far to the east and south. But she couldn't use that name either. Not while she was masquerading as a boy.

People had often told Leila that she resembled the Nima, those nomadic people who roamed throughout the Dominion (and possibly elsewhere on the continent as well) with their horse-drawn wooden wagons. They traveled from encampment to encampment, hiring out for the harvest here, mending pots or telling fortunes there. She had met some of them, as there was a semi-permanent population of Nima living in Marsine's poorer districts.

They had their own culture and their own language as well, though all of them appeared to speak Gasparto as well as any other native of the Dominion did. But though they lived within the Dominion, they never really seemed to be a part of it – keeping to themselves, maintaining their own traditions. So clearly she couldn't pretend to be one of them – she'd be busted the first time she came into a situation where real Nima were present. But maybe…

"My name is Luca," she rehearsed as she jogged along. There had been a Nima boy by that name living with an astonishing number of his relatives in a basement room in the harbor district when she'd been running with Tomas' gang. "No, I am not of the Nima, but my father was – or so my mother told me. His name was Nico, she said, and she met him when his band was passing through her village. A little north of here. He never knew he had fathered a child, and never returned. Now my mother has died, and I am off to see the world. I had hoped I would meet some of my father's people, and perhaps learn their ways…"

One of the many stories circulating about the Nima was that they stole children, taking them into their bands and raising them as their own. From what "Luca" knew of them, she very much doubted that was true. But while they were clannish, they could also be very hospitable. She hoped that the imagined blood connection might get her welcomed into a band, and as a boy of the Nima living in a traveling band she would be utterly invisible. No one would ever seek the girl thief Penumbra in such a place.

Chapter 24

Luca rode the driver's box of the brightly-painted caravan, clucking to the fuzz-footed cart horse as it stolidly pulled him along. Little Dika, five years old and with sparkling eyes as black as her curly hair, rode to his right while Kathal, the family's young pard, had tucked herself beneath his left elbow and was purring slightly – her golden eyes alight with interest. They were coming into the outskirts of Ylanda, capital of the county of Bourge and home to one of the largest Nima encampments in the Gaspari Dominion. Dika had never been here before that she could recall, and her excitement was so great that she was bouncing up and down on the hard wooden seat.

"Settle down, *jel'enedra,*" Luca said, and grinned at her. Little sister, one of many Nima terms he had learned over the past several months. Luca had been traveling with this band for the better part of a year, throughout the western part of the Dominion and then north and east again, winding over gentle mountain passes and through field and forest as they made the yearly circuit of the western Nima.

Pitti and Jaelle, a young Nima couple in their middle twenties, had taken Luca in – quite willing to buy his story of being a half-Nima bastard boy, orphaned now, and out on the road seeking his roots. After the birth of their daughter they'd hoped for a son. The small confines of the caravans didn't encourage huge families, but two or three children was the rule. None had come to them, and they'd welcomed this foundling in as if he had been sent by the gods. Leila felt a stab of guilt just thinking about it.

Her time with the Nima had been fascinating – learning their ways and the secret histories they told no outsiders, picking up enough of their language that she could converse in it, at least. And she had fallen in love with the little family. Pitti and Jaelle were so earnest and well-meaning, Dika so adorable. Kathal had been a half-grown kitten, youngest of the three pards the family kept, and irresistibly cute.

These forty to fifty-pound, long-legged cats behaved almost more like dogs, and the Nima bred them as companions and caravan guards. As defenders they were as effective as a dog twice the size, somewhat more intelligent, and kept themselves fed on everything from mice to pheasants and rabbits while their masters traveled along the road.

But as much as Leila adored her new family, the burden of knowing that she was deceiving them prevented her from giving herself fully to them. She was not truly Luca, and everything they thought they knew about her was a lie. Preserving the fiction of being a pre-adolescent boy, though, had proved far less difficult than she had feared. The Nima were a private and in many ways a restrained people, despite their reputation within the Dominion. Nudity, even among family members, was unknown. And as Luca was supposedly but ten years of age, nobody expected him to be engaging in the kinds of macho pursuits that would have been usual for an older boy – things she could not have done without blowing her cover.

Luca and the other boys of the band, which consisted of a dozen families traveling in fifteen caravans, mostly spent their days in chores – taking over driver duty on the caravans, helping with the livestock, or whatever else needed doing. The Nima traveled with horses, goats, chickens, and occasionally other barnyard animals – most of them theoretically not stolen. But stealing, of which the Nima were often accused, was indeed part of their lifestyle. Leila felt right at home. The other boys were in awe of Luca's skill, as he made off with anything that was left unguarded (and some things that were not) while the band traveled across the countryside.

Except for the constant awareness that she was living a lie, this had been one of the happiest periods of Leila's life. The people were warm, their culture rich in the enjoyment of life, and the almost-constant movement of the band meant that there were always new horizons to explore. After living her whole life within the confines of Marsine, life with the Nima had been freedom like she had never known.

But their time was coming to a close, and she could not deny it. Fourteen now, her development had continued and it appeared that she was, after all, taking after her mother. Though she was still slim and muscular, it was getting harder and harder for her to compress her growing breasts into the semblance of a boy's flat chest. Time to move on, before the situation became untenable. More than anything, Leila didn't want to see the look on the faces of Pitti, Jaelle, and Dika if they learned that she had played them all for fools.

So, the story had been building. Luca had begun talking about it as soon as he learned that the band was moving toward Ylanda and an early autumn gathering that would include dozens of other bands from all over the Dominion. "Perhaps I'll be able to get some word of my father!" he said enthusiastically. Pitti and Jaelle exchanged looks, then she spoke up. "Luca, you must know that Nico is a very common name among the Nima. How can you hope to find him?"

Luca appeared abashed for a moment, then a look of determination came over his face. "I know, it's going to be hard. But I have to find him. He's the only real family I have now, and he needs to know that he has a son. Mother said that they were very much in love, though they spent such a short time together. She would have left with him if she could, but her own mother was ill and needed constant care." What a crock, Leila was thinking, annoyed at herself for deceiving these kind people.

Jaelle's brows knit. The poor boy! To roll one of the local girls while passing through an area was frowned on by Nima culture, but it wasn't what you'd call unusual. Traveling with a band, where half the girls were probably your close relations, it was hard for a young man of the Nima to find an outlet for his passions.

That's what gatherings were all about, many bands getting together so that the young people could find mates. But that "very much in love" business had probably been very one-sided, and if Luca actually managed to find the Nico who had sired him it was likely the man would not even remember the boy's mother at all. She sighed.

Now here they were at the gathering, and it was time for Luca to detach himself from the band and move on – to become, once again, a girl called Leila. A young woman now, and possessed of skills that should easily see her into a comfortable lifestyle. She had no real ambitions at this point, other than a general aim to someday make her way to Palambo and look up Vandao. My, wouldn't he be surprised to meet her! And in the meantime, she had the whole of the Gaspari Dominion to explore.

Chapter 25

The Nima used coin in their dealings with outsiders – just as everyone else in the Dominion did, as was the case in the entire known world so far as Leila knew. But among themselves, barter was the usual medium of exchange. So the emerald necklace Penumbra had stolen from the Night Guild all those months ago still nestled within a secret compartment sewn into the bottom of Luca's pack. No goods or services on offer within the world of the Nima were worth what Leila could get for that necklace on the open market.

And she needed to sell that necklace now; but in order to obtain anything like its true market value, she needed to *spend* some money first. The scene at the gathering grounds outside of Ylanda was chaotic, with more bands arriving every few hours and kids swarming around, excited to meet new people or old friends while their elders met to discuss marriage possibilities. In the confusion it was easy for Luca to borrow a horse and slip away.

One of Leila's most valuable new skills, learned from the Nima during her months of traveling with them, was riding. Much as she had loved visiting with the coach horses at Madam Droma's, she had never done more than climb up onto Dobbin's broad, warm back. There was no riding tack at the stables behind the House of the Golden Fish, and in any case those horses had been trained to pull carriages – not carry a rider.

But horses were an essential part of the culture of the Nima. They used sturdy, heavy ones to pull their caravans and bred slim, graceful ones (descended from animals brought from the deserts of Palambo, it was said, by the ancestors of the Nima) for racing. Horse racing, and making book on those races, was one of the many activities by which they obtained coin from outsiders. So when Pitti discovered that Luca had never been taught to ride, he soon set about remedying the situation – to Leila's delight.

"Pitti, I want to visit the town. Can I take Barban for a ride?" She very nearly thought of him as a father, but had resisted calling him that. It would make leaving far too painful. He smiled at his adoptive son, but there was a hint of worry in his eyes. "That will be all right," he said, "but don't run him too hard. Don't forget he's racing tomorrow!" Luca grinned and nodded. He wasn't yet a skilled enough rider to be the nimble young stallion's jockey when money was on the line; and as he was leaving soon, he would never get the chance. But he wished he could!

"Another thing, Luca," Pitti went on. "Watch yourself in town. The residents of Ylanda are friendly enough to The People that they let us hold our gatherings here outside their city, and we bring much business to them when we come. But many are suspicious of us, and will take any excuse to accuse one of us of stealing or worse. Don't give them any reasons to do so, eh?"

Luca nodded again, more soberly. He knew full well that Gasparis were suspicious of the Nima for good reason. Not that he planned to be stealing anything in town. He had enough cash, picked up here and there over the past few months, to cover what he needed to buy.

Luca eschewed a saddle, just throwing a blanket over the glistening black stallion's back. He patted Kathal and shooed her back toward the caravan as she rubbed up against his legs, making the peculiar vocalization that indicated excited enthusiasm. Pards were as sociable as dogs, and they tended to bond with the people they lived with and want to follow them everywhere. But once trained, they would accept orders to stay and guard. Kathal was getting there, and with a wounded look she turned and slunk back home.

Luca mounted, and cantered Barban the mile from the crowded gathering grounds to the outskirts of the city. He could certainly have gone on foot, but he'd wanted to enjoy the feeling of being mounted atop the swift young animal. After all, he expected he'd be getting more than enough practice walking, once he parted company with the band.

As at Marsine and most of the cities across the Dominion, Ylanda had once had towering city walls. A few remnants of these still stood, having been incorporated into the sides of buildings that had been erected next to them. Those buildings were now more than a quarter mile inside the modern perimeter, a historical curiosity.

Luca had never been here before but it had been easy enough to get his elders talking about the place. It was one of the favorite gathering spots for the bands of Nima whose yearly migration took them through this part of the Dominion. As soon as he and Bandar had ambled into the city on a broad cobbled boulevard, he began looking around for signs that would tell him he was in the right part of town.

In a seaport like Marsine, the district he sought would have been easy to find. Here, in this city that got some river trade but found most of its economic lifeblood in the agricultural regions that surrounded it, he had a little more trouble. Finally he spotted a young man mounted on a plowhorse, following behind an enormous, creaking wain that appeared to be full of apples.

Luca nudged Bandar with his heels and came up on the young farmer, falling into step beside him. Leila's makeshift "boy" garb had long since been replaced with the colorful clothing favored by the Nima: blue trousers, a yellow ruffled shirt, and a red sash. She shuddered whenever she considered what an absurd peacock she must look in this getup; but in this case, it was protective coloring.

Luca asked the farmer for directions, and provoked a bark of laughter. "You Nima must start young!" he said, grinning. Luca colored, but on his dark features it wasn't so noticeable.

"Father says I should learn," he murmured with a shrug.

"Very well then," the farmer replied. "Turn left at this next intersection, go down… I'm not sure how many blocks, but there's a fountain in the middle of the intersection. Turn right there, and in another couple of blocks there's an area with several houses. Have fun!"

With that he waved and continued following his wagonload of apples as the Nima boy on his fine-looking stallion turned left and headed for the red light district. The directions were spot on, and Luca soon found himself clip-clopping along a block lined on both sides with three-story brick houses. From the upper-story windows, gaudily-dressed young (and not-so-young) whores leaned out, calling to passersby in the street below.

A woman with an unlikely-looking mop of bright red curls called to him as he was passing a few yards away. "Hello pretty boy,

ready to become a man? Come on inside, I'll show you a good time."
Actually, Luca thought in amusement as he dismounted and tied
Barban to the hitching post provided for customers, I'm ready to
become a *woman*.

He walked with jaunty confidence and a mischievous grin past
the bouncer at the door, and into the downstairs receiving parlor. A
trio of bored-looking whores dressed in scanty lingerie were
lounging around it on upholstered divans. The madam, a handsome
woman who appeared as if she might be anywhere from forty to
sixty, was wearing a respectable-looking frock that wouldn't have
been out of place on a countess.

She eyed him up and down as he came in and stood grinning at
her cheekily. Pretty as he was, Luca could charm the pants off you if
that was what Leila wanted to do. She had devoted most of her career
as a thief to stealthy operations that didn't require human interaction
– but she'd been trained in the art of the con game as well, and her
time with the Nima had honed those skills.

"How old are you?" the madam said suspiciously. "We don't
take children, here."

"I'm older than you think," Luca replied, flashing his white teeth
in vivid contrast to his dark features, "but that's not why I'm here. I
have a proposition for you of a different kind, and money to spend."

It was Luca who had gone into the whorehouse, but Leila who
emerged some forty-five minutes later. Or perhaps, she thought, as
she made her way down the street, she was now Musette. A rich
man's mistress, cut loose when his wife had learned of her and
threatened to divorce him if he did not end the relationship. He'd
been most regretful, but what could he do? He would no longer be
able to give her spending money, no longer pay the rent on her
apartment. But she still had the jewels he had given her, and she was
now forced to sell some of them in order to cover her expenses until
she found another "patron."

The whores had been delighted with the prank. This Nima boy
planned to put one over on the older brother of a friend, a bet that he
could lure the young man into a compromising position. But not only
must he be gotten up to look like a girl, he must look like a girl with
some class and distinction – not a cheap whore.

Along with the light red wig, they had whitened Leila's skin with their paints and powders until – with her green eyes – the notion of her being a redhead was almost believable. The wig, dress, shoes and accessories were all to be returned within a few hours, and in the meantime they had Luca's horse and clothing as surety. The horse was worth a thousand times the value of the items they'd lent her, so no one was worried that the Nima boy would not return.

Now Leila just needed to find a suitable jeweler to whom she could sell the necklace. It was a fine piece, and she planned to get a good price for it. She hoped it was not going to be a long walk. The shoes they had found for her, satin and rhinestones with little heels, were a good fit. But she had not worn anything so impractical on her feet, ever, and they were beginning to complain about it before she'd gone a block.

Once again, a local citizen was able to provide directions. As was frequently the case in cities run by the guilds, nearly all of the jewelers had their shops along one mercantile row – in this case, called Gold Street. Which was on the far side of the city from the red light district, of course.

Hang the expense, there was no way Leila was walking a mile in a whore's shoes! Smiling to herself as she realized the play on words, she concluded that having spent the first eight years of her life in a whorehouse was quite enough. There were single-passenger sedan chairs for hire throughout the city, carried by two sturdy porters each, and she flagged one down. A few silver shillings was enough to take her to her destination; and arriving out in front of the largest and most prestigious-looking shop on the street in a hired conveyance seemed more supportive of her story than would coming there on foot.

Leila (Musette, now) gave the lead man another shilling and asked him, with a sweet smile and a toss of her auburn curls, to please wait for her. Oh, she hoped this was going to go smoothly! Having plenty of training wasn't really the same thing as having plenty of experience.

She walked inside with her head up, an inch or two taller than usual in those heels. That helped her to capture the air of self-confidence she needed. An avid admirer of beautiful jewelry,

Musette let her attention be seized by one piece after another, her eyes sparkling nearly as much as the jewels themselves. The proprietor of the shop stood behind the counter, smiling slightly and eyeing her uncertainly. Might this woman actually be a customer?

Finally she approached the counter, an expression of serene happiness on her face. For a fourteen-year-old virgin to pull off the air of a young woman who had been around the block a time or two was no mean feat. Leila hoped the heavy makeup, the presence of which must surely be detectible from this distance, would suggest that "Musette" was not so young as all that and was fighting a losing battle against time. Better that than the truth…

The jeweler spotted that no wedding ring adorned her finger. "Good afternoon, mademoiselle, how may I assist you?" he asked suavely.

"I'm Musette," Leila said, extending a hand for a gentle squeeze. "I'm new to Ylanda, but I think I am going to like it here. Might I ask your name?" The jeweler swelled up a little, incidentally turning a pale pink.

"Francois Bardoux, at your service. I may call you Musette?"

She extricated her hand from his grasp and looked into his eyes. "Of course. May I call you Francois?" He nodded. "Might I have a look at that necklace there?" she went on, gesturing vaguely to a group of jeweled chokers that was spread on velvet below the glass countertop.

Unlocking the sliding door at the back of the case with a small key, he bent at the waist and began fumbling under the counter. "No not that one," Musette said petulantly, "the diamonds. I really don't care all that much for colored stones," she added, as if she routinely had her choice of whatever fine jewelry took her fancy.

With an oily smile Francois extracted the necklace in question from the case and held it up. At the whorehouse, Leila had insisted on putting on the dress in private, claiming embarrassment. Then she'd emerged wearing a shawl around the shoulders of the dress, hiding the fact that the "Nima boy" had real cleavage. Requesting a pot of the pale makeup to take with her in case touchups were needed, she'd lightened the rest of the skin that was revealed when the shawl was removed during the ride in the sedan chair. Now the

134

jeweler's eye was caught by that cleavage, as he leaned in to show her the glittering diamond torc.

"It's lovely!" Leila exclaimed, in her poshest accents. She might have grown up in a whorehouse, but she had been raised by an educated woman from the right side of town and she was now finding that she could *become* that woman, when she needed to. A woman who made a living as a rich man's mistress was really only a refined sort of whore. But the emphasis was on refinement. "Oh please," she added, "let me see it on!"

"Of course," Francois said, captivated. He leaned still further over the counter so as to fasten the fabulous object around her neck, all the while gazing at those ripe mounds on display down the front of her elegant dress. His middle-aged heart was beating faster. He thought he knew quite well what sort of young woman this must be, and he was wondering why *he* had not yet managed to acquire a mistress. He was a wealthy man, his children were nearly grown, and his wife was a fat harridan who had not shared his bed in years. Perhaps it was time…

There was a small oval mirror on a stand atop the counter, and Leila eagerly turned it so that she could admire herself with those glittering white gems on display. Truthfully, she much preferred the way the emeralds brought out the green of her eyes. But for now, she must play the part – and Musette liked diamonds.

"Oh!" she exclaimed, her lovely eyes wide with desire. "I must have it!" Leila turned her gaze to the jeweler, who was staring at her hungrily. Even if she was trying to come off as a woman on the wrong side of thirty, she apparently seemed quite delectable to him. Of course, he must have been fifty if he was a day. She dropped her gaze, demurely fluttering the long dark lashes that were part of the package with her dark skin and curly black hair. "How much is it?"

No doubt this lovely's patron would soon be dangling on a hook, eager to pay whatever the price might be to satisfy his darling. Might as well jack it up… "This is a truly exquisite piece," Francois began.

"Oh! I agree!" Musette declared breathily.

"I make many of the pieces you will see here in the shop myself," he continued with a gesture around the room, "but this one I imported especially from a supplier in Miradil. He has access to all the finest goods from the Hando realms and Palambo."

Musette's eyes got wide as she gazed into his eyes. He was so wise, so knowledgeable, and she was just an innocent young woman who knew scarcely anything of the world. "Then, the price..." she said softly.

"Is fifty florins," Francois concluded.

Musette's face fell, and a look of inexpressible sadness came into her eyes.

"What's the matter?" Francois asked. "Surely your patron could not deny you anything. You are so lovely!" She looked up at him, a hint of pleasure at the compliment not quite driving away the darkness.

"Alas!" she told him. "Bertrand's unspeakable pig of a wife has found out about us, and he has told me that we must part." Aha, I knew it! Francois thought. The poor girl...

"So," he said, trying to draw out the full story, "you have arrived in Ylanda only to find yourself out on the street?"

Musette looked into his eyes with an expression so plangent it fairly tore his soul. "Not quite out on the street, but close to it," she admitted tragically. A hint that she might start crying at any moment hovered in her eyes. "Should Bertrand's wife divorce him, he would be ruined. So he is no longer able to pay for my apartment, and if I do not pay the rent by next Mulday I will indeed be out on the street."

So much for a huge profit on the diamond necklace, then. But the girl's story wrenched at Francois' heart. How could any man so callously dump a beautiful young creature like this, just cast her aside? If she were *his* mistress, he'd have dumped the wife instead.

Before the jeweler could ask, Musette drew out the emerald necklace from a small embroidered reticule hung at her waist. "I am forced to sell some of the jewelry Bertrand gave me," she said sadly. "Though it pains me deeply. But I must have a roof over my head!"

She passed the necklace over to him as if she were handing over her firstborn child – eyes downcast and once again, a hint of tears threatening. He took it in his hands and spread it out. By the Seven! This Bertrand must have been wealthy indeed, if he had been able to gift his mistress with pieces such as this and yet avoid his wife discovering the situation.

In the Dominion, women were definitely subordinate to men and it was usually the husband who controlled the purse strings. But if there wasn't enough money in the household budget to pay the butcher's bill, or the servants, the wife would find out soon enough. And begin to ask some difficult questions…

Though half-drunk on the presence of Musette, Francois was not a complete idiot. He immediately extracted some of his professional equipment from a drawer below the counter on the back wall, and studied the emerald necklace he'd been handed. Amazing! The color, cut, and clarity of the stones, as well as the way in which they had been color-matched to form this necklace, was superb. He could probably sell this piece to one of his wealthy clients in town for considerably more than the fifty florins he'd suggested to Musette (the diamond necklace was really worth no more than thirty).

"Your Bertrand truly loved you I think," Francois said as he turned back to Musette with the necklace in his hands. Those enormous, deep-green eyes met his with an expression of gratitude.

"Oh!" she said sadly, once again it seemed on the verge of tears, "and I loved *him*. For nearly a year we were so happy. And when it was necessary for him to relocate to Ylanda, he brought me along. If only that bitch had not questioned the fact that he continued to be gone on Mulday nights in the new city as in the old!" She bent her head and put a hand to her eyes as if willing the tears not to fall.

Francois' bloated, weathered features took on a look of profound sympathy. "Alas, my dear," he said, "it is a sad tale you tell. But look on the bright side. You are now here in Ylanda, capital of the happiest and most fertile region in all the western Dominion! And you are young, and now free!"

Musette looked at him with a hint of optimism, as if his words had given her new hope. "Yes!" she said, "I will find love again, I know it!" Her gaze fell again, recalling the problem at hand. "But first, I must pay my rent before Mulday. How much can you give me for the necklace?" Her look suggested that love might be just around the corner for Francois, as it presumably was for her.

Dazzled, Francois gathered his wits. "I was thinking that I might be willing to give you as much as thirty florins." Her face fell. "But it will be a big investment for me, and I might not be able find a buyer for months!" he protested. Musette looked at him petulantly.

"I thought you said that Ylanda was the capital of the most fertile region in the western Dominion? Surely some of these farm owners must be quite wealthy?" She had hit the nail on the head, and Francois retreated.

"But still, such amounts are beyond the means of most," he pointed out irrelevantly. He only needed one customer willing to pay market value, and he could in fact think of half a dozen who might come through for a piece as magnificent as this one. Musette frowned.

"I like you, Francois," she said in a hurt-little-girl voice. "You are clearly a man of substance, and one who knows jewelry. And I was hoping that this chance meeting might have become the start of our friendship." He looked at her helplessly.

"But now I think," the lovely young thing went on in tones of betrayed trust, "that you are just taking advantage of me. You think that because I am a young girl I don't know how much this necklace is worth. So you would take it from me for nothing, just because I am desperate to pay my rent, and walk away laughing all the way to the bank while I struggle to live. It is cold of you."

She took the necklace back from him, and made as if to leave – her shoulders slumped, devastated by this betrayal from a man she had begun to think of as a friend. A pain rose up in Francois' breast. He could not bear it! "No!" he said in a voice strangled by emotion, "Don't go! How much do you need? I would truly like to become your trusted friend, if I can…"

Musette turned back to him in an instant, the necklace cupped in her hands at a level that happened to be about the same as her cleavage. She locked her eyes on his, an expression of childlike joy on her face. "Really?" she said, her voice high and girlish with delight. "Oh, Francois! It would mean so much to me, not to have to constantly battle with finances! If only I can get what this necklace is worth, then perhaps I won't have to sell any of the others. They have such sentimental value…"

Feeling like a man swaying in the wind atop a high precipice, Francois leaned across the counter once again and took Musette's hands in his, the necklace held within them. "Whatever you want," he promised, "if it's in my power, dear girl, it will be yours."

Chapter 26

Francois had a date with Musette, meeting in a café a few blocks from the jewelry store, for the Mulday after next. Alas for his hopes, she would not be there. For Musette, now far richer than she had been, had returned to the whorehouse never to be seen again. The Nima boy Luca, scrubbed and kissed and reporting complete, hilarious success in his prank against his friend's older brother, was once more astride Barban and riding back to the Nima encampment a mile away.

Everyone else seemed to have gone elsewhere, but Kathal and her parents were there to greet him when he rode up. Kirve and Tale were a little more reserved – they had already bonded with Pitti and Jaelle, and with Dika as well, long before Luca had arrived. But Kathal, just a few months old when he joined the family, seemed to have decided that Luca was *her* human. Leila wondered if, with the pard's superior sense of smell, Kathal knew along that she was a girl.

Though the trip had not been arduous, Luca removed the blanket and gave Barban a bit of a rubdown before removing the clip-on reins from his halter (the Nima scorned the use of bits, preferring to master their horses with close guidance and training from the age of a few months) and turning him out into the pasture area that had been fenced off when the gathering had begun. He would come when called.

Leila was now carrying more money than she had ever owned before, not counting the enormous pile of money her mother had stashed away over eight years of whoring – the coin that bitch Droma had stolen, meant to save Miriam's life. Much good might it do the old sow, she thought bitterly. Leila seldom fell asleep at night without a silent wish that the woman would be afflicted with a terminal case of boils. Or at least something as fatal as, and more painful than, the Ascari Pox that had killed her mother.

When Luca parted company with the band, an event that would be coming all too soon, he must carry all this money with him. At the moment it was all in gold, in a sack provided by the luckless Francois. It weighed several pounds, and was bulky enough that it was going to be hard to conceal about his person. It seemed that Pitti and his family were elsewhere in the encampment, probably socializing with some of their friends and acquaintances from other bands. This was the perfect opportunity for Luca to hide his stash.

Over the years Leila had become handy with a needle and thread. She now set about sewing some of the gold coins into the lining of Luca's cloak, and the rest into a secret compartment at the bottom of the pack that had come with her from the Night Guild. If anyone were to empty the pack and then lift it, they would immediately realize something was amiss; but she hoped it might be enough to deflect the casual eye. At least, packed down tight inside there with layers of cloth between, it did not jingle as the pack was moved.

By the time Luca was finished hiding the money his foster family had not yet returned, and he went out seeking them. Kathal was right at his heels, frolicking happily at the chance to be out exploring. She'd obediently stayed at the caravan for all the interminable hours while he'd been out in Ylanda, but now he was letting her come along. Oh joy!

Luca moved through the encampment, smiling and waving when he came across an acquaintance. Each band of the Nima followed their own route, usually repeating the same circuit year after year unless some unusual event or opportunity altered their plans. But the circuits of different bands frequently overlapped, an occasion for a communal evening (and some flirtation among the young people, whose chance for a deeper relationship would come at the next gathering) with singing, dancing, and the swapping of tales.

Eventually Luca found Pitti, Jaelle, and Dika sitting around a small campfire outside the caravan of a family he remembered from a brief meeting only a couple of months after he had joined Pitti's band. He and Kathal came up to the campsite and he made the gesture of greeting, both palms up and rising. "Ferkal!" he said, "We meet again!"

The old man (well, he looked to be in his middle forties, anyway) rose from his seat with a smile. He was pleased that the youngster had remembered his name after only one meeting all those months in the past. He and his niece (he was Jaelle's uncle, her father's brother) had been discussing the situation and he had some hopes that the boy Luca might stay on and become in truth the son of the family. Every family needed a son, for even among the Nima males were favored over females. And the gods had more than one way of providing one.

"Luca, good to see you again," Ferkal said with a welcoming smile. "Pull up a seat. I've invited your family to share our supper tonight." Luca grinned broadly, and took a spare stool. The "living room furniture" of the Nima consisted of folding three-legged stools, constructed of sturdy pine and held together with leather. They were surprisingly comfortable.

"I see Kathal has accompanied you," Jaelle remarked with a smile.

"I can barely drive her off," Luca admitted ruefully. How was he going to say goodbye to her?

"You've been gone a long time," Pitti chimed in. "Did you enjoy your trip to Ylanda?"

"It was amazing!" Luca enthused, shuddering inside at the deception. "Not since Marsine have I seen such a city!" They had picked "him" up on the road west, no more than twenty miles from Marsine, and part of his cover story had been that he'd gone there first after the death of his mother before deciding to try to find the Nima and learn more about his father's people. Pitti smiled. He remembered with fondness his first visit to Ylanda, when he was no older than Luca was now. They all thought he was now around eleven, though he'd claimed not to know exactly when his birthday was.

A convivial evening ensued around the campfire beside Ferkal's caravan. Ferkal's wife, Lyuba, set out a meal on two long boards laid across a series of folding stands in the area beside the caravan, and they all moved their stools over to partake of the food. As night was falling, all of them were gathered around the campfire once again.

"I found a lead to my father while I was in Ylanda!" Luca announced, and they all looked at him with interest. Ferkal, like Jaelle, was convinced that the boy's quest for the man who had fathered him was only a childish dream. The chances of actually finding him, let alone convincing him to acknowledge his by-blow, were slight. But none of them wanted to be the bearer of this bad news, and crush the boy's hopes.

Instead, they sat waiting for him to say more. Kathal, who had received some scraps from the table, was now curled at his feet asleep. This was the tough part, Leila thought. They must believe that Luca had received some accurate information, but it could not be from a source they would check on.

Luca went on, "I met one of the city constables, one who was not so unfriendly to the Nima, and I told him of my quest." Luca's relentless search for his missing father had been impressed on everyone he met, laying the groundwork for when he needed to depart. He went on, "He had heard of a man of the Nima, named Nico, who had been detained because he had been involved with the daughter of one of the locals!"

This behavior was frowned on, but the fictional Nico had an established pattern of getting in trouble with *b'or* – women not of the Nima. While it was a shame to Luca that the father he sought, so "deeply in love" with his late mother, would be moving on to other forbidden girls, it at least suggested that this particular Nico might actually be the one.

"What happened to him?" Jaelle asked. Her heart went out to this boy who had begun to seem as if he were truly her son, but she knew that the pain he felt, not knowing his birth father, was something that all her mother's love could not heal.

"The city let him go, but demanded that he leave town," Luca went on. "The girl's father was not happy at that, but nothing had come of their liaison so there was really nothing to hold him on. By then of course Nico's band had left, gone on their circuit."

"When was this?" Pitti asked. He was trying to work out whether they might find this Nico's band on their own circuit, and bring the boy's quest to an end.

"It was the gathering three months ago," Luca replied. The gathering ground was occupied usually every three months or so, each time by a different group of bands whose wanderings all had Ylanda as a common stop.

So Nico and his band, if he had caught up with them and they had not decided to expel him for his bad behavior, would probably now be as much as a thousand miles away in who knew what direction. Bands whose circuits did not coincide rarely interacted with each other, though all were part of the cultural identity of the Nima. Pitti let a small sigh escape his lips.

"The constable said that Nico told him he was going to Munch!" Luca prattled on happily, "He expected to reunite with his band there. That's only about three hundred miles from here – we could make it in a month if we hurried!" His expression of wide-eyed innocence suggested he assumed that the entire band would be willing to go hundreds of miles out of their established migration route just so he could go look for an apocryphal father. Who would probably already be long gone by the time they arrived…

Luca looked around the fire at his companions, his youthful face shining with enthusiasm. Even as Pitti and Jaelle's hearts sank, so Leila's was writhing in agony at the manipulation. But this had to be done! "Luca," Pitti said sadly, "it is not possible for our entire band to simply break from our accustomed paths to go looking for this Nico. It can't be done."

Luca's face fell for a moment. Then a look of optimism came across his face as it seemed another idea had occurred to him. But before he spoke, realization stole across his features and he said softly, "Oh. Of course. How stupid of me, I should have realized. I can't ask you to disrupt your lives just to help me find a man who doesn't even know I exist." He slumped on his stool, face downcast.

Jaelle rose from her stool and came over to stand beside Luca, hugging him to her. "You must understand," she said, "we don't believe that this quest of yours can end in anything but disappointment – even if you do find your father. Why not stay with us? Pitti can be your new father, a father who knows and loves you."

Leila had thought that the last of her life's tears had been shed on the morning that her mother died. But she had cried when she had lost her home with the Night Guild; and now once again she found her eyes stinging, hot salty drops flowing unbidden down her cheeks. She squeezed Jaelle back. "Oh Jaelle, I truly wish you were my mother and that we could be together always," she said from the heart. Then she got a grip on her emotions and went on.

"But my mother is dead, and Nico broke her heart. Before I can become a part of a family again, a true part, I must find him and make him know what he has done." So, the boy's view of his legendary father was less idealized than they had imagined.

"After you have found him, if you want, you could come back to us," Pitti said formally. It was tearing him apart to see the sadness in Jaelle.

Luca rose to his feet, and stepped forward to take Pitti's hands. "Thank you, Pitti. I hope that I may do that. I will return to the caravan and gather my things, then leave for Munch in the morning." The man gave him a quick squeeze, then released him as the boy and the cat turned away and moved off into the night.

Chapter 27

The cloaked rider, following a barely visible trail, came to the crest of the hill and beheld the good-sized town of Chanton lying below. "Stand, Nimble," the rider said softly, and the horse held a fixed posture as she dismounted and threw back the hood. She knelt and stroked the fur of the cat at her side, which was gazing at the town below her as if it held some fascination.

"Well, Kathal, there it is," Leila murmured. "One big score, and then we can dash south for good. I'll bet you're ready to get off your feet, eh?" Kathal nuzzled her and remarked, "Prrt." Pards had a wide range of vocalizations, from the banshee screech they were trained to emit when intruders were present to little clucking sounds that sounded almost like speech. Certainly, they seemed to understand much of what was said to them.

When Luca had left the Nima encampment near Ylanda the year before, he had said his goodbyes and then begun striding firmly along the highway that led a little north of east, toward Munch in the county of Bayern. With the amount of money Musette had realized on the sale of the emerald necklace he didn't intend to be on foot for long, though; and after walking along that road for a couple of miles he waited until no other traffic was visible before or behind him. Then he slipped off the road (one of the Dominion's fine arteries, wide enough for even large carts to pass side by side and paved with stone) into the woodland that surrounded it.

A thousand years of peace had allowed the people of the Dominion to apply themselves to many more useful pursuits than building up armies or developing new and ever more clever ways to kill each other. Commerce was aided by the well-maintained roads, by canals and locks, and by a complete lack of tariffs within the Dominion itself. There were no standing armies, no weapons beyond those borne by professional guards or what people carried for personal defense (or conversely, for personal offense – the end of war had not eliminated banditry and strong-arm robbery).

Leila mused on this as she picked her way through the woods and came upon a path that was well-trodden enough to have been made by the feet of men, not deer or other wild game. When she was far enough from the road to be sure that she was alone and unseen, she set down her pack and changed clothes.

Luca's colorful Nima garb, two sets of it, were stowed in the bottom of the pack. His cloak, into the lining of which she'd sewn a dozen gold coins, was a brick red color, far brighter than she would have liked. Perhaps she could dye it, or buy one in a more muted tone and transfer the coins. She put on her Night Guild garb, dark gray and form-fitting. A little *too* form-fitting, she realized. She had grown in the nearly a year since leaving Marsine. Damn, another thing to deal with.

Leila's hair was short and curly and boyish-looking. Without the cloth wrapped around her torso beneath the shirt her breasts were obvious enough that no one with eyes to see would mistake her for a boy close up; but from a distance it wouldn't be obvious she was a woman. Women alone in the Dominion were often troubled either by men who wished to step in and protect them – or men who wanted to take advantage of their apparent lack of protection. She could certainly defend herself, but it would cause complications if she had to kill anybody. I'd better just stay away from people for a while, she thought, and sighed.

Leila continued on her way, less conspicuous in the autumn woods in her gray garb. At the moment the weather was dry, and warm enough that she didn't need to wear the red cloak. She was making for the town of Auberge some twenty miles away, where she hoped she'd be able to buy a horse.

It was too far to walk in one day over the winding trail she'd chosen, and it was as she was sitting at a tiny campfire eating some of the food Jaelle had insisted Luca take with him that Kathal appeared. Leila nearly jumped out of her skin when the cat came at her in the darkness. "You scamp!" she exclaimed, after reclaiming her composure. "What am I going to do with you?" Kathal just butted her with her head and purred.

The next morning Leila, secretly glad of the company though she felt a pang that on top of deceiving her Nima family she had "stolen" their pard, walked into the outskirts of Auberge. Almost everyone in every town or city throughout the Dominion was familiar with the Nima and their pards, and to be seen with one would immediately raise questions. What was this girl, who looked so much like the Nima and was traveling in company with one of their animals, doing walking around without a band? Was she here to steal? Well, yes, could be... But Leila would prefer those questions never arose.

So Kathal was ordered to stay back, hidden in a small thicket that lay beside the trail as Leila went into town, searching for a horse seller. At the time she thought she had been taken by the old man, who looked her up and down and immediately added fifty percent to his prices – or so she suspected.

Bargaining was a skill the Nima were well versed in, but Leila as Luca had been only an apprentice Nima after all. Yet the chestnut gelding she'd bought and named Nimble had (though certainly, he couldn't hold a candle to Barban) proven to be sturdy, good-natured, and young enough that she'd been able to train him in the way that Nima horses were trained. Perhaps the five florins she had paid for him and his tack had not been so exorbitant after all.

So, the Nima boy Luca had vanished on the road to Munch, never to be seen again. Leila prayed that Pitti and Jaelle would not be too devastated that he would not return to them, and further that the Seven might see their way clear to provide the couple with a son of their own. It was the least of what they deserved for being the kind and loving people that they were. Her resolve never henceforth to give worship to the Seven, sworn at age eight, had faded a bit in the past six years. After all, unresponsive as they might seem, they were the only gods available.

Over the next several months Leila roamed without any real objectives, simply exploring the western Dominion and going wherever her fancy took her. Along the way she acquired more and better clothing, and a cover story that let her bring Kathal inside with her when she felt like staying at an inn for some cooked food and a hot bath, not to mention a soft bed – and perhaps, a little human interaction.

The pard, she explained, had been given to her as a kitten by a band of Nima in exchange for being allowed to stay on her family's land. This was a singular gift, as it was known that they did not ever sell the creatures. It had become a beloved companion, and though she was now forced to travel alone (for whatever reason came to her at the moment), Kathal helped keep her safe. It was not far from the truth.

They'd endured the previous winter in the area to the east and south of Ylanda, staying well out of the route taken by Pitti and Jaelle's band in their yearly migration. Leila thought fondly of the area around Catal, where the temperature seldom fell below slightly chilly even in the dead of winter, and orange trees blossomed on hillsides overlooking the Center Sea.

Here, inland, they were enduring days of driving rain, even a little snow at the higher elevations. An ancient mountain range, the Antels, lay southeast of Ylanda, running east and west. Its peaks were worn down to no more than six thousand feet at the highest, but that was high enough in the winter to make Leila long for sunnier climes.

She would never be able to return to Marsine, that was obvious – though she missed it with an inborn longing one can only feel for the place where one grew up as a child. Maybe after Fandal had died... But the guildmaster, who had been nearly a surrogate father to her before the calamity that had sent her flying for her life, had not yet been fifty. He might live another twenty-five years, for all she knew.

So, Leila and her animal companions had bounced around the west-central part of the Gaspari Dominion for close to a year. Never making real friends, never putting down roots, just rambling from place to place. Occasionally, after spending a little time in this or that location, she would identify a thieving opportunity that was too good to pass up – which of course meant they'd be quickly on their way once the job was completed.

Leila only stole from the rich. It wasn't just that they were obviously much more worthy targets, having so much more to steal. Growing up in poverty, and seeing poverty all around, some innate sense told her that the great masses of the poor were held in their poverty because of the same system that let the rich amass great wealth. Most rich people had never worked a day in their lives, the incomes that let them live like kings coming from people who labored like slaves just to obtain a bare subsistence.

Not that she donated the proceeds of her thefts to the poor, though – she had the feeling that would do little good. If she saw someone in danger of starving she would certainly contribute. But often, the poor knew no better thing to do with money than to buy themselves some mental relief in the form of a really good, rip-roaring drunk. After the trauma of her experience at the party celebrating her rise to journeyman, Leila was doubly convinced that alcohol was a gift of Betsalel – a dark gift sure to bring you fresh pain, and more of it, than what it took away.

The life had been good, in ways. Waking up not knowing – and not caring – where the evening might find you could be very freeing. Leila had nobody to look out for but herself and her animal companions, and their needs were simple enough. Except for when they were staying in inns, Kathal could usually feed herself with little trouble. Even in large cities, let her out the window at night and she'd return in the morning well-fed on fat sewer rats. But Leila had needs that were not being met.

She longed to be among friends again, or family. She had no living relatives but the grandfather she despised and the father she hated (assuming either or both of them even still lived), and traveling as she did there had been no opportunity to develop intimate friendships. She needed to settle down, to buy a house somewhere and become part of a community.

Lies seemed to be her constant companions, and Leila would no doubt have to enter such a community on a wave of fresh ones. "I'm independently wealthy thanks to robbing people blind" didn't seem like a good entrée to a place where she hoped to spend the rest of her life surrounded by loving friends. "I'm an orphan with a modest inheritance, enough to keep me" seemed a lot better. And it was just a little lie, really.

The orphan girl Leila Sampson was not known outside of Marsine, but she would not take that surname even if it was hers by right. Something else, some family name she could own... perhaps Leila Trovare, "Leila Found" in the dialect of the region she hoped to settle in. At night as she lay curled in a bed in some inn or in a bedroll in the woods, she imagined what her life would be.

She planned to buy a little house in the hills overlooking the harbor at Jena, far enough to the east of Marsine that she'd be safe from any Night Guild retribution. The journeyman thief Penumbra and the Nima boy Luca would be left behind. Leila Trovare would sit in her small garden in the mornings, sipping strong kaf (a drink made from the roasted beans of a small tree that grew in Palambo) and admiring the play of light on the waters of the Center Sea in the harbor far below. Or perhaps she would breakfast in a café, with a friend.

Leila would of course refrain from robbing her neighbors. That whole part of her life would have to be left behind. There must be no lies beyond the first one, nothing to stand between her and the intimate friendships she craved. She would be able to tell everything to these new friends she imagined having. Well, almost everything. Leila Trovare would be a new-born woman, a person with no past before the moment when she took possession of her new home.

But this dream of a peaceful life, a life without deceptions and danger, was one that Leila could only achieve if she had enough money. There had to be enough for the house, and to maintain a modest living for herself, perhaps invested at interest, for the rest of her life. As she was now fifteen years old, that was going to be a long time.

She still had a little of the gold Francois had paid for Musette's necklace, but a great deal of it had gone to the expenses of living: the purchase of Nimble, additional clothing she had needed, food, nights in inns, specialized equipment for burglaries. At least those had generally resulted in a replenishment of the coffers. But Leila was still thousands of florins short of what she would need to make her dream come true. So here she had come at last to Chanton, and what she hoped would be the big score to last her a lifetime.

Chapter 28

Wilhelm von Oester, sixteenth count of that name, had a reputation that had spread far and wide. People in Parat, capital of the Dominion hundreds of miles away, had probably heard of him. He was now in his sixties, wealthy beyond belief – partly because he was the scion of a family that had been wealthy since before Ostden I united the Dominion, and partly because significant mineral resources had been discovered within the boundaries of Oester over the past century.

Wilhelm's daughters had all been married off to the sons of other counts, and his own two sons – now in their thirties – spent their time caring for their wives and children and waiting patiently for the old man to die. They hoped that some of the money would still be left by then.

Some people, especially in the area around Chanton, were convinced that the count had misplaced a few of his marbles. For the past couple of decades, after his wife had died, he had devoted himself and his financial resources to turning Castle Chanton, the family residence and seat of County Oester, into the most outlandish building in the central Dominion – if not in the world.

The place had sprouted fairytale spires, sweeping buttresses, staircases that went nowhere, and other architectural fancies. Within the complex, an entire new wing was devoted to the display of the count's collections. And he had many. Ivory miniatures from the realms of the Hando had seized his attention for a time, then he had become enamored of the amazing layered metalwork of the craftsmen of Oleda. Once he had collected the best pieces he could find, his interest would wane and he would be on to the next thing.

His current passion, Leila had learned from casual conversations overheard as she made her way here, was tiny clockwork figurines crafted of solid gold and studded with jewels. It was said that they could walk about, duel with swords, or dance with one another. Not magic, but some kind of artifice. When all now living were dead and gone, Leila thought, future curators of museums would bless Wilhelm for providing them with so many amazing artifacts. Except, she planned that a suitable number of them would have vanished long before then.

But unlike any of the other burglaries Leila had committed over the past year, this one was going to take some time to set up. Castle Chanton, if not what you could call an impregnable fortress, was occupied by dozens of people – many of them armed guards. You could not just stroll into such a treasure house as this and walk off with a double armload of its contents, uncontested.

In the year since Luca had vanished Leila's hair had grown quite a lot, and she decided that it was best she establish her identity in Chanton as that of an innocent young woman, quite similar to that very orphan with the small inheritance who would one day be settling in Jena. She was hoping to make a life here in Chanton, and she would rent a small cottage while she settled in and began looking for work. She could not be Leila, of course, so who was she? As Leila rode Nimble down the trail to the main road leading into town, Kathal bringing up the rear, she closed her eyes and let inspiration take her.

The market square was off the main highway through town, centrally located with a large public fountain in the middle. This high in the Antels the growing season was short, and already there was relatively little produce coming in from outlying farms. The people of Chanton must rely a lot on pickled and canned fruits and vegetables, bread and cured meats, to see them through the winter.

There were a few stands in operation, though. Leila dismounted near the entrance to the square and tied Nimble to a hitching post that had been provided, though he would have stood there for hours without being tied if he'd been told to. She commanded Kathal, "Up! Stay put!" and the cat leapt to Nimble's saddle and curled up, ready to remain until instructed otherwise. Leila hoped she would not stand out too much.

On the far side of the square, shawl pulled around her shoulders for warmth in the stiff autumn breeze, Leila approached a fiftyish woman whose stall had apples, pears, and some late vegetables for sale. She was wearing a modest dress cut from a soft, lightweight woolen fabric – purchased in the last town for just this purpose. The skirt was divided for riding, but otherwise it was as respectable a garment as you could hope to see on the daughter of a burgher.

"Good day, mother," Leila said, admiring the stand's offerings. Actually, those pears looked pretty good. "Might I purchase some of your apples and pears?" The woman looked her over and decided she was all right, though from her dark complexion and her accent clearly a stranger to these parts.

Not all people in the Gaspari Dominion were fair, and not all those of a duskier hue were from Palambo or members of the Nima. All along the northern shores of the Center Sea were people with olive skin and black hair – usually with dark eyes as well. Leila could easily pass for one of the people of County Andala, far to the west and south of here.

The woman produced a muslin sack and Leila selected several each of the pears and apples, smiling happily. "Oh, these look so good!" she said with enthusiasm.

"Nothing to the fruit you must get where you come from I suppose," the woman fished. Leila grinned at her, a sweet expression with a hint of sadness lingering around its edges.

"You must mean Andala," she said, and the fruit seller nodded. "I surely hope I can go there someday," Leila said wistfully. "It must be wonderful to see the orange groves." The woman looked at her questioningly, and the dark-haired girl began babbling her life story as trustingly as a lamb.

"My father worked as a factor for one of the orange growers of Andala," she explained, "and his employer required him to relocate to Munch. He and my mother moved there before I was born, so I have never seen the place my ancestors sprang from. When I was small, before she died, my mother often spoke fondly of the beautiful trees growing across the hillsides above the sea." A look of sadness came into Leila's eyes at the wistful memory.

Leila had actually been to Munch, though months after Luca would have been expected there. She'd stayed a couple of weeks, exploring the small city and doing a few small burglaries. Unlike the case in Marsine, there was no central organization of thieves to discourage independents from operating there. She knew the place

154

well enough, at least, to be able to speak about it as if she'd lived there all her life.

The fruit seller looked sympathetic. "I'm sorry," she said, "I suppose it must have been hard for you." It went unspoken that the predominantly blond residents of Munch might have looked askance at the dusky-skinned transplants from Andala. Leila smiled again, shaking off the melancholy.

"It's all right," she said, "it's not as if I've known anything else." She reached across the table and offered the woman her hand, delicately gloved against the chill.

"I'm Rosa Estares," she said formally but with a little grin, "Pleased to meet you." Now the fruit seller cracked a real smile, and took Rosa's little hand in her own considerably larger, coarser one.

"Inge Mahler," she said, returning the smile. "What brings you to Chanton, Rosa? Are you on your own?"

Rosa smiled bravely. "I'm afraid so," she said softly. "Papa passed away last summer, and I've just been trying to decide what I want to do with my life now that I'm alone." Inge looked concerned. She was really quite grandmotherly-seeming, Leila realized.

"You have money to live on?" she asked.

Rosa didn't take offense at what some might call prying. "A little. Papa wasn't a wealthy man, but we lived comfortably enough. I'll need to find a job and save some money, but I hope to travel to Andala and see what it's like there. I think I might like the climate there better than here in the north."

Inge considered the statement, as she pulled the drawstring on the bag of fruit and placed the bag in the pan of a balance scale. "That's twenty coppers," she said, then added as Rosa handed over the money, "You're looking for work, then?"

Rosa nodded. "I wanted to come through Chanton because I heard about the castle, of course. I understand they open the collections to the public once per month?" Now it was Inge's turn to nod.

"Unfortunately you just missed the last viewing day. It was a little under a week ago. Three more weeks now until the next one, and it'll be getting cold by then. Do you have a place to stay?"

Rosa looked around her as if mystified. This town, the castle aside, could have been plopped down in the middle of Marsine and scarcely been noticed. But Munch was not much bigger, and Rosa was an innocent young woman with little experience of the world. "Can you recommend an inexpensive inn that's clean and respectable, someplace where I can stable my horse?" She gestured toward the far side of the market square, where Nimble stood patiently with Kathal, now curled up asleep, on his back.

Inge stood in thought for a moment. As a local, while she occasionally stopped into a tavern for some of the delicious local beer, she had little experience with the room rates charged by the inns. "The Huntsman is clean and respectable, around half a block down the street over there," she pointed. "And the Gnome's Lair is over on the far side of town, along the main road. I'm sorry, I don't really know how much they charge for lodging – or what you can afford."

Rosa continued to look unsure of herself, feeling very alone in this strange town with no one to guide her. "What I'd really like," she said wistfully, is to rent a small cottage, someplace with a little yard where I can keep Nimble, and cook my own meals to save money. I cooked for Papa for years after Mama died. Maybe I could even find work here, and stay for the winter. Then I could earn some money for my trip to Andala."

"You plan to travel with a caravan?" Inge asked. During the warm months, people with goods to haul or places to go overland banded together into caravans with long baggage trains. There was safety in numbers, and the cost of the caravan guards could be spread over all of them. Rosa nodded unsurely.

"My dear, you must be very brave to have traveled here even from Munch, by yourself! It's a wonder you weren't set upon and robbed of all you owned."

"Most of my inheritance is on deposit with the Bank of Gaspar," Rosa explained, "So I'm not in danger of having it all stolen from me. And for personal protection, I have my pard." Another gesture toward the cat and horse.

Inge's eyes widened. "You have a Nima pard?" she asked disbelievingly, her old eyes unable to see that far with any detail.

Rosa smiled prettily, and said "I'll show you!" She walked across the square and untied Nimble's lead, telling Kathal to "stay." Leila could have whistled the horse over – he knew how to free himself when tethered – but she resisted the impulse to show off. Such a feat would have been uncharacteristic for the naïve young Rosa.

When Rosa returned to the fruit stall leading the young gelding, she called to Kathal (now awake and looking around her alertly) "Come down!" With a graceful leap, the tawny cat touched down on the cobbles of the market square as lightly as a feather. Almost full grown now in her second year, she weighed nearly thirty-five pounds. The males were larger, some of them as big as fifty pounds; but the females were said to possess more ferocity – especially if their kittens were threatened. And as far as Kathal was concerned, Leila was her kitten.

Pride shining in her face, Rosa asked Inge "Is it all right if she hops up on the counter?" Fascinated and only a little fearful, the stall keeper nodded. Rosa tapped the counter and said, "Up, Kathal! Say hello." The smooth-furred creature leapt up onto the counter as lithely as she had come down from the horse's back. Then looking Inge in the face, she extended her right front paw, and said something that sounded like "lohk."

Inge gazed at the animal in amazement, then extended her right hand and squeezed the paw that had been offered to her. "Hello, Kathal," she said. The cat nodded to her politely, put her paw down, and then sat on her haunches on the counter, purring. She appeared to be smiling slightly.

Inge looked from Kathal to Rosa, her eyes wide with delight. "The Nima never sell their pards, I've heard it all my life! How did you come by her?" Rosa smiled with a hint of sadness, remembering good times now gone.

"As you may know," she said, "the Nima have a gathering ground at Munch." Inge nodded. "It must have been around four years ago," Rosa recalled, "at one of the summer gatherings, Papa and I had gone to see the races. I have always loved horses," she added with a pat to Nimble's neck.

Inge nodded, encouraging her to continue. "There was a crash – two of the horses collided on the field. They both had broken limbs and had to be killed, it was awful! One of the jockeys rolled away and was only bruised, but the other had his leg severely broken. The bones were sticking out, and I nearly died!" Rosa grimaced.

After catching her breath, she went on, "The jockey was just a boy a few years younger than me, perhaps eleven. Papa and another man hurried onto the track and Papa used his cloak to make a stretcher. Then they carried the boy away into town, a mile away, to a doctor who was a friend of our family. It was he that helped my mama through her last illness, and he was able to set the boy's broken leg. But he had to use a big plaster cast, and the boy wasn't going to be able to get up and down in the family's caravan, you see?"

This was a version of the story Leila had told several times during her year of traveling around with Kathal as a companion. But she was expanding on it now, partly for the sheer fun of doing so. Rosa went on, "The boy's mother was a widow with a young daughter, and she didn't know what to do. Their entire band could not stay in Munch for months while her son regained the use of his leg, but she didn't want to leave him. So Papa offered to let them stay with us. I think maybe he'd been a little lonely since Mama died, it being just us and the housekeeper."

Inge nodded sympathetically, and Rosa continued her tale. "The boy's cast came off in a couple of months, and he was recovering well. Their caravan had been left behind, parked in our carriage yard, and when the next gathering came she found that one of her relations was with one of the bands. She and her family were able to join with her cousin's band, and off they went with many thanks to us for our hospitality. I was sorry to see them go."

Inge was waiting for the other shoe to drop, Rosa remaining silent long enough to increase the tension. In another couple of beats, she spoke. "We didn't see them again for another two years. Papa and I had talked quite a bit with them about the Nima and their way of life. Them being dark-skinned people like we are, we felt some kinship I think. So we were a little sad that Jaelle and her family didn't come to see us again right away, as we assumed that they must be in Munch at least yearly."

Another beat or two, watching Inge's impatience grow. "Then in spring of last year, that was before Papa fell ill, there was a knock at our door and we found Jaelle and her family on our doorstep! She was holding a basket, and in that basket was a pard kitten – Kathal! She apologized for not having returned to us sooner, but she had been shuffling from band to band trying to get back to her original band and had not been in Munch since last we'd parted. Kathal was her gift to us, in thanks for what we'd done for her and her family."

Wow, what a story, both women thought. Leila hoped Inge believed it. "She's amazing, Rosa," the older woman said. "May I pet her?" Rosa addressed the cat.

"What do you think, Kathal? Can she pet you?" The cat looked at her quizzically, then at Inge, and leaned forward to rub her head against Inge's shoulder, purring loudly. Delighted, the stall keeper ran her hand over Kathal's smooth, silky fur and scratched her behind the ears.

"Oh!" she exclaimed, "She's just like my pussycat at home but a lot bigger!"

Rosa smiled, pleased that Kathal had gone along with her scheme. The fact that Inge had a cat at home and smelled like it probably helped, as the pard could be quite unfriendly to some strangers on occasion. A thousand generations removed from the deserts of Palambo, pards' light silky coat had become thicker, their ears smaller and lacking the tufts of hair their wild cousins sported. They'd become bigger and heavier, as well, and except for being relatively long-legged they did look very much like a tawny, outsized house cat.

Inge mused, "As sweet as she is, I don't know how the innkeepers will react to you bringing her into their inns. Perhaps the idea of renting a cottage is a good idea." Leila hadn't had any problems with the pard at most of the inns she'd stayed at over the past year, but as this worked into her plans she didn't contradict the older woman. She wanted to be able to come and go at all hours without having to parade past a roomful of inn patrons – or crawl in an upper story window.

Rosa looked at the fruit seller hopefully, urging her silently to come up with a plan. "Most of the properties available for rent in this district are the property of the count, of course," Inge went on thoughtfully. "And most of the jobs available for a young woman would probably be at the castle, for that matter. I think you should go and talk to the seneschal."

The girl looked a little fearful as the prospect of bearding such an important figure in his den. "The seneschal?" she echoed uncertainly, "Will he see me?" Inge gave her a big, motherly smile. "Oh, I think he will," she said slyly. "He's my brother-in-law."

Chapter 29

In the end Kathal agreed to remain at Inge's stall, where she would be selling her fresh produce for another several hours. Inge was happy to have her, still thrilled to the core to have made friends with such an amazing and legendary creature.

Rosa, following Inge's directions, took a left at the crossroads off the main highway some distance west of the market square, easily seeing that the road she was on wound up through gentle hills to the promontory on which Castle Chanton sat. It was an absurd place to live, perhaps, but it did look very picturesque perched up there among autumn oaks and the tall evergreens that grew in this part of the Dominion.

She trotted Nimble along the road, which was as well-paved as the main highway. Likely some of Oester's rich mineral deposits had funded its building and upkeep. They got snow here in the wintertime, thanks to the relatively high elevation of the Antels, and without paving the castle's lifeline would have been impassible for months at a time.

The weather had turned blustery, and Leila hoped that the rain that was threatening would hold off for a few more hours. She trotted right up to the castle, where the road spilled in through the main gate. There *was* a gate, at least; but in this world where siege engines had become unnecessary over a millennium ago the place seemed barely defensible. On the other hand, she wasn't an invading army...

A hitching rail and watering trough had been provided for visitors, and off to one side of the walled courtyard Rosa could see the entrance to the castle stables. She dismounted, giving a pat to Nimble and telling him to wait for her, and asked a boy dressed as a page where she might find the seneschal's office.

He grinned at her, and directed her to a door down along the far side of the courtyard to the left, some distance from the castle's official entrance. Count Wilhelm had had the front entrance redesigned, apparently after looking at a book of fairytales, with twin doors twenty feet high beneath an enormous round window, and a small drawbridge leading up to them. Moats were not practical in this terrain, so the drawbridge crossed a good-sized fishpond some four feet deep. The invading army would at least have to get its feet wet.

Rosa went in at the sturdy wooden door, which she noticed had an engraved brass plaque attached to it. It read "Heinrich Friedman, Seneschal." Inge's sister's husband must have held his post for quite some time, she assumed – although the way the Count spent money, perhaps every employee received such a plaque as soon as they were hired.

Inside she found a small reception room with half a dozen wooden chairs in it (only two of them occupied), and an earnest-looking young man seated at a massive wooden desk stacked high with paperwork. The Dominion's bureaucracy did generate a lot of that. He looked up as the young woman came inside, and did a double-take. Who was this exotic beauty? Rosa smiled shyly at him (Dieter Janson, she saw from the nameplate on his desk – maybe she wasn't wrong about those plaques?), and proffered the note that Inge had written for her.

"Please," she said, giving Dieter the full effect of her deep green eyes with their long dark lashes, "Inge Mahler sent me. She asked that I give this note to Herr Friedman." Dieter had been the seneschal's secretary for a year now, and he was acquainted with his boss' family. So without reading the note, he took it from her smilingly and stepped to the office door behind him.

Rosa stood there feeling thankful that he was giving her immediate service. From the look of the desktop, Dieter had quite enough to keep him busy. Yet he'd dropped everything to help her. That was kind. The young man rapped softly on the door. "Herr Friedman?" he called, "May I come in?"

The seneschal was in the midst of an interview with one of the castle's tenants, who was complaining that the roof of his cottage was in need of repair and winter was coming. He was quite happy at the interruption. "Yes, Dieter, please come in," he said rising to his feet. To the tenant, he said "Please ask my secretary for the repair requisition form, fill it out and return it to him. We will endeavor to get someone out there to replace your missing slates within a few weeks, though as I'm sure you're aware the roofing crew is very busy at this season. If you prefer, you can go over to Stores and they'll issue you some slates so you can make the repairs yourself," he added pointedly.

The tenant's face fell, and with slumped shoulders he thanked the seneschal and left the room as the secretary was coming in. Heinrich waited until the man had left and the door to the inner office had been closed, and grinned at his secretary. "Thank you Dieter, a timely interruption. By the Seven, does no one know how to perform the simplest household repairs anymore? It's not as if his rent is that exorbitant."

Dieter smiled in sympathy. He liked his boss, for the most part, though it sometimes seemed as if he spent as much time complaining about the castle's tenants as he did helping them. "A young lady just arrived sir," he said cheerfully, "bringing this note from your sister-in-law." He handed it over.

"Hmm," Heinrich mused, as he took the folded paper and opened it. "Why to me, I wonder?" The sisters were close, but it was rare for Inge to communicate directly with him instead of mentioning whatever was on her mind to his wife. He read down the page, then looked up with a grin. "Oho!" he said, "Might I get a look at this 'young lady'?"

Dieter grinned back, and opened the office door again. Rosa, hoping that she would not have to sit and wait, was still standing on the far side of the reception desk and looked up at him hopefully when the door opened. "Ah yes," Heinrich said, "I think we must see to her concerns immediately." The secretary motioned for her to come right in, and she smiled brilliantly and made her way past the desk to the inner office. The two people sitting on hard chairs in the waiting room glared at her behind her back.

Dieter stepped back to his desk and resumed burrowing through the stacks of forms, closing the office door behind him. Rosa stood in front of Heinrich's desk, looking very much the big-eyed waif. Her time as Luca had put a little flesh on her, eating well without the hard physical training that had marked her four years with the Night Guild. But she was still on the thin side.

"Please my dear," Heinrich said avuncularly, gesturing to a chair. It had a padded seat, more comfortable than the ones in the waiting room if not by much. Rosa smiled at him and sat down.

"So," Heinrich began, "you're looking for a cottage to rent? And also for a job?" She nodded shyly.

The seneschal leaned back in his comfortable desk chair and tented his fingers, thinking. "Many of our workers here at Castle Chanton live within its walls," he explained. "Room and board are part of their pay, and the castle kitchens turn out quite decent meals for everyone. Are you sure you wouldn't rather have something like that?"

Rosa seemed to consider. Such a position would probably be very desirable to a young girl on her own, having roommates of her own age to become friends with. And it would mean she was here twenty-four hours a day, supposed to be here – handy if she should be caught wandering the halls at a suspicious hour. But... "This would be in a dormitory situation?" the girl asked, so hesitantly Heinrich wondered just how sheltered a life she had led. She looked young for eighteen, but she wouldn't have been allowed access to her father's legacy if she were not yet of age.

The seneschal nodded. "All of the castle's live-in servants share sleeping quarters, girls with girls and boys with boys – though we do have a few private rooms for married couples. Those are all occupied at the moment, of course." Rosa's face fell. "Oh, I'm afraid that wouldn't do," she explained sadly. "Did Inge's letter mention that I have a pet pard?"

He studied it again. She *had* mentioned that, but he'd thought he must have misread her handwriting. In answer to Heinrich's questioning look, Rosa launched into a condensed version of the tale she'd told Inge, following it with "and that's why I was hoping to rent a cottage. Perhaps if I'm not getting room and board, I could get paid a little more in cash to help offset the cost of the cottage? I have my horse with me as well, and there would need to be a little land connected with the cottage for him. Maybe some kind of shelter for when the weather gets bad, too."

Heinrich was a kindly man, and Rosa's story had touched him. Her quest to return to the sunny climes her family had left before she was born seemed a worthy cause, and he became determined to aid her if he could. "May I ask what skills you have, Fraulein Estares?" She looked as if she'd been put on the spot, and in a way she had.

The skills Leila possessed were many and varied, and most were ones she couldn't admit to. But Rosa was supposed to be sweet and innocent, a sheltered girl only now having to make her way in the world. And not all that bright, either.

"Just the usual ones I suppose," she said deprecatingly. "I can cook and clean, and sew. And I can read and write, of course."

As enlightened as the Gaspari Dominion was in many respects, it had not instituted universal education. So literacy was not a skill owned by everyone. "The kitchen staff are all live-in, of course," Heinrich said, and Rosa kept her face looking a little anxious and unsure even as Leila was exulting. Thank the Seven! Her claim to be able to cook was greatly exaggerated.

"But I think we could easily find you a position with the Curator of the Collections," he went on. "All those thousands of art objects need constant dusting, of course. And correctly cataloging and documenting the provenance of items as they come in is something you should easily be able to pick up, since you can read and write." This time Rosa let her delight show on her face.

"That would be wonderful!" she said, her voice oozing gratitude.

"All employees of the Curator work days only," Heinrich explained. "At night the wing is locked up tight while guards with dogs roam the corridors. His Excellency is very concerned that his famous collection will draw thieves to steal it. And it is watched over by a large guard force during the day, as well. Can't have pilferage!" He checked to make sure she hadn't taken offense at his suggestion that she might be light-fingered and in need of guarding. She was smiling at him a little blankly, as if she hadn't gotten the implication at all.

"That sounds absolutely wonderful, Herr Friedman," Rosa said. "But about the cottage?" He pulled out a large ledger book from a bookcase beside his desk and flipped it open, then began checking its entries. Running a finger down the page, he stopped at one. Then he held his place with the finger while he checked the next two pages, before returning to the listing he had first marked.

The seneschal looked up at her with a frown line forming between his brows. "I'm afraid there's only one thing available at this time," he said apologetically. "Most of our cottages are for the tenant farmers, of course, especially the larger ones as they are usually occupied by families. But there is a gardener's cottage just outside the grounds. The late countess had a lovely garden, just a small thing really, and it required only one gardener to care for it. But Count Wilhelm's remodeling of the castle has included bringing a further twenty acres under cultivation as a park. You probably noticed some of that as you were coming in?"

Rosa nodded. Along with its astonishing collection of treasures, Castle Chanton had some of the most famous gardens in the central Dominion. "I hope I'll soon have the chance to explore the park," she said eagerly. "Are horses allowed within its grounds?" Heinrich shook his head.

"I'm afraid not," he smiled. "Old Wolfgang, our head gardener, would have a seizure if a horse's hooves took divots out of his manicured lawns or it left a pile of… fertilizer… behind. He and his army of assistants are out there almost all day every day keeping the place perfect, but it's for strollers on foot only. Not as beautiful at this season, of course, but in the spring it is truly something to see. You will be staying with us that long?"

"I hope to be on my way to Andala as soon as I can find a caravan to travel with – and assuming I've saved enough money to make the trip," Rosa said. "But I certainly hope I'll be able to see the gardens in bloom." The seneschal nodded.

"Anyhow," he went on, "the old gardener's cottage is quite small, only two rooms. It has a fenced yard around half an acre in size, which the last gardener to live there used to use for growing flowers and vegetables. It's all overgrown now, though. And the cottage itself is a little run down. At the least it'll need a good cleaning."

Rosa smiled sweetly, quite willing to live in a falling-down hovel if it meant she and her beloved pard and horse (given to her as a green-broke foal by her dear departed papa, of course) could all be together. "I'm sure I can have it shipshape in no time," she declared with what seemed to the seneschal like a brave attempt at an attitude of competence and efficiency. The poor girl was lovely, to be sure, but she was so young and naïve – such a babe in the woods, to be out in the world by herself.

"Under the circumstances I think we can let you have the cottage at no cost – provided you don't require us to keep it up for you. And as you will not be taking your meals at the castle, your pay will be higher. We can start you at one shilling a week, and if Gustav finds your work satisfactory, a small raise may be in order. If you're able to feed and clothe yourself without spending too much money, you should have a decent little nest egg by spring to see you on your way to Andala." Heinrich smiled, and was rewarded by an answering smile so brilliant it made his heart skip a beat. Ah, if he were forty years younger...

Chapter 30

After leaving Heinrich with heartfelt thanks Rosa hurried back to town atop Nimble to retrieve Kathal and tell Inge the good news. Then, thanking the woman even more profusely than she'd thanked her brother-in-law earlier, she hurried back to the castle. Only a few hours of daylight remained.

Unable to leave his office and his heavy workload, Heinrich had told off one of the castle pages (there appeared to be swarm of them; Leila was willing to bet that Castle Chanton was the town of Chanton's foremost employer) to show the new hiree to the cottage that would be her home during her stay there.

The castle had been built in a hanging valley, partway up a mountain slope. It afforded both a handsome perch for the picturesque castle, and a swath of nearly-level land around it more than a hundred acres in size. The area closest to the castle itself, twenty acres of it, had been converted into manicured parkland. Further out, tenant farmers grew everything from barley to grapes to vegetables for the castle kitchens.

Tucked in relatively close to the castle itself, around on the opposite side from the main gate, was the late countess' little private garden. And next to that, with a private door through the wall, was the old gardener's cottage with its small plot of land.

The page led Rosa there, both of them walking as she led the horse. It was a bit of a hike. The boy kept glancing up at the cat perched on the horse's saddle, her golden gaze taking in everything around them with interest. To him, it seemed as if she might be looking at him with an eye to his suitability as dinner.

"Well, here it is ma'am, uh, miss… There's a shed around back where you can put your horse, might want to do it pretty soon 'cause I think it's getting ready to pour… uh, will there be anything else?"

Maintaining Rosa's fixed smile of delight, Leila answered shortly "No thank you, you're so kind. I'll be quite fine."

The boy bolted off at a run, and Leila stood there shaking her head as he vanished from sight. From the looks of the place, Heinrich's characterization of it as needing "a good cleaning" seemed to be a gross understatement. With the overgrown vegetation in the yard, it was barely possible to tell that a house of some kind stood amid this half-acre patch of weeds and former cultivars. Not that Leila could tell a weed from a garden plant if it jumped up and bit her, beyond the herb lore that had been part of her training with the Night Guild.

She was still expected to report for duty at the Collections Wing before closing time, which according to Heinrich was at six – a short while past sunset, at this season. Leila had retained her valuable pocket watch along with many other useful items from her former life, and she'd made sure to ask the seneschal for the correct local time before leaving. It was now nearly four.

No time to lose! Leila led Nimble in through the garden gate and closed it behind her. "Down, Kathal, hunt!" she commanded, and the cat leapt from her perch and began exploring the jungle. Leila hoped it would soon be freed of vermin, at least. The vegetation in the yard was showing signs of going dormant, some plants already losing their leaves while their evergreen cousins were looking a little sickly. At this altitude, nights were already dipping below the freezing point.

"Stand, Nimble!" Leila commanded, and then picked her way through the vegetation. Her education had taught her very little about vegetables for the kitchen or flowers for the parlor – but quite a lot about poisons. And she saw no familiar poisonous plants growing among the chaotic mess that had formerly been a nice little garden.

She returned to the horse and led him around to the back, pushing through the undergrowth, to find a small lean-to shed running the width of the small ramshackle cottage. It stood perhaps twelve feet high along the cottage's back wall, sloping to eight feet at the far side. Double doors stood in the middle of it, held together with a rusted hasp, and she struggled to get them open – pressing against the encroaching plants to make a path.

Leila had feared that the shed would be full up with who-knows-what cast-off junk, turned into a storage area for unwanted garden equipment or something. But once she got the doors pried open, it stood almost empty. There were a few rusting implements in there – a rake with a broken handle, a hoe, two or three shovels and an impressive-looking scythe. But other than that, the shed held nothing but cobwebs and a few rats.

"Kathal!" she called, and after a few moments' rustling the pard appeared from amid the tangle of vegetation that stretched to the property's rear fence. The rats had had the run of this place for decades, sheltering from the mountain winters and using it to store whatever foods they could find. Probably, somewhere in that wilderness beyond the doors, there were squash plants growing wild and producing a new crop, unattended, year after year.

In a few brief moments their world came crashing down as the pard darted inside. She killed half a dozen of them in her first pass, and the rest fled shrieking through the holes in the walls that had granted them entry in the first place. Holding out a glowstone from her pack, Leila surveyed the results with satisfaction.

She removed Nimble's saddle and the blanket beneath it, unclipping the reins from his halter. Then she patted him on the rump and said, "Go see what's edible out there, buddy. And if it starts raining, you can come in here." Leila left the doors standing open and went back around to the front. There was a partially ruinous porch fronting the cottage, as if it had been intended for the gardener to sit there after a long day's work on a summer evening and admire the castle that stood in the front yard.

Heinrich had provided Rosa with a key, but as she beat aside encroaching vines and approached the front door, she wondered if one would be necessary. Was the door even still on its hinges? It was, and she turned the key in the lock though Leila could have gotten in there nearly as fast with the lockpicks in her pack.

Inside, the room was suffused in dim green-tinged light from the two windows on either side of the front door. Leila found that there were oil lamps mounted on the walls here and there, but any oil in them had possibly dried out before she had been born. Add that to the shopping list, then.

There was a small sitting area furnished with a dank-looking settee and a small table, plus a couple of wooden chairs. Beyond that was a little kitchen area with a two-burner wood stove and a sink. Cold water was provided, probably from a well, and when Leila leaned all of her weight on it the pump handle shrieked and a trickle of brown water came out. Repeated efforts eventually produced a clean stream.

Beside the kitchen alcove was a short hallway leading into the cottage's sleeping quarters. The tiny bedroom held a bed perhaps four feet across, made of iron and with a lumpy-looking mattress resting on a sagging spring framework. There was no bedding, and no wardrobe. One corner of the room offered a short closet rod suspended so that a few garments might be hung on it, and there was a small chest of drawers. Ugh! What had she gotten herself into?

Leila came to realize that Heinrich's "kindness" might not have been all Rosa had thought. This place was a complete dump, nearly uninhabitable – and its "free" status was contingent on her not applying to the castle for assistance in putting it to rights. Since any efforts she made would benefit the castle at no expense to the Count's coffers, she had been put in the position of either living in a rat-hole, or spending her own money to improve property belonging to Oester. Her guilt at taking advantage of their kindness while she plotted to rob them immediately shrank to a manageable level.

Rosa dropped her pack in the bedroom and hurried up to the castle. Surprisingly she was able to let herself into the late Countess' garden through the postern gate – the security around here was shit, Leila crowed to herself – and from there to a door that deposited her in one of the confusing castle's many corridors. Querying a passing maid, she soon found herself in the Collections Wing and in conference with Gustav Kohl, Curator of the Collections.

"And in this room are the Palambo statuettes," Gustav said as he led Rosa on a tour of the wing that housed Count Wilhelm's collections. The Curator was a precise, fussy man, not bad-looking, quite slender of build and elegant in his dress. He seemed to be in his early forties, and Leila knew immediately that he was not going to be receptive to Rosa's charms. Just as well, perhaps, as he was her boss and she needed to maintain a businesslike relationship with him.

The majority of women in the Dominion stayed home to keep house and raise their families, but it was far from rare for unmarried women, especially those in the poorer classes, to hold a paying job. Nor was it rare for their male superiors to require some "concessions" as a condition of continued employment. Much better this way. Besides, Gustav really knew his objets d'art. Leila could learn a lot from him. I'm going to like it here, she thought.

The tour concluded, Gustav went into the room near the stairs leading to the wing's second floor, the room where the staff took meals and stowed their personal items while they were on duty. It also contained a privy chamber. He opened a closet to reveal a row of identical dresses, each short-sleeved with a snug-fitting bodice, buttoned up the front, and an A-line skirt that looked as if it would hit Rosa a little below mid-calf. With a critical eye, he scanned them and selected one he judged would fit the slim, petite girl who was joining his staff.

"All the female staff must report for duty in these uniforms," he told her. "When it needs laundering, take a spare from this closet and you can drop the dirty one in this bin. The castle laundry picks up here once a week. I hope you won't take offense, but all of the day staff, including me, will be inspected by the guards before we leave for the day to make sure we haven't 'borrowed' anything from the collections. I'm sure you understand, this is just a precaution. The Count has put a great deal of money and effort into these collections, and he truly treasures them. He means this entire wing to become a public museum, a gift to the people of Oester, after he is gone."

Rosa accepted the uniform, showing no signs of having taken umbrage at the suggestion she might steal from her employer. Instead she smiled sweetly, and said "I have never heard of so noble a concept. To gather all these items of beauty and historical importance, and to give them to the people! Truly it is an honor to be working for such a man."

She took the dress Gustav had handed her and folded it carefully into a package small enough to be conveniently carried under one arm. The Curator ushered her out the front door past the guard, saying "Welcome aboard, Rosa. I'll see you on Mirday at eight, as tomorrow is our holiday."

Rosa returned to the cottage, retracing her route. Heinrich had made a point of mentioning that the Count gave his entire staff a holiday every Luzday. A few key people, such as guards in the Collections Wing, had a different day off so that the castle could be staffed at all times; but most of the employees, including Rosa, had the day off. And she needed it! She unfolded the dress and held it up, inspecting its details. It had no pockets, none at all.

Chapter 31

Rosa woke early, blessing the Seven in general and Count Wilhelm in particular, that she didn't have to go to work. There was so much to do at "home" that she couldn't believe it. Nimble had already gnawed his way through a considerable amount of the vegetation surrounding the gardener's cottage, and apparently without ill effect. Give him another week or two, and he might have it down to a manageable level. But she didn't want to wait that long.

Rosa (or perhaps it was Leila; neither of them had learned anything about gardening) used a honing kit from Leila's pack to put an edge on the scythe in the shed, then set about trying to clear the area in the front of the cottage so she didn't have to fight her way to the door. She'd never used a scythe before but had seen them used many times while driving past cultivated fields, traveling with the Nima. She soon figured out how to use it well enough to hack a clear path from the front fence back to the porch.

She saddled Nimble and took him into town, and was pleased to find that while the castle might declare holiday on Luzday, the merchants of Chanton town were not so inclined. The market square boasted more sellers than she'd found on the previous day, and Rosa was able to buy some supplies for her kitchen. She deeply regretted the subterfuge that had required her to claim competence in this area. Perhaps it was time to learn? A stall selling used books had a cookbook specializing in the regional dishes of Oester, and she bought it.

She'd found an old broom, half its straws rotted away, but no other cleaning supplies during the evening she'd spent "at home" yesterday. So in addition to some foodstuffs and the cookbook, Nimble returned to Castle Chanton loaded down with a bucket, a mop, a feather duster, some dishcloths, and a stoppered bottle of a mysterious fluid touted to be "the Dominion's foremost cleaning liquid – just add water." Not to mention a dozen other items intended to turn the gardener's cottage into a home.

At an age when most girls had already spent years helping around the house and were close to mastering the domestic skills, Leila found herself sadly out of practice. From the age of around five she'd been worked hard at Madam Droma's, cleaning whatever needed it and acting as a kitchen helper – but without any understanding of how the vegetables she chopped would fit into the plan for the meal the cook was preparing. Marta had not considered her juvenile helpers apprentices, just under-aged slaves there to do her bidding.

Now she was working for herself, Leila found that there was a certain satisfaction to the work. She was not doing this because she was required to, but because she would be living here for as long as it took for her to come up with a plan to steal Wilhelm's collection and she didn't intend to live in squalor that long. Sleeping rough under the stars was one thing, living in filth in a run-down hovel another.

By Luzday evening, as Leila collapsed tiredly on the settee (over which she'd thrown a sheet, purchased along with those she'd bought for the bedroom), much progress had been made. Nimble, feeling hungry after hauling all those items up from town, had eaten his way through another few cubic feet of the overgrown garden. Kathal had been left behind, and had amused herself driving the remaining rats from the property for good – eating quite a few of them in the process.

And inside the house, all of the floors had been swept and mopped; the walls and ceilings had been dusted and cleared of cobwebs; the stove, sink, and kitchen counter had been scrubbed and the cabinets filled with food; the mattress had been beaten and aired out, sheets and blankets added to it; and Leila's small collection of clothing had been distributed to the chest of drawers and the hanging rod. She almost felt like she was home.

The lack of any bathroom facilities was a bit of an issue. Hacking through the vegetation to the rear fence Leila had discovered a crumbling outhouse; but it looked as if its hole had been filled in years ago. There was not even any odor left behind. Digging an entire outhouse pit and relocating the enclosure, even in this soft soil, was beyond her abilities; but for the time being she invested half an hour with the best of the shed's shovels in a hole perhaps four feet deep and three across – giving her someplace to dump the chamberpot. She'd have to see if she could pick up some wood ashes at the castle.

The cottage had a tiny fireplace, but there was no firewood. Still another item on her "to buy" list. The free rent at this place was looking less and less like a bargain. But even so, Leila couldn't resist the emotional appeal that was creeping over her just having her "own" place. Oh, you've got it bad, she told herself. Hurry up and steal a few thousand florins' worth of Wilhelm's trinkets, so we can head for Jena!

Chapter 32

Rosa dipped her quill in the ink bottle and finished the line in the ledger. "One silver flute, six hands long, .925% pure. Made by Giuseppe Benedetti of Frinzi, 900 m.e. Purchased from the estate of Signor Aldo Fontana of Frinzi, Third of Breeze 1031 m.e. Price 25 florins." In the two months since she had come to work here for Gustav, Count Wilhelm had set aside his mania for the golden automatons and was now collecting distinctive musical instruments with a passion. He had also collected several musicians, and in the spare time from his quest for the finest of instruments he was trying to learn how to play them. From reports, that was not going well.

Having finished cataloging the flute, Rosa lifted it carefully in her hands and carried it with her up the stairs from the basement workroom and storage area to the main floor – then down a corridor and up a flight of stairs to the second floor of the Collections Wing. Gustav was in the room where the latest collection was to be housed, trying to decide exactly how the new acquisitions should be displayed.

The Count's current obsession was causing Gustav certain design problems, as the wide range of sizes and shapes of musical instruments did not fit into the neatly-ordered rows of glassed-in display cases that so handily housed most of the rest of his collections. These called for special cases to be built, and for an arrangement that was not only aesthetically pleasing but historically and musically appropriate. It would not do to have a third-century lute displayed beside a prehistoric drum, or in proximity to a complicated brass instrument from a hundred years ago.

Along with the flute, Rosa had brought a small card with her on which she'd neatly penned the instrument's details for the edification of the public when it was on display. Gustav had been quite pleased with the new girl's intelligence and abilities, and she was now earning an astonishing two shillings per week – more than twice what one of the kitchen girls received. But they of course got three meals a day and a bed as part of *their* pay.

Rosa of course had been cooking for her father and herself for years. Leila wished she were a real person, and would come and give her a few tips. She'd done all right for the previous year, when sleeping out in the woods, with items like camp stew and fire-toasted rabbit; but producing a meal in the cottage's tiny kitchen that would not give her indigestion had been harder than she expected.

But slowly, over the past couple of months, she'd learned. Wasn't she Leila, the quickest thief Tomas' gang had ever known? Penumbra, the Night Guild's youngest journeyman in a generation? Luca, darling of the Nima? Whatever she had to learn, she would master it. And before too long, Leila was beginning almost to look forward to cooking for herself – making the dishes she liked, in the way she liked them. Not that she'd decline an invitation to eat out!

Dieter, the seneschal's secretary, had approached her tentatively. It was not proper, somehow, for a young lady to be completely on her own and without any family support structure to vet her suitors and make arrangements if the relationship was going to lead to something further. The idea of a woman deciding for herself to keep company with a man, and taking that wherever it might go, was frightening for him. Still, he'd asked Rosa to join him a couple of times in the castle's dining hall at mealtime. Leila, three years his junior, thought him a sweet boy.

Winter had come, and snow now covered the grounds around the castle. The days were short, and Rosa spent most of the daylight hours at work in the Collections Wing – cataloging, rearranging based on Gustav's instructions, and dusting, for the most part. The day staff, guards excepted, worked from eight in the morning until six in the evening each day, with half an hour off to eat whatever food they'd brought for lunch, sitting at the table in the staff room.

Compared with the serious stone fortresses of a millennium ago Castle Chanton was a miracle of modern comforts; but it still got cold in the cavernous rooms with their high ceilings and poorly-fitted windows. And dust got in everywhere. In addition to Rosa, Gustav, and the guards, there was a staff of half a dozen girls – who spent nearly all their time just keeping the collections clean and sparkling.

Nimble pined being left alone every day, and after becoming friendly with some of the stableboys Rosa took the horse over to the castle stables. There he could be taken out for some exercise when the weather permitted, and spend time socializing with other horses.

The castle stables were warmer and dryer, too, than the shed behind the cottage. He was her getaway, when the moment was right, and she needed him to stay in the best shape possible.

But when would that getaway occur? Leila had had ample opportunity to study the layout and plan the job, and she was still trying to figure out exactly how to pull it off. She wished she had the resources of the Night Guild, and could just assemble a gang of thieves to clean the place out in the night. But it was just her by herself, and she sometimes wondered if, should she make off with all the loot Nimble could carry, whether the theft would even be noticed. Now *that* was a thought…

Chapter 33

Leila had hit on her plan, but it was going to take a long time to put into action. She felt a little unhappy that she was dealing falsely with the people she interacted with, especially those such as Inge who had taken Rosa at face value and extended her kindness; but her plans to rob Wilhelm of a few thousand florins worth of his treasures didn't interfere with her sleep in the least. It wasn't as if she were planning to take them *all*, or even a significant percentage of them. Just a goodly quantity of the most compact, valuable pieces – yet ones that were obscure enough they would not immediately be recognized as having been stolen from the famous Castle Chanton collections.

If anything, Leila thought, Count Wilhelm would probably be delighted at the opportunity to restock the stolen pieces by resuming his collecting activities. Or so she hoped. The possibility that Oester's almost limitless wealth might put a team of relentless investigators on her trail, refusing to give up their hunt until the stolen goods had been recovered and the culprit brought to justice, *did* interfere with her sleep.

So Leila was moving very slowly, taking her time. She began by taking an extra uniform home with her, as she had done countless times before over the three months since she'd begun working here. The staff were supposed to use their own discretion as to when their uniforms needed laundering, and the interval could vary depending on what sort of task you'd been involved with during the day.

That night, with a tiny pair of scissors, Leila opened up a hand-sized slit in the front seam of the spare uniform she'd brought home, a few inches below the waist. Many of the girls, Rosa included, added a simple white muslin apron to their uniform to help keep the dress clean longer, and it covered the slit. Should anyone notice it, it was just a place where the stitching had come out, probably from repeated washings.

Rosa now owned four pairs of bloomers and a similar number of camisoles, which she laundered herself by hand in the kitchen sink every few days – hanging them to dry in the sitting room near the fire. Into each pair of bloomers Leila sewed a long pocket, open near the front seam (in the same area where the dress was slit) and running down the inside of the right leg.

The search they all had to put up with nightly before leaving the Collections Wing was respectful and friendly, just an inspection of their outer garments and any packs or bags they'd brought with them, plus a light pat-down. The pocketless uniform dresses were form-fitting enough that anything bulkier than a coin or perhaps a small gem would have been obvious hidden beneath the fabric. The guards were shy and wouldn't usually run their hands up between the girls' legs, so she might have gotten away with filling the pocket with small items and then carrying them out the door under the noses of the guards. But Leila didn't want the risk, and she had another plan. One that she was soon to put into effect.

Chapter 34

Leila could tell you to the penny what a piece of jewelry was worth, but many other items – paintings, weapons, miniatures – had been outside her ken. Wilhelm had chosen his Curator well – Gustav was an encyclopedia of knowledge on the subject, and she (as well as Rosa) had learned much from him.

Pleased with Rosa's ready intellect and eagerness to learn, he had begun training her in the techniques that were sometimes used to restore items purchased for the collections – cleaning paintings without damaging the image, performing tiny, invisible soldering on broken jewelry, gluing statuettes back together so cunningly that you needed a jeweler's loupe to spot the break. Having no interest in women for the uses men usually put them to, he was willing to see her as simply a human being – one with a great deal of talent and potential.

Gustav not only curated the collections and designed the spaces in which they were displayed, but also sometimes accompanied Count Wilhelm on his buying trips – traveling to this or that city to inspect items being offered for sale to determine their authenticity and weigh in on the fairness of the price. Though money was truly no object for Wilhelm, he didn't like being cheated. Now, for the first time, the Curator felt that he might have an assistant who could step in for him during the times when he was gone.

Kathal had been allowed to accompany Rosa to work, as many had heard about the pard and were eager to see her. Not everyone appreciated the forty-pound cat prowling the corridors, though, so Rosa usually kept her by her side. She would curl up and sleep at Rosa's feet while she was in the workroom, or pad silently beside her, keeping an eye out for vermin, when she was cleaning and dusting. The guards (usually one per room except during the monthly public viewing, when there were two per room) had gotten quite used to her, and some of them were friendly enough to slip her morsels of dried beef or other treats.

Rosa was opening up the cases, carefully cleaning each piece and the glass beneath it in the Room of Rings, while Jurgen Becker stood guard at the door. He was a nice young man in his early twenties, unmarried but keeping company with a beautiful young blonde from Chanton. Rosa had met his fiancée, and she was a stunner. Small wonder Jurgen didn't let his eyes linger on Rosa's behind as she was bent over the display cases, cleaning and polishing.

Instead, he was smiling broadly and all of his attention was fixed on the antics of Kathal, as she rolled at his feet and writhed appealingly. "Play with Jurgen," Rosa had murmured to the cat as she came in and went to the far end of the room to begin with the cabinet containing a display of wedding rings. Each of them had once graced the finger of some famous woman from history, and along with the usual small placard each ring had a little miniature portrait of the woman who had worn it.

The rings themselves were lovely, worth a fortune for the stones and gold or platinum alone; but not all that distinctive. With her back to the room and Jurgen, after unlocking the case and setting its cover aside, Rosa set to work from the center of the case – lifting each ring along with its placard and portrait out and dusting them (and the space where they'd sat) carefully with a soft cloth.

Every fourth ring and its accoutrements found its way into the pocket of Leila's bloomers, however – not back into the case. The other items, after the glass on which they rested had had all dust removed, were repositioned so that there were no obvious gaps. Behind her Leila heard Jurgen laughing and saying "Cuckoo kitty!" as Kathal flirted and played with him. She kept those wicked claws sheathed, fortunately.

"Rosa!" Jurgen called, and Leila nearly jumped out of her skin. She set down the ring she was polishing (not pocketing) and Rosa turned to smile at him.

"What is it?" she asked, as if everything was perfectly fine. The grinning guard gestured at the cat, still rolling around on the floor, jumping up for a mock pounce on an imaginary mouse, dashing back and forth.

"Have you been giving Kathal catmint?" he asked. "My two cats at home get like this when I bring them some."

Rosa smoothed her skirts, the apron hiding the slit, and looked puzzled. "No, I don't even know where to get catmint. Unless there's some growing in that jungle of a yard at my cottage." After a moment's thought she added, "I suppose it would be dead this time of year? I don't even know what it looks like." Jurgen smiled and nodded.

"It dies off every year and comes back up from the roots in the spring," he explained. "My mother used to grow it, and then dry it. It has uses besides driving cats crazy, like making a tea that will calm nervous children."

She smiled at him. "Thanks, I didn't know that. I don't even know whether catmint has any effect on pards. She just gets like this sometime, especially in the winter. I think she doesn't like being cooped up indoors. Well, back to work." Rosa turned her back, and Leila resumed thinning the wedding ring population once again.

A little earlier than midday Rosa took her lunch break, declaring that she was extra hungry. That put her in there when no one else was around. She gulped the bread and cheese she'd brought, washing it down with water available at a pump in the staff room, and then used the privy. Gustav was in his office, where he spent much of every day researching new items to be sought for inclusion in the Collections.

A guard, one of two on the day shift who patrolled up and down the corridor and stood ready to relieve any of the room guards in need of a break (the other performed the same function on the floor above), was walking past the room toward the wing's front doors, his back turned. Leila slipped out of the staff room and went quietly down the stairs at the back, letting herself into the workroom that occupied much of the wing's basement level. Its ceiling was actually nearly three feet above ground level outside, and high windows around three sides of the room provided good light during daylight hours.

In addition to being used to maintain the Collections ledgers and perform restorations and repairs, the workroom served as a storage area for items that had been acquired but had later been judged unsuitable for display. Most of them were bulky and not worth much, which accounted for the fact that this room, unlike all of the rooms on the two upper floors, was not patrolled at night nor guarded during the day.

Leila went around a partition wall behind the work table and reached into a lower level cabinet that contained a collection of rather ugly urns from the fourth century b.m.e. Likely they were of great historical value to some scholar of those times, the turbulent years when the upstart kingdom of Gaspar was just beginning to come down hard on its neighbors. But they didn't cut the mustard from an aesthetic standpoint, and Count Wilhelm had refused to grant them display space. They'd been moldering in this cabinet for years, Leila guessed, from the amount of dust on them.

Taking a tip from her long-dead mother, Leila had made some very specific modifications to this cabinet. Beneath an urn at the very back of it, on the bottom of the cabinet, there was a small hole. And if you inserted a nail, which Leila had hidden at the back of an upper shelf, into that hole, you could pry up a knot some four inches in diameter to reveal a hole leading down into the space beneath the cabinet. The space was four inches high by three feet deep and four feet wide, and should be more than big enough to hold the amount of loot Leila intended to hide in it.

In moments she'd hiked up her skirt and emptied out the pocket in her bloomers, turning it inside out to disgorge its contents. Reaching in with her hand, ears sharply tuned for any sign of footsteps on the stairs, she removed the partially mummified corpse of a rat from immediately beneath the hole. Then she added the handfuls of loot she'd gathered this morning. Without the placards and portraits the rings would have taken up a lot less space, but that was just too bad.

This stash wasn't as ideal as Miriam's hiding place in the hollow behind Dobbins' stable wall, as it couldn't use gravity to keep the trove from being spotted when the knot was removed. Instead, Leila reached in again and pushed the hidey-hole's contents away so that, even should somebody find the hole, they would see nothing amiss. To complete the effect, she replaced the corpse of the rat.

Five minutes after she came down here, Leila locked the workroom behind her and returned upstairs. She'd washed the dust and dirt from her hands and face at the sink in the basement, checked before coming up the stairs that the corridor guard had his back turned, and tossed her apron into the laundry bin before getting a fresh one out of the cupboard. If anyone had wondered why she'd gone down there, she carried with her a supply of clean placards along with pen and ink. She'd noticed that some of the placards were too smudged with dust, and should be replaced as they could no longer be cleaned.

Rosa had locked the case she'd been working in before going to lunch, and she unlocked it again when she returned. Kathal had stayed with Jurgen rather than follow her, having too much fun playing perhaps. The young cat enjoyed returning to kittenhood now and again. Now she was curled up asleep at his feet, and as Rosa came in Jurgen said "Oh good, you're back. I'm getting hungry too." He leaned out the door and called to the corridor guard.

"Edward, how about relieving me so I can go eat?" Jurgen called, and Edward came into the room to take his station as Jurgen, smiling his thanks, set off down the corridor toward the staff room.

"Hello Edward, how are you?" Rosa asked, smiling.

"Could be worse, I suppose," he responded in tones that suggested he wasn't in the mood for banter. Edward was often morose, for such a young man.

Kathal had risen to her feet and rejoined her mistress at the display case where Rosa was once again cleaning and polishing rings. Leila thought better of resuming her thefts. It wasn't all that often she got assigned, alone except for the room guard, to clean in the Ring Room. But there would be other opportunities, she knew. It would be months before she was ready to leave.

Chapter 35

Spring was here at last, and it was singing in everyone's veins. With a little more daylight available, Rosa was able to retrieve her horse from the stables and take him for some early morning rides – cantering fast along dirt tracks, getting to know the countryside a little better. Arriving here as she had in the autumn, she knew far less about the back country than she'd have liked.

In any case, having spent much of the previous two years out of doors, Leila had found the long hours of confinement to the Collections Wing or her tiny cottage hard to bear. The work (well, the part of it that didn't involve cleaning and polishing) had been fascinating. But she now knew that steady indoor employment was not her cup of tea.

Kathal, now fully mature, went into heat. Oh, the noise! And the smell… Fortunately Luca had learned from the Nima of the herb they used to control the pards' breeding. It was readily available from an herb-seller in town, and after the infusion she made had cooled, she instructed the cat to drink it.

As pards found the flavor appealing, it was not a hard sell. And in a couple of days, her hormones had subsided. She would now be needing to drink the herbal concoction at the onset of symptoms every year, or until she was bred. Fortunately the desert cats' relatively sparse breeding cycle had not changed when so much else about them had.

Leila was now sixteen, which she supposed made Rosa nineteen. The older girl, so much more innocent than she was thanks to her sheltered life, remained pure and a little withdrawn. Dieter had attempted to pursue his courtship but had been politely rebuffed. "Soon I will be leaving for Andala, something I have dreamed of all my life. It would not be right to become involved with you, or anyone, at this time." He could only, if sadly, agree.

Even Count Wilhelm seemed to feel stirrings, though in what direction it was hard to imagine. Discouraged by his apparent lack of any musical talent whatsoever, he seemed already to be losing interest in rare instruments. Usually his passions lasted for around a year and this one had only begun the past autumn; so it seemed he was restless, having not yet found the new love of his life.

Gustav and the count had even gone on a hunting expedition this spring, leaving before the snows had melted from the castle grounds. Other counts in the Dominion might hunt the mighty stag, the fierce wild boar, or perhaps the savage lion (still to be found in the Dominion's southerly regions); but Wilhelm had gone looking for inspiration in the form of a tour of the workshops and art collections of Italia.

This large, bulbous peninsula, encompassing more than a dozen counties, jutted out into the Center Sea and had been the source of much art and culture over the centuries. More than five hundred years before Ostden the First had united the Dominion, a city-state called Roma had begun an attempt to take over and rule the peninsula and the lands beyond it as an early sort of empire. But they had met the forces of Gaspar in 417 b.m.e. and the entire peninsula had become part of Gaspar's hegemony instead. Now it was just a collection of Dominion counties, happily living their lives in peace and prosperity.

Gustav had left Rosa in charge of some of the Curator's duties while he was gone. The trip had taken several weeks, and during that time she had answered inquiries from people in possession of fine art objects offering them from sale, taken in a few pieces for professional appraisal (her expertise was nowhere near what Gustav's was, after a few months' training; but she could tell a blatant fake when she saw one), and performed repairs on quite a few small items from throughout the Collections.

Leila had used the time well. The hiding place beneath the cabinet in the basement workroom was now as full as she dared let it become, and she ceased her depredations. Not a single person, neither Gustav nor the bored cleaning staff nor the guards, had noticed that anything was missing.

Count Wilhelm was the biggest danger, knowing and loving his collection as he did; but he was always more interested in what he was collecting right now than in the things he had amassed before. They had only seen him twice in the time since Rosa had started work there, and on both occasions he'd only come to consult with

Gustav about new musical instruments that had arrived after being shipped from their former owners.

With a certain level of authority, Rosa assigned herself to spend hours each day in the workroom, making repairs to artifacts. Even the act of handling them repeatedly for dusting and polishing was enough to cause many of the ancient items to break, so it was not hard for her to find valid reasons to be down there now that she was the only person on hand qualified to make the repairs.

While Rosa was in the basement repairing artifacts, Leila pried off the kick plate below the cabinet and liberated her hoard of stolen treasures. She carefully packed them in soft cloths as needed, and into sacks small enough to be easily handled. Then she re-hid them in an empty cabinet with a lock, down in one of the basement room's most dimly-lit corners.

Working against time, anxious to have it all done before Gustav's return, Leila made a series of middle-of-the-night visits to the Collections Wing. The night guards were concentrated near the staff room close to the wing's castle entrance at around one a.m., during shift change.

By a little before one Leila, clad in a new set of dark gray burglar gear she'd sewn for herself (those she'd brought with her from the Night Guild were now hopelessly too small), was waiting near the shadowed corner where the wing joined the main body of the castle. Hugging the wall, she moved soundlessly along it toward the outer side of the building, where the main public entrance (the one through which she usually came and went to work each day) was situated at the top of a low flight of stone stairs giving onto the main level.

From there, she could see the lights of the guards' lanterns through the windows at the front. They patrolled the corridors (both upstairs and down, but never the basement) with dogs and checked each room hourly, making a nighttime raid on any substantial amount of the treasure impractical even if there were plenty of windows by which one could come in.

As soon as the lights receded toward the rear of the building, at just about one by her watch, Leila ducked back around the corner and let herself in through one of the basement windows near where the wing and the castle joined. She'd left it closed but unlatched when she was down there during her work shift.

Silent as a cat, Leila gently dropped the six feet from the bottom edge of the window to the floor. Then, pulling a glowstone out of a pocket and hooding it in her hand so that it cast only a faint pallor on the floor, she made her way around the partition to where the cabinet full of treasure lay. She took exactly as many bags as she could carry, locking the cabinet afterward. Next she carried them back around the corner, lifting them up and shoving them out the window one at a time before jumping up and wriggling out herself. She now stood five-feet-two, and thought it likely she would not be getting any taller.

Before Gustav and the Count had returned from their expedition in search of new art worlds to conquer, all of the sacks of stolen trinkets had been transferred from the Collections Wing to a space under the floorboards in the shed behind Rosa's cottage. It was nearly time to leave.

Chapter 36

Gustav was back, and the staff of the Collections Wing were all glad to welcome him. With only a teenage girl as a stand-in, it had not seemed as if there were anyone at the helm. "How did things go in my absence, Rosa?" he asked, as they walked toward his office.

"Pretty smoothly," she said, gesturing toward the stacks of paper and memos she'd left on his desk explaining exactly what she'd done (if not, certainly, what *Leila* had done) in his absence. "I had quite a few offers of items for sale, and I responded to all of those politely. The ones I thought were worthy of interest are in the stack on the left. And there were some things brought in for appraisal. I was able to spot a couple of fakes, but the rest I thought I'd better leave to you. I just don't have your level of expertise."

Gustav sighed. It was so hard, in this modern world where everyone seemed to be rushing around chasing money, to find someone with a genuine appreciation and understanding of historically important art. Yet this young orphan girl, out in the world on her own after leading what sounded like a very sheltered existence in Munch, had taken to the subject immediately and learned so much in only a few months. How could she just throw all this away to go running off to Andala?

"Did the Count find his new passion?" Rosa asked with a hint of mischief. Gustav shrugged his shoulders.

"I'm not sure," he admitted. "Sometimes it takes a while for his enthusiasm to build." Then he turned his attention to the topic that had been on his mind since he'd realized that spring was really here.

"Are you sure I can't convince you to stay with us, Rosa?" Gustav asked, sitting down behind the desk and leafing through the neat stacks. "You're the most able assistant that I've found since I started this job. Maybe I was just waiting for you to be born and grow up?" He smiled appealingly at her, showing her a lighter side she hadn't noticed before. Leila guessed he usually reserved this surprising personal charm for his "men friends," whoever they might be. His way of life was not illegal but certainly frowned on by polite society in the Dominion.

Rosa gazed down at him in sweet girlish innocence, a look of concern on her face. "Oh! I so wish I could stay. I have found these last few months to be the most exciting, fascinating time of my life. To stay here surrounded by such beauty, and objects of such historical importance, would be wonderful!"

Gustav looked at her questioningly, sensing he might be making progress. "Then..."

"I'm sorry," Rosa said, now looking as though she might be going to cry, "Seeing Andala, where my parents were born and where I was conceived, has been a dream of mine since I was a tiny child. And there are family connections I must seek out. Without my aunts and uncles and cousins, I am alone in the world."

He considered that. Of course, family – even family she had never met – would be important to a young orphan girl. Maybe she was hoping some great-uncle would pop out of the woodwork and arrange a marriage for her to a wealthy merchant. As much pay as he could offer her working as his assistant, it wasn't going to be enough to tempt such a beauty. Even if women didn't appeal to Gustav in that way, he could still appreciate them from an aesthetic point of view, and Rosa was lovely. Sweet and smart, too. She'd make some man a fine wife.

Gustav sighed. "Well, I can see I'm not going to talk you out of going to Andala. After you've been there and seen the place for yourself, is there any chance you might consider returning?" Rosa's face lit with pleasure, her smile lighting up the room like the sun.

"Oh! Could I? That would be wonderful!" Calmer then, she added "I can't truly say what will happen when I arrive in Andala. I may find that I have family who wish me to marry. And maybe it will be someone I don't *want* to marry. Would you take me back, if I return in another few months?"

Would he? Gustav had held this job for nearly two decades, and in all that time he had only twice or thrice had someone under him who showed promise for becoming the kind of expert who could one day fill his shoes. "I'll hold your job for a year, Rosa," he promised. "And if you come back, I'll see to it that your pay is doubled. How about that?" The impulsive young thing rushed around the desk and planted a kiss on his cheek.

A caravan had come to town, and would be waiting in Chanton's market square for three full days – taking on provisions, and offering any who wished to accompany them or ship goods with them the chance to sign on. The day staff at the Collections Wing threw Rosa a going-away party, complete with a fancy decorated cake and little presents, during the noon hour in the staff room. Rosa's dark eyelashes were spangled with happy tears, as Leila cringed at the love and kindness showered on her perfidious self.

From a seller of leather goods in Chanton Rosa had acquired an enormous leather valise, into which most of her worldly goods were packed. This was strapped across the back of Nimble's saddle, and he was hung about with saddlebags as well. Living here in in Chanton for less than half a year, the young orphan had acquired many things.

Kathal, annoyed at being booted from her usual riding spot, ran ahead of the horse and then turned to wait for him to come along. He was less than happy about all the extra weight. Having bid her goodbye at the party on her last day of work, none of Rosa's friends from the castle were there to see her off as she joined the caravan preparing to leave from the market square at nine on a Mirday morning; but Inge was there, and hugged the girl tightly before waving her off as the caravan began moving – out of the market square and onto the main highway west.

Chapter 37

Moving with the caravan was slow, so slow! Rosa got permission to add her valise, full of things she wasn't going to need right away, onto the back of one of the dozen wains being hauled along by teams of oxen. A few people rode on the wains, or on carts or wagons pulled by horses; but many people were on foot or horseback as well. It was going to take months for them to reach Andala, assuming neither foul weather nor bandits delayed their progress.

Rosa tried to keep to herself, moving up and down the line of wagons as if curious about what they contained and whom she might meet; but she spoke to no one. They had been moving for a couple of hours and the sun was high, but it had not yet reached its zenith, when Leila – on Nimble, accompanied by the cat, slipped off onto a dirt track heading due north. If anyone noticed, they didn't remark on it.

Leila had dealt with a couple of fences in Munch, and one of them in particular she trusted enough that she thought she would be able to let him handle the disposition of the trove of loot stolen from Count Wilhelm's collections. Almost without exception she'd pilfered items of high intrinsic value, not wanting to rely on historical significance or the fame of a former owner. Better these pieces remained merely anonymous bits of treasure, of dubious provenance but worth thousands in gold.

Nimble was restless from two hours of a pace far slower than he liked, and as she made her way up the trail Leila gave the young gelding his head. Munch was days to the north, and she might as well get some distance between her and the departing caravan. In her mind she was waving goodbye to Rosa Estares, on her way at last to fabled Andala.

Count Wilhelm had awoken earlier than usual, feeling off-kilter somehow. He was restless, and the trip to Italia – while enjoyable – had failed to engender the vibrant enthusiasm that had seized him, time and again, over the years since his wife had died. It wasn't that his treasures filled a gap left by the mother of his children, he thought. More likely, it was that without her at his side demanding he be sensible with his money, he'd been able to do whatever he liked – and he liked finding, buying, and owning beautiful things.

After breakfast he went to his office for a while and put his hand to some of the business of the county. But he had an able assistant in Heinrich, and his presence was not really required. Next Wilhelm wandered down to the stables and took out his favorite mount, Steadfast. The old fellow was getting up in years, but he still had a little bounce in his step on this fine spring morning. Alone of the citizens of Oester the Count was allowed to ride within the precincts of Castle Chanton's park – and he trotted up to the far border and then galloped back, divots be damned.

After returning Steadfast to the stables, to be rubbed down and cared for by the stableboys, the Count bathed and changed into fresh clothing, then took lunch in his rooms. He felt as if something was coming, something just out of reach. If he could think of how to coax it out, he would know immediately what new passion he could throw himself into – something to fill the void left by his waning enthusiasm for musical instruments.

Though it might appear otherwise, Wilhelm didn't emotionally abandon his treasures after tiring of collecting them. He still regarded all of them highly, and they were a great source of pride to him – the most famous collections in the Dominion, and some day they would be a public trust. Thousands would travel to Oester just to behold them, and these travelers would bring trade and prosperity to Chanton and its surrounding region. Generations to come would call him "Wilhelm the Good."

Wiping his mouth on a fine linen napkin after washing down his food with a draft of watered wine, the count rose to his feet. Perhaps that was what he needed! He would go and visit his collections, confer a little with Gustav. As he walked back through the magnificent ranks of his past enthusiasms, he would somehow know what he was meant to do now. With a little smile of anticipation on his face, Wilhelm set off along the corridors of the castle to the entrance of the Collections Wing. At this hour the doors between castle and annex were guarded but unlocked, and there'd be no need for him even to knock.

Gustav had also just finished his lunch, and welcomed his employer in heartily. Had he figured out what his new passion was to be? Would they soon be embarking on a new quest for, perhaps, Center Sea pearls or the unique pottery of the ancient Haelens? He was sad to have lost his promising assistant, but felt ready for a new challenge.

"Your excellency!" he said heartily, "what brings you here?"

"For Lucia's sake," the count grumped, "how long have we known each other, Gustav? I think you could call me Wilhelm." The younger man clapped him on the shoulder, a twinkle in his eye.

"Very well, Wilhelm!" he said with a smile.

"I've decided to seek inspiration in the past," the count explained. "Thought I'd walk back through the collections and see if anything will lead me in a new direction. Our recent journey gave me a few ideas, but… I just can't quite put my finger on it." Gustav smiled indulgently and took Wilhelm's arm.

"Very well, then," he said gaily. Spring was having its effect on him, as well. "Shall we start at the beginning?"

"Good idea!" the older man said jovially. "The Ring Room, I believe." The rings, everything from wedding and engagement rings of bygone nobles to signet rings, poison rings, and rings claimed by the former owners to have magical properties (though these had not been proven) had been Wilhelm's first love; and the amassing of the ring collection, followed by its disposition in the newly built Collections Wing nearly twenty years before, had occupied him for two full years.

The count greeted the guard on duty as he and the Curator made their way inside. There was no one else in here, this afternoon, but still his loyal staff of Collections guards remained vigilant. In the early years, before today's security precautions had been put in place, there had been some pilferage and a couple of more serious burglary attempts. But the wing hadn't seen a successful theft in more than a decade.

Wilhelm headed straight for the case holding the wedding rings of famous women of the past. There were even the rings of a few empresses here, fascinating bits of history as remarkable for their cultural value as for their beauty. But this case held personal meaning for him as well, for it contained the very first piece that had come to him, launching him on the course that he'd pursued for nearly half his adult life.

The count stood for a moment admiring the case, the room itself. Everything was immaculate, just as he liked it. The glass cases shone without a trace of dust, their contents sparkling from the regular care they received. It filled him with pride that he had brought all this into existence, this magnificent monument to his good taste and the cultural history of the Dominion.

Now Wilhelm bent closer, studying the glittering rings inside the case – each with its placard and portrait. It should be just there, he thought he remembered seeing it there the last time he was here. But that was more than a year ago, of course. After studying the case for several minutes, examining every ring in detail, he turned to Gustav with a look of consternation on his face.

"Have you been rearranging the collections?" he asked anxiously, "Or perhaps, are some things out being repaired?" Rosa had completed all the repair work while he and the count were gone, Gustav knew, and once a display room's contents had been displayed to Wilhelm's satisfaction they were rarely moved around.

"No, Wilhelm," he said with assurance, "there's been nothing like that. Why do you ask?"

His face going pale, eyes widening with speculation, the count said, "Will you please tell me, then, why I cannot find my grandmother's ring?"

Chapter 38

Gustav was in shock, his complacency shattered. They had spent an hour comparing the ledgers with the display cases, and it was not just Wilhelm's grandmother's ring – the very first item he had collected – that was missing. There were dozens, maybe hundreds of items not where they belonged; and no one had noticed!

But who, really, was to have spotted anything wrong? The cleaning girls were not particularly bright to begin with, and their job was monotonous drudgery. All of them had been working here for at least two years, some for much longer, and as one of them said "I just let my mind wander while I'm cleaning. Thinking about my Sigi, usually..."

The guards' job focus was broader, making sure that the rooms were secure and that there were no cases smashed, no cloaked figures stuffing bags full of treasures. Not a one of them could have told you any three specific small items that were supposed to be in any particular case, even if they'd spent years guarding the room in which those treasures sat.

And it was only small items that were missing, they realized. It would take days to go through all of the ledgers and determine everything that had been taken; yet it seemed clear that what they were looking at was slow, gradual pilferage by someone on the staff. But the girls were all searched every day! Could it have been one of the guards, or perhaps more than one of them, plotting together to carefully steal away treasures without being noticed?

Gustav himself, who must take full personal responsibility for the theft under his nose, had been so caught up in whatever Wilhelm was collecting now that he hadn't paid any attention to the older collections at all in years – only making sure that the rooms and the displays were kept spotlessly clean and constantly guarded. For all the good that had done!

The night guards would have had the best opportunity, Gustav realized, and he liked that idea. Already the entire guard force had been gathered and they were being interrogated, one by one, by the count's Captain of the Guards. The Collections Guards were a special team, but they were only part of the larger force that patrolled Castle Chanton.

Gustav had never seen Wilhelm so upset. When the extent of the pilferage had been realized, the man had actually sat down and cried! His seeming lack of interest in the treasures he'd amassed in years past was only an illusion, apparently. He had invested a little part of himself in each and every gleaming bauble, and he now seemed as perturbed as if one of his grandchildren had been abducted.

"All of the staff are being questioned," Gustav assured him, almost feeling like crying himself, "and their quarters are being searched. If any one of my people has perpetrated this crime and they have not been selling off the pieces as they were stolen, your treasures will be found and returned. But we can't say how long this has been going on – it could have been years, and whoever the culprit is they might have left our employ long before this discovery."

Wilhelm got a grip on himself. "I don't think it can have been that long," he said. "I saw that ring here the last time I came to visit the collections, it must have been eighteen months ago. You recall, I stopped by to greet visitors on Viewing Day?" Gustav nodded thoughtfully. A thought had occurred to him, but it was one he was loath to consider.

"Who among your staff is recently hired? Has anyone left in the past year?" the Count demanded. Gustav paled.

"Just the one girl," he said reluctantly. "From Munch, she was, but of Spanic origins. Very bright, literate, and a quick learner. I'd been training her to become my assistant, but she was orphaned and eager to visit Andala to see if she could find any of her relatives. She arrived here just as autumn was closing in, and left only today with a caravan heading west."

Wilhelm's eyes widened, and an excited expression took hold of his grief-stricken face. "This morning?" Gustav nodded morosely. "Then we can still catch her!"

"But, but…" the Curator stammered, "she's just an innocent young girl. And she was here such a short time. Surely, these thefts must have been going on for more than a year, at least…"

Wilhelm waved him aside, jumping to his feet and running out of the office, down the hall to where Hans Bohrs, the Captain of the Guard, was interviewing the staff. "You're probably right," he called behind him, "but we must talk with her to be sure!"

Leila crested a rise and reined Nimble in, letting him rest after climbing that last hill. He immediately began to show an interest in the lush spring grass that was growing on either side of the well-worn track, and she dismounted and unclipped his reins so that he could graze unfettered while she took a little break herself.

Kathal hopped down and was soon stalking toward a copse of small trees covered in white blossoms, while Leila decided that now might be a good time to change out of her "Rosa" garb and into something more comfortable and practical for her ride to Munch.

While she was digging into her pack, Kathal appeared with a dead partridge in her mouth and laid it at her feet with a self-satisfied "Mrhn?" Leila regarded the blood-spattered corpse. Two or three of those, plucked and gutted and roasted to a turn on a spit over a fire, might indeed be good. But she had no time for such things. There were hours of daylight left, and they needed to be on their way.

"Thanks, Kathal," Leila said affectionately, "but you go ahead. I'll just eat some of my waybread." She'd brought along plenty of foodstuffs, enough for the likely two-three day journey on horseback down the northern slopes of the Antels to Munch. The cat picked up the dead bird and took it a few yards away, where she had a good view of the little meadow they'd stopped in. Grinning around a mouthful of feathers, she sank her sharp teeth into the tender, still-warm breast meat.

Leila turned away, and began peeling off her riding dress and the bloomers beneath it. She left the camisole on, sniffing at herself in distaste. The past few months there'd been a definite shortage of hot baths, and after riding hard today she rather stank. Well, she'd put up at one of Munch's finer hostelries and soak for a week, once she'd unloaded her loot.

She donned a pair of leather trousers and an olive-colored broadcloth shirt. It was a man's shirt and big on her, but not intolerably so. She put on a pair of her favorite mid-calf boots, soft-soled, and a man's broad-brimmed wool hat to keep the sun off her head. Ladies in the Dominion favored a pale milky complexion and never left the house without a bonnet, to keep it that way. Not *her* problem, but she still didn't like the sun beating down on her face. Even here in the Antels, it was beginning to get hot.

All three of them got a drink from the little stream that wound its way through the meadow. Then, before mounting up again, Leila pulled an item from a side pocket of her pack. She'd discovered it at a curious sort of junk store tucked into an alleyway in Chanton, an impulse buy. It hadn't cost all that much, and she'd thought it might prove useful. It was a telescoping spyglass such as seamen used, watching for shoals or pirates or whatever it was you needed to look out for when sailing. Her life so far had still not provided any seagoing experiences.

Polishing the lenses on the tail of her shirt, Leila extended the spyglass to its full length and, screwing one eye shut, began admiring the view. You could see a long way from here, near the Antels' ragged summit. She wondered how far the caravan had gotten since she left it, and whether anyone had noticed her absence. Probably not – the caravan was strung out for more than a mile and anyone not seeing her there beside them would simply assume she was off at the other end.

Legs planted slightly apart, Leila turned her enhanced gaze to the south and west, trying to pick out the main highway. Was that it? That little ribbon of pale stone amid the trees of the forest that grew up close to the road in many places? Yes, it was! Alright, turn slowly to the right… There! She saw it. The magnification on the spyglass wasn't all that great, and it was hard to hold it steady – but she could clearly make out the colorful dots of the caravan's outriders, the bulk of the wains as they creaked slowly along.

Wow, this thing is great! Leila thought. It made her feel almost godlike, standing atop this ridge and surveying her domain – all-powerful as she beheld her tiny, ant-like subjects. She snorted to herself at the folly, and pointed the glass back toward the east. Could she see the spires of Castle Chanton from here? In fact the castle's setting on its promontory made it easy to spot, and it wasn't all that far to the east of her current position. She'd been traveling north most of the day, and the caravan had only made perhaps ten miles of its westward journey when she'd left it behind.

Leila sighed a little, thinking of how much she had liked working among mad Count Wilhelm's amazing collections, and of the people who had been kind to her there. Another bridge burned... She swept the glass west again, trying to estimate how far the caravan had traveled since this morning, when her eye was caught by rapid movement on the highway below. She sat down, knees up, and rested the spyglass on a knee to steady it as she took a more careful look. There were six riders down there, in the scarlet livery of Oester, and they were galloping west on the highway as if their lives depended on it. Uh oh...

Chapter 39

The caravan had been traveling steadily for most of the day at perhaps five miles an hour, a fast walking pace for a man. It had stopped shortly past noon for an hour so that the oxen and other animals could be watered, the humans fed. It was a warm afternoon.

Count Wilhelm's party of mounted guards had not left Castle Chanton until nearly three in the afternoon, by which point the caravan was lumbering along some twenty-five miles to the west of them. It took them around an hour to catch up. Hans Bohrs, who'd led the party at Wilhelm's behest, slowed his panting horse to a fast walk and surveyed the scene before him.

At the rear were some of the heaviest wains, pulled by oxen that were beginning to get tired. Some of them had horses hitched to them, and those horses' riders were now resting atop the cargo or riding on the driver's benches. Relatively few of those who'd begun the trip in the saddle (other than the hired caravan guards, who were on duty) were still riding, as it was so frustrating to be constantly overtaking the head of the caravan and then turning back. In the next few weeks, they would learn patience.

Bohrs pulled his horse up alongside the driver of the hindmost wain, startling the man out of the glaze-eyed boredom that had set in. Driving oxen, under most circumstances, didn't require a lot of constant attention. The man was not from Oester, but he recognized the mounted, armed man who approached him as some kind of local official. "Can I help you, sir?" he asked politely.

The captain touched his hat brim in a sort of salute. "Hans Bohrs, Hauptscharführer of the Oester Guard," he introduced himself. "I need to speak with whoever is in charge about one of the people who is traveling with this caravan. This *is*, I presume, the same caravan that left Chanton this morning?"

The driver gave him a crooked grin, eyes sparkling with interest. The day had been awfully dull so far. "Right you are, Cap'n," he said. "You'll be wanting to talk with Jack Thompson. He's the master of this outfit." He gestured forward, where the slow train of wagons disappeared around a bend. "You'll find him up near the head, probably about a mile from here."

Thanking the man, Bohrs put heels to his mount and led his party of five guards at a more measured pace, a fast trot, along beside the baggage train as they sought the caravan master. He didn't know what to make of this errand. Catch the girl, find her at all costs, and bring her back to the castle for questioning. But treat her gently, make sure no harm comes to her? Were they chasing a thief, or not?

In a few minutes they had skirted the length of the baggage train and found what looked for all the world like one of the caravan wagons of the Nima at the head of the line – pulled by a couple of sturdy cart horses. The man holding the reins was no Nima, though. He was tall and broad, in his mid-forties, with sandy hair and a neatly trimmed beard. He was soberly dressed, but his clothing looked dusty and he'd removed his jacket in consideration of the warm spring sunshine beating down on him where he sat on the driver's bench of his curious-looking wagon.

He appeared to be much more alert than the guy at the other end of the line had been, and the moment the six brightly-clad guards appeared beside his wagon he pulled on the reins. A leather-clad caravan guard mounted on a wiry-looking small horse came up on the other side and reined in, looking to his boss for directions. "Call a halt, Bob," the master said. He set the brake on his wagon and, identifying Bohrs as the captain of this group said, "All right, what do you need?"

They had been searching the caravan for more than an hour, speaking with everyone, before Hans Bohrs became absolutely convinced that the "sweet, innocent young girl" Rosa Estares was not among the dozens of people accompanying the baggage train. There were half a dozen chestnut geldings, but none of them were hers; nor had anyone noticed the cat in several hours. The girl herself might not be a standout, and her mount was ordinary enough – but someone should have seen that cat! So far as Bohrs knew, it was unheard of for a pard to be found traveling with anyone but the Nima.

Eventually one of the helpers on a baggage wagon admitted that he remembered the girl, and that she'd asked him to take her valise onto his wagon along with various trunks, bags and other luggage belonging to the people who'd signed up to travel with the caravan for personal protection.

Aha, Bohrs thought. If that's gone, we'll know that she deliberately left. They had certainly not passed her on the road, so she hadn't just fallen behind. He supposed it was possible, being young, that she might have ridden ahead for a while out of boredom with the slow pace and be a mile or two in front of them. But he doubted it.

Yet the valise was still there, exactly where the baggage helper had tied it. He hadn't noticed the girl since she'd left it with him, but here it was. Would it be stuffed with trinkets from Count Wilhelm's collections? It was locked, and for a few moments Bohrs had some hope they would find the stolen treasures inside. But when they got it open, it was full of clothing – just the sort of clothing you might expect a young woman like Rosa Estares to be wearing.

The guards' horses had recovered from their headlong rush, and the troop was now milling around waiting for their captain to tell them what to do next. The caravan was still halted, and Jack Thompson was cursing under his breath at the delay. The girl was not here, why could not these obnoxious officials simply go back and report that fact to their master?

"So you're certain, then, that no one saw the girl or her cat when you all stopped for lunch?" Bohrs demanded. He now knew for certain she was not here, but he needed to figure out how long ago she'd slipped away. The fact that she'd left the caravan, in his mind, was proof positive that Rosa was not what she'd seemed, and that she was the thief who had stolen Count Wilhelm's treasures. Did she have a male accomplice, he wondered? No one had reported seeing the girl with anyone except, once or twice, the seneschal's secretary Dieter. And he was not under suspicion.

Most of the people of the caravan had dismounted from their horses or wagons and were now standing around the mounted guards. There was a chorus of "Nope, didn't see her" and words to that effect. Then one fellow, a weedy little baggage cart driver in his fifties, spoke up. "She mighta' taken off at that track that leads north a few miles back," he suggested. "It's just a dirt road and it climbs pretty steeply crossing the mountains. You can't even walk it in the wintertime, but it's good enough now."

Bohrs gave the man his full attention. "How far back is this track?" he demanded. He hadn't grown up in the Chanton area and spent most of his time around the castle, so he wasn't as familiar with the byways as some might be. "A few miles back," the cart driver said. "It'll be on your left as you're going back toward town. We passed there around an hour before noon, as I recall. It leads pretty well straight north then takes a turn to the east and connects with the main highway to Munch. If your girl's from Munch like you say, maybe she got homesick." He winked.

Without dismounting, Bohrs nodded to Jack Thompson. "Thank you for your assistance, Herr Thompson. I apologize for the disruption. We'll let you get on with your journey now." With that, and a nod around to let the people standing nearby that the apology was meant for them as well, he wheeled his horse and his troop of guards set off at a canter down toward the eastern end of the caravan. About fucking time, Jack Thompson thought as he watched them go. Then he turned to those clustered around.

"Come on," he snarled, patience exhausted. "Let's get *moving!*"

Chapter 40

Once they'd left the caravan behind the Guard captain spurred his horse to a faster pace, and his men followed suit. They were not in the all-out gallop with which they'd started the expedition though, keeping their eyes open for signs of the dirt trail the cart driver had mentioned.

It wasn't hard to spot. There were dirt roads leading to farmsteads here and there along the main highway, but these generally had posts beside them announcing "Edelweiss Farm" or whatever. In many cases, the farm's fields were clearly visible from the road. But something around fifteen miles back, on the left just as they'd been told, the troop spotted a flood-scarred, bare dirt path perhaps five feet across leading north and up toward a pass through the mountains. There was no signpost, but there were the clear marks of a shod horse's hooves entering the trail from the road.

Pulling up and studying the tracks, Bohrs said "This is it! This has to have been where she went."

"Are we going after her now, sir?" asked one of his lieutenants. Their horses had already run for more than thirty miles this afternoon, and to push them at speed up this steep trail on top of that might have them dropping in their tracks. But if they didn't go after her now they might not catch her until she had gotten to Munch – where she easily might sell her stolen goods and vanish into the city's underworld.

"We have to catch her," Bohrs said firmly. "If we keep pushing, maybe we can make up the lost ground before dark." It went without saying that they would no longer be able to track her after dark, though there was a pretty good chance she would stay on the main track and not go off down some deer trail to escape pursuit. They turned their horses up the track and began following it at a fast walk, hoping their quarry would be unaware of the pursuit.

They did not catch Leila by dark. She'd known as soon as she spotted the guards dashing headlong down the road after the caravan that the game was up. Betsalel curse them, how had they figured it out? Everything had been just fine and dandy a few hours ago, yet now somehow the theft had been discovered and they were fingering her as the suspect? It was enough to make her wonder if magic were involved. If anyone could afford to have mages scrying out his enemies, it was Count Wilhelm.

Nothing for it now but to run, and run fast. The problem was that there was no place to hide, no confusion of roads for her to take. Nimble's hoofprints were clearly visible in the dust of the trail, and there was no prospect of rain. Leila assumed that the guards would be delayed for at least a little while discovering that she was not still with the caravan – unless that aforementioned mage had simply pointed her out on a magic map. No, she saw as she trained her glass on the highway one more time from a ridge another mile up the trail. They had ridden past the turnoff and were still dashing headlong toward the slow wagon train.

She'd been on the trail for nearly four hours when they'd appeared, Leila calculated. Add another hour to check the caravan, and she had a five-hour start on them. It was a slim enough margin, but Nimble was young and strong and he had not been run as hard as those guards' horses had today – nor anywhere near as far. She should be able to open up a good lead on them, though as the trail wound back down the mountains on the far side of the pass they might get line-of-sight on her.

Well, at least she wasn't likely to get within bowshot of them unless Nimble went lame or something. Better have a care for those hooves! Leila urged him on, encouraging him to go as quickly as he wanted to but not trying to push him beyond what he thought was comfortable. The trail ran in switchbacks as they approached the mountain pass, still some snow on those peaks even now in Flora. Little streams ran down every gully, carrying away the snowmelt to feed the rivers.

She wouldn't have tried to do this going downhill, but Leila urged Nimble up some steep slopes, cutting loops out of the switchbacks and saving some extra steps if putting a bit more strain on the heavily loaded horse. Kathal had been riding atop the saddlebags, but she dropped back to the ground and scrambled up past several switchbacks to sit watching them as they climbed to meet her. Her smile seemed to say, "Don't you wish you had claws, like me?"

To their west, the sun was sinking lower and lower and a chill was coming into the air. Leila dug a cloak out of her pack and a packet of pemmican-like substance as well, while she was at it. She ate it in the saddle, washing the dense, rich bar down with sips from her canteen. She hoped that the guards, presumably expecting to stop the caravan and arrest a thief after only an hour's ride, had not come equipped with spyglasses, cloaks, food, or water.

She was right. Far down the slopes of the Antels on the trail behind her, the guard troop was beginning to flag. They had stopped at the very same rise from which Leila had first spotted them hours ago, their horses blowing with the effort of the climb. Hans Bohrs grimaced. "This isn't going to work," he grated out, furious at having to admit defeat. "We have no food or water, no fodder for the horses, and no camping gear. We evidently can't catch her before dark and we can't stay out here all night, either. Let's go back to the castle."

The guards of his troop said nothing, but they were looking at him with speculation. It wasn't like their captain to just give up on something, especially something he'd been ordered very specifically to do. Looking around at them, he decided to offer an explanation. "We're still going to catch her," he assured them. "She's wandering around on this winding track through the mountains, and it'll be at least another full day before she gets to the main highway leading to Munch. We'll go back and get fresh men, fresh horses, and supplies. And then we'll take the highway north and just sit there, resting on our asses, until she shows up at the crossroads." A small, spontaneous cheer went up from the men as they turned their horses and happily pointed them back down the trail toward the south.

Chapter 41

Leila reached the pass as the last golden rays of the sun were casting long shadows across the land. She pulled her spyglass out again and scanned her back trail. As tired as their horses must be, she doubted the guard troop would have been able to gain on her. Nimble himself was clearly worn out, ready to get that saddle off and roll in the grass of some mountain meadow.

It was hard to make out color in the evening light, but her eye caught a glint of crimson – much further down the trail than she'd expected. And it seemed to be moving away from her… Yes! They were turning back! Just as she'd hoped, the guard captain (Hans Bohrs, she knew him by sight but had never spoken with him) must had concluded that it would do them no good to try pursuing her in the dark. They must all be tired, hungry, and thirsty by now – never mind the condition of their poor horses.

After assuring herself that the guards *were* truly turning back, Leila telescoped the spyglass back down to its folded size and returned it to its velvet bag. Then she faced ahead. Kathal was curled before her, making an effort to nap. "Come on Nimble, just a little bit further," she asked the horse. "Soon we'll all have a well-deserved rest."

They had come far enough down from the pass before stopping to bypass the snows, but it was still chilly during the night and Leila, sleeping fully clothed and wrapped up in her cloak, was glad of the warmth of the cat snuggled beside her. When dawn came, she stood up and stretched the kinks out. She hadn't thought much of the mattress in the gardener's cottage, but she kind of missed it now.

She spotted Nimble grazing a few yards away, and he raised his head to whicker at her before resuming his breakfast. Kathal stretched as well, then trotted off for a drink from the small stream before disappearing into the woods. She returned a few minutes later with a dead rabbit, as Leila was having another uninspiring meal of pemmican and spring water. "It's all yours, sweetie," she told the cat.

She suspected that it wouldn't be long before the Chanton guards figured out that she must be making for Munch, and came after her by the main road. They needed to get moving! Before long

Nimble had been saddled and they were moving down the trail – less steep on the northern side of the mountains – with Kathal again taking shortcuts through the switchbacks.

With only a single break, Leila and her animal companions came down into the foothills. The trail straightened out, and Nimble was able to pick up the pace. They cantered for a time, then walked, then cantered again as her anxiety began to increase. She had not formulated a backup plan, had no idea where to sell her trove if not to the fence in Munch. What gods-cursed luck, to have been found out so soon when the heist had gone so smoothly!

Resting only when necessary, stopping briefly for food and water and (for Leila, at least) toilet breaks, they came to the spot in the trail where another, similar trail came in from the east. The northward-running trail continued on, and according to maps Leila had studied it would connect with the main highway that ran east and west many miles north of Munch.

Sense should have told her that she was in a race she couldn't win, and she should have kept on to the north or lost herself in the hills until a couple of months had elapsed and the Chanton guards had abandoned the chase. But she was so close to her goal, the little house in Jena glittering just out of reach! And she had spent months working for this, too.

If she could just beat the guards to Munch she could unload the merchandise, then hide out while she formulated a plan to sneak away. Despite her "high" rate of pay, Rosa had had many unusual expenses and little had been saved from her wages. Leila's coffers were running low, and that was another reason she didn't want to wait two months or more for her payoff.

So, they turned east along the dirt track (undulating over the foothills, but mostly straight and with good footing) that led to the main north-south road. Once they reached that, it would be the better part of a full day's travel to the outskirts of Munch.

Dusk approached, and Leila urged Nimble up off the track and through a hilly woodland, looking for a place to camp that was not so exposed. The vegetation north of the Antels was thinner, less dense. They encountered a small stream meandering out of the hills and Leila followed its course upward to the south, until they'd wound out of sight of the track and had come to a small meadow. Then she hopped down and took off Nimble's saddle, as he sighed in relief.

Wet with dew, Leila arose stiffly again in the morning and spent a few minutes washing herself in the little creek before eating some more of the pemmican. By the Seven, she hoped the time would soon come when she would never have to taste, look at, or even think about the stuff again! Kathal was her usual cheerful self, but Leila detected a hint of resignation as she tightened the girths on Nimble's saddle. "Oh, don't be such a baby!" she chided him, leaning in to make him release the air he was holding, "At least the trail is mostly level and not full of rocks!"

They wound their way down the course of the stream, Kathal choosing to walk on her own feet first thing in the morning, and picked up the trail again. Leila took some time to examine it, but saw no footprints. This trail must be fairly well used, she thought. It appeared on maps and was not overgrown with weeds and saplings as you'd expect if no one ever came here; but during the past few days, at least, it seemed she was the only person riding on it. That suited her just fine.

As the morning wore on, Leila began worrying about logistics. Having never been this way before, she had no clear idea how much further it was to the main road. The rolling hills and wooded terrain didn't offer any clear vistas, yet she was beginning to think that it had taken her too long to get here. What if the Chanton guards were waiting to ambush her as she came onto the main road, or lurking along it to the north?

Her anxiety grew; and finally when she came up a rise and spotted a tall old pine tree growing on a promontory to her left, Leila decided to do something about it. She directed Nimble off of the trail to a patch of grass and let the reins hang down. "Stay here," she commanded him, and he happily began grazing.

Leila was still wearing the leather pants, shirt, and boots that she'd put on a couple of days ago. It had been her plan to get back into the "Rosa" outfit for riding into Munch, not wanting to raise any eyebrows at the sight of a woman wearing pants; but her fear that she was going to have to run for her life made her change her mind.

A girl who could shinny up a drainpipe and traverse to let herself into a third-story window wasn't afraid to climb trees. The pine was of a species with lower branches that died and broke off as the tree drew, and the first branches were more than twelve feet above the ground; but the bark was rough, and Leila nimbly scrambled up it until she could start grasping handholds.

She'd brought her spyglass along in its cloth bag, hanging from her belt, and after straddling a limb some fifty feet off the ground she pulled it out and began scanning the terrain to the east. *I was right, it's not far,* she realized. No more than two miles ahead over the rolling hills, the trail disappeared. Beyond it she could see the faint line of gray stone that marked the main highway, along which a fair amount of traffic was moving. Munch was a smudge on the northern horizon.

There were wains and carts, carriages, and riders alone or in groups moving along the highway in both directions. This was one of the main north-south arteries in the Dominion, and one of the few that ran through a good pass across the Antels. It remained open most of the winter, thanks to the efforts of the Dominion's highways department. They had developed horse-drawn plows especially designed for clearing snow from the road.

Glancing down and realizing with annoyance she was getting pine pitch all over her nice leather pants, Leila put the glass to her eye and studied the area of the highway nearest where the dirt track joined it. There! A flash of red, and another! The Chanton guards must have set an ambush for her. It was a good thing they were so enamored of those flashy uniforms – and a good thing she'd climbed this tree for a look at the land.

After stowing her spyglass Leila climbed back down the tree, dropping the last eight feet to the soft humus that surrounded it. Kathal had thought what Leila was doing looked like fun, and she'd climbed up the other side. But her desert-dwelling ancestors had probably never seen a tree, and it turned out she didn't like the experience. From the lowest branch she stood meowing at her mistress, asking for a little help getting back down. Leila frowned up at her. "You got yourself up there, you can get yourself down. Come on, it's time to go."

She stalked off toward the horse, and in another minute the cat scrambled awkwardly to the ground and followed – tail down. She hopped up onto Nimble's saddle as Leila was getting him under way, and they continued down the trail for another mile. Then, still well out of sight of the main highway, Leila turned Nimble off the trail and they began moving across country – heading north diagonally, with an eye to striking the road well beyond the ambush.

The countryside was fairly open, rolling hills covered in grass and brush with frequent oak, beech, and other deciduous trees plus the occasional pine. Leila hoped that the rolling terrain might hide them from her pursuers, and directed the horse along the course of yet another little creek that nestled in between the hilltops.

This was going to work out great, Leila thought. Though her life had begun badly, she had been born with an irrepressible tendency toward optimism that often got her into trouble. But it least it kept her from falling into despair and giving up. And it wasn't as if she hadn't had her triumphs.

Other than dips in the terrain, the main north-south highway ran mostly straight through this part of the Dominion. Leila had traveled stretches of it, though she'd entered Chanton by back roads. She wanted to make sure of traveling far enough north of the junction that the waiting guards wouldn't see her enter the road. It seemed reasonable to expect that, having had time to prepare, they might have brought spyglasses of their own this time. And perhaps bows.

The creek bed she'd been following veered off to the west, and Leila turned north and climbed a low hillside to see how she was doing. She was now much closer to the main road, and the trail she'd been traveling on earlier was now lost in the rolling countryside to the south. She turned more sharply east, as Nimble picked his way around copses of small trees and up and down hills.

Finally, there was the main road ahead – clearly visible through the trees. Leila clucked, liking the looks of the road ahead, and Nimble picked up his pace. There was no sign of any red coats, and the three of them (Kathal once again riding atop the horse's saddle) stepped onto the roadway. They drew glances from a carter coming south with a load of something that looked like onions, and a pair of horses heading the other direction, pulling a buckboard with a family riding it, shied as Leila urged her mount past them and began cantering up the road.

No time to lose, Leila thought. She guessed that the red-coated guards would have reached here from Chanton sometime this morning, and were expecting her to appear at any moment. When she failed to show, they might seek her down the trail – or turn north, guessing that she'd gotten past them somehow. She needed to be into Munch and selling her loot as soon as possible, before they realized she had slipped away.

She and Nimble could not possibly gallop all the way to Munch – the city was still hours away. But they could put some distance between themselves and the ambushing Chanton guards back at the junction. The horse lived up to his name as he slipped around carts and carriages, passed parties of mounted riders, and pushed up the road to the north.

Leila felt a swelling sense of freedom, of exaltation – they were going to make it! Then she and the horse squeezed around past an enormous hay-wain blocking the path ahead of them – only to find three red-coated riders awaiting them, on either side of the road.

"It's her!" one screamed, pointing, as he and his companions surged out onto the road and began moving toward her. Shit! Nimble reared, catching Leila's sense of urgency as she pulled hard on the reins. Without a bit, the reins were more like a suggestion than a rule – but Nimble was obedient to his rider's desires and in moments he had spun on his heels and was dashing south again. Kathal had barely managed to avoid being thrown off, and she was now holding on for dear life as the horse clattered down the road, skirting traffic.

Riding for her life, Leila looked ahead and saw red-coated figures far away, coming toward them. She was trapped! Near at hand to the east was the looming presence of the Blackwald, that deep forest of ill omen. During her stay in Munch Leila had heard many tales of the place: of the malevolent gnomes whose mischief plagued any who tried to ride through it; of mysterious storms that sprang out of nowhere and left you wandering lost, surrounded by shadows; and of a looming, amorphous presence of evil that lurked at the very heart, luring travelers to it – never to be seen or heard from again.

All utter superstitious nonsense, of course, Leila assumed. It was just a big, dark forest that had not yet been tamed by the hand of man. Likely it was full of deer, wild pigs, squirrels, foxes, weasels, badgers, and maybe a few wolves – things you needed to watch out for, yet nothing evil or sinister. But if the place's local reputation might aid her, she'd be willing to take her chances. With the Chanton guards closing in on her from ahead and behind, Leila reined the horse off of the road to the east. She spotted a narrow track leading under the forest's eaves and steered for it, urging him "Run, Nimble! Run as fast as you can!"

Chapter 42

The two parties of Chanton guards converged and galloped their horses after the fleeing girl, their blood up. She had thought to elude them, but they would soon have her – and the Count's stolen treasures, as well! They had all had a long ride up here from Chanton, but after that there had been several hours in which to rest. The girl and her horse had presumably been traveling all morning, though, and she had no more than a couple of hundred yards' head start on them.

As Nimble ran headlong into the trees, to Leila it seemed as if the bright morning had suddenly turned to dusk. "Blackwald," indeed! There was little low undergrowth, fortunately; but the trees grew close together and many of them had branches as low as six feet off the ground. She had to bend low over the horse's neck to avoid being swept off as he plunged into the dark forest.

The mix of trees here was similar to the much sparser woodland on the west side of the road, but for some reason here they had gathered tightly together – as if taking counsel with one another. Leila, panicked, didn't look back or even really forward. She just buried her head in Nimble's mane and let him take her – anywhere, as long as it was away from the pursuing guards. She could hear their cries of triumph behind her as they sighted their prey and gave chase.

The party of nine guards, despite their eagerness to catch the girl they'd been pursuing for days, found themselves pulling up just outside the opening in the trees where she and her horse had gone in moments before. It was as if some enormous invisible barrier, not physical but psychological, had come down and was holding them back.

One of the guards, youngest of the troop, turned pale. "She's gone into the Blackwald!" he said with alarm. His commander wasn't the type to let superstition prevent him from reaching his goal, though he too felt the eerie sensation as of some force urging him to stay away. It was if the trees themselves wanted to bar their passage. His hair stood on end.

"Yes, she's gone into the Blackwald!" Hans Bohrs said with exasperation, his face coloring with a mixture of anger and embarrassment at the way the forest had affected him. "And we're going after her! Get moving!" He had to fight his horse, as it shied and reared before allowing itself to be spurred onto the path ahead. The way was too narrow for more than one to ride abreast, so they fell into line behind him.

Though they wanted to gallop headlong, to catch up with their quarry, the guards found themselves fighting to get their mounts moving in the right direction. They were squealing, jinking, eyes rolling in evident terror. Were there wolves nearby? Before long Bohrs found himself well ahead of his men, keeping his horse to a canter along the barely-discernible trail through sheer force of will.

Behind him he could hear his troop bringing up the rear, the sounds of frightened, uncooperative horses and cursing riders. But aside from these sounds, the dark wood was silent – no birds calling, squirrels chattering, or any of the other wholesome sounds you should hear in a normal forest. A chill ran through him. Was there more to the tales than some silly folklore?

Then he realized that another sound was missing, one he had been sure he would hear: the sound of the heavy footfalls of Rosa Estares' horse as it ran ahead of him down this path. There had been a delay, but surely he could not be more than a few hundred yards behind? He reined in his horse and it stood shivering, head turning from side to side as if it thought something was about to pounce on it. Fearing to climb down lest the animal bolt and leave him stranded, Bohrs bent low over the saddle and peered down at the ground ahead of him in the dim light. There were no hoofprints.

Finally Nimble had run himself out; and his pace slackened to a canter, then a walk before he finally stopped, breathing heavily. His flanks were flecked with foam. Leila, coming to her senses, realized that she could no longer hear their pursuers behind them. Could they have lost the trail in the dim light? It must now be nearly noon, but no ray of sunshine struck the forest floor. Looking up she could see little bits of daylight through the leaves, but it appeared that the sky had gone overcast. How odd, when the day had been sunny what seemed like half an hour ago.

Perhaps a sudden spring storm was coming, Leila mused, as she urged Nimble to keep moving forward – if only at a walk. She doubted she'd have to worry about getting wet – how much rain ever reached the ground, here? By the Seven, this place was every bit as creepy as the tales had suggested! There was not a sound, not even the trickling of water to suggest a nearby brook.

It appeared Leila was going to have to travel all the way through the Blackwald and out the other side to escape her pursuers, a distance of many miles, and she hoped that she would be able to find some water for Nimble soon. Anger and frustration rose in her as she considered the gods-cursed bad luck that had led to her "perfect crime" being discovered so soon. By all rights it should have been days, weeks, or even years before anyone at Castle Chanton noticed that anything was missing.

Well, nothing for it but to press on. The trail they'd been following continued on, a faint paleness on the forest floor winding among the trees and up and down the gentle hills here north of the Antels' eastern reach. Leila sat like a lump on Nimble's back as he ambled along, recovering from his headlong gallop, idly stroking Kathal's fur as her mind roamed. She needed a new plan.

With any luck, this trail they were following would lead all the way through the Blackwald. Among many other useful items Rosa had bought a map of the entire Dominion (including the Center Sea and the northern shore of Palambo), and she'd studied it as much out of curiosity as to plan her route to Munch, and from Munch to Jena.

The dark forest of evil repute was roughly circular, stretching more than a hundred miles west to east, and on the far side of it the eastern part of the Dominion ran to the east for hundreds more before reaching the impassable barrier of the Killtops. Leila supposed that her best approach (assuming she and the horse and cat managed to make it out the other side of this place that seemed devoid of food and water) was to head for the nearest human habitation and find out where she was once she'd escaped the forest. Then move south and west for Vinizzi.

That tiny but well-populated county had been an independent city-state before being absorbed first by the hegemony of Roma and then by the Gaspari Dominion. In the thousand-plus years since then it had prospered mightily, a thriving seaport not dissimilar to Marsine. There Leila could linger for a while (provided she had any money left!) and build up her contacts in the underworld until she'd established a relationship with a fence who could move the trove of loot from the Chanton collections for her.

From Vinizzi it was not that far, a day or two's travel on horseback, to Jena. I'll have to be very careful not to ruffle any feathers in Vinizzi, Leila mused as she rode along, letting Nimble go where he would. Jena would not be far enough to run, and her carefully crafted new identity as an upstanding citizen would be ripped to shreds if anyone she'd crossed in Vinizzi came looking for her there. She sighed, and rode on.

Chapter 43

Lunchtime had come and gone, and Leila had still seen no signs of life in the Blackwald. No birds flitted from tree to tree or called in the wood, and the silence was becoming oppressive. They had definitely lost their pursuers, but what good was that if they were going to wander in here until they'd perished of hunger and thirst?

She reined Nimble to a halt, and patted his neck. "Sorry old boy," she said softly. Something about the utter quiet in here made you loath to raise your voice. He whickered at her, and began looking around for something to eat. No grass grew beneath the trees, but there was some small low-growing vegetation here and there and he sniffed it before biting some off and chewing experimentally.

Leila trusted the horse to know better than to eat anything poisonous, and after doing some stretching exercises she sat on the soft earth with her back against the bole of a huge oak and rummaged in her pack. She had two full skins of water and a third that was nearly exhausted. That would see her and Kathal through a couple of days in a pinch, but it wasn't going to be enough for Nimble. She closed her eyes and said a silent prayer to the Seven to lead them to a stream, and soon.

For all the good it would do, she thought sardonically. The Seven had certainly not come to her aid when her mother was dying, nor had she noticed them answering any of her other prayers. Perhaps they required a cash payment in advance, like old Meister Klingt? Or maybe they only answered the prayers of the truly faithful, those who devoted their lives to worship. Eh.

Kathal had hopped down from Nimble's back when Leila had climbed down, and immediately run off in among the trees. She returned around five minutes later as Leila was sinking her teeth into her second-to-last bar of pemmican, and looked her mistress in the eyes. There was no mistaking the plaintive "Mrk?" and Leila broke off a piece and offered it to the cat. Kathal sniffed it suspiciously then took it gently in her mouth and chewed it slightly before swallowing. Then she looked around for more.

Well, the stuff did have meat in it, after all. It was densely nutritious and required no fire for cooking, which was why Rosa had chosen it as food to take along on her journey. If only I'd brought more of it, Leila thought with regret. The idea of being stuck deep inside a forest where even Kathal could not find game was something that had never occurred to her when she was making her plans.

Leila shared the remainder of the pemmican with the cat, washing it down with the last of water in the third skin. She had a cup with her, and poured some of the water into that so that Kathal could drink. But she still held out hope they would find a stream or a spring for Nimble.

They continued on their way, and Leila's hopes were raised when the trail abruptly got wider. Then she began to see the remnants of paving stones here and there. This was once a real road, not just a thin trail, she realized. Where would it lead? What she'd read of the history of this region (a pursuit that had occupied some of Rosa's time in the long winter evenings a few months ago) suggested that while rumors of supernatural wrongness in the Blackwald dated from the dawn of human history, and the place had remained intact when many another forest had been cleared for agriculture or cut down for firewood, the presence of the lurking evil at its heart first began to be mentioned around two hundred years ago.

Abruptly the forest changed around them as the road became broader, most of its paving stones still in place though they were heavily overgrown with moss. There were signs of a forest fire here, not recent but still the trees were smaller, younger. Between them the crumbled remains of dead stumps claimed space, which should have resulted in a more open canopy. But somehow the dimness seemed still more pervasive. Or had Leila just been riding longer than she thought, and now it was getting dark?

The road widened still more, into a broad plaza. Saplings and larger trees grew between the stones here and there, but now Leila could finally catch a glimpse of the sky. It was nearly black, dark gray clouds roiling. Yet she didn't sense rain coming. It gave her a little shiver.

Ahead of her a large, ruinous stone building rose from the forest floor. It had clearly been burned out, but long ago. The walls still stood all the way around, forming a shell surrounding a stone-paved courtyard, but the roof was entirely gone. Creepers and other vegetation Leila hadn't seen earlier were growing over the stones, working slowly to pull the ruined edifice apart.

Leila dismounted once again, but Kathal didn't hop down. She crouched on the saddle, ears back and fur bristling. "You feel it too, don't you girl?" Leila murmured and reached up to stroke the cat's shoulder comfortingly. Kathal emitted a "Nak" and leapt down off of Nimble's back to rub against Leila's legs, purring tensely. Her fur was still standing on end.

As Leila approached the ruined building, curiosity warring with a sense of dread, she heard a sound that brought joy to her heart: the sound of water tinkling! Stepping through a ruined archway into the courtyard, she spotted a two-tiered fountain in the center of it. They were saved!

Nimble was shivering, ears twitching and eyes rolling, as she led him in to drink. He was clearly afraid of this place as he had not been of the ominous forest, but he'd caught the smell of water and his thirst was driving him on. The fountain, like a pair of broad bowls connected by a fluted column, seemed to be carved of marble and the inside of the bowls was coated in green algae.

The sun must shine here sometimes then, Leila thought, as she scooped up some of the water in her hands to take a drink. The water tasted sweet and pure, and she scooped another double handful for Kathal to drink. Nimble stepped close and began sucking the water up in long draughts, causing Leila to pull him back gently and admonish him, "Not too much at once! You don't want to get sick!"

Nimble shook his head, snorting, but stepped back. In between the stones grass was growing, further evidence that both rain and sunlight must sometimes reach this spot. He began nibbling it enthusiastically, his earlier uneasiness forgotten. Encouraged, Kathal went exploring the bounds of the courtyard, looking in the taller grass along the edges, and soon came up with a mouse. She didn't bother bringing it to Leila, but just gulped it down in one bite and began hunting for more.

I hope we can get out of here before I have to start eating mice too, Leila thought ruefully, then told the animals "Stay here!" and went in through a doorway to the inner part of the building. The place had once been huge, and with no roof it was as if she were wandering in a stone maze. The walls were mostly around eight feet high, but in places they had fallen in – letting her jump up and peek through to see what was on the other side of them.

It seemed that people, a lot of people, had been living here at the time that the building had burned. Unless she was going to find a couple of acres of cleared forest and an overgrown kitchen garden out back, happy thought, Leila guessed that the stone road must have carried a lot of traffic at one time – bringing supplies to the… what *was* this place, anyway? Why would you construct such a large complex out here in the middle of a gods-forsaken forest?

The rooms were full of rubble. Charred roof timbers, fallen masonry, were everywhere and beneath them were broken, charred furniture, smashed crockery, silverware… Ooh, silverware! The stuff was pure silver, blackened with age, and had a curious pattern stamped into the handles that Leila couldn't make out through the tarnish. But she gathered every piece she found and tucked them into her pack. It would be a lot easier to sell silverware, once it was polished up, than to move intricate art treasures of dubious provenance. Just the thing if she needed a little spending money when she got to Vinizzi.

Leila found her way to a broad chamber that looked like it might have been a dining hall, and there she discovered her first skeletons. She shuddered in revulsion as she approached one, though the bones were clean and dry. Shredded remnants of clothing, something plain like a monk's robe, clung here and there to the corpse. Its skull had been smashed in. A few feet away, another similarly-clad skeleton had a sword lodged in its rib cage, stuck tight. Monks' robes… Of course! This must have been a monastery, or a temple or something. Religion in the Dominion had had thousands of years to get organized, and Leila's education on the subject hadn't been all that detailed. But clearly, that was what this place had been.

Probably the monks had wanted to seclude themselves from the world so they could concentrate on worship, or some such nonsense.

But the world must have given them a lot of coin if they were able to sustain themselves out here in the middle of nowhere with no visible means of support. Maybe… maybe the organization itself, gathering offerings from its urban temples, had been able to fund this isolated location.

Yet they'd all been killed, and their monastery burned. Quite a long time ago, from the look of things. Leila began looking around with more interest. If the church was rich, might there not be some valuable religious icons lying around the place? She found nothing, but kept looking. At least she was accumulating a good supply of blackened silverware.

Leila was beginning to feel a little oppressed, emotionally. It had been a long, trying day and this sad ruin with its even sadder corpses was starting to get to her. Maybe the reason they'd all been killed was that the place had been sacked by an unusually large gang of bandits, who'd stolen all the church's riches before setting fire to it. Those riches must have been rich indeed, though, for bandits to leave lying a large quantity of perfectly good silverware…

Yet despite her funk, something seemed to be calling her – leading her on through the ruinous labyrinth. Near the rear wall she discovered a stairway, and realized that the place had a lower level. The floors she'd been treading on were solid stone, and Leila wondered at it. Could the lower level have been carved out of bedrock? It must surely have escaped the fire, else the ground floor would have fallen into the basement.

Down she went, on stone stairs worn with age. How many thousands of feet had trodden these steps, to have worn down the hard granite until each tread was cupped? Rainwater had run down those steps and pooled at the bottom, a thin brown soup that only wetted the soles of Leila's boots. She was astonished to find her way barred by a heavy, double wooden door. Each side had a rusty-looking iron lock.

Well shit, Leila thought. She had no doubt that her skills in lockpicking could have a lock as ancient and clunky as this one open in as little time as it would take to use the key – but not when it had been sitting out in the weather for however many decades or centuries. The mechanism was probably permanently rusted shut.

Maybe she could bring Nimble down here and have him kick it open? It couldn't be barred from the inside, unless somebody had volunteered to die of starvation down there. Just as a matter of procedure, she gave the right hand door a shove. With a shriek of rusted hinges, it swung open.

Chapter 44

A frisson of dread coupled with excitement surged over Leila as she stepped hesitantly over the threshold. Inside, the passageway leading away from the door was barely lit by the dim light coming in from above. Beyond that, all was blackness. She pulled a couple of glowstones out of an outer pocket of her pack, and held them before her as she walked hesitantly inside.

Since first acquiring these, Leila had made a point always to keep them charged. She stored them in a finely-wrought net bag, through which daylight could reach the stones. Their faint blue light wouldn't show detail, or color, but it could you from tripping over something or falling into, say, a pit lined with sharpened spears (she told her imagination to give it a rest) in the pitch darkness.

The corridor was around six feet in width, stone all the way around, and the air inside it smelled as if it had been trapped in here for eons. Leila turned her head from side to side, holding a glowstone out in each hand, to see what if anything was worth her attention in this forbidding, crypt-like space.

Mysteriously there was no sign here of the cataclysm that had destroyed the monastery's upper level. Carved wooden furniture, upholstered in shredded ancient fabric, sat here and there as if awaiting someone to sit on it. There were quite a few wall hangings, faded by time and frayed around the edges, too murky to make out in the dim illumination.

Leila was relieved to see no bodies lying around, but disappointed that she also saw no golden idols, jeweled religious pendants, or other valuable items. The fact that poor overloaded Nimble bore on his back sacks of glittering art objects worth more money than she could reasonably hope to spend in a lifetime didn't matter. She was a natural thief, with an inborn craving for treasure to steal.

It was impossible to tell in the darkness, but Leila thought from the feel of the air that this lower level probably spread below the entire length and width of the building above. Yet it seemed less labyrinthine, with a large central corridor running off toward the part of the complex where Leila and her animals had entered the courtyard.

There was less furniture in this corridor, but Leila discovered that there were a few sconces on the walls – and in each of them was a torch. Some of them seemed to have burned down, but others looked fresh and new – if ancient and dusty. Likely whatever oil these had been soaked in had long since dried to resin, but perhaps they would still burn. She pulled a box of Lucifer matches out of a pack pocket and struck one on the slightly rough granite wall. It flared to life, and when she held the match to a torch it burst into flames with a slight "pop" of exploding dust.

That's better, Leila thought, and carrying the lit torch she continued on her way with increasing confidence and anticipation. Surely, as well-preserved as this lower level was, she would find something here worth stealing. As she walked along at an increased pace, hoping the animals were doing all right back up in the courtyard, she spotted more unburnt torches and tucked a few of them into the top of her pack.

Rooms gave off the corridor on either side, none of them with doors set into the entryways. Leila quickly discovered that they were all the same, little cubicles maybe ten by twelve feet in size. Each had a single bed crafted of wood, a rotting mattress covered in the shredded remains of sheets, a chair and small table, and what looked like a shrine of some kind intended for private worship. They must be the private quarters of the monks, obviously designed to encourage them to consider themselves insignificant and interchangeable. She wrinkled up her nose at the idea. Individual differences were what made humanity powerful and interesting. Why try to squeeze people into a single mold?

At the end of the corridor Leila came to another set of doors, standing open, and beyond them what looked like an anteroom of some kind. How curious, there were simple wooden chairs standing all around the walls and a desk with a more comfortable chair standing to the right of a much more ornate set of doors set into the far wall. These were closed.

The sense that something was beckoning her was growing stronger, and she was eager to try those doors; but first Leila stood for a moment looking around the room. How bizarre, it looked almost like a larger version of Heinrich Friedman's outer office in Castle Chanton. Did the acolytes of this god (and she had yet to identify which of the Seven had been honored here) have to make an appointment to see him or her? There were a couple of reasonably new-looking torches flanking the doors, and she lit them with the one she was carrying. Then she set it down on the stone floor to free her hands.

She went over to the desk and rifled its drawers, coming up mostly with a snowdrift of fragments she guessed had once been paper or parchment. The ancients had used parchment for many of their important documents, the inner membranes of a lamb's skin scraped and dried to a whiteness suitable for writing on. She also found a couple of glass inkwells, the contents long since dried, some sealing wax, and an engraved seal attached to a wooden handle. The symbol on it resembled a dark circle with a single white ovoid in its upper quadrant, like an eye. Where had she seen that before?

But the pens Leila found on the desk looked almost modern. They were of carved and painted wood, smoothly rounded, and with a blued steel bracket set into the end to hold a replaceable steel nib. The nibs were rusted to the shafts, but otherwise in pretty good condition – down here out of the weather for who knew how long.

Leila had learned much history from her mother previous to her eighth birthday, but it certainly hadn't included details of when, in the thousand-year history of the Dominion, goose quills had given way to modern writing implements. Yet, she suspected, this place had not fallen as long ago as she'd first thought.

The doors were calling to her, and Leila turned her attention from the desk. It had annoyingly failed to yield anything of value. At the back of her mind a tiny voice was whispering "Danger, danger!" but the siren call of untold riches drowned it out. Hoping her luck might hold a second time, she gave the doors before her a shove. But they remained solidly closed.

Leila picked up her torch, which was still burning brightly, and held it up for a closer look at the locks. They were iron like the ones on the doors that led to this lower level, but unlike those they had never been exposed to any moisture. They appeared to be in perfect condition.

Wait a minute, if this was a waiting room and the guy sitting at the desk was the gatekeeper, wouldn't he have had the keys to the doors? Leila hadn't seen any keys, but then her inspection of the desk drawers had been cursory. Setting the torch in her hand back down, she moved back to the desk and began pulling the drawers out – dumping them upside down onto the formerly uncluttered desktop. When she reached the second drawer on the right, there was a clank.

Got you! she thought, snatching the pair of iron keys from amid the mound of paper flakes. She held them up so that they were silhouetted against the torch burning on the right side of the doorway. By the Seven, they were the most complicated-looking keys she had ever seen. The idea filled her with joyful anticipation. What was behind those doors, that was worth this level of craftsmanship in the locks?

Leila guessed right the first time, turning first one key and then the other to open the doors. They swung outward, and the room beyond seemed to be considerably smaller than this one. She picked up her torch from the floor again and rubbed the burning end against the doorframe on her right, removing some of the charred wrappings and bringing a brighter flame. Her heart was pounding as she strode in through the doorway.

By the Seven! No, by the Eight… Before her in the center of the fairly small room stood the statue of a man eight feet tall. He was perfect in every limb, bald, nude except for a loincloth, and standing with legs slightly apart, hands held forward palms up, eyes closed. Above the closed eyelids and centered between them a third eye, glittering bright red in the torchlight, stood open. Betsalel!

The skin of the statue was black. Not the black of the natives of Palambo, who ranged in hue from medium reddish brown to the color of dark kaf; but the black of charcoal, the black of a starless midnight sky. In the light of her single torch Leila could barely make out its details, save for the glowing red ruby that formed its third eye. There were six torches in sconces around the room and Leila went around lighting them. One was nothing but a ragged stump, and she tossed it to the floor before replacing it with the one in her hand.

Now the room was well-lit, half a dozen ancient but now-glowing torches filling it with a golden, flickering light. Two hundred years, Leila thought, this place must have died two hundred years ago. It gave her a shudder to think of all the time, back to pre-history, when the worship of Betsalel had been considered as acceptable as that of Lucia, or any of the other Seven who were still honored in the Dominion and beyond its borders. Such evil! No wonder the legends said there was a dark presence at the heart of the Blackwald. This hideous monastery and its perverted monks had been destroyed and forgotten, but the memory of the Shadow God (as Betsalel had ever been known) lingered on.

He was portrayed in the classic manner. Leila had seen a picture of it in a history book. The utterly black figure's two normal eyes were closed as if in sleep, symbolic of darkness and shadows and things that happened at night; while its monstrous third eye, symbol of the Shadow God's malevolent nature, burned red. Idols of Betsalel, just like this one, had once stood in every temple of the Eight throughout the Dominion, as well as in many separate places dedicated to the worship of this one god alone. Why anyone should choose to worship the god of shadows, antithesis of everything that was light and good, in preference to others of the pantheon, Leila didn't know.

But Lucia, acting through Emperor Fernand IV, had brought light to the Dominion and driven out the darkness. Betsalel's idols had been destroyed, his worshipers slaughtered if they would not recant; and for two hundred years no one within the Dominion had openly worshipped the God of Shadows, bringer of nightmares. Why would they? Leila's grandfather Josef had called her father a "black devil worshiper," implying that all Palambans were somehow involved in this perverted worship. It was only within the Dominion that Betsalel's worship had actually been outlawed, but surely no one anywhere would want to?

Leila recovered from the awe that had swept over her as she realized she'd penetrated the devil's sanctuary. Quite possibly, the last such in all of the Gaspari Dominion. While a part of her mind wanted to believe that Betsalel was evil incarnate, another cynical part wanted to point out that he had no more reality, no more influence on the modern world, than did any of the other seven deities. Betsalel hadn't done her any harm; and Lucia, Mira, Belantos, Mulia, Andros, Deline, and Dionos had not done her any good. They might well actually exist, but if they didn't impact her life what difference did they make?

Looking around the brightly-lit room, Leila was a little disappointed. Here in the inner sanctum, if anywhere, she'd hoped to find some treasure. She supposed that the idol itself ought to have some historical value – but finding a buyer would be impossible and the thing was far too big to transport. That "third eye," on the other hand, looked to be a perfect ruby half the size of her thumb. Drawing one of her daggers, she scaled the statue and clung to it, like a child hugging Daddy, while she pried carefully at the setting. Didn't want to damage that magnificent stone!

With a barely-audible "tink" the ruby came out of its setting, and Leila caught it with a lightning movement of her left hand before it should fall to the stones below. She released the grip of her legs on the statue and hopped nimbly to the ground, sheathing her dagger and holding her prize up for inspection. In the bright light of the six torches, it almost seemed to be glowing by itself. Nice!

Suddenly Leila's palm was suffused in agony as the stone burst into ruby flames, searing her flesh as it clung to her and began burrowing down into the flesh of her palm! All of the torches went out in an instant, plunging the room into darkness. Then before the afterimage had faded from her retinas they flared up again – but this time a baleful red.

Leila shrieked as the glaring gem sank into her hand, like some flesh-eating beetle seeking her core. The glow faded after it had disappeared below the flesh of her palm, which closed over it. In moments the pain receded, though she still felt a sensation of warmth in her left hand and arm. Was she hallucinating? In the red light she realized the statue was moving, its two closed eyes opening, as a voice – a deep, resonant, insistent voice – reached her mind without passing through her ears. "Leila," it said. "You are mine!"

Chapter 45

All right, Leila thought, I have to be hallucinating. What else could it be? Yet she could not identify any reason for that to be so; and she *could* unfortunately think of several reasons why she might have just awakened an angry dark god, one who had probably been waiting for somebody like her to come along for the past two hundred years. Oh, shit.

The torches continued to burn red, lighting the chamber with a glow that erased all colors. Leila looked little lighter than did the Shadow God, as they stood confronting each other. As Betsalel stood nearly three feet taller, not to mention that whole "omnipotent deity" business, she yielded him the floor.

"I have waited so long," the voice declared. Though the statue was moving as if it were alive, Leila saw that its mouth was *not* moving. The god's voice was coming directly into her mind. It scared the living crap out of her.

"Wh-wh-what do you want from me?" she quavered, keeping a tight grip on her sphincters.

"You are mine," Betsalel's voice replied, "body and soul. I am within you, and I am now a part of you – as you are a part of me. You will be my prophet, my emissary, my high priestess. Through you, I will regain my powers. And you, too, will realize powers you had not dreamed of."

Uh oh… "I don't *want* any of your powers," Leila squeaked. Then she cleared her throat and continued in her normal voice, "Please, just take back the gem. I'm sorry I bothered you. I kind of thought you were dead." Oh shit oh shit oh shit… There was a humming in the air, and the statue of the black god took a step forward and gazed down at her, hands on hips. Its two "normal" eyes were wide open, and glowing as red as the one she had (oh, so foolishly) stolen.

"What you want is of no consequence, little mortal," the voice rumbled. "You will do as you are told, or you will die. I am your god, and I command you!" Leila's terror was beyond anything she had ever known before, but within her slight form a core of inner strength arose.

"No!" she shouted back defiantly, "I will never serve you! You are evil!"

The god incarnate started back, as if scarcely believing the audacity of this tiny girl who came barely up to his navel. Hey, why did a god have a navel? Leila wondered. Weren't they supposed to have created themselves out of cosmic dust, or something like that? Then, to Leila's astonishment, he laughed.

"Oh, my sister did her work well!" he gasped, as if Leila had just told him the funniest joke in the universe. "She controlled that emperor of yours and fed him all her lies, and he poisoned the minds of every mortal on this part of the continent. That bitch," Betsalel added as if it were an afterthought, his mirth having evaporated.

"You-your sister?" asked Leila. "You mean Lucia? I thought she was your wife." The god burst into fresh laughter.

"Why," he asked, chuckling, "can you mortals never get it straight?" She looked at him blankly. "We told you all, once, entrusted it to those we judged to be our most sincere worshipers. They were supposed to write it all down, and forever after the new mortals who arose like mayflies to swarm and die would know the truth. Yet somehow the truth became twisted."

Leila couldn't believe she was having this conversation. On the plus side, he had not simply smitten her dead or obliterated her mind. If anything, she seemed to be thinking more clearly than usual. "Then what *is* the truth?" she demanded. Having been a small person her whole life, she was finding there was not, after all, that much difference between facing off against a human opponent twice your size and standing down an immortal being with unknown powers. Likely, you were dead either way. Hmm, that wasn't as comforting a train of thought as she'd intended...

Betsalel's disembodied voice took on tones almost of fondness. "The truth, little mortal," he said with infinite patience, "Is this. In the beginning of time, when this universe was born, was the One. The One was both male and female, our father and our mother, and s/he did not create the universe but was born with it. Alone of all that was born at that time, s/he had the power of thought, and of knowing, and of making."

Leila was spellbound, hearing from the lips (sort of) of a god the true story of her universe's beginnings. She forgot all her terror, drinking it in. He went on. "So s/he was alone, and it was thus for eons beyond your human imagining. But the time came, on this planet and on others in this universe, that little ape-like creatures began to walk on two legs, began to speak. And they cried out into the universe, with the power of their newborn minds, that they wanted gods."

Leila gazed up in the red light at the black god before her, waiting to hear more. "Their need for gods was so great that they worshipped anything," Betsalel continued. "Trees, the spirits of animals, the planet that had given them birth itself – though that was only an enormous ball of rock with a molten core, not a sentient being. The One felt compassion for these little apes who had begun to think and yearn, and in that compassion gave birth to the eight – two sets of quadruplets, one male and one female after the way of the humans for whom they were intended. My siblings and I were designed as a gift for the humans of this world, to satisfy your longing for the divine."

Leila's trance broke as she digested that last sentence. "What?" she asked in disbelief, "Your mother-father, whatever, *made* the Eight especially for us?" The dark god's red eyes looked down on her with sadness.

"Yes," he admitted. "We are yours, as you are ours. You give us form, and we respond to your needs to become what you desire."

"But…" the girl stammered, "What about your divine powers? What is it that makes you immortal gods? I don't understand."

It was a while before he answered. "We are immortal gods because we are born of the One, who contains all the universe within her/his being. Though every human should perish, we would go on – though greatly diminished. Because it is human belief and worship that gives us our divine powers. We are what you have made us, and as I am a part of you I cannot tell you lies." Leila pounced on that as Kathal would on an unwary squirrel.

"Then if humans give you your powers, you can't tell me what to do!" she declared with a little more audacity than she was sure she possessed. "I can refuse to do your bidding, leave you here to molder in this ruined temple for the rest of time!"

Now the Dark One took a step back, looking down at her with an appraising glance. What a creature had been drawn into his net! She was perfect for the task, but it would not be easy winning her to his side. "Do you believe me evil, Leila?" he asked softly, slipping past her defiance.

After thinking about it for a moment Leila responded, "Of course you're evil! Everyone knows it! That's why no one worships you anymore. Emperor Fernand learned what a monster you were, how perverted your rituals of worship were, and with assistance from divine Lucia he succeeded in wiping them from the Dominion. Your very *name* is synonymous with evil."

"Why?" Betsalel asked gently. "What evil have I done, or caused to have done in my name?" Leila sputtered for a moment, then seized on a fact she'd learned from her history books.

"Human sacrifice!" she crowed, "You had your followers throw babies into the dark fire, as a requirement for your favor!"

The god seemed taken aback. "Bullshit!" he roared at last, "that is complete and utter nonsense. I never did any such thing. Look within your soul, Leila, and tell me if I lie." She did, and realized with a shock that he had spoken the truth – the Shadow God had become a part of her, and as he could see into her soul so she could see into his. He was not lying.

Head down, Leila looked as if she were cowed, or forlorn as she stood before the towering god she had believed, her entire life, to be the very embodiment of evil. But her mind was working furiously. If everything she had been taught was wrong, where did the truth lie? Not just about the gods' origins, but of their attributes and powers?

After a minute or two she spoke. "But you *are* the god of shadows, of death and darkness and the things of the night, right?" He saw where she was going with this.

"Each of us is as you mortals have formed us," he acknowledged. "When we arose from the One, we were male and female, but otherwise formless. Mortals decided that we should be paired off, each goddess with a god whose attributes complemented her own. I became the god of shadows, and because you humans feared what stirred in the darkness, I was ever less favored. But my adherents understood that there is virtue as well as menace in shadows."

More thought. Leila peered up at him in the red light. "I'm yours, you said. Does that make me your worshiper?"

"I hope you will worship me, Leila. I cannot command that. But I can command your obedience to my will." He sounded almost apologetic. The girl ignored that statement for the moment.

"You do still have other worshipers, right? My grandfather said that all the dark people of Palambo were in your camp." Betsalel chuckled again, the sound both frightening and appealing. It was better than having him blast out her eardrums with a supernatural roar of rage, at least.

"No," he said, "Having dark skin has nothing to do with a preference for worshiping the god of shadows. In fact, my sister Lucia, in her role as goddess of light, must take some credit for that. The dark color in your skin helps to protect you from the sun's rays, which are far more harmful to you than any darkness." Leila had noticed that she had had no problem being out in the sun, no more than the Nima did. But many of the pale-skinned Gasparis suffered horrible burning if they went out with proper clothing. What a revelation!

"Yet Fernand's writ only extended within the Dominion," Leila pointed out. "Surely, you must have as many worshipers in Palambo now as you did before?" The god sighed.

"I would that it were so. I could manifest there and ignore the Dominion, though the loss of my worshipers here hurt me greatly. My brother Belantos, too, has suffered here. With no wars in a thousand years, very few within the Dominion pay him heed. But there is war aplenty in the little countries surrounding the kingdom of Palambo, and there are never fewer than six wars in progress at any one time in the realms of the Hando."

"So, why not just cleave to your worshipers in those places?" Leila asked. She didn't understand why this immortal being was bothering with *her*.

"Do you recall I told you that we gods are shaped by the beliefs of the mortals who worship us?" Leila nodded. "In Palambo, the established church – possibly influenced by the lies that were spread by your Emperor Fernand two hundred years ago – has become truly evil. Their rituals are cruel and perverse, and a sect of assassins has sprung up who claim to derive their powers from me."

The girl blinked, not understanding. "But they're *your* worshipers," she said. "Can't you just use your divine powers to smite them, tell them to knock it off, or something?" Again, a deep sigh.

"The change in the Palamban church came about while I was reeling from the blow dealt me by Lucia and her machinations," Betsalel explained. "By the time I realized what they were up to, they were no longer my worshipers. They say they worship me, but it is the darkness within themselves that they court. I can no longer even speak to them."

"And the Hando?" Leila asked.

"Diluted. I still have a few centers of power there, scattered around. Little more than secret cults, for the most part. I can manifest within the true idols in the inner sanctums of their shrines – just as I can do here. But the fewer worshipers I have, the less power I have to affect the world around us. And the less power I have, the fewer people there are who want to worship me. You mortals expect a return on your investment."

Well, if this wasn't the damnedest thing Leila had ever heard. For what felt like an hour at least she'd been having an intimate chat with the infamous god of shadows, and he seemed just like... Not exactly a regular guy, but someone who you could really talk with. And she knew in her bones that he told her no lies. She was even beginning to feel some sympathy for him, the wronged underdog, who'd been betrayed by his perfidious sister.

"There's one thing I don't understand," Leila said after digesting the latest bits of information. "Your sister, Lucia – why did she do that? History says she gave Emperor Fernand the power to perform miracles, to win people to his cause. Even though, since he was emperor, people pretty much had to do what he said, anyway."

The face of the god looked troubled. "She has... I fear that we all have, really, become too human. Though we are so different from you in a thousand ways we have become shaped in your image – our minds as well as the bodies we wear when we manifest for our worshipers. Lucia long felt that she was superior to me, for shadow requires the presence of light but not the other way around. She ignored the Balance, didn't see that there must be both light and darkness, war and peace, things of women and things of men, pure reason and mindless debauchery. And she thought she could become more powerful, come to rule us all, if she stole power from me. I was a target of opportunity for her, her polar opposite, and it was easy for her to convince humans to strike out against me."

Leila's face was awed, her green eyes dark in the red light. "It worked!" she said. "People these days believe that Lucia is the queen of heaven, foremost among the Seven, and that only the purest and most noble souls travel to her realm of the afterlife after death."

"The afterlife?" Betsalel asked, causing Leila's heart to sink further. Whatever reason there might be for her to need to explain to a *god* what the afterlife was, she didn't think she was going to like it.

"Um, please tell me that we have souls, and that when our bodies die our souls are set free, that we go on somehow?"

"Oh yes, of course," the god replied. "Your mortal form is just your manifestation in this plane. But your immortal essence, the part that goes on, is not really you, exactly. It's hard to explain. While it resides within your flesh it is molded by that flesh, and by what happens during your mortal life. But freed from the flesh, it quickly flees and all that it had learned during its time in that mortal form begins to fade."

"But… what happens next?" Leila asked sorrowfully. All her life she'd been told that there were rewards for good behavior awaiting her beyond the grave. Though considering her behavior so far, maybe it was just as well that were also no hells – as Betsalel seemed to be saying.

"Some, most, will immediately seek to be enfleshed once again. It becomes a habit, though they might choose some other form than human. For some, experiencing the entire range of life in its myriad forms is the most wonderful adventure there is."

"So, the ones who don't take another body?" Leila prompted.

"They join with the One, where they mix all together and may become the essence of new gods." New gods?! So far as she knew, her world had never known any gods but the Eight. Betsalel smiled, revealing bright teeth that looked red in the glare of the torches. "Did you think this was the only world in our universe that had given rise to life, little one? Though I and my siblings came from the One, I cannot even say for sure if we were his/her first creation. On each world with life, as creatures arise who need gods, the One gives of his/her essence to create them."

Leila's horizons expanded as she considered the size of the universe, and she suddenly felt very insignificant. In her science books she had learned that astronomers believed the myriad stars in the night sky to be suns like their own, and they were uncountable. How many of them had planets with their own people on them – and their own custom-tailored gods? What an astonishing concept.

"Always Eight, then?" she asked. It seemed a surprising number.

"However many seem to be required," the god replied. "Humans have two sexes and four limbs, hence Eight is a mystical number here. On some planets there are three sexes and the sentient inhabitants have a dozen limbs." Leila eyed him suspiciously. Was he having her on? But there were more important things to discuss.

She drew herself up to her full height, a little less than three full feet shorter than the god. "Very well," she said, summing up, "there's no divine punishment or reward for our actions in this life. And the Eight are not bonded pairs, but siblings. And humans' belief and worship are what give all of you your powers." Betsalel nodded. "So *what*, exactly, do you want from me, then?" The god smiled.

"Simple, little Leila," he said. "I want you to restore my worship to all of the Gaspari Dominion."

Chapter 46

Leila snorted. "You want me to *what*? I'm a sixteen-year-old girl thief on the run from the Chanton authorities. How am I supposed to manage that? You do realize that it's still technically illegal to worship you within the Dominion?" The god's posture suggested that her response had stung him.

"Leila, outside of this forest my powers are weak. I cannot manifest myself anywhere but in this chamber, my inner sanctum, and this is only thanks to the sacrifices my loyal priesthood made when this place was sacked and destroyed. But a part of me is now carried within you, and with that I can go anywhere you can."

Leila shuddered imperceptibly at the reminder. "So, you need a lift somewhere? Is that it?"

"I need you to go to Parat, the capital of the Dominion. It was there that Lucia and her puppet, Fernand, struck the first and most telling blow against me when they removed my idol from the Temple of the Eight."

Leila had read something of that. It was the first overt act after a campaign of propaganda against Betsalel worship that had lasted for months. After that, mobs had happily leapt to do the Emperor's goddess-inspired bidding – smashing temples, pulling down idols, killing the worshipers who resisted. From beginning to end, it had taken less than five years for all evidence of the Dark One's worship to be wiped from the Dominion.

Parat! That was in the completely opposite direction from Vinizzi. Was she never to sell this loot and realize her reward for Rosa's several months of patient effort? Well, she supposed it would be no problem finding a fence in the capital, when it came to that. "What do I do when I get there?" Leila asked, her frustration plain in her tone of voice.

"The idol I'm inhabiting now and the one in Parat are the only two of my focal points that were not destroyed in the purge," Betsalel explained. "Only at one of these points, and in the presence of at least one believer, can I manifest and affect the outside world."

"The one in Parat was not destroyed?" Leila asked in puzzlement. Surely, it should have been broken into a thousand pieces, once the ruby eye had been smashed.

"Fernand would have liked to destroy it, certainly," the god explained. "And my sister was lending him much power. But my priests at the temple there in Parat, the foremost nexus of our power in the Dominion, had warning of the approaching attack. They gave up their life essences for me, joining that power to mine, so that we were able to make the idol indestructible. Try though Fernand's troops might they could not break it, could not pry out my third eye. So they did the next best thing – they carried it away from the well of power and hid it in the deepest recesses of the Imperial Treasure House, tucked behind locked doors. But before they carried it inside they enclosed it in bricks, as if it were nothing but a decorative column to be set in some forgotten corner. And then, I think, they forgot."

Leila considered the tale. She was already planning the break-in, she realized, though she had never been to Parat. Betsalel had appealed to an irrepressible part of her nature, it seemed. "So, you can't enter this other idol?" she asked.

"I can extend my consciousness into it," he explained, "but all I can 'see' is the inside of the bricks. I can't tell you anything of the room in which my idol is hidden, or how to get there. You must somehow get into the Treasure House, learn where my idol is hidden, break in and free me from my prison. Once I can manifest again, I can do the rest – begin the task of restoring belief, which is the first step."

The girl looked troubled, and Betsalel knew that it was not just the physical difficulties of the task that were bothering her. But he preferred to take this one step at a time. "Other than the fragment of me that nestles beneath your heart," he said, "I cannot be with you on your journey. But before you go, I can provide you with some aid. Embrace me."

Leila looked up at him, startled, as he knelt and held out his arms to her like a parent might do with a small child. Almost without her volition, her feet moved and she stepped into his embrace. She tentatively put her small, thin arms around his naked torso, felt the smoothness and suppleness of the utterly black skin and its slight warmth. He seemed cooler than most people, but then she had hugged relatively few people in her life.

The Shadow God bent his head and kissed her brow, saying "Child of Shadows, accept this gift. When you wish to be unseen, think of the shadows and you shall become as one with them. None shall see you unless you want them to, save only the priests of Lucia. She has granted them light that can penetrate any darkness, so beware." Releasing her, the god stepped back and stood looking down at her benevolently. "One more gift I have for you, a companion to aid you on your way. But he awaits you above. Go now, for time is short!"

"Wait, I have more questions!" Leila called, but Betsalel had returned to the pedestal and frozen in the position he'd been in before she had stolen his eye. The god had departed, and only the maimed idol was left behind. She stepped forward, hesitantly reaching out a hand to touch its leg. It was hard, and smooth, and cold.

Chapter 47

The torches were blazing golden again, and Leila reached up and took one out of its sconce to light her way as she went out. Feeling that it was important somehow, she locked the doors to the inner sanctum behind her and pocketed the keys. Certainly Betsalel's long-dead priests had no further need of them. And perhaps she was now the first of his new priesthood? She resented his taking over her life without so much as a by-your-leave, but she also felt... not pity exactly, but some sense that he was no better or worse than anyone and had gotten badly screwed by his power-hungry bitch of a sister. She was never going to look at Lucia in the same "light" again!

She was young; and life was an adventure, was it not? Leila made her back out through the corridors of the lower level to the doors she'd come in by, noticing as she approached them with her torch that they did indeed have a bar. Since it had not been thrown, how had the horde of iconoclasts been prevented from coming through them? Some god trick, she supposed, and thought no more about it.

Leila had been down in the inner sanctum talking with the dispossessed god for what seemed like hours, and she'd expected to need the torch she was carrying to find her way back to the courtyard. Surely night must have fallen, after all this time. Yet when she came out through the doors (closing them again, as she had with the others) she found that the sun was still high. And she could see it! The overcast that had loomed over the Blackwald since she and her animal companions had entered it had vanished, and sunlight glinting down through the trees that ringed the temple grounds clearly indicated the time to be around three in the afternoon – and west was *that* way.

If perhaps time had been suspended during her interview with Betsalel, still Leila was anxious to get back to the courtyard. So after trotting up the stairs, she looked for a shortcut through the labyrinth and vaulted over walls in a couple of places where fallen masonry permitted. In minutes she was striding into the courtyard through a different doorway from the one she'd used earlier.

Nothing much seemed to have changed. Nimble was still idly nibbling blades of grass from around the perimeter of the courtyard, where the grass grew more thickly. Kathal seemed to have had her fill of mice and was sprawled in the shade, cleaning her paws. Leila decided to test out the new power the god had given her, and willed herself to invisibility. Then she approached the fountain, walking silently.

Leila felt no different. Was it all a crock? But holding her hands out before her she realized that, though she was standing in daylight, a murky blur of shadow was gathered around her. Huh, she thought, probably the middle of a sunlit courtyard is not the best location to pull this off. But it'd surely work well if she were pressed up against the wall in a poorly lit corridor, for example. Wonderful!

She continued to the fountain and cupped up some more of the water to drink, and Kathal immediately jumped to her feet, ears pricked and nose quivering, and stalked toward the spot where Leila stood. A few drops of water were falling from her hands onto the dusty stones at her feet.

The cat walked around her, a puzzled expression on her face, then sniffed at Leila before putting out a hesitant paw to touch her. Relenting, Leila willed herself visible again and the cat jumped backward four feet, fur bristling. Then she approached again, rubbing against her mistress' legs and saying "mackle" in complaining tones. "Sorry, Kathal!" Leila laughed. "I just had to see for myself if it worked. You would not *believe* what I've been doing since the last time I was here." She crouched down to rub the cat's fur and scratch behind her ears, which elicited a contented purr. All was forgiven.

Nimble looked up to see what all the commotion was, then went back to eating. He'd been working hard lately, and could really have used some grain. But as he had to settle for this grass, he needed to keep working at it. As Leila was loving up her feline companion there was a rustle of feathers and an enormous black bird fluttered down to perch on the rim of the fountain's upper basin – some six feet off the ground.

Kathal tensed, and Leila put a restraining hand on her. This was the first creature bigger than a mouse they'd seen since coming into the Blackwald, and the only bird. Now that she'd agreed to Betsalel's

244

mission and the sun had come out, were they about to be mobbed by friendly woodland creatures like something out of a children's book?

The raven eyed the cat critically, and croaked "Better keep that hand on her. I don't like the way she's looking at me." Leila was dumbstruck. She knew ravens could be taught to speak, because there had been an old conjurer and storyteller who worked the marketplace at Marsine when she was a child. He'd had a raven he claimed was a hundred years old, and could speak three languages; though she'd only ever heard it repeat a few words when he spoke them to the bird and offered it a treat.

Looking around in case someone might have crept up and decided to play a trick on her, Leila saw no one. Aha, not what she was expecting... "You must be the companion um, our dusky friend mentioned?" she asked. The bird bobbed on its perch, turning its head to fix her with its beady eye.

"Got it in one," it said. "You must be smarter than you look."

"Perhaps I should let Kathal go play," Leila mused, as if to herself.

"No! Sorry!" the bird said. "I was just making a joke. You can call me Yeil. I'm here to help you, so don't let the cat eat me or you'll be out of luck."

"Very well," the girl said, turning to her furry companion. "Kathal, that's Yeil," she said pointing. "Don't harm him. Unless I tell you to..." she added. Two could "make jokes."

During the time they'd been speaking no bluebirds, fuzzy bunnies, or cute spindly-legged fawns had made an appearance. "Uh, Yeil?" Leila asked, looking up. The bird cocked its head and looked down at her inquiringly. "Speaking of eating you, I'm almost out of food. What are the cat and I supposed to eat, exactly?" A little roasted bunny was beginning to sound good.

Yeil took to the air and lifted above the monastery's ruined walls. He circled above the courtyard, then announced "Our master has withdrawn his influence, and you should be able to find some game in the woods once you get a little way away from the ruins. Dibs on the entrails!" He dropped down and alit once more on the rim of the fountain.

Leila turned to the cat, getting her attention. "Kathal, go hunt!" she commanded, beckoning out through the complex's main entrance. In addition to using the pards to bring in small game the Nima, who spent much of their time traveling through unpopulated regions, used bows to hunt deer and creatures like young wild pigs. The boy Luca had received some training in archery, but Leila had not brought a bow with her. Traveling light and alone except for her animal companions, she hadn't thought it worth buying one to add her nascent skills to Kathal's instinctive talents. Maybe she ought to pick one up soon, though, if she was going to be traveling hundreds of miles to Parat.

The afternoon was wearing on, and there didn't seem to be any point in traveling further today. Especially as there was water here, and grass for Nimble, and Leila expected it would take them at least several hours to get to the other side of the Blackwald. That this temple should be in the geographic center of the forest seemed right somehow, but it was certainly not marked on her map so she was only guessing.

Leila untied the bedroll from her backpack and laid it on the stones of the courtyard near one of the ruined walls, where it would receive some shelter from the wind. Then she went inside the ruins and began gathering firewood from the smashed furniture lying among the fallen stones. Not every stick of wood had burned in the fire that had brought down the roof, some two centuries ago. Likely the blaze, enclosed by the stone walls, had been starved for air.

Kathal had been gone for nearly an hour. Nimble was still cropping the grass, the raven (still perched on the fountain) had gone to sleep with its head tucked under its wing, and Leila the eternal optimist had laid a fire of broken chair legs ready to light when the cat returned with something for her to eat.

The pard had evidently already had her own supper, but had not stopped to clean herself before finding something for her mistress. She trotted into the courtyard, tail up, with a large and very dead hare dangling from her jaws and blood all over her muzzle, chest, and front paws. Leila stroked her head and said "Thank you Kathal, good girl!" as the corpse was dropped gently beside where she sat. After lighting the set fire with a Lucifer match Leila set to work with one of her daggers to gut and skin the hare. "Yeil!" she called up at the sleeping bird, who woke with a start. "Din-din!"

He must have been hungry, for he fluttered down and began pecking at the entrails without the slightest bit of concern for the nearby cat. Kathal was sitting a few feet away, busily cleaning the blood off her fur, and she gave him a level golden glance as he came down. But she was comfortably full, and had been told the black bird was off-limits. She went back to her grooming.

The hare was a bit tougher and gamier than the fluffy bunnies Leila had been imagining – but it was hot and juicy, and the first food she'd had in days that wasn't pemmican. She devoured it with enthusiasm, leaving little behind but gnawed bones. Kathal had shown renewed interest by the time it came off the spit, and had received a few warm morsels. Now she was curled up on Leila's bedroll, fast asleep.

The sun was far down now and darkness would soon be coming on, but it seemed to Leila that it was too soon to lie down and sleep. Instead, she walked over to the fountain and engaged the raven in conversation. There were so many things she'd forgotten to ask the dark god.

"Where exactly in the Blackwald are we, Yeil?" While Leila would take Kathal over the lippy raven as a companion any day, it had occurred to her that having eyes in the sky might prove a useful thing.

"Dead center," the bird said smugly. "The heart of the darkness, so to speak. Darkness is our master's specialty, and he's kept your kind out of here for centuries by making it a place where everyone fears to tread."

"But the animals?" Leila asked, puzzled at how utterly dead this place had seemed earlier and how alive it was now.

"It's a forest like any other," the bird explained, "though more densely grown than most. The darkness is in men's minds, and in their eyes. Yet our master can drive away the forest creatures as well, if he extends his reach."

Leila pondered this, then recalled something else that had been on her mind. "When Nimble and Kathal and I came in here," she said, "we were being closely pursued by a troop of mounted Chanton guards. I was sure they were right on our heels, but then they vanished behind us. What happened to them?"

Yeil made a "kuk-kuk-kuk" noise, halfway between a raven's croak and a chuckle. "They've been wandering, lost, for quite some time now," he said with amusement. "First your tracks vanished from the trail, then the trail itself became lost and with no sun above they didn't know where to turn. Their horses, too, were seized by an unreasoning panic that made them hard to control."

"But the sun's been out since I returned from below," Leila pointed out. "Won't they have gotten their bearings again? Suppose they find the road and come here while we're sleeping?"

"What you see," the raven explained, "is not what others see. Our master's powers currently do not extend much beyond this wood, but within it he reigns supreme. Fear not, little thief. Your pursuers will not find you."

How does he know I'm a thief? Leila wondered. Was Yeil a real raven, ensorcelled somehow by Betsalel's power to have the power of speech and reason? Did the god tell him everything about me? Or was he, perhaps, a construct – a fragment, perhaps, of the god himself, shaped into the form of a large black bird? Certainly, his speech mannerisms were not those of Betsalel. She decided not to ask these questions of the bird. Who knew whether he would answer them truthfully?

Hauptscharführer Hans Bohrs, thirsty and hungry and exhausted, led his ragged band of mounted guards along a narrow trail through the forest. He felt sure that this was the same one they had somehow lost hours before, and though he saw no tracks on it to suggest the girl had come this way he was determined to follow it and see where it led.

The others straggled behind him dispiritedly. The horses seemed to have recovered from whatever had been driving them mad with fear when they first entered the wood, at least. But all of them were tired and discouraged, anxious to find water. Up ahead between the densely packed trees, Bohrs spotted light. Were they coming to a clearing, at last? The oppressive dimness around them, the sheer psychic weight of all those trees, was beginning to get to all of them.

He eagerly spurred his horse forward, and it responded with a jolt and then moved up from a plod to a trot. Then it scented water ahead, and began moving faster of its own accord. There was whinnying up and down the straggling line as the other horses in the band surged forward. Bohrs galloped forward, coming out of the trees, and then reined to a halt as he beheld a startling sight. The forest had thinned to a sparse woodland, the clouds were breaking up, and a few hundred yards ahead of them traffic hurried along the main highway between Chanton and Munch.

Chapter 48

In the morning the sky above the courtyard was clear, the sun's first rays suffusing it with pink. Leila packed up her bedroll and ate her last bar of pemmican. Kathal had slept beside her part of the night, then gone prowling and seemed uninterested in sharing her breakfast. As Leila was filling her water skins and saddling Nimble, preparing to leave, Yeil was pecking the last well-aged bits of hare guts from the stones beneath their feet.

"I guess you're our navigator for now," Leila told the bird as she swung up into Nimble's saddle. "I assume we have to head east, then north quite a bit to get started toward Parat."

"I've never been far from this wood," Yeil admitted, "so I can't help you with directions once we leave it. But for now, stay on the trail to the east. It goes pretty much straight through, and there's a town another five miles further along it on the eastern side." Leila threw him a jaunty salute and reined Nimble out of the courtyard and off to the left.

As it widened coming from the west, so the broad paved road soon narrowed and became once again a simple, meandering dirt track as Leila and her curious party followed it to the east. The forest seemed much more wholesome now, with birds (yes, even a few ravens) calling among the trees, patches of sunlight streaming down, small creatures moving in the underbrush. Once a deer came down the path toward them, then started in alarm and went crashing off into the forest to their left. Leila regretted the lack of that bow. It might even be worth the time it would take to cook up some venison steaks, to have a supply of meat that might last a few days.

As it was, Kathal walked most of the way and frequently dashed into the woods on either side of the path after prey only she could hear. She brought a dead squirrel to Leila, and her mistress thanked her politely for it but just tied a cord around its tail and hung it from the saddle. She was beginning to get hungry, but she neither wanted to munch on raw squirrel nor take the time to make a fire and cook one. Maybe something else would turn up.

They came upon several small streams, so water was not a problem. And once, a waterway large enough to be called a river split the forest running north out of the Antels. Fortunately the spring runoff was mostly over by now, and though the water was cold it was not terribly deep. Kathal clinging to the saddle anxiously, Leila rode Nimble across with the water coming up only just above his belly.

There was sunlight along the eastern bank, and as the afternoon was coming on Leila decided to accept the inevitable and stop for a while. Yeil had been following along with them by air, stopping occasionally to perch in a tree and wait for them to catch up. Now he landed at the riverside, toes in the gravel where the waters lapped in passing, and peered into the water for almost a full minute before suddenly darting his sharp beak out to catch a little fish around three inches in length.

Leila, who'd been busy laying a fire from dead branches and driftwood lying along the shore, looked up and said, "Good job, Yeil! Here I thought you were a raven, and it turns out you're a heron."

Swallowing the little fish with a single gulp, the bird said somewhat stuffily "One uses what resources one has. You of all people ought to know that." Hmm, what did he mean by that? Leila was inclined to take offense, but decided against it. Better she didn't let the bird's comments get to her. She was saddled with him, it seemed, and it would be good to keep things friendly.

There was plenty of fresh grass springing up along the banks in the area where the early floodwaters had receded, and Nimble was happily munching it while Kathal prowled among the trees. She returned with a second squirrel as Leila was gutting the first (much to Yeil's delight), the fire already well enough underway that she could start cooking. After both squirrels were skinned and gutted, she sharpened a couple of green twigs cut from willows along the bank and thrust them into the scrawny-looking corpses. Instead of the usual slow-roasting over coals she went for a quick toasting over the hottest part of the flames, singing the flesh a bit but getting it at least partway cooked and warmed through in a hurry.

Blowing on her fingers between bites, Leila dug into the first squirrel while the second cooked a bit more in proximity to the already-dying fire. There wasn't a lot of meat on these little guys, and it was lean. She ate all of the meat that was easy to get at but didn't take the time to pick the bones. Meanwhile Kathal had fed herself from more game caught nearby and was now cleaning her fur. Leila tossed the remnants of the carcasses into the embers and the fire flared up again briefly. When it had died down again, she brought water from the stream with her cup and doused it before climbing back aboard Nimble and continuing their journey.

Now that they'd all had a bit to eat, Leila had leisure as she rode to consider how she was going to make it all the way to Parat. It must be nearly 750 miles from here by the main highways, which were likely the shortest route since she couldn't take to the air like Yeil.

But she didn't for a minute believe that she'd seen the last of the Chanton guards. They might have been stopped from following her through the Blackwald, but since they could only assume that she'd abandoned her goal of reaching Munch it would not be long before it occurred to them to go back south to the main highway leading east, then north on the far side of the ill-omened forest until they picked up her trail again.

They couldn't be sure which way she would go once she left the forest, though, so they would probably be watching for her and asking after her as they rode north. She needed to figure out a way to lay a false trail, one that would send them off in the wrong direction; and then she needed to disappear, unremarked as she moved north and east by the main highways to Parat.

As she considered how to do this, Leila picked up the pace. They needed to get to this town Yeil had mentioned before the close of the business day. She set Nimble to a canter, going back to a trot every couple of miles, and the trail wound away beneath his hooves.

Chapter 49

On its eastern edge the transition between the Blackwald and the surrounding countryside was much less abrupt, presumably because there were fewer people on this side and the woodland that surrounded it had not been cleared as extensively. The main road north and east on this side was five miles away, not a few hundred yards.

As the woods thinned the trail broadened and straightened, though it remained unpaved. Leila began to see farmsteads on either side. Then the trail abruptly became a broad, unpaved wagon road between cleared fields, which gradually led into the town of Rosen. There was no sign along the road she'd come in by, but Leila soon began to see signs on shops touting "Rosen Smithy" or "Rosen Meats." Mmm, meats... Actually what she wanted was some less perishable foodstuffs, and plenty of them.

Kathal was walking again, trotting along beside the horse as he slowed to a walk coming to the crossroads where the farm track met the main highway. She was looking around her with interest, but aloofly ignoring the stares of passersby. The afternoon was wearing on, and likely most people would soon be at home having dinner with their families. But a few people were still out and about, and most of the shops were still open.

With no one around to hear Leila hissed to the raven, "Stay out of sight, you, but keep an eye out. We'll be heading north on the main highway as soon as I finish my business here. And don't talk to anybody."

"Caw?" he replied with wounded innocence, and flew off to perch atop a nearby two-storey building with a peaked roof.

Leila spotted a general store and climbed down, hitching Nimble to a post outside. The proprietor, a man in his late thirties, greeted her politely enough but it was clear from his curious stare what he thought of the sight of a dirty and disheveled, leather-clad young woman with a mop of curly black hair and dark skin, accompanied by what he recognized as one of those Nima cats, walking into his shop. The Nima occasionally patronized stores in towns they were passing through, but no Nima woman he'd ever seen dressed like *this*!

"Evening," Leila said briskly, anxious to conclude the errand. "I'm in need of some traveling supplies. Enough for a few weeks. Something light – my horse is already pretty well weighed down." She gestured through the window, to where the chestnut gelding stood patiently – his saddlebags bulging. "Very well," the man said, and began going along the shelves behind the counter gathering items. He assembled some hard crackers, dry cheese, jerky, dry-smoked sausages, and some apples.

"How about some grain for porridge?" he suggested, but Leila shook her head. "No, I'm traveling fast," she told him. "Just stuff I don't need to cook will be fine." When he'd assembled as large a pile of edibles on the counter as it appeared could be loaded onto the horse, he said "That'll be six shillings. Do you need anything else?" Glancing around the store, Leila said "I don't suppose you sell bows and arrows?"

He goggled at her. His store was full of foodstuffs, both fresh and preserved, as well as work clothing and various household items such as pots and pans. Weapons were quite outside his line. But while there'd been no war within the Dominion in centuries, bows could be used for hunting as well as for fighting off one's enemies. "There's a bowyer up near the north end of town," he said. "Eisen's place. He's probably still open now, stays up half the night making 'em sometimes. But they're good bows, from what I hear. Not cheap, mind you…"

"Money's not a problem," Leila said. "On the road north, you say?" The man nodded. "Good, I'm heading that way in any case. I understand the road east to Buda is another three miles north?"

"Closer to four," he admitted. "There's an inn at the crossroads, if you want to wait until morning to turn east. Then it's another thirty miles or so to Gmund."

"Good idea," Leila replied. "Thanks, you've been very helpful." She smiled at him what she hoped was winningly, but guessed she must look a fright and her girlish charms weren't likely to buy her much at this point. "Say, can you change a florin? I'm running a bit short of silver shillings and coppers." The shopkeeper's eyes widened, but he nodded. It was the end of his business day, and he had quite a lot of cash on hand.

The supplies went into a sack, and Leila thanked the man again and strode out with it slung over one shoulder – a purseful of small change jingling in her other hand. Behind her, the shopkeeper watched her go with amazement. A young woman, more like a girl really, all wild and dirty and carrying around gold to pay for a few silver shillings' worth of supplies?

You didn't see that every day, that was for sure. He supposed that the cat would be protection enough so carrying that kind of money was safe, though. He made ready to lock up, planning to go to his favorite tavern for a couple of beers after work. Tonight at least, he'd have a tale to tell his friends.

Leila rearranged Nimble's load so that the added weight of the supplies was more evenly balanced, and climbed aboard. "Sorry, old friend," she told him, "but you won't have to carry all this stuff much longer." She gave him a pat on the neck as they walked along the road. Though this road was a major north-south artery, there was little traffic at this hour.

She hitched the horse again in front of a smallish wooden building in front of which a handsomely carved and painted wooden sign sported a bow lying sideways with crossed arrows, above the legend "EISEN." Leila tried the door but found it locked. Then she knocked loudly, calling "Herr Eisen? Hello?" She put her ear to the door and heard footsteps approaching, so backed off and stood on the doorstep, hip shot. There was a rattling of the lock and the door swung inward, to reveal a bald, burly middle-aged man in a sawdust-spotted shop apron standing in the doorway. He topped her by close to a foot.

Though she'd presumably interrupted him at his work and must look bedraggled, he was reasonably polite. "Yes Fraulein? What can I do for you?"

"You're the bowyer?" Leila asked bluntly, and he nodded. "I'm in need of a good bow and some arrows, and I'm afraid I'm in a bit of a hurry. I have gold," she added, in hopes that would tip the scales in her favor.

Whatever the case, he backed up and gestured her inside. He started a little when Kathal strolled in behind her. "That a pard?" Eisen asked in surprise. Leila nodded impatiently. "Never saw one except on a Nima caravan," the bowyer said, fishing for an explanation.

"I'm not Nima, but I'm friends with them," Leila said shortly. "It's a long story, and I don't have time for it right now. Could you please show me a bow in an appropriate size for me?"

Bows came in different lengths and thicknesses, as well as in different designs that delivered different results. Some of the mounted tribesmen among the realms of the Hando favored short, composite bows they could shoot from horseback, Leila had read. But she was looking for something that could take down a deer or a small wild pig – and be a weapon with a longer range than her daggers had, if the Chanton authorities caught up with her.

The front of Eisen's shop was hung with bows of all different sizes and several different designs, all of them resting on pegs and without strings. "For a little thing like you," he muttered, and began searching the wall for something the right length. After looking her up and down, with particular attention to her arms, he pulled down a laminated recurve bow that was nearly as long as she was tall, and strung it.

He handed it to her, saying "Pull that, and let's see if it's right." It looked similar to the one Luca had practiced with during his travels with the Nima, but a little longer. Well, that *was* nearly two years ago. She had presumably grown. The length of the draw seemed right, but it was awfully easy to pull. She glanced up at Eisen and saw him watching her, assessing her familiarity with the weapon. She'd had a few months of training and practice, and had been told that it took years to make an expert archer. But at least she wasn't a complete neophyte.

"This seems awfully light," Leila told him, "do you have anything with a little more draw weight? I need to be able to take down game. And maybe bandits…" He gave her an appraising look, took the bow back and unstrung it before returning it to the peg on the wall. Then he pulled down another, strung it with somewhat more effort than before, and handed it to her saying, "This one's forty-five pounds. I doubt you'll be able to handle it, but give it a try." She pulled it easily, the wiry strength she'd acquired having not left her though she'd spent the past half year engaged in more sedentary pursuits.

"This is pretty good," Leila told the bowyer. "How much?"

Looking her up and down, he replied "Two florins. But I'll throw in a waterproof case, a quiver of broadpoints, and a sack of strings with that." She sensed that was his opening offer, the starting point of negotiations – but she had no time for that. And she wished to be seen as in a hurry, besides. Though her supply of gold was dwindling fast and she hadn't yet figured out how she was going to replenish it any time soon (polishing and selling silverware while on the run didn't seem likely), Leila reached into her purse and pulled out the coins that had been requested. "Here you go," she said, "Wrap it up."

Chapter 50

After mentioning the road east once again and being told about the inn at the crossroads, Leila left Eisen with the impression that she might now be considering bypassing the inn and pushing on toward Buda into the night as she put heels to Nimble and galloped him up the highway to the north.

The sun was now setting, and Leila let the horse find his own pace after their mad dash out of town. Yeil had picked them up just beyond the outskirts and had been following along in the air. On a deserted stretch of the highway a mile north of Rosen, with dusk approaching, she turned Nimble off of the highway to the west where a small stream ran below the road in a stone-lined culvert, heading downhill into a grove of trees.

In a few minutes they had arrived within the shelter of the grove. "Are we staying here for the night, or what?" Yeil asked a little peevishly.

"Not all night," Leila replied, "just until I get a few things done. Why do you ask?"

"I'm no good in darkness," the bird admitted. "Can't see shit, it's not like I'm a nighthawk or a bat. I need to roost and rest, after flying all day."

Leila snorted. "For a jet-black bird who's the servant of the God of Shadows, you seem to be missing a few job skills. Go ahead, pick a tree. I'll wake you up when it's time to leave." She set about removing Nimble's saddle and the heavy items hung about it, stashing all but the food deep within a thorny thicket. In the dim light, at least, it seemed to be invisible. She gave the poor horse a currying, cooing to him and thanking him for his patience.

Next she squatted on the ground and gobbled down a sandwich made of a couple of hard biscuits with some dry sausage and cheese, washed down with water from her skin. Ugh, she thought, I should have gotten some fresh bread while I was at it. She used the rope she carried with her to sling the food up off the ground between two trees, hopefully safe from hungry critters.

Her impromptu supper concluded, Leila began stripping off the filthy leathers. She almost considered just throwing them away, but thought she might need them again sometime. So she tucked them into the bottom of her pack, before pulling on her burglar gear. She might be able to make herself and whatever was in contact with her skin invisible at will, but she still preferred the anonymity and ease of movement the outfit offered.

As darkness fell across the land, Leila was mounted on Nimble again, the saddle empty except for a couple of spare sacks, and moving as quietly as possible back toward town – through the surrounding woodland, this time. Kathal rode the saddle, eyes dilated and nostrils twitching. She sensed that an adventure of some kind was about to unfold.

On their way in from the west Leila had been keeping her eyes open, and she'd identified several possible targets for her night raid. The back door of a washhouse yielded to her lockpicks easily enough. The proprietress was likely asleep upstairs, and she didn't hear the girl slip inside and begin rifling the laundry. Leila emptied out several sacks of clothing and linens that had been dropped off by the customers but not yet laundered before she found what she sought. She hastily stuffed everything she'd dumped out into whatever sack was handy before making off with one containing the items she wanted. There'd be some confusion and customer complaints in a few days, but she doubted anyone would notice one sack was missing.

Leila tied the sack onto Nimble's saddle and continued on her way – the horse's hooves muffled by four pairs of her underdrawers, stuffed with dried grasses, that she'd tied to them. Near the town's western entrance, along the unpaved cart road, Leila had spotted a jobber's yard with several small farm carts parked in it. Later in the season, she guessed, these would be out canvassing the local farms in the radius of several miles, buying produce direct from the farmers and getting a better price.

So early in spring though, there wasn't enough fresh food available to be worth the trouble of hiring horses and drivers. Leila suspected that the jobber kept the carts himself only because it would be hard to find any to rent when the harvest season was in full swing. They sat forlorn in his rear yard behind a six-foot wire fence, gathering dust until it was time for them to be put into use.

There was a dirt lane running behind the yard, and a broad gate in the fence that could be opened when it was time for the carts to go out. The gate was secured by a chain and a padlock, fortunately not too rusty for her to open. A small quantity of cooking oil had been included in her supplies, and she applied a little to the gate hinges as well as to the lock. The gate swung open soundlessly.

Bidding Nimble and the cat to wait and be silent, Leila crept into the yard. The cart nearest the gate would do fine, she thought. It was of a size to be pulled by a single horse, and two not very large, quite friendly people might sit side by side on the driver's bench. As near as she could tell in the starlight, it was several years old and quite worn-looking, unpainted. But the wheels and axles looked all right, and the shafts were intact.

Now, if only she was right and the jobber also maintained his own supply of harness! Luca had learned about harness as well as about horses during his time with the Nima, and Leila felt confident she could find a set that would fit Nimble provided there was any to be had.

A lean-to shed stood at the back of the building fronting on the yard, and its door was no more difficult to open than the padlock had been. Inside, the smell of old leather greeted her. Yes! Another door at the back of the shed led to the building, where the jobber no doubt gathered his goods before distributing them to his store customers. But she had found what she wanted.

Some half an hour later Leila had put Nimble's saddle and her sack of dirty laundry into the back of her target cart and had managed to buckle the collar and harness onto him in the near darkness. Unlike Marsine, the town of Rosen did not pay for streetlights and except for the stars and a few glowing windows where some residents had candles or lanterns burning, it was dark as the inside of a black bag.

The horse had never drawn a cart before, but Leila had trained him well and he was willing to go along with pretty much whatever she wanted. Eyes rolling a bit, he obediently backed up between the shafts and she attached the harness to the cart so he could pull it. She didn't try sitting on the seat and driving him, though – that was going to require some further instruction. Instead, she led him forward out of the yard by his headstall.

The cart was *not* silent, creaking as it rolled away from the spot where it had probably sat through the winter. Leila had found some canvas tarpaulins in the shed with the harness, and she threw a couple of those into the cart's bed on top of the saddle and laundry. Kathal hopped in and curled up atop them, at home anywhere it seemed.

After the gate was locked behind her Leila led the horse and cart through the back alleys of Rosen, staying away from buildings with lighted windows. She'd applied a little of the cooking oil to the wheel hubs as a temporary measure and it seemed to be helping, but she was going to need to buy some real axle grease soon or it would drive her crazy.

One more stop along the way as they headed north out of town on one of the lanes that served the farms surrounding it. Leila had spotted a walnut orchard on their way in, and she told Nimble to stop as she took one of her spare sacks and began filling it with green walnuts. This had been another part of the specialized herb-lore taught by the Night Guild, but they had been working with hulls that had been removed and dried. She hoped these would work for what she needed to do.

Horse and cart continued on in the darkness, the load increased, and took a right at a lane that led up to the main highway. Then Leila turned north on it. This was going to be the tricky part, leaving the cart on the road while she completed her preparations. Pulling up beside the culvert a couple of hundred yards from her temporary campsite, Leila bade Nimble "Stay and be quiet," and to Kathal said "Stay and guard." The cat looked at her alertly, and then moved from her comfortable position atop the tarpaulins to sit on the driver's bench. Leila carried the sack of laundry with her as she headed for the woods.

Chapter 51

Dawn light stretched once more across the eastern reach of the Dominion, and illuminated the main highway north and east toward Parat with a rosy glow. It fell upon a rickety-looking farm cart, pulled by a surprisingly sleek-looking horse – not the kind of cob you would expect to see at the front of such a conveyance. The animal was a somewhat blotchy-looking dark brown color.

The space in back was not full or turnips, of other farm produce, but rather with what looked like a load of junk under a worn canvas tarpaulin. There seemed to be a couple of oil lamps with cracked shades, a broken chair or two, pieces of a music box, and a small circular table with part of its top broken away.

The driver was even more curious to behold, a little old woman as round and wrinkled as a late-winter apple. She was covered from head to foot in smudged-looking garments, a kerchief on her head completely covering her hair except for where some dark curls streaked with white peeked out above her forehead. She wore soiled cotton gloves, and the only part of her skin visible was her face. It was dark, but overlaid with a pale filminess as if she had some skin disease. Deep wrinkles furrowed her cheeks and brows. She appeared to be dozing as the cart lurched down the road, the horse seemingly needing no directions from the driver.

The cart's left wheel bounced down into the gap left by a paving stone that had cracked over the winter, disintegrating into rough-hewn gravel after repeated assaults by rain and freezing temperatures. Leila started awake, a terrifying sense of disorientation sweeping over her until she recalled where she was and what she was doing. Betsalel, daylight already?

Kathal lay curled beneath one of the tarpaulins, but it seemed that the jolt had awakened her and she let out a plaintive "mak?" "All right," Leila said wearily, "you can come out now. But get ready to hide if anyone comes looking." The cat wriggled out from beneath the tarp and sat swaying as the cart continued its progress, looking around her and trying to straighten her mussed fur.

The raven perched on the rear of the cart, bobbing up and down on his legs and occasionally flapping his wings to maintain his balance. "Could you possibly have chosen a less comfortable way to travel?" Yeil carped, considering whether it would be better to take to the air, even with the energy expenditure that entailed, than to ride on this infernal contraption.

"Sorry if you're inconvenienced," Leila replied sweetly. "I'm finding it a little uncomfortable myself. Why don't you use your magical shadow powers to drop a pot of gold on us, and I'll swap our 'impoverished old granny' disguise for that of a mysteriously veiled noblewoman traveling by private coach, at the very next town."

"I'm here to give you guidance and advice," the raven croaked grumpily. "Finances are up to you. Why don't you just sell some of this fabulous loot you're packing?" A wave of regret passed through Leila at his words. If only! She might be on her way to Jena by that aforementioned private coach by now, stepping into a life of ease and happiness, had not a series of calamities befallen her. With a sigh, she sent it away. No use fretting about what might have been...

It had taken Leila far longer than she'd hoped to craft the disguises for herself and the horse. Turning her chestnut horse into a dark bay, transforming a skinny teenage girl into a plump granny, had taken almost the entire rest of the night. Not to mention lugging all those sacks of loot up from the campsite!

Betsalel be praised (considering she was now, so to speak, on his payroll, Leila had begun naming the Shadow God in her unspoken references to divine intervention; she would have to be careful not to speak such things aloud), not a single cart or lone rider – or, for that matter, troop of Chanton guards – had come along the road while all of that was going on.

Nimble might well have dozed in the traces while she worked, and Kathal and the bird had certainly slept; but Leila herself had not gotten a wink of sleep until long after they'd begun rolling along the road heading toward the crossroads. She passed the inn by in the pre-dawn darkness, and set Nimble to pulling the cart up the road at whatever pace he felt like doing. Pulling the load was certainly less work for him than carrying it on his back, and she now realized that he seemed to be getting used to the idea.

Fortunately he'd been accustomed for the past year and more to respond to voice commands rather than reins or foot nudges – though either would work when she was riding him. So Leila held the reins and told him "Let's go, stay on the road," and they were off. She hoped and expected that the horse, who seemed pretty bright by the standards of his breed, would soon connect the motions of the reins with the commands and would become as capable as any cart horse bred to the task.

There was no disguising that he was not a cart horse, though, whatever his color. Her cover story took that into account. Leila longed for nothing so much as the chance to remove this preposterous costume and fall into a soft bed, followed by a large hot meal; but she needed to get as far along the road toward Parat as she could, today. Pulling the cart, Nimble could do no more than two-thirds the speed he would have managed were she riding astride him (and were he not weighed down with all that loot). It was going to be a long trip.

Soon they began to encounter traffic on the road, going both directions, and Leila had to command Kathal to get down and permit herself to be hidden among the piles of junk in the back of the cart. Those had been "stolen" from a midden heap behind the inn at the crossroads, and she hoped to add more to them as the journey progressed.

None of them were enjoying themselves, but Leila was particularly uncomfortable. Though today there were storm clouds on the horizon and a cool breeze had sprung up, it was warm at this season and the wads of fabric that created the illusion of plumpness on her muscular frame were already sweltering though it was not yet noon.

The latex (created from the sap of certain wild plants) that she'd used to create the illusion of wrinkles on her smooth dark face burned and made her face feel tight, a discomfort she was constantly aware of. Leila knew that old people's wrinkles usually formed around the eyes first, with crow's feet and under-eye circles and bags, and had done her best in the dim light available to create that effect. But it wasn't going to withstand close inspection.

Tonight, when it was time to stop at an inn, Leila hoped to improve on the disguise. In the light of day, she was able to see that the dye job on Nimble could also use some work. In the meantime, she hoped, their best hope was to remain inconspicuous. Just a fat old woman with a load of junk in a dilapidated cart, on her way someplace with a horse that had probably been borrowed from a neighbor. No large cat, no talking bird. Yeil, too, had been ordered to make himself scarce when people were around.

Leila ate her breakfast from among the provisions she'd bought in Rosen, and after midday they pulled the cart to the side of the road so that she and the cat could relieve themselves. Kathal soon returned from the nearby woods with a squirrel, but her mistress forbade her to eat it in the cart. Bloodstains were right out.

While relieving the crossroads inn of some of its trash at around four this morning, Leila had also crept into the inn's stables and "borrowed" a feedbag and a few sacks of grain. Now Nimble finally had nourishment appropriate to the level of effort he was putting out, but water was still an issue. Yet the Dominion had provided: at frequent intervals along the main road, stations had been set up where hand pumps and troughs of water quenched the thirst of weary travelers. Civilization was grand!

As the sun was well down on the western horizon Leila and her entourage found themselves pulling into the outskirts of Salz. They had been passed quite a few times during the day, many travelers preferring to move at a pace faster than that of a farm cart; but none of those had been a party of red-coated Chanton guards. Leila prayed (again, to the Shadow God) that they would have learned of the young woman with the cat and the chestnut gelding, and their plans to travel east to Buda.

Chapter 52

Leila became more comfortable with her disguise as her journey toward Parat went on. She was Halina, a grandmotherly woman of Gaspari descent (with a rumored Nima ancestor to explain her complexion), whose husband was long dead and whose only son, Pyetr, had left twenty years before hoping to seek his fortune in Parat –where his ancestors had sprung from. They had fallen out of touch years before, but she had now been turned out of her cottage by a cruel landlord who meant to raze it (along with half the homes in the neighborhood, near Buda) to build himself a palatial estate.

Having nowhere else to turn, Halina had sold everything she had of value to fund this expedition to Parat in search of her son. She'd bought the cart on the cheap, but the horse had cost her nearly everything. Now she was traveling with all her worldly possessions – a sad collection of refuse which, in her eyes, were treasures – to track down her wayward boy.

Her tale was met with pity from nearly all who heard it, though a few people tried to point out that her plan was folly. But it was clear she was not right in the head, and those people soon gave up trying to talk her out of continuing on her quest. Besides, she told them, if she was unable to find Pyetr at least she could visit the fabulous Temple of the Seven, foremost place of worship in all the Dominion, and die happy.

With lamplight to work with and better supplies, Leila was able to craft a version of her "old lady" makeup that was not so painful to wear nor so obtrusive to behold. The dappled markings where Nimble's dye job needed work were smoothed over, until he truly was a dark bay horse. Far too young and beautiful to be pulling a cart for an old lady, unfortunately – but she avoided explaining him away unless she was required to. For the most part, people glanced their way and saw what they expected. She was nearly as invisible as if she'd used her Shadow power to fade from sight.

Yeil usually escaped the cart before they pulled into a hostelry for the night, flying off to roost nearby. Kathal sometimes spent the night in the stables with the horses, sleeping comfortably within her jumble of junked furniture in the back of the cart and stealing out in the early hours to reduce the population of rats raiding the horses' grain. Other times she would hop out before they arrived, slipping into the shadows; and at some point during the night climb in through the window Halina had left open for her, to spend the rest of the time before dawn snuggled in her mistress's bed.

Though Leila had become more adept at applying her disguise, and inured to the hours spent sitting on the cart's hard bench (though the cloth stuffed inside her clothes to simulate Halina's plumpness helped with that), she finished each day exhausted and ready to fall into bed – feeling as old in truth as the woman she was portraying. She always took the time to have a hot supper, though, before hobbling off to her room. By preference she slept on the top floor, ready to slip out the window and be away should a troop of Chanton guards suddenly begin pounding on her door.

Each day Halina spoke to as few people as possible, but what little she'd heard suggested that Leila's ruse had worked – the guards when they came up the road from the south had picked up her trail and gone east toward Buda in hot pursuit. It worried her, though. That trail would vanish as soon as they got a little way down that road, and no one would have seen her. On the other hand, no one would have seen a young girl with a pard at her side, riding a chestnut gelding, on the north road either.

Would they assume she'd cut across country, and was now lost to them? Would they slink back to Count Wilhelm with their tails between their legs to report failure? Or would they continue scouring the eastern Dominion, searching for the slightest clues to tell them where their quarry had gone? The crucial importance of her disguise helped to mitigate Leila's discomfort with it.

At least, once her room door had been locked and Leila had wedged it at the bottom to prevent unwanted intrusions, she was able to remove her hot, uncomfortable clothing, peel off the irritating wrinkle makeup, and just relax. In minutes, usually, she would be drifting off to sleep. Her first night, in Salz, she'd insisted on a tub of hot water being delivered to her room, as she "couldn't abide bathing in public rooms." Days of grime had come off, then she'd been forced to don her makeup and far-from-clean garments again to let

267

the inn staff come and take the tub away. Still, she felt much better for the bath.

Following her second day of travel Leila had slept the night at an inn in Weisen, and had stayed up late with needle and thread turning her wadded padding (various soft garments and some sheets) into a sort of undergarment she could wear. That let her get into her "fat suit" much more quickly, and without any day-to-day changes in the contours of Halina's avoirdupois.

The woman had enormous, sagging breasts, a round belly, and massive hips with a large and lumpy behind. Whenever she was in public she always covered herself in layers of clothing from head to head to toe, gloves concealing her youthful and slender hands as a scarf wrapped around her head and neck helped to hide the fact that her face was far too thin for one of her girth.

By the fourth night, as she and her animal companions approached the small city of Pisk, Leila's funds were beginning to run low. She found herself regretting having spent her gold so freely when she was laying her false trail in Rosen. Now she was down to a small handful of gold coins, and a fairly large purse of silver and copper.

She considered pulling out one of the Chanton treasures from its bag buried beneath the junk furniture in her wagon, selling it to get enough money to assure her arrival in Parat without having to sleep out in the countryside. She might try to pass such a thing off as the last valuable item among Halina's possessions, reluctantly parted with only because she must eat. But the treasures were so exquisite, and so valuable, that she doubted anyone would believe the old Gaspari woman had come by it honestly. That might bring trouble down on her head. Better to slip out in the night and see if she could find a nearby merchant's cash box to rob. In the meantime, she'd play her part.

Spying a likely-looking hostelry within the outskirts of the city, off the main road far enough out from the city center that there would be little traffic during the night, Halina pulled her cart into the stableyard at the side. At this hour, approaching six, the gates still stood wide open. A gawky-looking teenage stableboy came out and approached her.

"Yes ma'am?" he said politely, his voice starting low and rising into the upper register on the last part of the phrase. He must be around fourteen, Leila realized. "Please bring my cart inside the stable and lock it up for the night, and unhitch my horse," Halina quavered. Yeil had flown off to perch on the stable roof, unnoticed by the boy, and Kathal had hopped out and skulked off out of sight just before they turned in. "Make sure he's rubbed down and given some food and water, then stabled for the night."

There wasn't all that much extra floor space in the stables, and the stableboy wondered at the request for indoor storage of the cart. "Um, that'd be extra for putting the cart inside, ma'am. It should be safe enough parked in the yard, and I don't believe we'll be getting any rain tonight."

"Oh, no!" the old lady replied, shocked. "It must be kept locked up. All my treasures, my family heirlooms are inside, don't you see?" She gestured to the interior of the cart, where (atop a false bottom she'd laid down) the collection of broken and cast-off furniture had been growing steadily. "My boy Pyetr slept right there in that cradle when he was a baby," she said fondly. "It would kill me were anything to happen to it."

"Um, all right, ma'am. Will this be added to your inn bill?"

"Yes, thank you," Halina replied. "If you can help me down, I'll be going in to speak with the innkeeper next." The boy gave her an arm down, and the old lady groaned as she lifted her bulk out of the wagon and stepped unsteadily onto the packed dirt flooring the stableyard. "Oh, my old bones!" she exclaimed with a sigh, "By the Seven, I'm so stiff I can scarcely move after riding the cart all day."

Seeing the old lady's bag (Leila had transferred the contents of her pack to a well-worn, flowered valise as part of the disguise) looked far too heavy for her to carry by herself, the boy whistled to a still younger boy who'd popped out the rear door on some other errand. "Fredi!" he called, "Come help this lady in with her bag!"

Fredi screwed up his face at being deflected from his purpose. "Papa told me to fetch more wine!" he yelled back, defiantly.

"Help the lady first, then get the wine, or I'll pound you!" his older brother replied. Furious but cowed, Fredi came forward and lifted the valise with one hand, then took Halina's arm and helped her hobble back out of the yard and around to the inn's front entrance. Bent as she was, she stood no taller than him though he couldn't have been more than eleven.

After he'd deposited her in the common room her wizened face twisted in a smile. "Thank you, Fredi," she said sweetly. But she did not tip him. He soon dashed off on his original errand before Papa should catch sight of him. Wobbling a bit, Halina approached the bar where a man she took to be the innkeeper was polishing glasses. He was more than a foot taller than her, and there was a clear resemblance between him and the two boys. Probably a family enterprise, Leila guessed.

Still polishing, he looked down at her as she slowly and shufflingly approached. From the look of her, he wouldn't be getting much coin out of *this* one... "Good evening, son," the crone began. "Your boy out there is seeing to my horse and cart, and I'll be needing a meal and a room as well. Do you have something not too expensive?"

With a mental sigh, the man pulled the register from under the bar. The inn was a large one, with rooms on this floor and two above it. There was also an attic space, divided between extra storage and a small dormer room with a fairly low ceiling. This old lady might not have any problems with bumping her head up there, but surely she'd never make it to the top of the stairs?

"We're somewhat full at the moment," he admitted. "I have a room on the ground floor, but that's got two beds and it's six shillings. That's on top of the stabling fees, which are four shillings if you're storing your cart inside. I assume you'd prefer not to be in the second floor dormitory?" Most inns of any size had one large room with multiple beds in it, where single travelers who didn't mind sharing with strangers could get a cheap night's sleep. Halina looked shocked.

"My, that is higher than I'd hoped. And I certainly couldn't share a room with strangers! Isn't there anything else?"

The innkeeper looked concerned. "I do have a room up beyond the third floor, in the attic, that I could let you have for two shillings," he admitted, "but there are several flights of stairs." He left it at that, judging it rude to mention that she looked like she'd keel over just walking across the room. The old lady straightened up a little and looked at him in outrage.

"I'll have you know, young man, that I'm not a cripple! I've spent more than sixty years working a smallholding and I've been doing everything for myself the past fifteen. I'm a little stiff at the moment from riding on the cart all day, but I can certainly walk up a few flights of stairs if someone will carry my bag for me."

She gave him a challenging glare, and the innkeeper shied away from it. Ugh, what an ugly crone! Well, it was her choice. "Very well, ma'am," he said stiffly – holding out his hand. "That will be six shillings for the stable and the attic room, and that includes a bowl of stew and a bread roll, plus there's bread and butter in the morning if you want it." Halina smiled, an expression that increased the number of wrinkles in her face but didn't show her teeth. Leila had drawn the line at working over her own white, strong teeth to resemble something a woman four times her age would have. The old woman produced a fairly large leather drawstring purse, and began rummaging in it – pulling out coins.

"That's one, two, three, four… You did say six? My, that's more for my horse and cart than it is for me…"

"Six," the innkeeper said firmly. He'd dealt with these penny-pinching oldsters before. They'd play on your sympathies and try to get you to cut your prices until there was no profit for you. But from the looks of that purse, the old bat could have easily afforded the most expensive room in the place. Either she was pathologically miserly, or she had to make that purse last for a long while yet to come.

After handing over the coins and causing the purse to vanish within the voluminous folds of her clothing, Halina made an effort to stand straighter, stretching and rubbing at herself as if trying to ease her arthritic joints. She peered up at the innkeeper again. "Does that stew come with a drink?" she asked casually.

"I'll get you some water," he said with a laugh. "Go ahead and have a seat at the table there next to your bag and I'll have my wife bring you some food."

Halina went over to the table and sat down, fussing with her valise until the bowl of stew and a plate with a small bread roll and a pat of butter had been deposited in front of her. She ate with good appetite, savoring the meaty richness of the stew and enjoying the heat of it even though she was feeling overly warm this close to the common room's fireplace. A great many people were in here, many of them also eating the stew, and she glanced around at them surreptitiously between bites. None of them were wearing uniforms, or paying any attention to her that she could see.

After the meal young Fredi trotted up to the attic room with Halina's valise, but she refused his help on the stairs a bit snappishly. There were handrails all the way up, and she was slowly and methodically climbing – clinging to the rail, lifting first one foot to a new tread and then the other beside it. Rests were frequent.

Fredi returned below after dropping her valise on the attic room's bed, and pressed the key into her hand. "Are you sure I can't help you up the stairs, Grandmother?" he asked politely. She smiled gamely at him.

"No, no, I've got to do it myself," she wheezed. "Just give me time, and I'll get there. But thank you again, Fredi."

Once again she did not tip him. He shrugged and hurried back down the stairs, ready for his next assignment. His parents had him and his brother jumping, and their older sister as well, even though the inn also employed several people who were not part of the family.

Leila looked after him when he'd gone, clinging to the handrail as though it were her lifeline. Most of the inn's clientele, those who were not already in their rooms, were down in the common room enjoying the start of the evening's carousing. Listening for a moment to assure herself that no one was near, she lifted her skirts and trotted the rest of the way up the stairs to the attic.

Within half an hour, the door securely bolted, Halina had become Leila again and she was lying down to get some sleep. Later on, when all was dark and quiet, the journeyman thief Penumbra would pay a visit to the sleeping town below. Before tucking herself in, Leila unlatched her dormer window and pushed it open a few inches, peering out as dusk crept over the city. She saw no sign of Kathal, but left the window open. The exterior of the inn was covered in dark wood shingles, and the cat should have no trouble joining her.

Below in the common room, a young man in his later teens sat nursing an ale. He was getting his money's worth, it seemed, for he'd been sipping this same ale since coming inside two hours before. He was clad as a traveler, in dark leather pants and a long dark cloak, but had not paid for a room. Less than an hour earlier he'd watched as the fat little old babushka had tried to beat the innkeeper down on the price of her lodging. The size of her purse had not gone unnoticed, nor had the mention of the room she was occupying. Finishing the ale at last, he pulled his cloak around him and strode out into the gathering darkness. Time to find a good place to stand and wait.

Chapter 53

The sound of scrabbling below her opened window roused her, and Leila quickly woke and sat up in bed. She had laid her pocket watch and a glowstone on the nightstand earlier, and reached for them so she could see what time it was. Close to one a.m. That meant she had nearly five hours of sleep under her belt, and for tonight that would have to do it.

As she was about to climb out of the narrow bed Kathal came in through the window and bounded up onto the bed, purring. Leila hugged the big cat, stroking her fur and scratching her behind the ears. "Been having some fun, have you girl?" she asked softly. "You might as well keep the bed warm for me while I'm gone." She slipped from between the covers and put her feet on the threadbare rug that was all the room offered in the way of a floor covering. The cat happily curled up in the warm spot left behind and seemed to fall instantly into sleep.

Leila had gone to sleep in her camisole and bloomers, not owning a proper nightdress, and stood shivering as she bent over the valise, digging out her burglar's gear. At this latitude nights were cold, even this far into spring. She was retrieving her daggers from the pockets in Halina's fat suit she had sewn for them, when she heard the furtive sounds of something – something a lot larger than Kathal – climbing up the side of the building.

Clutching a dagger in one hand and a glowstone in the other, Leila stepped silently back to the corner of the room and willed herself to invisibility. Only the glow from the glowstone, she'd learned from experimentation, would be visible when she did this – and then only when she removed the hand holding it from behind her back. Then it would look like an eerie, disembodied blue light floating in space and surrounded by impenetrable shadow.

It was nearly black in the room, but there was a faint amount of ambient light coming in through the window and a dark figure was silhouetted against it. It put both hands on the sill, the window now standing wide open, and hoisted itself silently up over it and into the room. It was clad all in dark colors, a hood over the face, and was not a huge amount taller than Leila herself. The figure's head almost but not quite brushed the room's low ceiling.

Aha, Leila thought, come to rob a helpless old lady of what little coin she possesses? Shame on you. Penumbra would never have stooped so low. In the dimness the thief spotted a mound on the bed and approached carefully for a closer look. He'd thought the old babushka was bigger and fatter than that. Could he have gotten the wrong room, after all?

The dark figure came a little closer to the bed, reaching out toward the nightstand to see if perhaps that fat purse had been laid there overnight. He hoped the old woman hadn't hidden it beneath her pillow. Suddenly the sleeping mound sat up, far smaller than the woman should be but frightening large in the dim light as it opened glowing golden eyes and emitted a "Reeyowl!" tailing off into a burbling growl.

Frightened out of his wits, the thief jumped backward – only to feel the sharp point of a dagger pushing through his cloak and the shirt beneath it, and nearly breaking the skin on his back. The Black One curse it! This was supposed to have been easy money!

"Hold perfectly still," a soft voice murmured low behind him. "Kathal has just fed this night, but she'd be perfectly happy to sharpen her claws on you if you don't mind your manners." A hand came up behind him and dragged his hood back, revealing his head. A boy, Leila thought. He might not even be much older than she was, from his slight build. But the profession of sneak thief was one most often taken up by those who remained small their entire lives. This guy could be in his forties, for all she could tell in this light.

He was around five inches taller than she was, slim and muscular-seeming. Leila checked around the neck of the cloak to make sure there was no back-of-the-neck sheath for a dagger, then commanded her captive, "Put your hands on top of your head." By now she'd released her shadows – else contact with the would-be thief would have rendered him as invisible as she was. Slipping the dagger into the waistband of her bloomers, she used both hands to reach around the intruder's neck and unclasp the cloak. She tossed it across the room, to be searched after there was some light to see by.

The thief twitched slightly, and in half a second Leila had her dagger out and digging into the flesh above his kidney again. "I told you not to move. The cat *will* rip your face off if I tell her to." A cat? But it was huge… Realization was beginning to sink in. He remained motionless as she once again sheathed the dagger and ran her hands all over his body. She removed a dagger from his belt and another from a sheath strapped to his leg beneath his leather trousers. But he seemed to have no other weapons.

Only two daggers? Leila hurled them across the room one at a time, where they buried themselves in the wooden wall with a "Thunk! Thunk!" This guy must not be much of a thief. Perhaps that explained his being desperate enough to rob old ladies of their purses.

Holding her dagger again, standing between the thief and his cloak lest he make a lunge for it before she could search it, Leila stepped off as far from him as she could go in the room's small confines and held out her glowstone. "All right you," she commanded, "turn around and let me get a look at you."

He rotated anxiously, not knowing what to expect though he'd been able to tell that his captor was a small woman. He was astonished to see, in the blue glow from that curious stone she held, that she was young – nearly his own age – and that she was beautiful. A thicket of dark curly hair surrounded her elfin face, dark as one of the Nima, yet she had eyes lighter than his own. And she was wearing nothing but a camisole and bloomers! He cast his eyes down shyly.

"What's your name?" Leila demanded, "And what makes you think you can sneak in here and rob an old lady of what little she owns? That's despicable!" "Tevo," he stammered out. "I'm Tevo, and who are you, her bodyguard? What, is she hiding under the bed?"

Leila laughed, a low chuckle. She'd just as soon not have the innkeeper or one of the other guests up here wanting to know what the commotion was about. "Halina's… not here at the moment," she replied. "I still want to know what you thought you were doing."

Tevo's shoulders slumped, and he thrust out his lower lip. Though small he was well made, and his face was boyishly handsome with a mop of unruly dark brown hair (as near as she could tell in this light) spilling over his forehead. He looked young and vulnerable standing there, in her power, and Leila felt a wave of sympathy wash over her despite his bad behavior.

"I was hungry," he said so quietly she could barely hear him. "I left home in Buda two weeks ago trying to get to Parat, but I was nearly out of money by the time I got to Pisk. And I couldn't get more. This town has, well, it's sort of like a guild for thieves. They just call it the Brotherhood. But they don't allow any thieves to operate in their town unless you join the Brotherhood, and the initiation fee is ten florins. By the Dark One's navel, how am I supposed to get ten florins without stealing it?"

Leila digested this in silence. Was she hearing a pack of lies? She stooped behind her and picked up Tevo's cloak, fastening it around her neck so that she was no longer standing there clad only in her underwear. She felt around the inside of the garment and discovered it had many pockets hidden in its depths. But they all seemed to be empty, and there were no more knives. Maybe the kid was telling the truth.

"Why didn't you just leave town?" she finally asked. "You've got legs. Surely you could make it to the next town and do some thieving there?"

"That was what I was going to do," he said forlornly. "I just needed a little cash so I could buy some food before I left. I haven't eaten in two days, and it's likely a two-day walk to the next town. I spent my last five coppers on an ale downstairs so I'd have a reason to hang around in the warmth of the inn and check out the patrons. I figured if I robbed a traveler, likely it wouldn't get back to the Brotherhood at all. Or at least not until I was long gone. After I saw your old babushka's purse, I was dreaming about maybe even riding on a coach instead of walking."

Leila sighed. The boy's story had the ring of truth to it. He seemed so pathetic. She decided to test her theory by going over to her valise, on the far side of the room, and pulling out a couple of the apples she'd brought inside with her in case it turned out the inn didn't supply breakfast. She tossed them to him, and he forgot all about her admonition not to move as he snatched them out of the air and began devouring them. As the juice ran down his nearly beardless chin, she began to believe he was telling the truth.

She dug a packet of beef jerky out of the bag and tossed that to him as well. "Kathal, stand and guard," Leila told the cat, and she went from her tense crouch to a more relaxed but alert stance. Leila took a Lucifer from the top of the nightstand and lit the bedside lamp, putting the glowstone she was holding back into her valise.

By the time she had done this, Tevo had already eaten all of the jerky and was licking his fingers. In the much brighter light from the lamp, she could see that he was, really, quite cute. If you liked them young and on the small side, which she did. Not that she'd abandoned her vow of eternal maidenhood, mind you – but a girl could look.

"I'm inclined to believe you're telling the truth, Tevo," Leila admitted. "But don't try anything funny or I'll gut you like a hog. I've done it before, you know," she added ominously – turning one of the most traumatic events of her young life into a bragging point. He eyed her warily, and put his hands up at shoulder level, palms out. With a disarming grin he said, "Thanks a lot for the food. You've saved my life. I promise, I'm not going to try anything."

She nodded dismissively. Kathal could be on him before he'd taken two steps, if need be; and there really didn't seem to be much harm in him. He was nowhere near as dangerous a criminal as *she* was. "So," she began in friendlier tones, "you came from Buda. You're from there originally?" Tevo nodded.

"My mom died when I was little," he explained, "and my dad raised me. He was… well, he was a professional thief is what he was. He was pretty good at it too, before he took sick. We had a comfortable enough life until he fell ill and couldn't work anymore." Leila felt a pang of sympathy. His story had some similarities to her own.

"Is there something like this 'Brotherhood' in Buda, too?" she asked. Until now, Marsine was the only place she knew of with such a widespread criminal organization. But she'd never been in the eastern part of the Dominion before. Tevo shook his head. "There were a few gangs, but nobody forced you to be a member of one. Dad was independent, said he didn't like taking orders from anybody. He started teaching me the trade when I was maybe like, thirteen, and I was starting to get better at it."

"And you're how old now?" Leila asked.

"Seventeen, last Sunreturn," he said.

"So, why were you going to Parat then," came her next question. Tevo hung his head, looking down at the floor as if ashamed.

"It seemed like a good idea at the time," he mumbled. She looked at him questioningly, and he went on. "Dad was sick for about a year, and I was taking care of him. It was really hard for me to bring in enough money to support us. We had to move to smaller quarters and sell pretty much everything we didn't need in order to pay for rent and food. Then he was dead, and I had no one. Since we weren't part of a gang and also weren't part of 'normal' society, I'd never made any close friends – and now all my relatives were dead. I just decided to move to the big city."

Leila smiled at him. "You've been hearing stories about it all your life, and you thought it would be a place where you could really make it big?" He nodded, half convinced she was mocking him. She didn't look any older than he was, if anything younger; but she sure *acted* like she was his senior.

"Don't feel bad, I've felt that way too," Leila admitted. An inspiration had seized her, and she'd decided to open herself to this forlorn young thief. She had suddenly seen her way clear to escaping the daily discomfort the Halina disguise caused her.

"You're going to Parat to seek your fortune?" Tevo asked wide-eyed.

She nodded slightly, but said "No, not exactly. You see, I'm on a mission from God."

Chapter 54

Halina shook up the reins, and Nimble pulled the cart out of the inn yard and turned down the street, striking the main highway three blocks up. The sun was barely rising, and few people were on the streets at this hour. No one noticed the tawny cat that came darting out of an alley and leapt up into the cart, burrowing down amid the jumble of broken furniture in it. Nor did anyone see the huge black raven that launched itself from the inn's rooftop and swooped to follow as the cart rattled down the cobbled street.

The old woman Tevo had referred to as a "babushka" (a term, he'd explained to Leila, that was used to refer to grandmothers who habitually wore head scarves in the region where he'd grown up) sat slumped on the driver's bench, looking straight ahead, as they followed the main road through the center of Pisk and out the other side. None of the shops were open yet, more's the pity, but she'd had her reasons for getting an early start.

After the buildings of town had thinned away, the countryside on either side of the road became a mixture of farm fields and woodland, slightly rolling country that offered plenty of hiding places for bandits. The Dominion's Imperial Lawkeepers did a pretty good job of keeping bandit gangs from preying on travelers along the main highways, but a woman traveling alone always ran the risk that she might encounter a lone bandit, or just a fellow traveler who thought he could take advantage of the situation.

This was one of the reasons why Leila had chosen to disguise herself as a fat, ugly old woman carrying around a load of obvious junk that only she saw as treasures. She had not been molested at all, as who would expect such a creature to be carrying any money? Of course if they had been desperate enough to stop her, they would have received a few nasty surprises.

Out in a stretch of woodland east of the road, a dark figure had been waiting. At the sound of the cart's approach, it rose up out of the copse it had been sheltering in and began jogging toward the road. There was no other traffic in sight. The figure, clad in dark leather clothing with a swirling dark cloak, ran to the side of the cart and hopped up onto the driver's bench beside Halina.

"Anita, is that you?" Tevo asked disbelievingly. He could still hardly credit that the lithe young woman he'd talked with for hours last night and this blob-like, repulsive old babushka were one and the same.

She grinned at him, showing her teeth for a change, and said in Halina's voice, "Mind your manners, young fellow. Show a little respect for your elders!" He smirked.

Earlier this morning, long after Leila had laid out the essentials of her mission to Parat, it had occurred to Tevo that she had still not told him her name. That hardly seemed fair, so he asked for it. Leila had a good feeling about the young thief, believed that there was no harm in him; but she wasn't quite ready to trust him with all her secrets yet. "Call me Anita," she'd said, not quite telling him a lie. She wondered how her old roomie Anita was doing, back there in Marsine at the Night Guild.

Tevo had looked her over in the warm lamplight, and a flash of realization suddenly came over his open, cheerful-looking face. "Your name's not Anita," he said, "it's Rosa Estares! You're the girl in the flyers." Leila looked at him blankly, an uneasy feeling creeping over her.

"Flyers?" she asked hesitantly, fearing the answer.

He was looking at her, then Kathal, as if seeing them with fresh eyes. "I saw one my first day in Pisk," he said. "It seems you robbed the Count of Oester of a bunch of his precious art objects? Good going!" The professional admiration in his voice was so clear that Leila's fears of imminent exposure (or the need to knife the likeable young man in order to silence him) were immediately relieved.

Tevo removed a rumpled, folded flyer from a back pocket of his trousers. It seemed that the count had used some of his vast riches to hire a portrait artist to work with those who had known Rosa best. His pencil portrait of her, in one of the outfits she often wore, had been converted to an engraving and used to illustrate a flyer offering a reward of two hundred florins, an unheard-of sum, for information leading to the apprehension of the female thief Rosa Estares. The recovery of the treasure she had stolen was not mentioned, since who would trade five thousand florins worth of art objects for a two hundred-florin reward?

These flyers had apparently been printed up and distributed by a horde of messengers, all over the Dominion for all that Leila knew. The count certainly had the resources to do so, and she sensed that the monetary value of the collection meant nothing to him compared with the personal effort he had put into gathering the pieces. Gustav was probably pretty mad at her too, a thought that filled her with an uncomfortable sense of guilt.

The likeness had been frighteningly good, and both Nimble and Kathal had been mentioned as well. The pair had discussed their plans until only a couple of hours before dawn. Then Leila had lain down in bed hoping to catch another couple of hours' sleep, but the anxiety had been too great. It was no use, and long before light had begun to suffuse the sky to the east she was up and getting into her Halina disguise.

Now the pair of them were rattling along the deserted road. If anyone asked, Tevo was her grand-nephew. Halina was now no longer traveling to Parat seeking her long-lost son. Instead, she was relocating there to live with her niece and her family, and this elder son had been sent to escort her. This story would do for the time being, but Leila was firmly determined to leave the old woman behind. It might be an excellent disguise, but it was beginning to irritate her beyond belief.

So was the raven. Once they were out away from prying eyes he'd perched on the cart near the driver's box and begun giving her his opinion of her change in plans. "I'm afraid I have to revise my earlier opinion," Yeil croaked. "When I said that you were smarter than you looked. What were you thinking, bringing a thief in on our master's plans?"

"Uh, hello? Yeil?" Halina replied in Leila's voice. "*I'm* a thief. It's *because* I'm a thief that I ended up mixed up with our master in the first place."

"Oh, so all thieves are part of a vast brotherhood of trust and amity, then? I hadn't realized that was the case. Never mind, then…"

"Kathal," Leila called. "Are you feeling hungry, sweetie?" The cat, who'd been curled up asleep in a pile of cast-off throw rugs at the bottom of the pile of broken furniture, stirred and poked her head out. "Mrp?"

The raven took to the air, calling "Nice, real nice! Sic the cat on the bird every time he opens his beak to tell you something you don't want to hear, why don't you? If I hadn't been ordered to accompany you by Betsalel himself, I would *so* be back in the Blackwald now…" He wheeled away toward a nearby stand of trees, where likely there were songbird nests full of eggs or succulent hatchlings.

Tevo watched him go. "That's a little hard to get used to," he remarked. He looked around at Kathal, who was still trying to figure out why she'd been called. She thought she'd heard something about food? He clucked to the cat and she came to him and sniffed his fingers, then politely allowed him to scratch her behind the ears. They were already starting to hit it off, which Leila saw as a good sign. Kathal seemed to have an unfailing instinct for separating the good from the bad, when it came to people.

It was close to noon when they came to the next settlement, a small town called Badzig. In the meantime, Leila was finding it immensely more enjoyable rolling along in the jouncing, creaking cart with Tevo's company. They encountered traffic frequently as the morning wore on, but when no one was there to see she could shed the mannerisms of old Halina and be herself, more or less. At least Tevo was a fellow thief, and that meant she could talk with him about subjects she'd been unable to speak of with another human being in nearly three years.

Maybe I don't need an entirely new identity and a new life as an ordinary citizen, Leila thought. Maybe all I need is a few close friends who know me for who I truly am and love me anyway. Of course Tevo still didn't know her true name, and though she was coming to like him more and more she was not quite ready yet to trust him with that. Maybe in time it would come.

The two of them had discussed more than anecdotes from the world of thievery, though Tevo was quite anxious for details of Leila's big score. She had also not revealed to him that the loot was as yet unsold, and was in fact residing in a secret compartment at the bottom of the cart behind them. When they arrived in Badzig, Tevo had a goodly shopping list of items he was to purchase on behalf of his "great-aunt." She'd been greatly pleased to know that he could read and write.

Parting with a couple more of her gold coins had been painful for Leila, but she was sure that they'd soon be able to get more. She felt herself to be a superior thief to Tevo, having benefitted from a more effective training program; but he was not completely useless in that regard. She doubted he would be very good at a con, though – his face was just too open, his emotions written on it plainly for all to see. Yet she hoped he'd be able to carry off the simple deception she planned to take them the rest of the way to Parat, at least.

They treated themselves to a hot lunch at the town's one inn on the change left over after their purchases had been made, the young man solicitously helping his great-aunt to a chair. If anything, the presence of the anxious young nephew seemed to bolster the old lady's credibility.

Leila looked on in amazement as Tevo shoveled down four times the amount of food she ate. He'd made a few inroads on her traveling stores as well, after they'd gotten on the road – the "meal" of apples and jerky in the early hours of this morning having been all he'd had to eat in days. But apparently young men his age had an infinite capacity for food. It seemed like a disadvantage, to her.

Traffic was heavy on the main road in the early afternoon, as they made their way along heading north by northwest toward Kohl, the next city of any size. It wasn't until nearly four in the afternoon that they found themselves alone on the road, with no other travelers visible in either direction, and pulled the cart off the road along a dirt track leading off to the west.

According to Leila's map there was a tiny farming village in that direction, some twenty miles out. The unpaved road was wide enough for a farm cart, and was used by the farmers taking their produce out – probably to the markets at Kohl, as it was closer. At this hour of the afternoon, it was very unlikely that anyone would be coming by; and they were down in a depression, out of sight of the main highway. They pulled the cart off the road in amongst a grove of trees beside a small creek, and Leila unhitched Nimble and removed the harness. This would do nicely!

Chapter 55

Nimble shuddered in delight, shaking his hide to relieve itches caused by the harness rubbing. Then he bobbed his head and whinnied at Leila in joy. He recognized her by her smell, even if she did look a bit funny. She patted him on the neck and told him, "Go eat, but stay close." He'd had a feedbag of oats while they were in Badzig, but that was hours ago. He took a drink from the creek, then moved over along its banks and began cropping the new grass.

Kathal and Yeil had both immediately headed into the trees, looking for something to catch and eat. Ravens will happily eat anything, though cats are fussier; and the black bird had some hope he might soon be enjoying fresh offal from one of Kathal's kills. He had a healthy respect for the cat, but was beginning to see that her presence wasn't entirely negative.

Anita and Tevo had their own work cut out for them, and they'd been discussing the details of it for hours; so as soon as the animals had been taken care of they set to work. First off, Halina removed her kerchief. Also her shawl, gloves, blouse, skirt, petticoats, heavy boots – and finally, the fat suit.

Tevo goggled as Anita stood once again clothed only in bloomers and a camisole. But this time it was broad daylight, and the details of her delectable form were revealed as they had not been before. He blinked as he realized that her figure was considerably more developed than he'd thought, then looked away in mortification.

He'd had very few opportunities to meet girls during his life in Buda. Anita was the first one he'd ever spent longer than a couple of hours with at a time, and assuredly the only one he'd ever seen in her underwear. An embarrassing swelling in his trousers began, and he hastily untucked his shirt and let it hang down over the top of the pants to hide it.

Leila would have liked to see the last of the still-unwashed garments she'd stolen from the laundry in Rosen, but they'd proven so useful she was loath to toss them away. Instead she tucked them into the cart, down by Kathal's pile of carpets. Then she handed her scissors to Tevo and sat down on a boulder. For the second time in her life she was shedding her locks to escape pursuit, but at least this time she had help.

Tevo stood behind Anita with the scissors. He had cut hair before. In the years when it was just him and his papa together at home, they had often given each other haircuts. But being so close to this beautiful, beguiling, hurricane of a young woman was making it really hard to concentrate on the task at hand.

It's hair, he told himself. I'm just cutting off her hair, so she can take her new disguise. And I'll be an important part of that disguise. We'll be together, and I'll be helping her. And I'll help her when we get to Parat, and she'll help me, and everything is going to be better than I ever imagined it. I hope.

Anita's tightly curled locks were softer than he'd expected, not slippery-silky like straight hair (such as his own) but more like down, like the caress of a breeze as Tevo ran his hands through it. He almost hated to bring the scissors down, snipping a lock here and a lock there, his hands shaking as he struggled with desire and the shame it caused him. But eventually, that mop of glistening black curls had become a short fuzz no more than an inch in length, standing up all around her head.

Women should have long hair, Tevo had always been given to understand. He was surprised to find that the short haircut made Anita look even cuter and more desirable, closer to what he imagined to be her real age. She hadn't yet told him what that was, and it didn't really matter. As far as her mind and skills and life experience went, she appeared to be years ahead of him.

They disposed of the cut hair, then it was Leila's turn to work on Tevo. When they'd first discussed the plan, he'd suggested they masquerade as man and wife, a young couple traveling to Parat's Temple of the Seven to ask Mulia to grant them a son. She had quickly vetoed that proposal. While it would have saved money for them to share a bed, she'd seen how Tevo looked at her with those flashing dark eyes of his and there was *no way* she was going to be sleeping with him all the way to Parat.

Instead, they would be a brother and sister from a small farm near Deggen (a village some distance to the west and south of Pisk). Their father was of the Nima, but had met and fallen in love with a farmer's daughter and left his band to marry her. They had inherited it from her parents, and now worked the farm together with their four children.

"Why can't you be the one with the head injury?" Tevo had asked. He didn't like the idea of being a useless invalid for the entire trip, at least during daylight hours when the eyes of the world were on them.

"It just isn't as plausible," Leila had patiently explained. "With three strong sons, why would the daughter of the household be out working with the livestock? Besides, I have more experience than you do of going in disguise. It's better if I do the talking."

Tevo was powerless to overcome her arguments. She was such a fierce little thing, so... well, bossy was an apt description. Yet he found her take-charge attitude somehow comforting even though he felt that, as the man, it should be him making the plans and issuing the orders.

So, what had emerged from their hours-long planning session were the half-Nima farm kids Rolf and Gerde. Rolf had injured his head falling from a horse and though the wound had not looked serious he had been struck blind. His mental confusion lingered as well, and Gerde was the only one of the family who could be spared. They'd loaded him into their farm cart, hitched to their riding horse (the plow horses were needed on the farm), for the several-day journey to Parat. There, surely, divine Lucia would grant Gerde's prayers for the full recovery of her brother's sight and mental faculties!

Tevo's hair was straight and dark brown, his eyes even darker; but his skin was relatively pale. Leila suspected that if he were to spend a season out in the sun he might easily darken to a shade to match hers – but they didn't have time for him to get a tan. So she was giving him one fast, using some of the dye she'd kept for touchups on Nimble mixed with a skin cream. She very carefully applied it to his face, neck, hands, and arms up to the shoulder. Soon they were close to the same color.

Now that Tevo's dye job was finished he started on the next task, lifting everything out of the farm cart and giving it a coat of paint. It had been raw, weathered wood before but soon sported a dark green finish. He didn't notice that the floorboards were quite a bit higher than the apparent bottom as seen from the outside.

Tevo next carried a bundle of clothing down into the woods and behind a tree before he changed into the simple farm garments they'd bought, far too shy to let Anita see him in his own underdrawers. Leila didn't want any spots of dye or bits of clipped hair on her clothing, so continued to go about her business in her bloomers and camisole – seemingly quite unembarrassed. That wasn't actually the case, but she was determined to pretend as if nothing was amiss. It helped her, and might possibly help Tevo after he'd gotten used to the idea. She was going to have to train that boy, and fast. His discomfiture while he'd been giving her the haircut had not gone unnoticed.

Before changing into her own farm clothes and becoming Gerde, Leila had one more chemical operation to perform, She called Nimble up from where he was grazing by the creek, and he sauntered up to her with his nostrils flaring. She'd mixed up some bleach, similar to that she'd used to create the white streaks in Halina's hair, and applied it to him with a paintbrush. The chemicals stung his skin beneath the short hair and he didn't like the smell, but he was truly a patient, loyal, and sweet-natured beast. By bedtime they had a dark bay horse with four somewhat stained-looking white stockings and a prominent blaze on his forehead – different enough, Leila hoped, from the plain bay that had pulled the old lady's wagon.

Supper was provisions from Leila's dwindling sack of supplies purchased in Rosen, and they made no fire though the evening was cold. They'd bought a thin, second-hand straw pallet in Badzig, and Tevo chivalrously insisted that Anita be the one to sleep on it while he mounded up fallen leaves and threw one of their blankets over it, before rolling up in his cloak.

In the morning they arose stiff from their night out. The cart was dry, and they set to work distressing the paint job with sand and dirt so that it looked less freshly done. The broken furniture had been carried off into a nearby thicket and dumped, along with the small cask the paint had come in. They laid a couple of boards across the cart from front to back, supporting the pallet. This left a hollow beneath it where Kathal could hide.

Leila added one last item to her disguise, a wig of long straight hair a shade lighter than Tevo's own. She tied a small kerchief over it, which went perfectly with her homespun garments. After hitching their horse to the transformed cart, Leila tied a bandage around Rolf's head and over his eyes. She figured there was no way Tevo was a good enough actor to pull off the illusion of blindness unless he was truly blind, and he had to agree with her – though he hated being unable to see. "Ride on the box with me for now," she told him, "and I'll squeeze your hand if anyone looks like showing interest in us. Remember, Rolf, you're very confused in your mind and have a hard time speaking. But don't overdo it."

He grinned at her from beneath the bandages. "Whatever you say, sister."

"Smart-arse!" she shot back, with a grin he couldn't see. With Kathal tucked into the space below the pallet, well-fed on her night's hunting and more than happy to den up and sleep the morning away, Gerde shook up the reins and Nimble pulled them up the dirt track and back onto the stone-paved highway. The sun was well up, but no one was in sight.

Chapter 56

The cart rolled into the medium-sized city of Kohl near noon with the injured Rolf, head swathed in bandages, lying limply and apparently asleep on the pallet draped in blankets. A worried-looking Gerde drove through town on the main highway, moving slowly as she looked around at the buildings. Many in the downtown area were of yellow brick and two to three storeys high, and from the look of the place it was quite prosperous. Most cities in the Dominion were, thanks to the wonderful highway system.

Near the far side of town Gerde found a somewhat run-down inn, able to supply the siblings with a pair of second-floor rooms – one beside the other. With help from the female innkeeper, she roused Rolf from his slumber and assisted him, reeling and querulously asking where they were, up to his room. "Thank you, mistress," Gerde said, her Gasparto slightly tinged with the accents of County Sachs – the region where the Petulengro family made their home.

After seeing her ailing brother settled, once again asleep, Gerde explained "Ever since his injury, besides the blindness and confusion, he sleeps a great deal. I suppose it's a blessing, really. But I'm sure that divine Lucia will answer my prayers – they say that her connection to her worshipers is stronger in the Temple at Parat than anywhere else on earth." The innkeeper smiled kindly at her.

"Please let me know, dear, if you need anything. I'm sure your brother will be fine again once you reach Parat."

Gerde smiled weakly, a waifish expression. "You're very kind, mistress. I think that I'll just lie down for a while now. Maybe I can get a little sleep as well before suppertime." With that, she went into her room and locked it. Within moments Leila had the door wedged, and had dumped the contents of her pack out on the bed. The room was shabby, but clean enough.

In another few minutes Leila had removed her wig and her farm clothing, and was dressed in her burglar gear. Then she faded from view and went out the window. This was her first opportunity to test her Shadow power in broad daylight (though the day was a bit gray and overcast, with rain threatening), and she slipped across the side of the building to Tevo's window next door.

The window was latched, and Leila didn't want to jimmy it. She tapped softly on the window, clinging to the sill; and in a minute Tevo appeared, the bandage pulled back from his eyes, and was peering through the window with a confused expression. He unlatched the window and made to push the casement open. Leila dodged to the side, still clinging like a spider to the side of the inn, and hissed, "Tevo! Go back inside!"

Startled, unable to figure out where the voice was coming from, he did as ordered. Moments later Leila had crawled in over the sill and was standing on the floor of his room. "Can you see me?" she murmured.

"Anita? You're there?" Tevo answered as softly. She released the Shadow power and peeled back her hood, so he could see that it was truly her. Tevo grinned at her in amazement. "Whoa!" he said, still keeping his voice down, "How'd you *do* that?" She smiled back.

"Remember when I mentioned that my master had given me a special power to help me fulfill my quest?" He nodded, recalling now. That night had been full of surprises, and he hadn't been playing close attention to details.

"Watch," Leila said, and became shadows once again. "What do you see?" she asked. He peered at her. There were no lamps on in the room, as it was early afternoon, but there was daylight coming in the window behind her.

"It's just a pool of murky shadow," Tevo said thoughtfully, "not shaped like a person, just sort of a blob. It blocks out the light from the window like there was smoke in the room." He put a hand out and felt for her, trying to determine where in the "blob" she was standing.

Leila reached out and seized his hand, and the pool of shadow immediately spread to engulf Tevo and his clothing as well. Anything she was touching, including her clothing and items she was carrying, would apparently become enshadowed as well. This could be really useful!

She released the shadows again, and Tevo reeled away. "That was really weird," he said in awed tones. He had never had any

291

experiences with the supernatural before, though he'd readily enough swallowed Anita's tale of her encounter with the Dark One and her discovery that he was not, after all, as black as he'd been painted.

"Your door is locked," Leila said quietly, "so you might as well just take a nap for now. You'll be needing the sleep for later tonight, anyhow. I'm going to go scouting now, make sure there are no guild monopolies on thieving in Kohl, and pick us out some likely targets. I'll be back in time to lead Rolf down for supper."

"All right, Anita," Tevo sighed. He'd much rather be out exploring, but he lacked the skills she had. "Be careful out there."

Cloaked in shadows, Leila climbed down the side of the building to a lean-to shed at the back, and from the roof of that to the ground. Their rooms overlooked the rear dooryard, which was one reason they'd been so cheap. The shed was open at the front, and their cart was parked within against the possibility of rain. She'd have to rely on the false floor and the camouflage of the straw pallet to keep her loot safe now, Leila realized. But the thing certainly didn't look worth stealing.

Kathal had already wriggled out of her hidey hole beneath the pallet and was hunting for mice amid the shed's other contents. "You'd better stay out of sight, Kathal," her mistress murmured to her. She looked perplexed to hear the voice coming from a pool of shadow, but then seemed to accept that this was something she'd seen before. She slipped under the cart and curled up to sleep some more.

Nimble had been unhitched and rubbed down, and was now tied to a post in the yard beside a pile of hay and a watering trough. The inn didn't have a stable, as most of its clientele didn't have horses. He'd be all right there, and if the threatened rain came he could always slip the loose knot she'd put in the rope and come into the shed with Kathal.

Convinced that her animal companions were safe and comfortable (Yeil had flown off about his own business, as soon as they came into town), Leila continued on her exploration of Kohl. This end of town, along the main highway on the northeastern edge, seemed a little less prosperous than the central area they'd driven through on their arrival. Not a likely spot for a good score.

Leila turned southwest and headed toward the center of town, taking back alleys whenever possible. Kohl was an ancient settlement, founded long before the Dominion as a stronghold along the Vizha, a major river that ran roughly north from the Antels to the Northern Ocean. It had grown up first along the riverfront, and had then spread helter-skelter in a western direction, resulting in a warren of streets that curved, wandered, joined each other at odd angles, or stopped only to pick up again a couple of blocks later under the same name. A very confusing place for a first-time visitor, but Leila had a good sense of direction.

As long as she avoided rapid movement or standing in direct sunlight, she found, people tended to notice nothing out of the ordinary as she traversed the city. They'd had only a few bites of traveling rations for lunch, and Leila helped herself to some fruit from a sidewalk stand while the greengrocer was taking money from a customer. The fruit in her hand and in her pockets immediately became part of her personal pool of shadow, and she walked off eating the early plums with no one the wiser.

Leila needed to avoid close quarters, as just because somebody couldn't see her didn't mean they wouldn't notice if they bumped into her. Being small and lithe helped, here, and she was able to slip into several stores that looked like likely targets and wriggle into corners where she could watch, unobserved, as business was conducted and cash tucked away.

Unable to resist, when Leila found herself alone near the counter of a clothing store while the proprietor helped a customer to find garments in his size, she crept behind it and lifted a goodly handful of silver shillings and even a couple of gold florins from the unlocked cashbox. Then she slipped to the rear of the store and out the delivery door, which had been locked but didn't take much to open. If they failed to find a real score, one that would see them through to Parat, at least they now had enough money to buy them another couple of nights' lodging and some more food.

The whole time she'd been out, more than an hour now, Leila had been searching for signs that something like the Brotherhood or the Night Guild was operating in Kohl. There had been none; and even if there was, with her shadow power how were these thieves to catch her – any more than her targets or the authorities sworn to protect them were? She felt safe enough, and she had identified a jewelry store that seemed like a likely target. But she wanted to make sure, so she returned to the seamier side of town and went looking for a pawn shop.

In Leila's experience, fences usually used a pawn shop as the front for their business of accepting stolen goods. But certainly not all pawnbrokers were fences. She lurked in the shadows in the mouth of a nearby alley until she saw a shady-looking character heading for the door. Moving quickly and silently on her soft-soled boots, she was right behind him as he went inside, a bell on the door announcing his entry.

Leila immediately slipped off to the side, losing herself amongst the used merchandise on display. The pawnbroker, a worn-looking, balding man in his sixties, came out from the room at the back in response to the bell. "Afternoon Alf," he said in friendly tones. "What have you got for me today?" Likely a legitimate businessman would be eyeing this Alf character with suspicion. He was small, greasy, and resembled nothing so much as an oversized, bipedal rat. Yet apparently, he was a regular customer here.

Alf looked around furtively, though so far as he could see there was no one else in the shop. "You're going to like these, Bohdan," he said, reaching beneath his short cloak to pull out a small cloth bag. He poured its contents onto the counter, and Leila edged silently closer for a better look in the dimly lit shop.

What the ratlike character had deposited on the counter was a mound of plain gold chains, a common enough jewelry item sometimes worn by men as well as women – especially among the Nima. Leila wondered where he'd gotten them, but she was willing to bet it wasn't from his dear departed mother's hope chest.

Bohdan put his hands into the pile and began separating the individual chains. They were of different weights, lengths, and link designs, and represented a considerable amount of craftsmanship as well as the value of the gold with which they were made. The pawnbroker bent below the counter and brought up a two-pan balance and a bowlful of weights, then scooped the chains off the counter and into one of the pans before adding weights to the other side.

The old man jotted some notes on a piece of scrap paper, then announced "Two pounds, three ounces. I can give you ten florins." Alf was outraged

"They're worth more than that for the gold alone!" he whined.

"Yes, and I might need to melt them down and sell them as that, depending on where you got them," the fence replied patiently. "I need to make a profit, you know."

"I got 'em from a jewelry case in one of them mansions up in the hills," the thief said resentfully. "Batty old lady's completely lost her marbles, I don't think she knows her own name anymore never mind what jewelry she's got. I hired on for some yard work and just crept in and grabbed a handful. They'll never be missed, besides it's not like they're unique or anything. Just plain old gold chains." Bohdan sighed, but nodded.

"All right," he said, "twenty florins. Fair enough?"

"It'll do," Alf mumbled, a hint of resentment in his voice. The fence removed the weights and scooped the chains back into their bag before putting the scale back under the counter. He left the loot sitting on the counter while he went into the back room and returned, a minute or so later, with a handful of gold coins.

After Alf had left the shop, Bohdan turned and went back into the room behind the shop. There was a gap in the counter with a hinged section of countertop that could be lifted for walking through. Leila, still invisible, crouched and sneaked under it. Then, moving as silently as possible, she followed the elderly fence to see where he'd gone.

Alone in the shop, as he thought, he was in the process of stowing his latest acquisition in a safe mounted in the wall. It was up high, and he had pulled up a stool and pulled aside a drape. Not quite as sophisticated a setup as the safe in Josef Samson's study, which Leila had raided not quite three years before; but this safe had something she had never seen before: a combination lock.

She had heard of these ingenious mechanisms, but they were a new thing and not all that widespread. The folk of the counties in this part of the Dominion were famous for their abilities with mechanical devices. Clocks and watches, clockwork automatons, and apparently also combination locks were all made here.

The dial, made of brass with numbered lines engraved in it, was enormous – half a foot across at least. There were no windows in this part of the shop and Bohdan had a couple of lamps lit, nicely illuminating the dial as the pawnbroker turned it right to 35, left to pass 17 once and then stop on it the second time around, right to 68, left to 43, and right once more, up over the top, to 25. Leila watched in fascination, committing the numbers to memory.

After determining that the pawnbroker was a fence and that there'd been no mention of guild membership in his discussions with the thief, Leila had been planning to go visible and arrange with him to take in stolen jewelry from her later on tonight. Gerde and Rolf needed to be on their way toward Parat as quickly as possible, not hanging around Kohl until business hours tomorrow morning. But now, another idea had come to her. Why not cut out the middleman and just steal the gold she needed from the fence? If anybody in this town kept a goodly quantity of gold on hand it was him, and now she knew where he kept it.

Chapter 57

The blind boy and his solicitous sister ate a surprisingly delicious and hearty meal at a table in the inn's common room, lovingly served by the proprietress. "I had a boy and girl like you two once, myself," she said.

From her tone nothing bad had happened to them, but Gerde asked with concern, "Once, Magda?"

The woman smiled. "All grown up, years ago now," she said with a touch of wistfulness. "I'd hoped after my husband passed on that I could get my boy to return to Kohl with his family, and help out with the inn. But he's an accountant, making good money in Parat. I've got two grandchildren I've never even seen."

Seemingly, though the Dominion was full of thriving towns and cities, the lure of the capital still claimed its share of young people chasing their dreams. It wasn't just farm boys who ran off to see the big city. "That's too bad," Gerde said sympathetically. "What about your daughter?"

Magda smiled. "Lives down in Badzig with her husband and three boys."

"Do you see them often?" the farm girl asked.

"Often enough," the innkeeper replied. "They come up once a year to stay for a week's visit at the inn, and nearly tear the place apart. I'm thankful I only had the two."

Gerde grinned at her, and went back to helping Rolf eat his stew. A big pot of vegetables and savory broth with some kind of meat in it was about all you ever got to eat at most inns, or at the least at the sort of inns where the teenage siblings could afford to stay. Leila thought with nostalgia of the excellent meals she'd had while living in the dorm at the Night Guild. But this was good enough, full of big chunks of chicken with lots of carrots and turnips and young spring peas. It had some kind of little dumplings floating in it, too.

Tevo had been bored out of his mind since assuming the role of Rolf, and had napped for several hours while Leila was out planning their heist. Now he was wide awake and eager for some stimulation. After being spoon-fed the delicious stew and gnawing on several slices of a flavorful, hearty black bread he would happily have hung out in the common room just drinking water and listening to the conversations around him for the rest of the evening.

But Anita was in control of the situation, and when she hauled him up onto his feet again soon after they'd finished eating and told Magda that Rolf had better rest, he'd been unable to raise any objections. Rolf was supposed to be living in a fog, too confused to understand what was going on around him.

As Gerde helped her poor, blind brother up the stairs Anita murmured to Tevo, "Sorry – I know you must be going nuts with boredom. But you stand out a little too much with that bandage. I don't want to be under the eyes of a roomful of people who might remember us later, if anyone comes asking." Gripping her arm in one hand and the handrail in the other, Tevo sighed.

"You're right, but I sure would like to get out and *do* something!" Gerde helped her brother up onto the landing, and as she led him down the corridor to her rooms, she kissed him on the cheek.

"I'll come in and sit with you for a while. Besides, I haven't had time to tell you about our forthcoming adventure!

After stowing the bag of gold chains, Bohdan had closed the safe and relocked it, then pulled the drape back down. He'd climbed down from the stool and put it to one side before going to the front of the shop and locking the door. Leila wondered what he was up to, but took advantage of his absence to go silently down the dimly lit hallway toward the back. A narrow wooden staircase there climbed to what she guessed would be living quarters on the second floor. The shops in most cities were built like that, the shop owners and their families living right above their places of work.

Leila heard the old man coming back, and scrunched back into the shadows in the stairwell. But he didn't come as far as that, instead turning off at a door in the hallway. He was in there for several minutes, tinkling sounds suggesting he might be using the privy. In a town like this one, it was probably not just the mansions of the wealthy that had water closets. Her guess was confirmed when she heard the sound of the flushing toilet followed by water running in a sink. Very modern!

Bohdan went back down the hall to the shop and unlocked the front door again, then returned to sit on a stool behind the counter, picking up a book. Leila took some time for a more thorough examination of the back room. It appeared to have locking doors on both sides of it, and was probably where the old fence kept most of his valuables. She and Tevo were only interested in cash, though, unless there were some items that they could use personally.

Another customer came in, this one looking like a middle-aged woman down on her luck. Possibly what she had to sell had come to her legitimately. As Bohdan began haggling with her over the price, Leila went down the hall to the back door. Hmm, a complication: the back door had a heavy hasp and a padlock – mounted on the inside of the door. The old man must make sure it was locked up tight before going upstairs to bed in the evening. She could pick any lock, she felt confident, but not one she couldn't reach.

"So you see," Anita concluded, "We're going to have to figure out a way to get in there without waking up the old man. It shouldn't be a problem getting into the storeroom, and once we're in there I can open up the safe" – she waved a piece of paper on which she'd written down the combination before she should forget it – "and we'll just grab whatever coin is on hand. I'm sure he's got more than enough florins in there to see us comfortably to Parat and set up a base of operations when we get there. But first, we've got to get in."

They were speaking in hushed tones, and Leila had brought one of her slim collection of books with her so that she would be found "reading to her brother, it helps to soothe him" should anyone chance by and wonder why she was in his room. Tevo was just so glad to have Anita here, keeping him company and setting him problems to solve, that he didn't care what anyone thought.

She'd complained about what a pain the Halina disguise had been – the sweltering garments, the irritating wrinkle makeup that had left her face still broken out days later – but though there was little enough physical discomfort in portraying Rolf, the tedium was really getting to him. If only he were as clever as Anita, and could come up with some alternate cover story for why the two of them were traveling with a farm cart.

"Say Anita, why *did* you get a cart to go with your Halina disguise? Wasn't that a lot of trouble to deal with?" Leila still had not told him they were carrying five thousand florins worth of art treasures around under the straw mattress and dirty blankets, and was not yet ready to do so – though as they spent more time together, she was coming to believe that she could trust Tevo even with that secret. Huh, next she'd be telling him her real name!

"For Kathal, of course," she replied as if she couldn't believe he had to ask. "Everyone knows that Rosa Estares had a Nima pard with her, and there are very, very few of those cats around. Almost all of them can only be found in Nima caravans, acting as companions and guard animals. The Nima don't sell their pards to anyone."

Oh of course, how silly of him. "You know a lot about the Nima," he said, "and you look a bit like the Nima too. Are you really part Nima, like in our story?"

"I traveled with them for a few months when I was younger," Anita replied. She didn't mention that it was as the half-Nima boy Luca she had been among them. Had they been willing to take her in as herself, she might still be with them. "I needed to leave, so I told the band I was traveling with that I was off to search for my long-lost father," she explained. "I was already miles away and dusk was coming on when Kathal showed up at my camp. We'd bonded when she was a kitten, and she decided to follow me."

"Great story," Tevo said somewhat enviously. He had now learned he was a full year older than Anita, yet all he'd done in his life so far was a little minor thieving in the town where he'd been born. She wasn't even seventeen yet, and already she'd traveled with the Nima and stolen a king's ransom in treasures from the notorious Mad Count of Oester. "Say, I'm guessing you haven't been able to sell Count Oester's treasures yet, or you'd already be in Parat dining on hummingbird tongues. So what happened to it?"

Betsalel save me, Leila thought, the boy asked that question as innocently as if he were asking me what I had for breakfast. It wasn't that she thought he would scheme against her to steal the treasure if he knew, he was more likely to blab about it to a random stranger while passing the time of day. "Oh, when the Count's guards chased me into the Blackwald I knew right then I wasn't going to be able to sell everything as planned. So I stashed it where nobody can find it. I'll get it after I take care of my master's quest, I guess. Or after things settle down. Maybe in a year or two."

Without actually lying to the boy, Leila had managed to imply that the treasure was hidden in the Blackwald. Now that she understood the source of the "lurking evil" in that dark and tangled forest, she knew that it was real enough to keep out anyone who might enter there with ill intent.

Tevo's thoughts next flitted back to the problem at hand. Outside the window of his narrow room night was falling, but it would still be many hours before they could venture out, precisely like two thieves in the night, to rob the fence's treasure room.

"Did you check the fence's upstairs quarters?" Tevo asked Anita. She nodded.

"After realizing we weren't going to be getting in through the back door I sneaked upstairs. The door to the apartment wasn't locked, and I just walked right in while he was still haggling with that customer." Outside the window, Leila caught a flicker of motion and spotted Kathal, off on a nocturnal prowl in the darkness. Poor kitty was probably starving, after hiding out all day.

"That building's pretty ratty," she went on, "just two storeys and it's sandwiched in between two other buildings so there are only windows at the front and the back. But the apartment was a lot nicer than I expected. A good-sized bedroom, big sitting room with some really good furnishings in it, a bathroom with hot and cold running water and a flush toilet. It looks like he usually cooks for himself, as the kitchen is pretty well stocked. There's even an icebox."

In Kohl, as in many cities in this part of the Dominion, ice brought from the mountaintops or cut from frozen lakes in the wintertime was stored with salt in insulated ice houses, and householders could get regular deliveries of block ice to keep their food fresh at home. Marsine could really have used something like that, Leila thought – but the trip to the nearest glacier or frozen lake was simply too far.

"What about the windows in the back?" Tevo asked, having a thought.

"There's one on either side of the back door," Anita said, "lighting the hall and the stairs in the daytime, at least. But those both have steel latches and padlocks on them, just like the door."

"And what about the upstairs ones?" he went on, his mind still thinking about details.

"One window is in the bedroom, looking out on the alley behind the building, and the other is in the bathroom right across the hall. They just have regular latches on them, no padlocks. But I don't like the idea of breaking in upstairs. The guy is old, and might need to get up and pee a lot. I don't want to kill anybody." Tevo grinned at her, recalling how terrified he'd been at their first meeting with her threatening to run him through or sic the cat on him. He knew Anita well enough now to realize that though she was one hell of a thief, she was no killer.

"But if you can get at the locks in back, you'd be able to pick them without any problem? Quietly?"

"I haven't met a lock yet that took me longer than five minutes to pick," Anita bragged. "I had four years' training from the best experts in Marsine." She had admitted to him that she'd spend time with the Night Guild, but not explained why she was no longer with them.

Tevo had been sitting on the bed, ready to lie down with his bandage pulled over his eyes in the event it was necessary to become Rolf in a hurry. Now he rose, dark eyes twinkling in the lamplight, and walked over to the bench on which he'd set his pack. After some rummaging he came up with two curious looking items. One looked like a short, blunt steel wand maybe six inches in length. The other was four inches in diameter, and resembled a narrow roll of cloth. "I have just the thing," he announced.

Chapter 58

It was now the wee hours of the morning, and a light drizzle was falling. Kohl did have streetlights that burned all night, but few of them were to be found in this run-down section of town – and none at all in the alley behind Bohdan's pawn shop.

Two dark figures approached down the alley, counting the doors as they made their way silently along the filthy cobbles. Behind them, a tawny figure darted among the shadows. Kathal had wanted to come along, and Leila had decided it would be all right to bring her. She was good protection, if they ran up against anything unexpected.

At the back door to the pawn shop, the taller of the figures pulled two items from the folds of its dark cloak. "Here, hold the cutter while I use the tape," Tevo murmured into Anita's ear. She did so, and he peeled some of the narrow cloth strip from the roll with a slight tearing sound. It was cloth, sort of like coarse ribbon – but it had been coated on the inner side with a gummy adhesive.

The window consisted of several panes, each around five by seven inches, held together with strips of lead inside the steel frame. He chose the pane closest to the padlock, which was clearly visible through the glass by the light of the glowstone Anita held up.

Tevo tore off four strips of the tape and stuck them temporarily around the edges of the frame, not burnished down. Then he took the cutter tool from Anita and made a smooth pass across the surface of the pane at the top, deeply scoring the glass. Leila watched, intrigued. She couldn't believe that nobody in the Night Guild had known about this technique. But then, Buda was a long way from Marsine.

After each swipe of the cutter, Tevo laid one of his strips of tape across the cut with one end firmly secured to the adjoining pane and one to the pane that had been scored. When the pane had been scored and taped on all four sides, he used the hardwood knob at the end of the cutter to tap gently, almost soundlessly around the edges of the rectangle. With a slight "tink" the glass broke the rest of the way.

Tevo carefully pulled the cut section of pane out of its leaded frame with the tape, and laid it gently on the stones of the alleyway at his feet. There had been no loud noise, no fragments of glass scattered around to become a hazard, no alarm raised. Leila beamed at him and handed the glowstone to him, murmuring "Brilliant! Hold it up so I can see the lock…"

A couple of minutes later Leila had slipped into the back of the pawn shop through the now-open window, and a couple of minutes after that she'd opened the back door and let Tevo and Kathal come inside as well. They left the door closed but unlocked, in case they needed to make a quick exit. There was no light inside but the faint blue glow from the glowstone, but it was enough to make their way down the pitch-black corridor to the rear door of the pawnshop's storeroom.

Once again Tevo held the stone for Leila as she picked the lock. He'd had some training and practice in this art, but it was clear that she had had far more. His envy of her skills warred against his liking for her, and the ever-growing desire she inspired in him. He was falling in love, and he suspected he was doomed.

In less than a minute they were inside the storeroom. The room, perhaps fifteen feet square, was full of interesting stuff. Under other circumstances they could have happily spent a couple of hours exploring, and made off with enough loot to fill the farm cart; but now they were on a focused mission: open the safe, get the cash, and get out.

Leila led Kathal back out, halfway down the corridor between the back door and the storeroom. "Stay and guard," she said quietly, and the cat settled onto her haunches, facing the direction Leila had been pointing, and gazed alertly down the hall toward the door.

Returning silently to the storeroom, Leila closed the door behind her. The door from this room to the front of the shop was closed, and she presumed locked. As a precaution, giving them another means of escape if they were discovered, she unlocked it and peeked out briefly before closing it again, preventing anyone peering in from the shop's windows at the front from seeing anything amiss.

They were almost finished! In a couple of minutes, they should have what they came for and be ready to leave. Leila pulled another glowstone from a pocket and held it out, looking for the stool she'd seen earlier. With both doors closed, they could almost have lit some lamps and worked with plenty of light to see by – but she was leery of bars of light showing below the doors where no light should be.

The room was so cluttered she almost missed it, but then spotted the stool shoved away beneath a counter that was piled high with miscellaneous merchandise. Leila pulled it out, careful not to make any noise, and put it in position beneath the curtain on the wall that hid the door of the wall safe. Tevo was suitably impressed at her efficiency.

Needing both hands, Leila whispered "Hold your glowstone right up by the dial, Tevo." He did so. She tucked her own glowstone back in a pocket and pulled out the paper with the combination written on it: 35-17-68-43-25. While Tevo held the glowstone for her to see by, she turned the dial right, left, right, left, and right again. No click was heard, and when she tugged on the handle, the door held tight.

Oh shit, what had she done wrong? Then like a hot wave surging over her, Leila realized her error. She spun the dial a couple of times as she'd seen Bohdan do when he locked it, then repeated the sequence – this time spinning *past* 17 on the first left to strike it on the second pass. The safe door opened.

By the Seven (no, Eight! Leila told herself), the safe was enormous. It was far wider than the door, extending for another foot on either side, and so deep Leila nearly needed to hoist herself up and crawl inside to touch the back wall. This must have cost Bohdan a pretty penny, indeed!

A great deal of the contents were valuable treasures like the necklaces the ratlike thief Alf had brought in yesterday afternoon. Also loose cut gems, little ingots of gold and silver, piles of far fancier jewelry, bank notes, and some of the kinds of art objects Mad Count Oester was fond of collecting. There were also, clearly visible after Leila brought out her glowstone and set it inside the safe, quite a few stacks of gold florins and silver shillings. Enough, far more than enough, to see them through to Parat!

But the banknotes were worth having, too. Leila was halfway into the safe, reaching for a stack, when there came a familiar "Reeyowl!" from the far side of the closed door to the corridor and the back of the shop. Oh, shit! The pards' wild ancestors had probably used that cry to warn off rivals, but the Nima had trained them to use it as an intruder alert that had the added benefit of causing all but the boldest of intruders to wet their pants in terror.

From behind the door they heard a voice, recognizable to Leila as belonging to Bohdan, crying "Back, fiend!" There was a fierce barking, and she realized that Bohdan had a dog with him. What? She had trod every area of the shop, and searched the apartment. There had been no sign of a dog – where had it been hiding? Maybe he picked it up somewhere for night duty, not wanting to keep a messy animal in his small quarters...?

Leila hissed to Tevo, "I'm going invisible! You open up the door to the shop and flee in that direction!" An instant after speaking these words, the girl vanished – another shadow in a room full of shadows. Having some sense of her intent, Tevo pocketed the glowstone – plunging the room into pitch darkness.

He felt his way to the door they'd unlocked earlier and slipped through it, then crawled under the counter at the opening to the right and stole down an aisle, past stacks of dubious merchandise, to the front door. This too was latched and padlocked from the inside, and he dug out his lockpicks to begin trying to open it. There was enough light in the street outside that he was silhouetted against the glass.

Bohdan was terrified by the strange creature that had invaded his shop. The simple pull cord on the safe door, hidden by the hinges, had rung a little tinkling bell in his sleeping chamber. The precaution had paid off. Half the thieves in Kohl were aware that he kept money and valuables in his shop. Of course it was bound to occur to someone to break in and steal them. What puzzled him was how anybody had managed to open the combination lock on the safe. It was his single most valuable possession, and the genius artisan who had crafted it had showed him how to set the combination himself so that no one, absolutely no one beside himself, would know it.

And now there was this other problem. After hearing the alarm he'd dressed hastily and roused the dog, which was delivered nightly for his protection. With a loaded crossbow in one hand and a lamp in the other, he was ready to skewer the intruder. And then he'd discovered this demon from hell in the corridor at the bottom of the stairs. What was it, some kind of huge cat?

Bohdan had been operating his pawn and fencing business in Kohl for many years, had in fact taken it over from his father who'd run it before him. So he'd had little truck with the Nima and didn't recognize one of their famous guard cats when he saw one.

That screech had nearly given him a heart attack! He was not a young man. And Vrah, his four-legged security service (a sixty-pound Bulgar, the short-coated breed known for their ferocity – and also the most popular non-estate guard dog in the Dominion) had retreated up the stairs several steps and was cowering behind Bohdan – all of his hair standing on end. He emitted a piteous whine.

Well, whatever that thing was, it was probably not immune to crossbow bolts. The range was no more than twenty-five feet from his position halfway up the stairs to where it stood, watching him with those golden eyes, in the hallway. Holding the lamp up with one hand, he took careful aim with the crossbow. It wavered slightly, a heavy thing with its steel mechanism and hardwood stock. At the last second, as Bohdan pulled the trigger, the cat darted down the hallway. The bolt slammed into the wall near the baseboard, not far from the door to the water closet.

Leila, anxious about Kathal (she might be ferocious but she was only a little cat, after all) had just opened the door to the storeroom and the cat streaked through it. The only light in the room was a faint blue glow emanating from the glowstone inside the safe, and the yellow light coming from Bohdan's lamp on the stairs at the rear of the building. Tevo had left the door to the front of the shop open when he'd fled, and she now ordered Kathal, "Go hide," with a gesture that sent the cat scurrying through the door into the darkened shop beyond.

Bohdan was close to having an apoplexy from all of the excitement. He'd confidently expected that with Vrah at his side he'd be able to handle anyone who tried to break in here and steal what was his. But the apparition, some kind of huge cat it must have been, had unnerved him. It was as if it had understood what he was doing with the crossbow, and had just waited for him to pull the trigger!

It might *seem* like a demon from hell but the fence had seen no fingers, no opposable thumbs. That creature had not gotten in here by itself, and that meant there were human thieves. A glance to his right showed that the window to the right of the back door was standing open, and the back door's latch was open as well. He assumed its internal lock had also been bypassed.

The padlock was not in evidence, and he hadn't brought his keys with him in any case. Cranking the crossbow back and fitting another bolt into the groove, Bohdan rallied his courage and continued the rest of the way to the bottom of the stairs. He took the time to light the wall lamp nearest the back door, throwing more illumination down the hallway, and commanded "Vrah! Guard!"

With another whine the dog came down the stairs and stood behind him. Its nose was twitching, and it didn't like what it smelled. But some of its fortitude returned, and it began stalking down the corridor beside the old man – legs stiff, lips curled, and growling deep in its throat.

Oh crap, Leila thought, as she beheld the shop owner and his guard dog coming her way. She'd already learned that her Shadow power would not completely hide her from creatures with a good sense of smell. She left the storeroom behind, glowstone still illuminating the interior of the safe and its door still standing open, and after passing the counter she took the aisle to the left. Ahead of her, she could just see Tevo frantically working to open the front door, and Kathal pacing in front of him with her golden eyes aglow, emitting little yowls of warning.

Bohdan, lantern held in one hand and the cocked crossbow in the other, came into the storeroom and found it empty of intruders. The safe was standing wide open, but he didn't stop to check its contents. He hadn't heard the front door bell ring, nor any glass breaking, so the thief and his cat must still be here. In the front of the store trying to get through the locks, he'd be willing to bet.

He came through the door and set the lamp on the counter. It threw shadows, but with both hands he'd have a better chance of making his shot. Bohdan came around the counter and peered down the center aisle, the one most illuminated by the lamp. A not over-large figure clad in dark clothing was visible down there, desperately trying to open the locks on the front door. Hah, got you!

The cat was not visible, hidden by the shadows. "Vrah, attack!" the fence commanded, and the well-trained dog leapt to do his master's bidding – though his nose told him plainly that the cat was still nearby. He had gotten no more than halfway down the aisle when it suddenly appeared out of nowhere, screaming at him and raking his tender nose with its razor claws. With a yelp of terror, the dog turned tail and ran, nearly knocking his master over in his panicked attempt to flee. The pair of them scrambled past the counter and ran toward the rear of the building.

Fucking useless dog, the fence cursed silently as he watched them go. Maybe the cat would do him a favor and have the mutt for breakfast. But now, the thief was undefended – and Bohdan still had a loaded crossbow in his hands. The laws of the Dominion, and of Kohl, made it perfectly legal for anyone finding an intruder in their home, bent on theft, to kill the malefactor without further discussion.

Bohdan's own body was casting a shadow over the thief, blocking the light from the lamp on the counter. But there was enough light from the street to let him see the silhouette and at this distance, not ten feet away, he could hardly miss. The criminal must surely be aware of his presence, yet he had his back turned – still trying to unlock the front door.

Ignoring the sounds of the cat attacking the dog far behind him, the fence took careful aim with the crossbow. A bolt dead center should just about do it... Suddenly the weapon fell from his hands, bolt firing into the shelving unit to the left, and Bohdan collapsed bonelessly atop it. Leila had hit him over the head from behind, hard, with a decoratively-carved wooden cylinder around four inches in diameter and three feet long.

Tevo had been crouching on his feet as he tried to pick the locks, and had gotten through the padlock but was still having problems with the main door lock. He fell back onto his butt and sprawled, legs out into the room, with a sigh of relief. "Shit, Anita – I thought you were never going to get here!" he gasped.

"Sorry," she said, "it was hard finding the right item in the dark, but I guess that one did the trick. Is he still alive?" Tevo bounded back up onto his feet and inspected the pawnbroker where he lay sprawled atop his crossbow. He fished the weapon out from under the old man and hurled it across the room to crash in the darkness, knocking down more of the shop's merchandise.

A moment later Tevo reported, "There's a pulse. But I don't think he's going to be waking up any time soon." As he rose to his feet Anita rushed forward, threw her arms around him, and planted an enthusiastic kiss on his face. She missed his mouth by about an inch.

"Oh, thank Betsalel!" she exclaimed. He wasn't sure whether her actions or her words were more startling.

They found the dog cowering at the top of the stairs, while Kathal crouched watching him in the light from the lamp Bohdan had lit earlier. He was whining in abject terror. One on one, a cat could take a dog of up to twice its weight without much problem – dogs lacking those razor claws.

Leila smiled. "Stay and guard, Kathal," she said unnecessarily. Then to Tevo she added, "Let's finish robbing the safe, shall we?" They cleaned the safe out of all its gold and silver coins, and all the "pay to bearer" banknotes as well. All the rest of Bohdan's hoard remained, and was soon locked up again. The two thieves, jubilant, locked both the door to the front and the door from the hallway, leaving the storeroom secure, as they moved toward the back door. Then they called the cat away, and vanished into the night.

Chapter 59

They'd left their inn room windows closed but unlatched, having gone out that way and intending to return by the same route. But they were now carrying a heavy haul of coins, and decided to stash the loot before making the climb. Utterly unobserved at this hour, they tucked it all the way down at the bottom of the cart under the pallet and blankets.

Leila joined Tevo in his room, before going to her own. After getting inside they pulled off their hoods and stood grinning at each other like maniacs, by the dim light of a lamp on the bedside table. Gerde had explained to Magda that though Rolf slept most of the time he would sometimes awaken in fear and confusion and cry out. She needed the lamp left lit so she could be ready to go to him, night or day.

"We did it!" Leila squealed quietly, throwing her arms around her cohort in crime. The adrenaline rush of their narrow escape had left both of them ecstatic with relief. Tevo hugged her back, showing a surprising wiry strength. Then he leaned back a little, smiling into her eyes for a moment, and kissed her.

Not counting the time she'd nearly been raped, Leila had never been kissed by a boy. She was surprised to find that the kiss, from this boy she liked a lot and was coming to trust, didn't bring up any painful memories. It felt good, it felt wonderful, and she wanted more. Pressing herself into his arms, she kissed him back.

Moments later though, she pulled away panting – a look of fear on her face. This was no time to be swept away by passion! Tevo looked at her with a hurt expression, not understanding what was going on. "Are you all right?" he asked worriedly.

"I... I've vowed to remain a virgin for life," she offered by way of explanation. Now he looked not only hurt but disappointed.

"Forever?" he asked disbelievingly. Didn't all women want to marry, some day? Anita nodded, eyes downcast. "But, Anita... I love you," Tevo admitted. Leila nearly burst into tears. How could she treat this sweet, honest boy so unfairly?

She drew herself up to her full height, and said "Tevo, I haven't been completely truthful with you. There are some things you need to know."

"The god's quest? The robbery? Were those lies, then?" he asked, pain showing in his dark eyes.

"Oh, no! Those were the truth," Leila assured him, leaning up to kiss him gently on the cheek. "But for starters, my name is not Anita. Or Rosa, or Halina, or Gerde for that matter. It's Leila. My surname would be Sampson, but I refuse to take that name. For now, it's just Leila."

The kiss had taken away some of Tevo's concerns, and he held out a hand. "Pleased to meet you, Leila," he said politely. "I'm Tevodar Karmarzin, born and raised in Buda. Might I ask where *you* come from?" She solemnly shook his hand, then gestured for him to sit on the bed while she took the chair beside it.

"It all started in Marsine a little over sixteen years ago," she began.

Though Gerde and Rolf were anxious to get on their way to Parat and the hoped-for divine cure for Rolf's illness, this morning they slept in a little. They breakfasted amidst quite a few of the inn's patrons, then set about getting ready to leave and were back on the main road, heading northeast, at an hour when traffic was heavy and getting heavier.

Leila had revealed everything to Tevo last night, before slipping over to her own room to sleep: her mother's teenage tragedy, her early years in the whorehouse, life as a street urchin, the Night Guild. And that was just the first thirteen years of it, before the incident that had sent her on the run. No wonder she'd sworn off sex, Tevo realized. But despite this blow to his hopes for their future together, it only made him love her more.

The biggest revelation, and the one he'd had the hardest time digesting, was that he'd been riding atop five thousand florins' worth of art treasures that were actively being sought by an army of investigators hired by the Mad Count of Oester. It wasn't so much that she hadn't trusted him with the information – in her position, he wasn't sure *he* would have trusted him with the information. But Tevo now felt as though, as he reclined with eyes bandaged on the worn palette in the back of the cart, he were sitting on one of those explosive devices road engineers used for cutting their way through mountains.

They'd thought it best to begin the day in the midst of heavy road traffic, with the injured Rolf lying in a daze on the pallet and brave Gerde driving the cart. At the next opportunity, they would pull up the cart's false floor and hide away a portion of the loot from Bohdan's for safekeeping. Each of them now had fifty florins in gold and silver hidden about their persons, which should be far more than enough to see them comfortably to Parat.

The old fence's safe had yielded an astonishing bonanza, more than four hundred florins in addition to the banknotes; yet that was only the least part of the treasures he'd had in that safe and elsewhere around the storeroom. At his age, Bohdan could have retired to a country villa and never worked a day in his life on what he'd amassed. It made the two young people wonder what motivated him to continue in his dangerous, frustrating, and illegal business.

Leila thought, hoped anyway, that Bohdan would suspect the thieves to have been some of his customers – local thieves who made use of his services and knew he had a lot of cash on hand. One of them might well have managed to watch him opening the safe from beyond the counter in the front of the shop… perhaps with a pair of opera glasses?

He had never seen Leila at all and had caught only a dim silhouette view of Tevo as he'd crouched trying to get the front door open. It wouldn't occur to him to look for the thieves among the constant flow of travelers passing through the city. And indeed, as they set out, she saw no signs of any obvious watchers. Leila was very anxious not to add another wealthy, powerful enemy to the list of those who already wanted her hide, and she heaved a sigh of relief as their cart rolled along the highway – Kohl receding in the distance. She felt relieved, too, that she had finally told Tevo everything. Now she truly had an intimate friend, someone she could share everything with. If only being with him didn't provoke such uncomfortable longings!

Chapter 60

Now that they had coin to spare, it would have been nice if Gerde and Rolf could have enjoyed it more. Fancier accommodations, lavish meals, perhaps some better looking, more comfortable clothing than the rough homespun garments the two farm youngsters wore every day – having no others to change into.

But any sign that the pair had more money than they ought to would raise suspicion; so nearly all of the money in their pockets stayed there. At least there was no further need to camp out, as towns and cities in this part of the Dominion were spaced to allow an easy day's travel along the highway (even in a slow farm cart) between them.

Yeil was making himself scarcer and scarcer, to the point where Leila wondered if he might have abandoned them. He'd expressed himself in no uncertain terms about the unwisdom of her recruiting Tevo to the cause, and she had told him to stuff it; so now they were at an impasse. But every time they thought they'd seen the last of the black bird, there he would be launching himself from atop the inn's roof as they set off in the morning.

"I think he's supposed to be my minder more than my assistant," Leila admitted as she and Tevo were sitting together on the driver's bench. There was no other traffic on this stretch of the highway, and they were able to talk.

"But Betsalel is inside you, you said? Why would he need Yeil to keep an eye on you?"

"I'm not sure," she replied, troubled. "If I concentrate, look inside, I can feel him there. And I believe he knows my mind. But I don't think he can see out of my eyes, so he doesn't necessarily know what's going on around me. The bird must have some way of keeping in touch, but I don't know how that works."

Their next stop, Nowa, was the first point inside the borders of the original kingdom of Gaspar. For hundreds of years, blessed by a dynasty of exceptional rulers, that kingdom had grown larger and larger by absorbing its neighbors until no rival on their part of the continent could stand against them. And the peace this empire had created had certainly been good for the entire populace of the Dominion.

Most people were proud to be counted as citizens of the Dominion, pleased to be able to pursue their lives without the turmoil and destruction of war that had plagued their ancestors. All parts of the Dominion must hold to the constitution, a body of laws that had been built up over the centuries by Imperial decrees ratified by the Grand Assembly – or in some cases, initiated by that body. But local rule in the counties allowed for cultural differences and kept people from thinking they were being oppressed by a bunch of foreigners in far-off Parat.

Any country will have its malcontents, and certainly both women and the poor had less freedom and prosperity than they might have wanted. But overall the Dominion had proven to be a good thing. It had lasted for more than a thousand years, after all.

After Nowa traffic on the highways got heavier, and Gerde and Rolf found themselves unable to cover as many miles in a day. Their farm cart was slow, but enormous hay wains were slower – and hard to pass, with a constant stream of vehicles moving in both directions.

Ostrow, Kalze, Lenga, and Skiern passed by without incident. In each town, Gerde searched the used booksellers' shops for more reading material. This was theoretically so she could read to her poor, blind brother – but the books provided entertainment for both of them in the long evenings after supper. Tevo and Leila were both bored, wishing they could be enjoying the convivial atmosphere in the common room but knowing they needed to stay out of sight. They almost considered sneaking out at night to perform a few robberies, just for fun. But they successfully resisted the temptation.

Gerde selected a somewhat nicer inn for their night's stay in Prusz, the last stop before reaching Parat. They expected to be there by early afternoon tomorrow, if they continued at their current pace; and it was time to plan what they were going to do when they got there. The three-story wooden building, painted white and decorated with colorful flower motifs in the Gaspari style, looked nearly new or at least recently refurbished.

After going around to the stable yard and arranging for Nimble to be cared for and their cart with its pallet and blankets parked indoors out of the rain, Gerde led her blind brother to the side door. In this inn, the stable yard could be reached from the common room as well as from the kitchen. Inside there was the usual long bar, and a room full of chairs, tables, and benches. Not one but two large stone fireplaces heated the place in winter, but the hearths were now cold. Summer was coming, and the weather was heating up.

Along the wall between this side door and the inn's main entrance was a sort of concierge desk. This was manned from six in the morning until midnight, when the outside doors were barred, and inn guests could not only check in but also go there if they needed additional blankets, pillows, or towels. Each floor of the inn featured two bathrooms with hot and cold running water, an astonishing luxury, and Leila was looking forward to taking a long soak.

There was a youngish man at the desk when they came in, at around five in the evening, and he smiled at Leila with a hint of question in his eyes. What was up with the young man wearing bandages around his head and eyes? "Good afternoon," Gerde said politely, "I'd like two small rooms for my brother and me, please. And I need them to be next to each other so I can go to him if he wakes in the night." The concierge looked puzzled, and Gerde leaned across the counter and whispered, "Rolf injured his head falling from a horse. He has been struck blind, and is confused in his mind as well. Sometimes he wakes up and I need to come and comfort him."

Well, that was a new one, thought the concierge. These two looked like brother and sister, right enough, and he couldn't imagine they'd go to so much trouble if what she really wanted was to sneak across the hall and hop into bed with her lover. They could just as easily have requested a double bed and registered as man and wife – it wasn't as if the inn required copies of one's marriage certificate.

"I'm sorry for your trouble," the young man murmured sympathetically. "I suppose you're going to Parat to pray for his recovery, then?" Gerde smiled at him so sweetly his heart nearly skipped a beat. A little dusky, maybe – probably Nima or maybe Spanic ancestry – but those eyes!

"We've travelled from our family's farm for just that purpose," the girl assured him.

After consulting the register book the concierge's face fell slightly, and Gerde looked at him with speculation. "I'm sorry, panienka," he said, using the Old Gaspari term for "young woman," "but we have no single rooms free. At least none that are close together. The inn is very nearly full at this time." Gerde's face fell.

"Oh!" she said softly, "I've already had your stableman unhitch our cart. What shall I do?"

"If you wouldn't mind sharing a room with your brother, I have a medium size room with two single beds in it. It's actually quite comfortable, and no more expensive than two single rooms would be. Do you think that might work for you?" It tore his heart to see the sweet young thing, who couldn't have been much above seventeen, in such distress.

Gerde looked at him in consternation, then appeared to have realized something and her smile returned. "Oh, of course that will be all right. Under ordinary circumstances I would never consider getting into my nightdress in front of Rolf – but until divine Lucia answers my prayers, that's not going to be a problem – is it? I'll take that room, thank you!"

After brother and sister had eaten supper in the inn's common room (a choice of half a dozen entrees on the menu, including some Gaspari specialties neither of them had tasted before!) Gerde helped her poor blind brother up the stairs to their room and they went inside. They had much to discuss.

"What's next?" Tevo asked, broaching the subject that had been on both of their minds. "Do Rolf and Gerde continue to Parat and pray to Lucia to help them free the rival she crushed two hundred years ago?" Leila grimaced at the idea. She'd been chewing the problem over in her mind during spare moments throughout their journey, and she still had not come up with a workable plan to find and free Betsalel's stolen idol. And even assuming they were able to do this, then what? Having the Shadow God walking free in Parat wasn't going to bring back the worshipers who'd been slaughtered centuries before. She believed, and Tevo did; but while two might enable him to manifest, it wouldn't be enough for him to recover his former strength.

"I hate to say it," Leila replied, "but I think it's time we asked for some advice." She went to the window, which overlooked the stable yard, and saw no one stirring. Likely the stable hands were in the kitchen having their supper. Throwing open the window, Leila looked up toward the building's roof and called "Yeil! Come!" In case anyone did spy them, she hoped they would assume the raven was a pet – like the one she'd seen in Marsine all those years ago.

Almost immediately there was a fluttering of dark wings and Yeil came down and landed on the sill. "About time!" he croaked. "I was beginning to think it would never occur to you to ask for my help." Leila stepped back, and the bird hopped inside and perched on the nightstand beside Tevo's bed. She closed the window, then sat beside Tevo on her own bed – both of them facing the raven.

"Sorry we didn't consult with you sooner," Leila said apologetically, though it irked her to kiss up to her annoying tag-along, "but you already said that finances were up to me, and finances were our main concern until recently. But now that we're almost to Parat, we need some instructions. What does Betsalel expect us to do, besides find and free his idol? Are you able to communicate with him?"

The bird bobbed his head, fixing her with a bright eye. "Similarly to you, I am linked with our master," he attempted to explain. "But I have no physical conduit embedded within my body, as you do. Rather, I carry a piece of our master's mind. Through my eyes he can see what I see. And if I concentrate, I can speak with him silently."

Yeil then bowed his head and closed his eyes, as if he were demonstrating the technique. The two young thieves sat watching him spellbound. The bird's recent speech had been less sarcastic than anything either of them had heard from him before. Was he about to prove his worth?

After a couple of minutes the raven opened his eyes and spoke again. "You need to consult with the High Archon," he said. The High Archon! Leila had had little enough to do with the Dominion's established religion in her life, but her readings in history had taught her the basics of its structure.

Throughout the Dominion, at least, if not perhaps in Palambo or the realms of the Hando, there were temples of the Seven (formerly Eight) operated by a hierarchical structure of acolytes, novices, priests or priestesses, and arch-priests or arch-priestesses. Progression through these ranks was determined by consensus within the church's ruling members. But the High Archon, head of Great Temple of the Seven in Parat, ruled over them all – every church official, every temple whether of the Seven or of the mysteries pertaining to a particular member of the pantheon. And the High Archon was elected not by the men and women of the church, but by the gods and goddesses themselves.

How was she supposed to get in to see *him*? The current High Archon, she knew, was Gabriel Sforza – a man who had served in the post since before Leila's mother had been born. High Archons, by definition having the favor of the gods, tended to outlive ordinary mortals. "What am I supposed to do, assuming I can arrange an audience?" she asked the bird.

"Enlist his aid, of course," Yeil said, reverting to the dash of sarcasm with which he usually salted his remarks. "I'm sure if you ask nicely, he'll be happy to listen to the story of how our master got a bad rap. We need to prepare the way for his return to power, so we might as well start at the top."

Ignoring the snarkiness, Leila was pensive. After a few moments she asked, "Do you think it possible that the other gods, the six remaining in power besides Lucia, might support our master's return?" All of them were avoiding mentioning Betsalel by name, for fear of being overheard.

The bird went silent again for another minute, then replied "There's a possibility. Our master is unable to communicate with his siblings directly, but perhaps through the High Archon they could be contacted and reasoned with. They should all fear Lucia after what she did, and she is now the most powerful of them by far. But if they band together, they can defeat her or at least hold her back and prevent her from doing any more damage to the Balance. And Dionos, in particular, is in danger of being her next target if she decides to seek still more dominance."

319

He had a point, Leila realized. Dionos had been cast as the god in charge of lechery, debauchery, and drunkenness, popular enough with young men but frowned upon by most solid citizens. It wouldn't be hard for Lucia to paint him as a disgraceful bad influence whose worship should be rooted out for the good of society, and Leila could easily imagine many of the people she'd met in her life lining up with axes to begin the task. By his very nature, Dionos was not a god who drew worshipers ready to lay down their lives in his defense.

Leila now had some ideas, but she needed to work out the details. And as Yeil was not going to be much use with those, she could let him get back to whatever he'd been doing. "Thank you, Yeil. Tevo and I need to discuss our plans now, but we'll consult you again after we've figured out the details." She walked over to the window again and pointedly opened it.

The raven glared at her with his beady eyes, then hopped to the sill. "Yeah, bring me in as a conduit to your god, then kick me out again. Let me know what's going to happen next, before you plunge us into any more disasters." With that he took to the air. Disasters? As if! Without Tevo, Leila would have had to endure that godawful old lady disguise for another week, and would have been forced to work alone to replenish their coffers. Not that she couldn't have done it by herself, she admitted, thanks to her Shadow power – but working with a partner, one she liked and trusted, was so much more… satisfactory.

Chapter 61

In the morning Gerde and Rolf checked out of the inn, having caught a decent night's sleep after hours spent in consultation. The girl shook up the reins and the two, with their creaking farm cart, set off in the direction of the main road to Parat.

Soon after, Leila turned the cart up an alley and began driving Nimble in the opposite direction, heading toward the seamier side of Prusz – along the riverfront. The Vizha, the same river that flowed through Kohl and also through Parat before winding back toward the northwest and eventually spilling into the ice-laden Northern Ocean, ran wide here and made Prusz a thriving seaport.

They stopped at a shop that catered to river traders, and Tevo (having removed the bandage from his head as soon as they were out of sight of the inn) went inside. He returned fifteen minutes later clad as a sailor, and carrying a large canvas sea bag. Then they wandered the alleyways of the port district until they found one that dead-ended.

While Leila guarded the open end, Tevo pulled the pallet off of the cart and tossed it aside. He put their extra loot from the pawnshop heist in the bottom of the bag, then pried off the boards making the false floor. Next he added the several well-padded sacks of treasures from Count Oester's collections to the bag. Atop those went his pack, followed by the contents of that pack.

Kathal, evicted from her hiding place, stalked down the alley to explore the far end of it for rats – while Nimble stood patiently in the traces. Now sailor Tevo took guard duty while Leila, standing between the horse and the alley's end, hastily changed out of her homespun garments and into something a little more low-cut, a little lacier. She'd been accumulating quite an assortment of clothing as her journey went on, wanting to have plenty of costume choices as new disguises became necessary. Oh, if only Count Wilhelm hadn't gotten onto her theft so damn quickly! Life would be infinitely easier if she didn't always have to hide.

Some work with mirror and makeup, and in minutes sailor Tevo was joined by a painted floozy, one of many who worked the riverfront area. She was dressed somewhat conservatively for one of her profession, but on the other hand it wasn't yet ten in the morning. Kathal had been told to stay and guard, and anyone thinking to make off with the horse and cart might well find himself clawed to pieces – or trampled by the horse, for that matter. Leila trusted Nimble not to let anyone he did not know lead him away.

The pair came out of the alley and strolled down the block, arms around each other and laughing uproariously as though they'd had brandy for breakfast. They staggered into one of the several hotels (unlike inns, these offered rooms but served no food and had no common room for guests to relax in) along the block that catered to sailors and the women who accompanied them.

There was an office off to one side of the dingy corridor, with a small window looking out on it. The man behind the window was middle-aged, scrawny, and had a red bulbous nose that suggested he, too, might often have brandy for breakfast. He also had some kind of a scrofulous skin condition creeping over his bald scalp and down his cheeks. "Just the hour, then?" he grated, hardly bothering to look up from the pulp novel he'd been reading. At least he could read!

Leila squeezed Tevo's waist and looked up into his eyes flirtatiously. The sailor boy grinned back at her with the glow of anticipation. "The whole night!" he declared, "Maybe two, we'll see. I've got until Andday before I have to be back on board..." Leila tittered, thrilled that her new-found friend was so fond of her company.

"That'll be three shillings for the night," the man said, "in advance. You want to stay another night, you come pay me tomorrow." Tevo handed over the coins, and the man pushed a rusty-looking key across the counter. "Two-fifteen," he said, gesturing with a thumb toward the staircase at the end of the hall. "Turn left at the top of the stairs, fifth door on your left." He went back to what he'd been reading.

The laughing, amorous couple made their way up the stairs, sobering somewhat as they reached the second floor landing and made their way to their accommodations. The room had a double bed, a washstand, and a chair in it, but that was all. Clearly, the management did not expect long-term customers. Leila kissed Tevo on the cheek. "That wasn't half bad!" she congratulated him. "I think with a little practice we'll make a con artist out of you yet."

He smiled his appreciation and began unpacking the sea bag, spreading its contents on the bed. Leila began peeling off her lacy dress and getting into her burglar gear. With her Shadow power, she could just as easily have dressed up like one of the colorful mummers who traveled from place to place putting on shows; but she liked the "night work" costume for its comfort and ease of movement. Next she removed the makeup she'd hastily smeared on, using the basin to wash her face and hands.

Tevo handed the emptied sea bag to Leila, and she put more clothing into it – this time the sort of outfit that might be worn by a maidservant. Then she rolled it up into a manageable bundle and attached it to one of the clips on her belt with a length of rope. "Back soon," she promised, before vanishing from sight and slipping out the window. It looked out over an alley at the back.

Climbing to the ground, the invisible girl made her way silently back to where they'd left the horse and cart. Nobody had apparently disturbed them in the few minutes they'd been gone. Kathal scented her and came prowling over, rubbing against her legs just as if she'd been something more than a nebulous pool of shadow in the air.

Still enshadowed, Leila changed from her night gear to the maid costume. She put the burglar outfit into the bottom of the bag. Then she held it open. "Into the bag, Kathal," she beckoned. The cat gave her a questioning look but obediently crawled into the bag. The "maid," leaving the top of the bag open, laid it carefully into the bottom of the cart.

With some difficulty Leila got the cart back out of the alley and Nimble on the way again, this time turning uphill away from the riverfront. Before long they intersected the main highway and turned down it heading southwest, looking for the livery stable she'd noticed on their way into town yesterday. It should be on the right... there it was!

A teenage boy was dumping a cartload of manure in a corner of the yard as Leila pulled in. He downed his pitchfork, dusting his hands on his overalls, and came over to her – giving Nimble a pat on the neck as he came up. "Can I help you, panienka?" he asked, surreptitiously giving her the once-over. In her long medium-brown wig, she looked a little older. And her maid's outfit put her in his economic class.

She gave him a slight, tense smile. So much work to do, so little time! "My master will be staying in Prusz this week conducting business," she told him, "and I'm to find stabling for the horse and storage for the cart until his return cargo is ready to haul."

"One week?" he asked. She nodded. "Does the cart need to be out of the weather, or can we just park it in the yard?" he asked, gesturing around at the generous walled space.

The maid looked blank. This had not been covered by her instructions, but the cart was empty after all. "In the yard will be fine," she said, "but the horse is to have plenty of hay and grain and water. And it would be good if he could be out in the paddock for a few hours every day instead of locked up in a stall the whole time."

"No problem," the boy said. "That's eight shillings, or you can give me a deposit of four and pay the rest when you come back."

She smiled at him, and handed him the full eight. "Thanks," she said. "Sorry, but I'm in a hurry. The man can't do a thing for himself! See you in a week," she added, and hefting the sack (which looked a lot like a sailor's sea bag, and was curiously lumpy) she immediately left the yard and set off on foot.

"Wait!" the boy called, "I didn't get your name!" but she was already gone. Oh well, he thought, a pretty girl like that should be easy enough to remember. And she already paid for the full week. He was the only employee on duty at the moment, so he pocketed the eight shillings and set about unhitching the horse.

Leila turned invisible again, as soon as she had rounded the corner leaving the yard and seen no one nearby on the street. On the way here from the riverfront she'd taken note of several shops, and she visited them during the return trip on foot. Bless her, Kathal gave scarcely a mew of protest as she was joined in the invisible bag by a bolt of thin black fabric, several packets of black dye, a scimitar with a jeweled hilt and scabbard (probably never intended to be used as a weapon) and a quantity of garish-looking costume jewelry plated in gold and studded with cut-glass gems.

Maintaining her invisibility, loaded down with stolen items and a cat who was on the verge of losing her patience, Leila tiptoed into the transient hotel and made her way up the stairs. The same man sat at the registration desk, leaning back on his stool and engrossed in his book.

A slight tapping at the door alerted Tevo, and he had it open in a shot. Leila dispelled her shadows and hurried to get Kathal out of the bag. "Oh, poor kitty!" she exclaimed, showering the cat with affection and apologies. "You were so good, you were mama's little angel!" Tevo looked at her askance.

Accepting her mistress' apology, Kathal strolled around the room with her tail up, sniffing at everything before hopping onto the bed and curling up to go to sleep. "Did everything go alright?" Tevo asked. The fact that she, the cat, and the stuff in the bag had all arrived safely would seem to suggest so, but he was feeling anxious.

"Fine," Leila said briskly. "I left Nimble and the cart at that stable we noticed on the main highway as we were coming in. It shouldn't be any problem getting him away from there when we're ready to leave, except maybe for the noise." Tevo nodded. "I guess we'd better do me first," he said reluctantly, "but how about we eat something first?"

They'd enjoyed a couple of fine, hot meals at last night's inn, but it would be back to trail rations for another day or two – depending on how soon they could book passage on one of the boats plying the passenger trade along the Vizha. Not all of them were set up to take horses, after all. Why pay to transport your horse on the water, when there was a perfectly good road?

After eating some of their provisions and giving some to Kathal as well, they were ready to begin on their new set of disguises. These should last them until they had completed their quest, they hoped. "All right, strip," Leila demanded, and Tevo cringed. While they had established a new relationship when she had confessed all her secrets to him, that had not done away with the problem that she had vowed to remain a virgin – while he was very eager to remove himself from that status.

"Oh, get over it, Tevo!" Leila said with exasperation. "I just need you in your drawers so I can apply the dye, and there's nothing sexual about it." "But you have such an effect on me!" he moaned, giving her a lopsided grin that quite nearly stole her heart. She shoved him on the shoulder. "Go on, strip. Where's your razor?"

Though shaving was not something he needed to do all that often, Tevo did own a razor and shaving brush. They were among his most prized personal possessions, and he'd taken them with him when he left his home in Buda behind. While he removed his sailor's garb, and sat on the bed in his linen underdrawers, Leila arrayed her scissors, the razor, and the brush and soap on the nightstand beside the bed.

Tevo's shoulder-length dark brown hair was the first to go, cut short with the scissors. Then Leila applied a foam of shaving soap to his head and began carefully taking it down to the scalp. He was quite a bit paler where the hair had been removed, a curious contrast with the dye-darkened skin of his face and neck.

Next, she had a very artistic job of brushwork to do, blending the paler skin of his denuded scalp with the darker skin of head and neck, taking the rest of his skin a shade or two darker until he was the color of polished bloodwood. With his dark eyes and narrow nose, he resembled the desert people of eastern Palambo. It would do.

Leila had already been aware of Tevo's wiry strength, but it was a surprise to her to see him stripped to his underclothes. His skin was smooth and fairly pale except where she'd dyed it or it had been exposed to the sun – laid over nicely defined muscles that rippled when he moved. Mmm.

She planned for both of them to be covered from head to toe when they started out, but they might also need to appear with considerably less clothing later on – and all exposed skin must be the right color. With a black father and a blonde mother, Leila was not as dark as a Palamban either; so she would need a dye job too. But Tevo would be meeting the public first, and there would surely be hours at least if not days between finding transport and sailing.

Having Tevo stand now that she was finished with his head and shoulders, Leila began carefully applying the dark-brown skin dye, mixed with oil, to his back down to the waist. He stood there patiently, thinking how good it felt for her to be touching, stroking him. Motherless for so many years and never having had a woman, there'd been very little physical contact with anyone in a long time. And she was right, it wasn't sexual – it just felt good.

Then Leila did the arms and hands, down his ribs and up into his armpits, which provoked whoops of mirth. "Stop squirming! Do you want to end up with stripes?"

"I can't help it!" he choked, twitching away from her. "I'm ticklish." At last she was ready to start on his front, and Tevo suddenly realized that maybe, just maybe, the activity was a teeny, tiny bit sexual after all. At least his dick seemed to think so.

Bumping into his "tent pole" as she was trying to apply the dye to his chest area, Leila glanced down. "Hello," she said, like a cook chiding a puppy who was underfoot in the kitchen, "who invited *you* to this party?" She gave it a flick with her forefinger, and Tevo managed to avoid soiling his drawers. Barely.

She pierced his haunted dark eyes with her deep green gaze, a friendly smile on her face. "Hang in there, we're almost done." Gradually, Tevo's excitement receded. But oh, he wanted her so badly! In another few minutes Tevo was a deep brown everywhere that wasn't covered by his drawers, and for an inch or two beneath them as well. The dye had soaked into his skin with the oil and would soon be drying. She rubbed it in a little more with a scrap of cloth, then took up the bolt of black fabric that was lying on the bed.

Rather than take the time to sew them garments like the *kad'r* the desert tribes were said to wear, Leila had decided to go for something more like the *siri* worn, so the book had told her, by women in one of the large south-central realms of the Hando. Those were of colorful silk, a single long length of fabric wrapped around and around to cover the body. This, of night-black cotton, would perform a similar function. And she very much doubted that anyone in this part of the Dominion would know that nobody in the vast kingdom of Palambo actually dressed this way.

Now that his skin was dry Leila had Tevo stand, one hand holding the loose end of the cloth at his shoulder, as she unwound it from the bolt and began looping it around his body. There was far more fabric than should be needed even for both of them, so she made it generous – the idea was that in this public garb the person should be covered in cloth from head to toe – only the eyes showing.

When she'd achieved the effect she was looking for Leila cut the fabric from the rest of the bolt and tucked the cut end into a fold. She used an elaborate gold-colored brooch with a large "ruby" in it to pin the cloth, helping to keep it from unraveling as Tevo walked; then further secured it with a heavy "gold" chain around his waist. The effect was rather striking, even more so once she'd affixed the jeweled scabbard of the scimitar to the chain.

"Have you ever used a sword?" Leila asked. While there'd been no wide-scale war in a millennium and weapons research in the Dominion had ground to a standstill, armed conflict was something that continued to happen and there and many people – bandits, strong-arm robbers, castle guards, constables – were trained in the use of swords, bows, crossbows, and other traditional weapons.

Tevo lifted a hand, exposing his arm to slightly above the wrist, and pulled down on the section of cloth that was covering his mouth and nose. He could still breathe with it in place, but it was better to remove it for conversing. Grinning, he said "Never touched one. I thought I was pretty good with daggers, until I met you."

She grinned back. "Well," she said, "it's only for show anyhow. I doubt blood of any kind has ever stained that gleaming blade. But let's see you draw it." Tevo glanced down to his left hip, where the hilt of the weapon was riding a little above the belt line. He grasped it and drew it out, finding that the curve of the sword (the blade of which was only a couple of feet long) made drawing it more awkward than he'd expected.

He brandished the weapon in his right hand, turning it to the light. It glinted menacingly. Leila, cloaked in shadows, had stolen it from beneath a pawnshop counter while the proprietor was in the back visiting the privy. He'd locked the front door before taking his break, and hadn't realized he'd locked someone in with him.

Tevo's eyes widened. "Sure looks sharp to me," he remarked.

"Well, try not to cut yourself," she replied. "Practice doing that a few times while I get a few things together." The boy repeated the maneuver until it was beginning to seem familiar and comfortable, though the idea of actually using the sword on someone seemed absurd.

Leila turned back, and put a broad gold-toned bracelet engraved with interesting designs onto his right wrist. It contrasted nicely with his deep brown skin. Ah, that was better! "I can't foresee any situation where your actually pulling the weapon and using it will bring a good outcome," she said, "because you'll only have to do that if you're surrounded by armed men and they'll probably just shoot you down with crossbows or something. But let me see you glare menacingly and just put your hand on the hilt as if you were tempted to use the scimitar."

Her student did as instructed. "Not bad at all!" Leila crowed. "Just one more thing…" She reached for her makeup kit. "Close your eyes for a moment. That's good, all right, open them, hold still…" She applied some kohl to his lids. The contrast against his now-dark skin wasn't that great, but it made his dark eyes seem bigger and more noticeable. The effect was to make the cute young thief look slightly menacing and devilishly handsome, and Leila bit her lip.

"Perfect!" she said. "Now remember, you are very arrogant. While you are just a servant, you regard all foreigners as essentially inferior. You are traveling in their land, and you are trying to be polite; but you are very touchy about your dignity and quick to take offense. So if anybody tries to give you any shit, you glare menacingly and just reach across to touch the hilt as if you were only *considering* drawing the weapon. Actually drawing it should be a last resort. Understand?"

"Yes, mistress," Tevo said, that boyish grin seeming totally out of character in his current guise.

"Cut it out," she commanded shortly. "All right, let's hear your line." Despite his lack of experience in con games, Tevo had a good memory. After they'd worked out their plans last night, they'd run over what he was to say and he had not forgotten it.

Tevo pulled the swath of black cloth up again, so that it hid his mouth but didn't interfere with his breathing or muffle his speech. He drew himself up to his full height, which could have been more impressive… but hey. In a passable Palamban accent he said, "Greetings honorable sir. I am Ademji, servant and acolyte to the

Palamban high priestess Laleihala. We are traveling to Parat to give homage to the High Archon, and our carriage has become disabled. So in the interests of speed, we require river passage for ourselves and our sacred animals to the Gaspari capital. Can you assist us?"

"That was great, Tevo!" Leila crowed, suitably impressed. Just a few days before she'd been convinced this boy would be hopeless in a con, but he was starting to show some real talent. Maybe after all this Shadow God business was over they could roam the continent together, bilking fortunes from the rich and stupid. Maybe she'd even rethink that "vow of chastity" thing.

"They're certainly going to ask you about the sacred beasts," she said, "so what do you reply? "The sacred color of our order is black," Tevo said in his Palamban accent. It wouldn't be likely to stand muster with anyone who'd been to a place frequented by Palambans, but here they were hundreds of miles from the Center Sea.

The menacing figure swathed in black continued, "With us on this journey are a black leopard cat, rarest of the breed, and a black *djimdjim* bird, native to the jungles of Palambo and possessed of the power of human speech. It resembles a bird I believe you Gaspari call a 'raven.' Also of course we must transport our horse, that poor beast which pulled us all the way here from the shores of the Center Sea after our ship docked in Jena. Our carriage has broken both a wheel and an axle, and repairs will take days. But we are anxious to go forth and meet with your High Archon after traveling these many miles for that purpose."

Leila's grin nearly split her face in two. "Perfect!" she declared. "You are going to *nail* this!" She threw her arms around his neck and gave him an enthusiastic kiss through the cloth. Tevo was pleased, but wished his lips had been exposed. The outburst had woken Kathal from her post-lunch nap, and Leila told her "Stay and guard."

Slipping the room key into her pocket, Leila went invisible and escorted Ademji down the stairs and out the front door of the hotel – her contact with him rendering him as invisible as she was. It was now getting on to mid-afternoon, and there was a fair amount of traffic along the street. Careful not to bump into pedestrians, she took her accomplice to the dead-end alley where they'd stopped this morning – or was it a month ago?

When no one was passing the alley mouth Leila released her grip and suddenly Ademji was standing there. He pretended to adjust himself after urinating, careful not to disturb the complicated folds of his "garment." "Go knock 'em dead, kiddo," Leila murmured. "You've got the easy job. I still have to go dye a cat."

Chapter 62

They boarded the Amalie at eight in the morning of the following day. This far from the sea tides were not an issue, but the boat had had to wait for cargo to be delivered. Finding a boat willing to take the two Palamban visitors and their animal companions had proven harder than Leila had hoped, but Ademji had done a sterling job.

Leila had both hugged and kissed him when Tevo had returned a couple of hours after he'd departed. He had delivered the same basic script, with some well-executed ad-libs when necessary, to nearly a dozen boat captains or their underlings before finding one willing to take his gold.

Considering that had their theoretical carriage been in working order they could all have been in Parat by highway in less than six hours, the fare had seemed steep. But the river journey took rather longer. The plain on which both Prusz and Parat had both arisen was broad, and the river running through it – also broad – was slow and winding.

The high priestess Laleihala, swathed in black cloth like her acolyte and also adorned with gleaming gold jewelry well-studded with gems, spent much of her time in contemplation within her cabin. Most of the Amalie's passengers, especially the few who had signed on at Prusz, chose to make the trip standing or sitting on deck. But the high priestess was not as these commoners.

This was Leila's first trip on water, and while it was not the Center Sea, it was definitely not as smooth or as predictable as traveling over land. She experienced no ill effects from motion sickness, but regretted the need to remain closeted in her cabin with the cat and the bird. Nimble, now as black as Yeil from poll to fetlock, was hitched to a post at the rear of the boat with food and water – and a pan to catch his droppings. The farm cart had been left behind.

The raven, of course, had a few choice words. After being requested to ride on Laleihala's shoulder and spout random phrases in Palamban – and not to shit down her back, thank you very much – he had been outraged. "What do you take me for, a talking parrot?"

he demanded. "And I'm accustomed to shitting where and when I please!"

"You're a highly intelligent, sentient being," Leila had said soothingly, as their party was preparing to go to the docks. "Surely you have some control over your bodily functions?" The bird considered for a moment, as if plumbing his inner depths for a response.

Finally he came up with, "*He* shits wherever he wants," indicating Nimble. The horse had undergone his third color change in less than three weeks, but he was maintaining both his cheer and his dignity.

"He's smart," Leila admitted, "but he's still an animal. You're a person." While Yeil thought that being put in the "person" category was a good thing, he still had objections.

"Look," he said in exasperation, "I'm not built the same as you. I was hatched from an egg, and I've only got one orifice down there. I just don't have the physical control you have, all right? Give me a break!" She hadn't really considered that there were major anatomical differences between birds and mammals.

"Do you have any warning when you need to defecate?" she asked curiously.

"There's a sort of a warm, wet sensation just before," Yeil admitted. "But then two seconds later it's just coming out. I don't really have any control over it."

"Tell you what, then," Leila said firmly, "While you're riding on my shoulder, if you feel that sensation you fly off and crap someplace else. On the heads of my enemies, would be good. But you only have to ride on my shoulder when we're out in public doing the high priestess bit, all right?"

"All right," the raven agreed resignedly.

The "spouting random phrases in Palamban" had been another issue. Leila had wanted the raven to be a marvel, a sign of her mysterious high priestess powers, but didn't want people to realize he was as sentient as they were. "Where did you learn to speak Gasparto?" she asked, and Yeil replied, "It was a gift of our master." "And our master's worshipers in Palambo, at least those he had before a couple of centuries ago, spoke Palamban and he was able to communicate with them. So, just ask him to gift you with Palamban. It might come in handy if – gods forfend – we should run into anybody who's actually familiar with the language."

Yeil had communed again with their master, and now he had as full a grasp of the principal Palamban language as he did of the one spoken throughout the Gaspari Dominion. Not that he was happy about it. Leila suspected that the phrases he was spouting as he rode her shoulder probably meant something like "Somebody save me from this obnoxious little bitch" or "I'll shit wherever I like first chance I get." She didn't let it worry her.

And Kathal, too, was not a happy camper. She looked quite lovely in her dye job, black from head to tail with darker black spots scattered across her body. The pards' desert ancestors had a rare black morph, sometimes called a "black panther." But the trait wasn't a good evolutionary fit for the tan and sandy environment the cats lived in. And it seemed to have been bred completely out of their domesticated descendants. Yet here, stalking beside Leila with a look of resentment in her golden eyes, was the very rare "black leopard cat" itself.

Leila was concerned about Kathal cleaning herself while wearing her disguise. The dye was not supposed to be toxic, but at the least it would stain her tongue black – and likely that effective, rasping instrument would soon be turning her back to her natural tawny color. So she'd told the cat not to lick herself. Which was like telling a horse not to graze, when grass was right there at the side of the road. It was a constant struggle, so thank the Eight their voyage would be a short one.

Ademji spent much of the voyage sitting cross-legged before the door of his mistress' cabin, or occasionally pacing about the deck. He looked suitably dark and menacing with his glittering scimitar and his black garb, and people kept out of his way. It was with great relief for everyone when the Amalie pulled into the docks at Parat, huge and sprawling capital of the Dominion, at a little past five in the afternoon. Summer was approaching, and at this latitude there were hours of daylight yet to come.

The party disembarked after the other passengers were let off, in a stately procession. The jet-black horse, its halter also adorned with shining gold and glittering gems, was led off the boat by the acolyte. After standing more or less motionless on the moving boat deck for nearly ten hours, Nimble needed no encouragement from Leila to prance and toss his head. Behind them came the aloof, mysterious figure of the black-clad Palamban high priestess, black bird on her shoulder, as the black cat strutted with tail high – bringing up the rear.

From the second-floor window of a building overlooking the docks, Cyryl Kubasz turned from the fruitless inspection of a party leaving another craft coming from upriver to the arrivals from the Amalie. He peered through his binoculars, a recent improvement on the spyglasses and opera glasses that had been around for over a century.

He'd been at this post for over a week, since being hired by the agents of Mad Count Oester. Cyryl took days, an associate took nights, and they had two more counterparts watching the main road from the southeast as well. The reward should they manage to capture the Estares girl was huge, and in the meantime Cyryl and his fellow thief-takers were being paid well for their hours of patient vigilance.

But the tedium was beginning to get to him. Cyryl was a man of action, skilled with blade and bow, and to sit on his ass twelve hours at a time for day after day, breaking only for food and drink and the occasional trip to the privy, was stultifying. At least he had it better than Janosz, on the night shift. There was enough traffic on the river even at night that a watch must be kept, but at least in the daytime there was always something moving, something to look at. Though not what he was *hoping* to look at, so far.

Nothing but the usual lot of mixed travelers, nothing matching the pattern he was looking for. Cyryl set the binoculars down and rubbed his eyes. As he was squirming in his seat, stretching and cracking his back, he spotted the last of the travelers coming down the gangplank from the river transport Amalie. They were unusual enough to make him pick up the binoculars again and peer through them in astonishment.

What a remarkable group! Certainly not the dark girl with the heavily laden chestnut horse and the golden cat he was looking for, but the newcomers were definitely enough to liven up his dull day. The black-shrouded man and woman looked to be foreigners, Palambans probably considering the dark skin. The horse the man in front was leading, prancing and fidgeting as if it couldn't wait to get ashore, was a glossy black as dark as he'd ever seen on a horse. It didn't look like one of the desert breed, too tall; but perhaps these visitors had bought it after coming to the Dominion across the Center Sea.

The smaller figure, whom Cyryl took to be a woman from her size (though she was shrouded almost head to foot in the same black wrappings as the servant leading the horse), strutted proudly with an enormous black bird on her shoulder. Remarkable! Then he saw something that sent a chill down his spine, and the hair on his head rose.

Behind the woman a large cat scampered, tall and slender. Forty pounds at least, he judged, and from its conformation it had to be a Nima pard. It was black, not golden, but the coincidence was enough to send him to his feet. Setting the binoculars down again, Cyryl ran to the stairs and hurled himself down them. "Vlad! Get up there and take over for me *now*!" he shouted to the boy who acted as his backup. He buckled on his sword belt and rushed to the door. He had to follow them before they got away!

Chapter 63

Parat was huge! Both Tevo and Leila were glad of the yards of black cloth hiding most of their faces, as it was impossible not to gawk. Yet they continued in their small, ebon procession just as if they knew where they were going. Leila had examined a map of the city, so she did have some slight idea. But being here in the midst of the late-afternoon chaos was a completely different experience from studying a piece of paper in the quiet solitude of their room.

She, too, now had a shaved head, her skin darkened slightly to a shade a little lighter than Tevo's. She had had to do her front by herself, with him guiding her as to spots that weren't smooth. Even that had been nearly enough to give the poor boy heart failure, as the high priestess Laleihala intended to show some cleavage if/when it seemed appropriate – and that meant her breasts had to match the rest of her. Oh, how men suffered because of their cocks, she thought – and it occurred to her that women, too, suffered because of men's cocks.

On the far side of the river, reached by a tall and impressive stone bridge that had been built three centuries before, was the industrial part of Parat. Businesses that generated noise or bad smells were restricted to that area, away from the residences of most of the capital's citizens. Traffic back and forth across the bridge was thick throughout daylight hours and heavy even at night, to the point where the Grand Assembly was now debating building a second one a mile further downstream.

The Temple of the Seven, foremost nexus of the gods' power on the planet, stood like a beacon partway up the hillside above the river. Seven smaller temples, scattered around the city, were each devoted to the worship of only one of the four goddesses and three remaining gods. The eighth had been utterly razed two hundred years ago and the site left bare. No one wanted to build where once the Shadow God had ruled.

At the very summit of that hill stood the Imperial Palace, like a miniature city within a city. It had extensive gardens on the grounds, open to the public, and more than two dozen individual buildings. Leila's quest on behalf of Betsalel required her to go there and somehow find his idol where it had been bricked up and locked away within the Imperial Treasure House. But first she must somehow obtain an audience with the High Archon and begin paving the way for the dark god's return. So the Temple district was her goal, the area she planned would become their base of operations. It was quite a walk.

She paced behind Nimble, the bird riding her shoulder (except for occasional brief flights to crap, if not on the heads of her enemies, at least not down the back of her black *siri*). The cat scampered at her back, and Leila wondered why they had brought the horse with them.

Caring for him here in the city was going to be a problem, and it was out of character for the high priestess Laleihala to ride astride. A palanquin carried by four burly black acolytes clad only in gold jewelry and skimpy black loincloths seemed more like her speed, she mused with a faint smile (hidden, of course, by the *siri*). But she couldn't imagine parting with Nimble. He had been with her, one of her two close companions, for more than a year. He wasn't just a possession, something to be sold off when no longer needed. So they'd have to find a way to stable him.

They had arrived at last, after climbing at a stately pace for nearly an hour, at Temple Street. The broad boulevard, paved in glistening light gray stone, ran for nearly a mile and dead-ended at the Temple of the Seven off to the left. There were many hostelries along it, serving the thousands of pilgrims who came each year to pray at the temple for favor from the gods.

Also on the street were eateries, general stores, greengrocers, butchers, and apartment buildings. No hotels of the type Tevo and Leila had spent their last night in Prusz at, that was for certain! While the planet's pantheon mostly offered no rules governing humans' sexual activities, only Dionos among the Seven actively encouraged unbridled romps. Where Dionos' personal temple sat across town, pleasure houses lined the street – or so Leila had read.

After stepping onto Temple Street the procession ground to a halt. Which way now? Any of the hotels here would probably do for their first night's stay in Parat, but they needed one that offered stabling for their horse. The buildings here were mostly three and four storeys tall, and it was difficult to tell from the front what facilities might be available behind.

As they stood trying to appear impassive while peering around, a small boy of perhaps ten, or an underfed twelve, approached Tevo. He looked like a street urchin, and Leila was immediately on her guard. When she was in his shoes, she'd have happily robbed nearly anyone if it meant food in her belly at the end of the day; and the high priestess and her party certainly looked like rich pickings draped as they were with eye-catching "gold" jewelry.

Tevo had grown up in the underworld of a city himself, and had some experience of his own with street urchins. "What is it you want, boy?" Ademji asked sharply. The ragged boy swept a low bow.

"Honored sir," he said, "I see that you and your party are visitors to our city, and I wish to offer you my services. I can guide you to wherever you need to go, guard you against sneak thieves, and provide you with much information about the history of Holy Parat."

Part of Laleihala's mystique was that she rarely spoke directly to anyone, making her wishes known to her acolyte and letting him be the spokesman when they were in public. But she couldn't resist stepping in. It would certainly be useful to have a native guide here, but how likely was it they could trust this young rapscallion?

Kohl-rimmed eyes scowling from within the dark cloth swathing her head, Laleihala stepped forward and stood before the boy, hands on hips. "You are addressing my servant, the honored acolyte Ademji, and I am the high priestess Laleihala – Mysterion of the Palamban Cult of the True Shadow." The boy's face paled beneath the dirt. "The True Shadow"? That could only mean…

He turned to flee, but Laleihala snaked out an arm and got him by the shoulder in a grip of iron. How could what appeared to be only a small woman have such strength? "Let me go!" he cried, struggling futilely. "I wasn't going to steal nothing!" She glared at him, her grip tightening. "Don't feed me to the Dark Fires!" he cried, utterly panicked now. A wet spot had appeared on the front of his trousers, and urine was running down his leg. His filthy feet were bare, hard and callused.

"Stand still," Laleihala commanded. "I intend you no harm." The boy's face was reddened, tears cutting streaks through the grime.

He snuffed hard and wiped his nose with the sleeve of his tattered shirt.

"No?" he asked hopefully. He figured she could probably have struck him dead with a thought and sent his soul off to roast in the black one's fires for an eternity, if she'd had a mind. But he was still standing here, breathing.

"What's your name, boy?" Laleihala asked gently. Leila's heart was overflowing with pity. There but for chance go I, she thought.

"M-maksim Walesa," he stammered out, "but everyone calls me Maks." She nodded, a movement barely detectable within the folds of cloth.

"Everyone?" Laleihala asked. "You are a member of a, what is it you call them here, gang of street urchins?"

He shook his head. "I know some of them, but I'm not a gang member. I'm not a street urchin, either!" Maks added in insulted tones. Leila looked him up and down. Right, *sure* you're not a street urchin, kid.

"Do you see this bird on my shoulder, Maks?" the black-clad Mysterion asked. He nodded. Hard to miss the thing, it was damn near as big a swan. "This bird," Laleihala went on, "similar in appearance to your ravens I believe, is the *djimdjim* bird of Palambo. They are usually white, but black ones like Yeil are sacred to my cult. Yeil possesses the power to see into your soul, and know if you speak truth. So do not lie to me, boy, or Yeil will pluck out your heart." The bird took his cue and, glaring menacingly at the boy with his beady little eyes, croaked *"Seti ya mjambo kistalo!"*

After this pronouncement Laleihala remained silent, until the boy couldn't stand the pressure and went on. "The urchins, see, they're all orphans. Or, some of 'em ran away from home because their da was beating on 'em or something like that. The orphanages are no good, they make you work all day and don't feed you hardly anything."

"So," the high priestess said slowly, "you're not an urchin because… ?"

"I've got my ma!" he exclaimed. "And we've even a place to live, sort of. My da's out there someplace too, I suppose, but I ain't ever met him. Things was all right for us until last year, Ma was

340

working as the housekeeper for a family in the Temple District and we had a little place to live out the back, all to ourselves like. Then the old master died and the family moved away from Parat, put the house up for sale."

Laleihala interjected, "Why didn't your mother just go look for another post? If she'd been working for that family for years, surely they would give her a reference?" She was forgetting to use her "Palamban" idioms, but the boy didn't seem to notice.

"She took sick, the same time the old master did. It was some kind of fever. They prayed to Lucia for him to get better, but he died anyway. Ma was real sick, and we didn't have no money for the temple. But she lived, in spite of that. Except she's been real weak. She's getting stronger now, and pretty soon she'll be able to look for another job. But in the meantime, we didn't have anything except what I could scrounge. We sold almost everything we had first, then I started to spend my days out looking for whatever work I could get, so Ma and I could have food."

The high priestess nodded thoughtfully. Maks was thin enough to give credence to the tale, and Leila thought it likely he'd been cowed by her bullshit with the raven into hewing to the truth. "So where have you been living, then?" Laleihala asked.

"In the same place, at home," the boy explained. "The family was shaken up by the death of the master, I think they thought Lucia owed it to them to save him. They packed up and went off to live with the missus' brother's family in Ceske."

Leila, in her disguise as the crone Halina, had passed through Ceske early in her journey. It was many miles from here by the main highway. "And the new owners didn't kick you out of the servants' quarters?" The boy grinned a little, the first cheerful expression they'd seen on his face since he was trying to con them into accepting his "services."

"There ain't no new owners!" Maks said. "At least, not yet. The family put the sale of the house and grounds into the hands of an estate agent before they left for Ceske. But he doesn't seem to be trying very hard to sell it. The house has been vacant for nearly six months now."

"Is the place run down, then?" Laleihala asked sharply. After six months vacant it would probably be damp and mildewed inside, at the least. The boy considered. He had never lived anywhere else in his life but the detached servants' quarters of this one house, and had no basis for comparison.

"It seems all right to me," he said at last. "It's no mansion, but it's sturdy and well-built and the roof doesn't leak. Maybe it's a little small, though. It was just the master and mistress and their two children, a little older than me, living there. Ma and I lived in the little cottage out back, on the far side of the garden."

Leila was now grinning brilliantly behind her *siri*, some of which must have shown in her eyes. Thank you, Betsalel, she prayed silently. Surely of all the gods of this holy city it must be he who had come to their aid. "Maks," Laleihala said somewhat sternly, "I have decided that we will hire you after all. And I must say, it is shameful how you have let yourself become so ragged and filthy. We will have to address that as soon as possible. But first, please take us to meet this estate agent."

Watching from a recess between two buildings across the street, Cyryl Kubasz wondered what he had just witnessed. He had not been able to make out what was spoken between the small figure he'd assumed was a woman and the ragged street boy, but her tone of voice had reached him and he was now sure the figure was female. Yet in that black shroud, he could tell little else about her. Her hands were the only thing visible, and they were dark brown – as were those of her companion.

The only similarities between this party and the quarry he'd been hired to find were the woman and the cat, and even they seemed wrong. Rosa Estares was known to be riding a chestnut gelding and accompanied by a tawny Nima pard, wearing the kind of tidy and conservative clothes you might expect from a daughter of the middle class.

Here was a Palamban man leading a black gelding (and geldings were the second most common sort of horse in the Dominion), a woman of indeterminate age shrouded in black cloth, with an enormous talking bird that looked like a raven perched on her shoulder. There'd been no mention of any bird in the information the

Count's agents had provided to him and his men. And he had never heard of Nima pards being any other color than tawny.

These people were seemingly from Palambo, and the ancestors of the pards came from there as well so probably there was a black species similar in size and shape to the pards, which the mysterious strangers had because it was part of their religious observance to collect black animals, or something. The fact that they'd come here to Temple Street first thing after disembarking suggested they had something to do with religion, but they certainly looked nothing like the usual run of pilgrims. When he considered what religious cult might be so fond of the color black, a little shiver ran down his spine.

Cyryl sighed. It was pretty damned unlikely that these people had anything at all to do with the thief Rosa Estares. But the Palamban man was carrying a big black sack full of something over his shoulder. Most likely their luggage, of which they'd have needed a lot traveling all the way up here from Palambo. But still, there was something about them that nagged at him and piqued his curiosity. As the ragged boy began leading them off down the street to the north, away from the Temple, the thief taker followed at a safe distance behind.

Chapter 64

Leila was jubilant. This was absolutely perfect! The Temple District estate agent, who had truthfully done nothing more toward selling the property in question than paying to have a "For Sale" sign put up months before, had been completely astonished when a party of outlandishly-dressed foreigners arrived at his office and offered him cash on the barrelhead in gold florins, if he was willing to accept some ten percent less than the asking price he'd set.

As there'd been no prior interest at all, at that (admittedly high) figure, he was delighted. After the buyers had inspected the house and grounds and concluded that there were no serious flaws, they returned from a brief sojourn in the master bedroom with the money in a sack. Astonishing!

After the coin had changed hands the agent had produced a receipt and a deed to the property. It would be up to them, he explained, to duly register the deed with the Imperial Registrar's office in the palace complex within thirty days, in order to finalize the transaction. But in the meantime the keys were theirs, and they were free to occupy the house.

There was hot and cold running water, but the boiler had been cold for a long time. Tevo got it lit, while Leila went out through the garden (where Nimble was happily cropping the overgrown grass of the lawn) to the servant's cottage to meet with Maksim's ma.

He had of course run to tell her the good news as soon as the party had come here from the agent's office. While money and paperwork had been exchanged, the boy and his mother, tears of joy in their eyes at the amazing good news, had been tidying up.

There was running water in the cottage, but only cold. There was no bathtub, either, and only a single fireplace in the tiny house's main room. Marcelina lit the fire with the small amount of firewood remaining from last winter, and put a kettle on to heat. Then she commanded her filthy son to strip. She felt ashamed that she had let him get into such a state, but she had been so sick, so weak – and he was bringing in what little they had in the way of food. Boys are often not fond of washing, and Maks was no exception.

By the time the high priestess and her acolyte went out to the
cottage to formally introduce themselves, they found a very pale,
thin, and faded-looking woman who looked fifty at least but was
probably only in her early thirties, wearing a worn and similarly-
faded housedress. At her side was Maks, several shades lighter and
with his fingernails cleaned and trimmed, hair washed and combed.
Like his mother, he had hair of a medium brown color with some
lighter streaks in it, and pale blue eyes. He was still not wearing any
shoes.

Laleihala performed a very small, complicated genuflection
which the Walesas, mother and son, took to be the Palamban
greeting to an inferior. Maks had told her in hushed tones that the
house's new owners were foreign religious officials of some kind,
and that it would probably be a good idea not to pry into any details
of the church. But they had been kind enough to him and his mother,
and were bailing them out of a serious jam. If the situation had
continued, they might well have starved or frozen when winter came
again.

"Maks tells me that you are now well enough to resume your
duties as a housekeeper, Marcelina?" Laleihala asked. The woman
smiled tensely and nodded.

"Yes, I am much recovered now," she admitted. "But I'd be
stronger if I had more to eat..."

Seemingly the boy wasn't the only one in his family with an eye
out for the main chance. Laleihala, still shrouded in her *siri*,
concealed a smile. "We would like to hire you, and your son as
well," she said. "We need someone to cook and clean for us, and to
look after the sacred black horse. He must be treated with the
greatest of respect. The bird and cat will look after themselves, I
think, and will also keep watch on the house."

Marcelina and Maks exchanged a glance. "I would like you,
Marcelina, to go and buy us some food for supper. We will need
quite a few supplies, as well, and as there is no furniture in the house
except for the bed in the master bedroom we will need to purchase
some soon. Perhaps, Maks, you know of somewhere we could go and
arrange for furniture, rugs, and so forth to be delivered?" He nodded
eagerly.

Laleihala drew forth a purse from somewhere in the folds of her black garment, and deposited ten gold florins in Marcelina's palm. "Please return the change to me, or let me know if you need more," she said as the woman's eyes widened. She had never seen that much money in one place in her life. "In addition to your meals and the cottage where you're already living," the high priestess went on, "the two of you will receive a stipend of ten shillings weekly. Will that be adequate?"

"Oh, yes! Most assuredly," the woman said with joy. Her son looked equally ecstatic. This had truly been their lucky day.

"One more thing," the high priestess said as if it were an afterthought. "Our cult has certain religious observances, you understand, which must remain private. When we are home, if the door is unlocked you are free to come in. You, Maks, may use the bathtub from time to time – just ask first and I'll arrange it. But if you find the door latched from the inside, please respect our privacy. Thank you."

With that the black-clad Mysterion turned and, side by side with her acolyte, returned to the house. And latched the door.

Chapter 65

Inside the house Leila threw herself into Tevo's arms, ripping the coverings away from her head and face to reveal her shiny brown scalp. Planting a big kiss on his lips, she spun away from him and ran to the master bedroom. There was an enormous carved wood four-poster bed in there – undoubtedly judged too heavy for the previous owners, with their long journey ahead of them, to carry along. It had a decent looking feather mattress on it, with a somewhat dusty duvet cover over it. Likely they'd just be camping out on the floors of the upstairs bedrooms for tonight though, until more furnishings could be obtained.

Keeping her voice down lest it be heard outside the walls, Leila crowed "Isn't this wonderful, Tevo? I can't believe we just stumbled into something so perfect!" Both Kathal and the raven were now out in the yard with Nimble, exploring their new domain. The back yard was perhaps thirty by one hundred feet, with the cottage at the rear inside an eight-foot stone wall that completely surrounded the property. The house, which really was fairly small, occupied most of the width of the lot and had a small front garden, also walled, with a set of iron gates leading to the front steps. A hatch for coal deliveries led into the basement from just beside those steps.

Stairs outside at the back led down to the basement, which had a small workshop area with storage for tools or whatever. There was some scrap lumber down there along with a hammer with a broken-off claw, a rusty saw, and a brace-and-bit that looked like it might have been manufactured a century before.

Also down there was coal storage and the boiler, which provided hot water to the taps in the bathroom and kitchen and also to the ultra-modern steam heat system. Pipes throughout the house supplied steam to metal radiators in every room, though there was also a large fireplace in the main living room – clean and cold.

The previous owners had left just as winter was beginning last year, so there was still the greater part of a load of coal in the basement. It should certainly be enough to see them through the rest of their mission. It seemed probable that winters here were long and fierce, and southern-bred Leila had no intention of remaining here that long.

The ground floor had a decent-sized living room and a formal dining room, now bare. There was also the sort of large country kitchen you might expect in any house built in the last five hundred years, a generous sized master bedroom, and a comfortably large bathroom with a big clawfoot tub and sink. The flush toilet was in a separate small room. All the modern conveniences, and located not a mile from the Temple of the Seven. Leila was over the moon, and began a spiraling dance around the master bedroom, unwinding her *siri* to trail behind her.

Tevo had partly unwound his own garment to expose his head and shoulders, but he was gaping at her as she was revealed before his eyes, soon down to her underwear – and her boots. Leila had thought that sandals would be more appropriate footwear for Palambans, but there'd been no opportunity to obtain any. They weren't a popular item in the northern Dominion. "Leila, what are you doing?" he asked plaintively, as his groin area surged to attention. They had spent much time together since they met, and had become close friends, but she still had that effect on him whenever he caught a glimpse of that so-delectable flesh.

She grinned impishly at him. Even bald, she was still astonishingly cute and desirable. "I thought I would take a bath," she said. "Do you think the hot water's ready yet?"

"Uh, probably I guess… Let me check." Tevo hurried from the bedroom, but rather than go into the bathroom he went to the kitchen and tried the hot tap in the sink.

He returned to the bedroom, where they'd dumped their belongings, to find that Leila had stripped off her underwear as well and was now clad in some kind of lacy robe-thing. It came down to her knees and actually covered more of her body than her underwear did, but still! He put a hand up over his eyes, turning red beneath the skin dye, and said "It's nice and hot. Go ahead and take your bath, if you want. I think we need to go furniture shopping pretty soon, though."

Leila was in a fey mood, spilling over with delight at their good fortune, and she felt an impulse to tease. "Why don't you join me?"

she suggested lightly, "I'm sure you could use a bath too, and that way we'd save hot water." She strolled across the room toward him, where he stood covering his eyes with one hand while he attempted to keep his *siri* up with the other.

She pressed into his body, pulling at the top edge of the cloth and sniffing his chest. For one with hair so dark on his head, Tevo was remarkably smooth and hairless over much of his body – a bare dusting on his chest, and a little on his lower legs. A very pretty body, really...

Tevo was now resting both hands on her shoulders – gazing into her eyes. "Leila..." he murmured low in his throat, with such tortured longing that her urge to tease him evaporated. It was wrong to treat a friend so cruelly, and Tevo was the only friend she had. At least the only one who could speak...

He seized her in his arms and crushed her to him, his mouth hard on hers, his tongue going into her mouth. She felt his cock stiff and insistent beneath the fabric wrapped around his middle, pressing into her belly, and it did not frighten her. This was Tevo, her friend, who would never do her harm. And she felt an answering passion rising in her, a desire she'd been subconsciously aware of almost since they'd met. She wanted him, as he wanted her. And they were alone in the house.

Leila began pulling at Tevo's clothing with her hands as her mouth devoured his, breathing hard. His hands had slipped inside her robe, stroking her warm flesh... and then he drew back, panting. "Leila, no!" he gasped, "this isn't right! Remember your vow?" She reached for him again, her green eyes dilated with desire.

"Fuck my vow," she said coarsely. "I want you, Tevo. I love you!"

A look of joy shone in his eyes at this unexpected news, but still he was backing away from her though his balls ached. "Think!" he hissed. "Think, Leila! I love you and I want you, but now is not the time. Don't you see?" She looked at him blankly, a little hurt. She had expected that all she had to do was crook her finger and he would be hers for the taking.

She still didn't get it. "What happened to your mother, Leila?" Tevo asked. "She and your father were deeply in love, supposedly, and they acted on it, and look what happened. It ruined her life, and it very nearly destroyed yours as well. We can't risk that, not while we still have a dark god to free and a religion to re-start."

Leila stopped trying to climb him and stood thinking. A look of realization, of what she had nearly done, washed across her face. "There are herbs," she said after a moment, "herbs that will prevent a child from starting." Tevo had heard of them.

"You have to take them every day for a while before they work, right?" She nodded. This sort of herb lore had been part of her training as a member of the Night Guild, as it had been for the girls at the House of the Golden Fish.

"And have you been taking those herbs, my impossibly delicious little Leila?" he asked with so much love and affection, and such an irresistible smile, that she wanted to jump into his arms again in spite of it all. Instead, she shook her head and cast her eyes down. But a smile was growing on her lips.

"How about if I start tomorrow?" she suggested.

He threw his arms around her again, but the hug was one of affection and not passion. "Excellent idea!" he said, "We'll take care of this little religious issue, and make a date for right here as soon as that's been wrapped up. All right?" She hugged him back and grinned up at him. Tevo was being amazingly sweet and self-sacrificing, and wise. But she noticed he still had a very hard problem. Stepping back a little, she asked shyly, "Would you, uh... like a hand with that?"

Chapter 66

Within an hour Marcelina and Maks had returned with armloads of groceries, some pots and pans, and the location of a shop some distance from Temple Street where the house's new owners could buy furniture for delivery. She prepared the Palambans a late supper, which they ate sitting atop bedrolls on the floor.

They slept in those bedrolls, each of them in one of the two upstairs bedrooms. No point in testing their new-found resolve, now that both of them must fight the urge. In the morning the acolyte and his Mysterion, bundled once again in their black wraps, walked over to the furniture shop and selected enough furnishings to turn the bare house into something like a home.

They'd taken Nimble along, leaving the cat and bird behind, and loaded him up with purchases from other shops in the district. Seemingly, you could buy almost anything in Parat. Having plenty of money, they did. They returned from their errands to find a van pulled by four heavy cart horses pulling up outside, and within hours there were beds, mattresses, chairs, throw rugs, a dining table, and more spread throughout the house.

For the main living room they had gone with a Palamban motif. Instead of traditional furniture, large cushions had been set around the room on the floor, surrounding a low black-painted table. The cushions were, of course, black. Laleihala set Marcelina to making the beds (the two newly acquired single ones as well as the larger master bed) with the linens they'd purchased. There were towels hung in the bathroom, and the servants had been dismissed while the Mysterion and her acolyte engaged in some "religious rituals."

On this occasion, the rituals involved the painting of some lengths of black fabric (more from the same bolt that had gone into fashioning their *siris*). These had a pocket sewn into one end, hemmed at the other, with a dowel attached to string at either end running through the pocket from side to side so that they could be displayed as wall hangings.

Tevo laid down some paper obtained from the butcher on the living room table, and painted each of the black hangings with red paint, using symbols of Betsalel. No one now living in the Dominion except for a few scholars of religious history had any idea what the symbols of Betsalel were – every one of them had either been destroyed or hidden away six generations past. A consultation with Yeil was needed, and some trial and error as he attempted to describe what they were to draw.

One of these was hung on the front door, the other on the back as if to ward off intruders. Yeil assured them that this would have a real effect. Casual passersby would wonder at the strange hangings, but anyone who tried to enter the house with ill intent would find themselves possessed of an eerie sensation of dread and the urge to leave. It was similar, he said, to what Leila's pursuers had felt when they tried to go after her into the Blackwald. But he assured her it would not affect their servants, provided those servants held no bad intentions.

The other two hangings were placed on the walls of the living room, creating a stark and slightly menacing effect with the black cushions. They hadn't bought any artworks or framed prints for the walls, so anyone who entered the house with good or ill intent might be left feeling a little uneasy. It was not a warm, comfy, inviting place. But for now at least, it was home.

A small writing desk had been purchased for the parlor, along with blank stationery and some pens, sealing wax, and other paraphernalia. Leila's calligraphy had improved during her time working as Gustav's assistant at Castle Chanton, and while Tevo was working on the wall hangings she penned an elegant letter to the High Archon.

"To His Holiness Gabriel Sforza, High Archon of The Dominion of Gaspar, Greetings. I am the high priestess Laleihala, Mysterion of the Palamban Cult of the True Shadow, and I have traveled to Parat to consult with you on a matter of great religious importance to our two countries. As a token of my regard for the Church of Gaspar, I have come bearing a great gift to be donated to the Temple of the Seven: two dozen exquisite bloodwood figurines carved a thousand years ago by the people of my land. I am sending one of these with my servant, the acolyte Ademji of my Mystery, so that you may see what I am offering. In return, I ask only that you grant me an audience so that I may tell you of the information I have learned.

Please reply by messenger to 320 Pleasance Street, Parat, at your earliest convenience."

Leila blotted the letter and folded it neatly into thirds. She'd carved a sort of seal from soft wood and used it to impress one of Betsalel's symbols into the red sealing wax she dripped over the fold. On their shopping expedition they'd picked up some black velvet bags of the sort often used by jewelers, and into one of these the letter went – along with a palm-sized, exquisitely carved jungle cat. The bloodwood was burnished and almost black with age, the cat's eyes picked out with rubies and the spots on its body with tiny, perfectly faceted onyxes.

This and its fellows were, of course, part of Count Wilhelm's collections that Rosa had stolen over the course of the months she had worked there. Leila guessed that while the flyers distributed everywhere made no mention of the treasure, a detailed account of the stolen items would have been circulated to constables in every city and town, and to the Imperial Lawkeepers as well. Perhaps such lists had even been handed to pawnshops and known fences, with the promise that a big reward would be given, no questions asked, if the Count's agents were notified of anyone attempting to sell the treasures.

However, she reasoned, it was not likely that such a list would have been given to the staff of the Temple of the Seven. What sane thief would make off with such riches, and then give them away to the church? And as Laleihala and her acolyte were from Palambo and the statuettes were of Palamban origin, surely no suspicion would be cast on their provenance. They were the property of the Palamban church, now being donated to the Gaspari church, in a gesture of good will and friendship.

Leila prayed to Betsalel that the old man would prove to be free of the superstitious bigotry held by so many Gaspari citizens, and would not immediately send Church Guards to arrest the foreign devil worshipers without at least hearing what she had to say first.

She returned to the living room with the pouch in her hands, to find Tevo just finishing the hanging of the second emblem on the wall nearest the front of the house. "Done?" she asked, and he nodded cheerfully.

353

"A devilish good job, if I do say so myself." Leila grinned at him.

"I've got the letter done, so you'd better get dressed and go deliver it." He'd been working in normal clothes during their "rituals," while she was already wrapped in her *siri* over a regular blouse and long skirt – also black.

"Yes, Mysterion ma'am, I'll get right on it!" Tevo said, saluting jauntily and taking the velvet pouch from her hands. She watched him go, fondly, then wrapped her garment up around her head and shoulders before going out the back door to find Marcelina.

Leila caught the housekeeper cleaning her own house, while Maks was working with some newly acquired garden tools in the garden. It was probably too late to start a kitchen garden this year, but she'd asked him to prune back the wild growth of shrubs a little and spade up the overgrown vegetable beds. Several large evergreen trees and a couple of shade trees that would be bare in the wintertime helped to screen the yard from prying eyes in the upper storey windows of the houses surrounding them.

"Marcelina, I just wanted to let you know that we're finished with our rituals for now. I have sent Ademji on an errand, and I will be meditating for a couple of hours. But I have a list of some things I need you to buy, and you'd better bring Maks along to help carry them." Leila had learned that in Holy Parat, unlike the case in most other regions of the Dominion, the church ran schools where even the poor could attend. Almost everyone learned to read and write, and it tended to reduce the disparity between the rich and the poor.

She handed Marcelina the list and some money, and the woman smilingly wiped her hands on her apron and gathered her hat and a shoulder bag. "Dinner at seven, then?" she asked, as she made ready to go out of the cottage.

"That will be fine, thank you," Laleihala replied with a smile in her voice. She stepped back out of the cottage and the housekeeper came out behind her and locked the door.

"Maks!" she called, and the boy turned from his spading. "Come help me with the shopping!" He knocked the dirt off his spade and returned it to the small garden shed built off the rear of the house. Marcelina took him by the hand, and the two of them bowed slightly to the mistress of the house before leaving. What strange people these Palambans were, the Gaspari woman thought as they made their way through the front gates and turned in the direction of the nearest shopping district. They ate so late, for one thing. And look at this list! It was probably going to take her two hours to find all this stuff. When was she ever going to find time to clean the main house?

Chapter 67

Leila watched them go, then went in through the back door and upstairs to her bedroom. She removed the length of cloth wrapped around her and brushed it off. The cloth was beginning to look the worse for wear, but she was afraid to have it laundered. She feared it might run and come out looking gray instead of black – diluting the mystique of their shadowy religion.

There was no Palamban presence at all in Parat, unless you counted the two bogus representatives of the "Cult of the True Shadow." But maybe Ademji, on behalf of his Mysterion, might be able to find a dress shop that could whip them up a couple of night-black *kad'r*. He was less than half a foot taller than she and they both had slim, muscular builds. Probably two identical robes would work for both of them.

At the moment, though, Leila had an urgent task to complete. Stripping to her underwear, she put on the soiled leather pants and shirt she'd worn during her escape from Chanton. She'd just *known* they would come in handy again someday. Then she headed for the garden, going invisible before stepping out the door, and retrieved the shovel from where Maks had stored it.

Had an observer in any of the buildings surrounding the Parat branch of the Palamban church managed to see through all the vegetation to the spot where Leila was digging, they would have beheld a very odd sight indeed. The digger and the spade she held were cloaked in shadow, and so was the spot near the wall where she was digging. But every once in a while a spill of soil would cascade down from the pile beside the hole, suddenly appearing as if the earth itself had vomited it up.

They'd obtained a couple of large oilskin bags, and Leila placed all of the Oester loot except for the remaining Palamban statuettes in one bag, pulled its drawstring tight, then placed that bag mouth-end-first into the second and pulled that one tight as well. The treasures were already well-wrapped for protection, and the girl who had stolen them prayed they would remain undamaged. She'd never dreamed she would need to be keeping them so long.

Leila carefully shoveled the dirt back into the hole atop the bag, nearly a foot of it. Not too heavy, she hoped. There was extra dirt left over from the hole, space taken up by the bag, and that she scattered under the eaves of the fir trees along the back wall behind the servants' cottage. Then she moved pine needles over the top of the area where she'd dug.

Nimble did, indeed, "shit wherever he pleased." But Leila had been able to encourage him to make his deposits in one particular area, near to where she had buried the loot. Now she shoveled that up and told the horse, who'd been watching her activity with a great deal of curiosity, "Over here, Nimble." She led him into the little alcove and he sniffed at the pile of dung that had been moved there. Then she took him by the headstall and led him around, backing him up toward the pile. "That's the idea, good boy!" she crooned, as he added a little to the top.

Chapter 68

Cyryl Kubasz, stationed in the shadow between two decorative shrubs outside the wrought iron fence of the house at 385 Pleasance Street, was in a quandary. He had left the boy Vlad, never intended to be more than emergency relief and a runner, at his post along the waterfront for the rest of the time until Janosz came on last night. Then this morning he had left the boy there again, taking his place on the day shift, while he set himself to watching the mysterious party from Palambo. If that was indeed where they were from.

What was he doing? He needed to be back at his post! Vlad lacked the experience to tell a likely suspect from a run-of-the-mill passenger, and the waterfront was the most challenging detail. His men watching the main road from the south, and the one watching from the north in case by some freak chance the girl had gone that far and then backtracked, had only the relatively narrow width of the road to keep an eye on – while Parat had river traffic coming in at half a mile of docks, on both sides of the river.

If Rosa came in on an ore barge and crossed on the bridge, he would have her in his eye. But would Vlad do as well? Truly, he should be back at his post – but these travelers had struck a chord in Cyryl, and all of the instincts he'd honed after two decades of being a thief taker were quivering. There was something *wrong* about them, he knew it!

They had come into town on a boat from Prusz, and less than ninety minutes later they'd been negotiating the purchase of this small house across the street. Clearly they did not lack for funds, but who knew what resources the Palamban church had at their disposal? Most in the Dominion believed all the Palamban elite to be rich beyond mortal dreams, and the blatant gold jewelry with enormous cut stones the travelers had been wearing certainly seemed to back up that belief. Cyryl couldn't necessarily condemn them just for having questionable taste in personal ornament.

He had arrived here this morning after making a few inquiries. The house had been owned by a citizen of Parat, who had been a senior member of a legal firm prior to dying of the fever that had swept through the city last winter. It had been some kind of influenza, and many had died though most had recovered. The man's family had almost immediately packed up and left with no thought for the housekeeper and her son. She had been with them for years, apparently since before the boy was born. Cyryl wondered idly whether her son might also have been the son of the late head of household. Such things were not unheard-of, and if the widow suspected it that might account for her callousness.

There'd been little enough to see, and none of it had confirmed Cyryl's suspicions – or allayed them. For hours after he'd arrived, parking himself in the shade between the two bushes, there had been no activity at all down at number 320. Then, suddenly, the man he'd seen leading the horse had darted outside briefly dressed in black trousers and shirt, revealing a bald head as dark as the rest of the skin he'd so far shown. He'd tacked up an ominous-looking black banner with some kind of arcane red symbols on it, then returned inside.

Something about that banner gave Cyryl the shivers. It was just black cloth with red paint splashed across it – why did it make him want to abandon his enterprise and run back to the riverfront? Maybe these people really *were* Palamban religists involved in some kind of dark rituals.

Not very long after that the man appeared once more, this time covered head to foot in that curious garment that seemed to consist of a long piece of black cloth wrapped around and around his body. He had the jeweled scimitar the thief taker had noticed earlier, and was walking with purpose, on some kind of errand apparently, off to the south.

The day's excitement, so far, had culminated with the appearance of the housekeeper and her son. The boy was looking considerably cleaner and less ragged than when Cyryl had first beheld him on Temple Street yesterday, and he guessed that they had been re-employed by the foreign visitors. They hurried off to the north, on a shopping errand he guessed. And that had been that.

Wait, here came the Palamban man returning. He was swaggering along as if he didn't have a care in the world, and went through the gates of number 320 and up the steps to the house's front door with its ominous hanging. Then he let himself in with the key, and nothing else happened. Cyryl had not seen the horse or the cat since yesterday evening, though he thought he might have caught sight of the bird. He took it to be a raven, but who could say? Perhaps it was some obscure species from Palambo, chosen by the church for its color.

Another couple of hours passed, and the thief taker's butt was beginning to get sore from sitting on the damp ground. There had been absolutely nothing to see. Then the housekeeper and her son came up the road, returning from the direction in which they'd come. Their arms were loaded with packages, mostly groceries and household supplies – Cyryl suspected, after studying them through the binoculars he'd brought along. Nothing out of the ordinary at all.

Two more hours passed with no movement of any kind from the house, and the sun was now sliding toward the horizon. With an oath, Cyryl hung the binoculars over his shoulder and rose stiffly to his feet. He was no longer a young man, to be sitting on watch hour after hour! Enough already, he thought, as he hopped down from the low retaining wall and headed off in the direction of the river. I'm returning to my post!

Chapter 69

The Mysterion and her acolyte shared the new dining table, enjoying the last of the delicious meal Marcelina had prepared. Laleihala had informed the housekeeper that she should always make enough extra food for herself and her son, but that they'd prefer she would take it back to their cottage to eat. Cleanup of the dinner dishes could wait until morning, the high priestess assured her, as she and her acolyte preferred to have their privacy in the evenings.

Marcelina was beginning to wonder if the relationship between the high priestess and her servant were perhaps a bit more than what you might expect in a religious hierarchy. Something about the way they responded to each other... She'd certainly had some experience in her life of master and servant being more to each other than it seemed; but who knew what the Palamban church thought was appropriate?

Maybe the priestesses were required to sleep with their male acolytes as some kind of twisted religious practice. All she knew was that she and her son had three square meals a day and money in their pockets, and hadn't been worked unduly hard or subjected to any abuse. Those two Palambans could spend all day and all night shagging each other ragged, as far as she was concerned.

Leila lifted her glass, half full of a truly marvelous red wine, in a toast. "Great job, Tevo!" she said, grinning. That "never touch alcohol" vow had been broached once, with severe consequences. But that had been years ago, and she was an adult now. Well technically, not an adult by law in most parts of the Dominion. But she *felt* like an adult, and she was alone with her closest friend on earth, and the wine was delicious. It complimented the roast medallions of lamb with mushroom sauce nicely.

And, she'd had her first dose of the contraceptive tea this morning. She'd have another before bed, and as her last period had been a week ago she should be protected in another few days. Tevo grinned at her, that crooked smile that set her heart racing. Damn, even with his head shaved and his skin four shades darker, he was still just so *cute*! Their glasses clinked.

"I didn't actually set eyes on the High Archon," he pointed out, not wanting too much credit. "But his acolyte came back and said that he had received the note and the statuette with interest, and would be sending a reply soon!" Leila was enthusiastic. Her childhood might have been stolen from her, but she could still access it from time to time.

A knock came at the door. The dining room was at the front of the house, with the kitchen behind it, but heavy new drapes blocked the view out to the front yard and the wall beyond it. The two of them had begun the meal swaddled in their *siris*, as Marcelina had served the meal. Then after she'd gone out the back door, they'd unwrapped the cloths until their heads and shoulders were exposed. Now, Tevo hastily wrapped himself back up and Leila stood to tuck in a few loose corners, before he went to answer the door.

A young man of perhaps fifteen years stood there on the doorstep, dressed in the robes of an acolyte of the Temple of the Seven. Each of the gods and goddesses had been assigned a color: white for Lucia, blue for Mira, red for Belantos, and so forth. Betsalel's color had been black, and that had surely not been lost on the personnel of the temple when Ademji had appeared with his message. The boy's robes were white, striped with blue, red, yellow, green, purple and orange.

"Honored Ademji, I have your reply from His Holiness the High Archon. I am instructed to wait here for your acknowledgement." He bowed his head, hands held together in an attitude of prayer. Tevo accepted the paper from the kid (a whole two years younger than himself) and gestured him inside.

"Please wait here while I consult with my mistress," he said, and left the boy standing in the hall while he let himself back into the dining room through the door in the hall and held it out to Leila. She was grinning ear to ear. Good news, it must be good news, to have sent a runner so late!

Making a stab at dignity and failing at it so miserably that Tevo was very glad the High Archon's acolyte was on the other side of a shut door, Leila ripped the message open. It had an elaborate seal on it, presumably made by the ring that was part of the High Archon's holy regalia.

"To the high priestess Laleihala, Mysterion of the Palamban Cult of the True Shadow, from His Holiness Gabriel Sforza, High Archon of The Dominion of Gaspar, Greetings. I am most pleased by your token, and am curious to learn of the information you wish to impart. On behalf of the church of the Dominion of Gaspar I am happy to accept the offer of your gift, and I invite you and your acolyte to dine with me in my chambers tomorrow, the 26th of Flora, here at the Temple of the Seven at six o'clock. Please inform the bearer of this message if you are able to attend. "

Mindful that sound could penetrate walls, Leila settled for throwing her arms around Tevo's neck and kissing him soundly through the layers of cloth that covered his face. His eyes were smiling. He bowed deeply, and turned to open the door to the hallway. More little bows between him and the acolyte. Then Ademji pronounced solemnly, "My mistress is happy to accept your master's invitation. Please tell him to expect us at six o'clock tomorrow."

Chapter 70

Leila awoke the next morning ready for action. She had a long day ahead of her, and for this first part of it she'd be getting no help from her "team." She found Tevo up before her, wearing his *siri* and sitting cross legged on one of the living room cushions. His eyes were closed, and he gave every appearance of communing with his god.

Leila could hear Marcelina bustling around in the kitchen, cleaning up after last night's supper and preparing breakfast. Having useful, paid work to do seemed to have completed the last steps in the woman's recovery from her illness of the past winter. She was already looking younger, and beginning to move with more energy. She was humming an unfamiliar tune, high and sweet, as she fried sausages and toasted bread.

Taking a similar posture on the cushion to his left, the Mysterion lowered her head and murmured a prayer in Palamban. Or so you might think, if you were unfamiliar with that tongue. Then she spoke softly to her acolyte. "I'll be going up to the Palace Complex this morning to talk to whoever has care of the archives," she told him. "It'd be good if you could go over to that tailor shop you saw and have them run us up a couple of black robes, like a Palamban *kad'r*."

Tevo concluded his "prayers" and eyed her sidelong. "Is that the thing that covers you from head to foot and just has a slit for the eyes, with a veil you can pull down so even the eyes are hidden?" He'd seen a picture in a book, once upon a time.

"That's the one," Leila replied quietly. "Just have them make two to your size, but take up the hem on the second one another five inches. And we won't need the veils, I don't think."

He grinned slightly. "Good idea. It'd be nice to have something I can get on and off in a hurry, and easily wear other clothes beneath it. I'll do that after breakfast."

"Breakfast," Marcelina called from the kitchen, then moved to serve the food on the dining table.

Laleihala and Ademji made a show of examining the food with interest, as if it were something they hadn't seen before. They ate it with enthusiasm and compliments, though. As Marcelina was about to depart though, the high priestess told her "Marcelina, we will busy around the city today and going out this evening to dine with the High Archon." The Gaspari woman's eyebrows rose. These curious employers of hers evidently had connections in high places!

"So after the kitchen is tidied up and the beds made, please feel free to take the rest of the day off."

"Thank you, Mysterion," Marcelina said, bowing slightly, and left the room. Leila and Tevo, having pulled their *siris* down far enough that they could eat, tucked into the hearty breakfast.

It was fortunate for the travelers that Cyryl Kubasz had abandoned his surveillance for the time being – concerned that his real quarry might be slipping into Parat unobserved, while he wasted days staring at the house on Pleasance Street where nothing much ever seemed to happen. For he would have been quite startled, and suspicious as well, to see a somewhat prim-looking young woman emerge from the house at around ten in the morning, and hail one of the hansom cabs that roamed the streets throughout the city.

Sophia diFontana was a short, slender young woman of perhaps twenty, her straight, medium brown hair held back in a bun and silver-rimmed spectacles on her nose. Though the late spring weather was on the warm side, she was wearing an expensive ladies' traveling dress that covered her from her chin to the tips of her boots. Her hands were gloved and she had a largish brown leather satchel slung over her shoulder. Her complexion was a light tan, though a close inspection would show she was wearing rather a lot of makeup.

Leila was intrigued by the slow cab ride up to the promontory on which the palace and its associated buildings sat. Traffic on the streets was heavy at this hour of the morning, with people scurrying about on foot or horseback or in horse-drawn conveyances, enormous wagons making deliveries, small children darting here and there. The sights, the smells of this new and unfamiliar city were fascinating to her, and she was starting to regret she wouldn't have more time to stay here.

But still, the idea of wintering here held no appeal. And after she and Tevo had successfully completed the god's mission, she would be free at last. They could go anywhere together, do anything. Maybe even get so far away from the Count of Oester that they could cash in on her big score and live like kings.

"This here is the Imperial Archives building," the cabbie said. He set the brake and helped her down, and Sophia tipped him – generously, but not to the point that he would be likely to recall it hours later. She climbed the marble steps and went up to the entry, which had columns out in front. Two men in the livery of the Imperial Guard stood flanking the door, looking bored and sleepy. The one on the left was eyeing her with interest, and she dimpled at him.

"Good morning, Miss," he said with a grin.

"Oh! Good morning, uh, officer? What do they call you?"

"Guardsman, Miss," he said – pleased that she'd stopped to speak with him. Most of the women he tried to get friendly with just walked on by with their noses in the air.

"You look tired, Guardsman," Sophia said. "Do they make you guard the building all day and all night? That must be very hard…"

He chuckled. "Guard *this* place all night? Not hardly. Who'd want to steal a bunch of musty old books? Nah, I'm just tired because I had a late night last night…" he winked at her, then continued. "Guards are only assigned to the Archives building during business hours, in case anybody gets rowdy." He snorted with laughter. The idea of any of the scholars and pedants who visited the Archives getting "rowdy" was absurd. Sophia joined in the laughter, a polite and ladylike titter. Then she said

"Good day to you," continued in through the large double doors, and looked around. The entry hall was enormous, faced all in marble and carved with scenes from the history of the Dominion.

Despite the size of the place it didn't seem to be particularly well-attended. She was the only member of the public in sight, and the only other person in the room was a young clerk sitting at a carved wood desk. He looked up at her eagerly. No doubt most of the people who came here were men over fifty, so the sight of an attractive young woman was welcome.

Sophia returned his gaze as she approached the desk. "Good morning," she said, with a trace of the accents of Italia. "I'm hoping you can direct me to someone who can tell me whether a certain item is stored either within the Imperial Palace or in the Imperial Treasure House, and if so how it came to be there. I'm compiling a family history, you see, and must verify whether our traditional story is true."

He smiled at her. "You'll want to speak with Fyodor Rastnikov," he said. "Come, I'll escort you to him."

"Oh, thank you!" Sophia said with a melting smile. The clerk, whose name she hadn't gotten, took a placard from a desk drawer and set it on the desktop facing out. It read "Will Return Shortly." Then he took her by the arm and led her through a doorway, into a long corridor with many rooms leading off of it.

Leila kept careful count of the doors they passed, and noted as well that there was a sign over the door they eventually entered, reading "Art and Treasures." Instead of a desk there was a long counter here, room enough to have a dozen books at once open for research across its top. Bookshelves lined the walls of the main room, and those of corridors going back into dimness. They rose some fifteen feet high, and there was a staircase on wheels to allow access to the upper stacks. The smell of old paper filled the air.

Standing at the counter was a tiny old man, perhaps in his late fifties. He had wisps of graying hair surrounding a mostly bald pate, and was wearing thick gold-rimmed spectacles. He probably had perfect vision thirty years ago, Leila thought. She loved books, but not *this* much! "Doktor Rastnikov, I've brought someone to see you!" the clerk said cheerfully, and the old man looked up at them with interest.

"Doktor Fyodor Rastnikov, this is… uh, sorry, I didn't get your name?"

"Sophia diFontana," Sophia said, extending a gloved hand.

"I'm Ladislaw, by the way," the clerk added, and shook her hand after the learned doktor was finished with it.

"Thank you Ladislaw, you've been most kind," the young woman said. He stood there for another few seconds just taking her in, then started.

"I'd better get back to my post," he said reluctantly. "I hope Doktor Rastnikov can help you with your research."

Sophia gave him a smile and a cheerful wave as he fled the room, then turned her attention back to the old doktor. He was scarcely any taller than she was, somewhat pudgy in his scholar's robes, and so cute Leila just wanted to reach out and chuck him under the chin. Sophia resisted the urge, instead saying, "The reason I've come, Doktor, is to ferret out the truth behind an old family story. I'm working on a four-volume history of the diFontanas, who as I'm sure you must know have been prominent merchants in Vinizzi since the time when it was an independent city-state."

This was in fact true, which was why Leila had chosen the name. Rastnikov nodded. "For generations," Sophia explained, "the story has been told in our family of my great-great-great-great-grandfather Paolo diFontana, who made a pilgrimage to Parat in around 812 or 813, we're not sure which. He brought with him a priceless art treasure, a Hando carved jade vase six feet tall, that had been in our family since 26 b.m.e. He donated the vase to Emperor Fernand IV as a token of his loyalty to the Dominion. It is said that the emperor awarded him the Order of the Dominion for this service, and that the vase was proudly displayed in the Great Audience Hall in the Imperial Palace thereafter."

Rastnikov frowned. "I don't recall seeing such a vase," he said, "but then of course the décor in the palace is constantly being updated. There's certainly a possibility it was moved to some part of the palace that's off-limits to the public, or to the Imperial Treasure House for safekeeping." Sophia's face lit.

"That's what I'm hoping!" she said. "I visited the palace and saw that it wasn't there. But I understand that the archives record the whereabouts and provenance of all of the Imperial assets. Is that true?"

"Certainly," the doktor said. "But we have a staff of scholars, people like myself, who will happily search the archives to answer questions in exchange for a small fee. Couldn't you have saved a lot of time and expense by submitting your inquiry in writing, instead of coming all the way from Vinizzi?"

Her lovely eyes widened, then she looked down and a little smile formed on her lips. "You've caught me, Doktor!" she said gaily. "In fact, when I first announced my plan to travel to Parat in search of this information my uncle told me I was insane. But I am an adult, and of independent means. And I just had to see this place for myself!"

Sophia took a turn around the room, arms spread wide, clearly ecstatic to be in the presence of so many books. "Just think of all the history contained in these books! They can have their gold and silver over at the Treasure House, this is the *real* treasure!" She turned to find the old scholar grinning at her in wonder. Here was truly a girl after his own heart.

Chapter 71

Some two hours later, after an extensive search of the archives of the Palace and Treasure House for the years between 800 and 850, Sophia kissed Doktor Rastnikov sweetly on the cheek and thanked him for his efforts. He flushed. "I'm so sorry, my dear," he said, "that we were not able to prove your ancestor's story of the jade vase. I wonder if the story got garbled over the centuries." She smiled at him.

"Well," she said resignedly as if the disappointment had not been too great, "history is history and truth is truth. Maybe great-great Paolo made the whole thing up to explain to his wife where he'd been for the past three months!"

With that Sophia took herself out past the front desk, waving to Ladislaw and to the friendly guard outside, and went down the steps to the promenade. In addition to all the government buildings there were quite a few eateries on the grounds, and she went to a nearby café and had some lunch. Food in Parat certainly seemed to be on the heavy side, but she guessed even she might acquire a taste for it if she had to spend six months of the year slogging through snow.

Thus fortified, the attractive if scholarly-looking young woman strolled along through the grounds admiring the magnificent architecture and lovely gardens. The latter were at their peak right now, and they were truly beautiful. The enormous Imperial Treasure House loomed to her right, and she joined a small throng of sightseers going inside.

One of the most fabulous attractions Parat had to offer, after the Temple of the Seven and the Palace itself, was the museum sited in the front section of the Treasure House. Heavily guarded both day and night, it housed some of the most unique and exquisite treasures the Dominion (and therefore, the people of the Dominion) owned – on display for the edification of the public. Had not great-grandpa Paolo's vase been completely fictional, one might have come to see it here.

There was a small fee for entry, children under ten free, and at this hour the place was crawling with visitors. Hmm, that was going to be something of a problem. Leila's Shadow power worked well even in daylight, provided there were at least some shadows around for her to blend in with – but in crowds it was a danger.

"Pardon me," Sophia asked the young guardsman standing at attention near the entrance to the exhibit halls, "Could you please tell me if there are… uh… facilities?" She lowered her head as if embarrassed.

"Oh, you mean the privies?" he asked genially. "Ladies' is down the hall there on your right."

Leila had never seen such a thing in any of the other cities she'd visited, and she had visited a lot. By the Eight, such opulence! The convenience set aside for female visitors was a large room with basins set along one wall, and a row of six stalls along the other. Each of these contained a flush toilet like the one at their home. Wow, I feel like I'm living in the future, she thought. The building was centuries old, but clearly much renovation work had been done. She let herself in, lifted her skirts, and sat on the stool. Might as well pee while she was at it!

The stalls had no ceilings, so that light could get in from lamps set along the walls. Leila pulled the plan of the Treasure House that she'd stolen while Rastnikov was up on a rolling staircase pulling down another volume, and studied it. She hadn't known what to expect going into the Archives building, and had been prepared to break in there in the middle of the night to find the information she needed – after casing the layout. But no such trip would now be needed.

The archives were kept chronologically, with items entered as they came in or were reassigned. Similarly to the information Rosa had recorded regarding each of Count Wilhelm's new acquisitions, there were spaces for date, physical description, provenance, price, and eventual disposition. This meant that everything from a set of silver cutlery destined for the Palace dining room to a shipment of carved columns to be set in place when the portico of the Bureau of Taxation was remodeled would all be recorded in the same book. And if you knew the exact date that an item was acquired or relocated, finding it would be a snap. But of course Sophia had been unsure when it was her ancestor had made his putative gift to the emperor.

Having failed to find the vase listed within either of the years she'd first mentioned, they had had to go back and forward in time, studying every book for a record of that missing vase. And in the book for 810, the year that Fernand IV had launched his pogrom against the church of Betsalel, there was a faded notation in a crabbed hand: "12 Fevrus 810, One brick pillar, crated, delivered by Imperial Guard. Hold for storage. Assigned to room M227, top floor, Imperial Treasure House."

That had to be it, Leila knew, and Doktor Rastnikov found her scribbling down notes in the thick notebook she'd brought with her when he came back down the ladder with the books for 815 and 816. "Find anything interesting?" he asked. "I'm afraid not," Sophia said ruefully, "just updating my research journal. I'll need to cite all my references when I submit my works for publication." He nodded sagely and laid the latest acquisitions on the counter so they could renew their search.

Leila had discovered that each volume of the archives included a back pocket full of folded maps, allowing researchers (once they'd learned the location of a searched-for item) to pinpoint it on a map for whomever wanted to find it. It had been the work of a couple of seconds to pocket one of the Treasure House maps as she was returning some of the already-searched volumes to the shelves.

The Treasure House seemingly had only one story, the sprawling ground-level edifice that housed the public museum as well as a great many quite large rooms where treasures were kept. But it went down into the ground beneath the hilltop for another two levels, a warren of smaller rooms where Leila assumed small, valuable items (like the actual gold coin in the Imperial treasury, the crown jewels that weren't on display, and so forth) were kept.

Leila guessed that the idol of Betsalel, encased in bricks (and crated as well, according to the archive notation) had been too big and bulky to get down the stairs and into one of the lower level storage rooms. Fernand should have hauled it off on a wagon and had some ship carry it out into the Northern Ocean and drop it to the bottom of the sea, she thought. But then she recalled that the pogrom had been launched in Fevrus. Likely the Northern Ocean was solid ice at that season.

Well, the fact that the idol was hidden on the main floor was good news, she supposed. Easier to get at than the basement, at least. But there was no way she and Tevo would be able to go in there in the daytime with crowbars and wreckers' hammers to free the idol – the noise would be heard far and wide. She wasn't sure whether they'd be able to do it at night, either; but she needed to go see this room M227 for herself.

Memorizing its location on the map, Leila waited until she heard no one else in the room. Then she shrouded herself in shadows and exited the stall. Carefully slipping out the door, keeping near the wall to avoid colliding with passersby, Leila came to a decorative iron door blocking the way to the corridor she wanted to go down. It was firmly locked.

At this hour of the day most of the Imperial Guard force was concentrated on the main floor, in the area open to the public. A smash-and-grab raid, breaking one of the glass cases and making off with an armload of treasures, was a much bigger danger than somebody trying to sneak into the fortress-like storage areas at the rear of the building, let alone those on the floors below.

There was a guard standing with his back to the wall, around twenty feet to the right of the door – the same one, in fact, whom she'd asked earlier for directions to the privies. His attention was on the stream of visitors going into the museum, answering questions (and probably, keeping an eye out for anybody who looked suspicious). In moments she had picked the lock and, still cloaked in shadows, slipped inside.

Leila carefully pushed the door shut behind her. It did not latch, so she locked it again from the inside. A high-ceilinged, dimly-lit corridor stretched before her and she could hear the sounds of the people in the museum outside – plus, closer at hand, the sounds of measured footsteps. Likely they had guards patrolling the corridors here day and night.

Room M227 was down the corridor ahead of her, then down another broad corridor to the left, and about three-quarters of the way down that corridor on the right side. There were no windows in the building at all, and the corridors were lit with wall lamps spaced at wide intervals – just enough light to walk down the corridor without tripping over your feet.

Moving silently, and utterly invisible, Leila ghosted along the corridor keeping eyes and ears open for approaching guards. Along the way she passed the doors of storage rooms. As the rooms on this floor were large she doubted there were really hundreds of them, so what did the numbering system mean? The first room on her left, behind a heavy bronze door set in stone, was marked "M120." Eh, it didn't matter, since she had the map. As she approached the intersection of corridors where she was to make her turn, she was barely able to see a guard walking this corridor far down toward the end. He had his back to her, and before he should reach the terminus of his route and come back this way she was around the corner.

The corridor vanished in the dimness before her, stretching out of sight. Nobody in it as far as she could see, and she heard no one walking. Leila peered behind her, to where the corridor ran into shadows in the other direction, and saw no one there. The coast is clear, she told herself – trying to work up a little gleeful enthusiasm for the task at hand. But there was something so… oppressive about this place. The dim lighting, the endless corridors, the towering ceilings that made her feel like a crawling bug all conspired to make her very anxious to leave again.

Leila continued stalking silently along on her soft-soled boots, making almost no sound even on the cold stone floors. The guard's boots, when she noticed them, seemed loud against the silence. Stifling a gasp, she threw herself into the slight recess where the door of room M214 was set, in between two of the wall lamps.

The guard, a man in his late twenties from the look of him, walked along in a gait that was almost a shuffle. Bored out of his mind, probably, after patrolling a corridor where nobody ever came for who knows how many precious hours of his dwindling life. He glanced around a little, but expected to see nothing. And he saw nothing. Leila was just another pool of shadow in a corridor full of them.

After he'd walked to the end of the corridor and returned past her, Leila slipped back out of the recess and made her way hurriedly to the door of M227 on the opposite side of the corridor. The bronze door to this room looked exactly the same as every other door she'd seen in this place. Without the room numbers posted above them, she imagined, one might wander the place lost until one had died of hunger and thirst.

The guard was on his long journey back to the far side of the building, already lost to sight. Leila had her lockpicks out and went to work. This was not your average shopkeeper lock, that was for sure – but on the other hand, lock technology had advanced quite a bit in the hundreds of years since the Treasure House was built. And no one had replaced the locks. It was a little over a minute before she heard the final tumbler click, the lock release.

Leila hesitated for a moment before touching the door again. What would she find? Would the fragment of Betsalel lodged beneath her heart call out, somehow, to his most important idol? The god had not explained all the details of how he and his "siblings" were able to manifest in the physical world – or how they existed when they were not doing so. It was an intriguing subject, and she hoped she might be able to pump the god for more details before they parted ways. Steeling herself, she pushed on the door. It moved slightly, perhaps an eighth of an inch – and stopped. The door was barred from the inside!

Chapter 72

After getting back down the hill from the Imperial Compound as Sophia, Leila went shadowy a few blocks away and entered the house through the back door. I was foolish to walk out the front in broad daylight this morning, she had realized during the ride home. Who knew what eyes might be watching the house where the exotic and mysterious visitors had taken up residence?

Though having Tevo as a friend and companion was helping to preserve Leila's sanity, the constant need for disguise and subterfuge and lies was beginning to wear her down. Sure it was great fun, getting over on the marks. But she was coming to realize that the long con was not her cup of tea. She just wanted to relax and be herself – for a while, at least!

She found Tevo in the living room, propped up on one of the cushions and reading a book. He was dressed in ordinary clothing and looked perfectly relaxed. "You're back!" he crowed, rising to his feet and coming over to give her a hug. "Mmm," he said, assessing her Sophia drag. "Hot schoolteacher! You want to give me some homework?" he suggested with a leer.

Still shaken by her discovery, Leila hugged him perfunctorily and then pushed him away. She peeled the wig off her head and hurled it onto the cushions, then began removing the jacket of her dress. The need to have as much of her dark skin covered as possible in order to impersonate a woman of the Italic region had been agonizing, riding back in the hansom at the peak of the afternoon's heat.

Tevo, still playful, took the jacket from her. "Keep going," he suggested, still looking at her as if he was planning to fall on her in a mad passion as soon as she'd stripped down far enough. She wasn't the only one who could tease, it seemed. Leila smiled weakly at him.

"Stop!" she begged. "I've had a kind of unsettling afternoon, and I just want to stop sweating."

"Sorry!" he said, and began gathering up the wig and garments as she peeled them off until she was standing in her underwear. He couldn't help admiring her, even so – though the contrast between her relatively pale face and the extra-dark brown of her revealed limbs was a bit discordant.

"There's a pitcher of water in the icebox," he told her. "Why don't you grab a cool drink and I'll take your things upstairs."

"Thank you," Leila said, giving him a sweet look of love before turning and hurrying into the kitchen. She was thankful they'd given the help the afternoon off. Along with the rest of its modern conveniences this house boasted a decent-sized icebox – and they'd had their first ice delivery yesterday.

Leila poured herself a tall stein of ice-cold water and returned to the living room to fall atop one of the cushions. She dipped her fingers into the stein and patted some of the water on the bare top of her head. A slight stubble was already starting to come in – she'd need to have Tevo shave it for her again before their dinner engagement.

He bounded down the stairs in another moment and sat on the cushion at her right hand. "I got the *kad'r* you wanted," he reported. "The tailor looked at me funny, but I was all 'grim-looking-foreigner-might-be-touchy-better-not-cross-him,' and he got right to work. They're not all that hard to sew compared with a modern outfit. It's amazing what you can get done without speaking a word, if you just look ominous enough!"

Aw, my baby is growing up, Leila thought whimsically. When she had first met the boy (was that truly less than two weeks ago?) he had seemed so hopelessly incompetent and innocent that she'd despaired of using him in any role that didn't involve someone in a coma. But now he was out on his own, intimidating tailors. She felt proud.

"I found out where the idol is," Leila said.

"That's great!" Tevo responded; but then got a look at her face. "What's the matter?" he asked. "Is it hidden under the Emperor's throne with a hundred armed guards around it twenty-four hours a day?" She smiled, jolted out of her sour mood. It seemed he could always make her smile.

"Not quite," she explained. "Actually, I don't think it would be all that much trouble for us to get in there and start breaking Betsalel loose. Except for one thing…"

A little while later, Tevo sighed and sat back. These cushions could be pretty comfortable once you got used to them. "Just like Betsalel's priesthood, the ones who gave their lives to make the idol impregnable, there must have been somebody on Lucia's side who was willing to die to make it so the Shadow God couldn't return," he said thoughtfully.

"Maybe several somebodies," Leila replied, "if that bar is as heavy as it felt." She lapsed into silence for a moment, before adding "To just sit there and die of starvation, or of thirst! How horrible!"

"Aw, maybe they took poison or fell on their swords," Tevo suggested. "It'd be quick…"

Leila sat up again. "You're probably right," she said, rolling up onto her feet. She was a sixteen-year-old, lithe as any gymnast. She wondered what it might be like getting up from these cushions if you were someone like Doktor Rastnikov. "I'd better go get this makeup scrubbed off and get into my outfit. Could you go call Kathal and Yeil inside?"

There was still more than an hour before they needed to leave for the Temple of the Seven, so Leila took a quick bath. The warm water, coupled with a special cream, helped to remove all traces of the pale makeup that had lightened her dye-darkened skin to a tone a couple of shades lighter than what she had naturally. If I'm going to keep changing color, she thought as she scrubbed at her skin, it would be nice if I could just do it with a wish the way I become shadows. She'd been granted a supernatural gift by a disgraced god a few weeks ago, and already using it had become as commonplace as eating.

They re-shaved each other's heads, then went to get into their costumes. Leila returned from her bedroom wearing the deep black *kad'r* Tevo had obtained for her over an outfit she'd specially chosen for tonight. The fabric of the over-garment was quite opaque, and it operated like a cloak. But instead of a single closure at the neck, it had a series of frog closures from across the nose down to below shin level. Clearly, not something you were going to get out of in a hurry.

Her cohort in crime, aka the acolyte Ademji, was also dressed in a *kad'r*. But he was planning on keeping his on all evening, only throwing back the hood so that he could eat; and beneath it he wore normal clothing. He and the cat had been occupying cushions in the living room, waiting for her, for some time.

"Ah, my Mysterion!" Ademji cried as she came down the stairs. "You are looking very… Mysterion-ous, this evening." Leila smiled, a gesture utterly lost on her audience. Kathal was sprawled, black cat on a black cushion, and seemed oblivious to her arrival. The raven was perched on the room's central table, looking disgruntled. But then, that was his usual expression.

Leila unfastened the top couple of frogs on the *kad'r* and pulled the hood back, grinning at her acolyte. Then she took a seat on an unoccupied cushion. "You have the figurines packed up for travel?" she asked.

"I forgot to mention," Tevo said, "while I was waiting for our oh-so-ebon garments to be made I visited a shop where they sell curios, and I chanced upon the perfect carrying case." He gestured to where a dark-stained bloodwood box, around two feet tall by a foot by a foot, sat on the table.

This damned outfit restricted vision, Leila thought irritably. How else could she have missed it? The box had a carrying handle on the top, and a series of clasps that held it closed. Once the clasps were released it opened out into a display case two feet wide, two feet high, and six inches deep – with twenty-four square six-inch cubicles within. All but one of them was packed with a cunningly wrought, ancient-looking bloodwood figurine, wrapped in wool for protection within its cubicle.

Leila jumped to her feet and hugged Tevo, kissing him soundly. "Oh, Tevo, it's *beyond* perfect! This is wonderful!" The two dozen figurines Rosa had lifted from Count Wilhelm's collection were only a small part of the total number he owned, few enough that they had not been missed for weeks after she'd stolen them. Now they truly looked as if they had always been a collection of twenty-four. The bloodwood case even showed enough wear to suggest it had traveled here, carefully guarded, from Palambo.

"What's your plan, Leila?" Yeil asked, fixing her with a beady eye. At some point in their journey, the raven seemed to have abandoned his overt hostility to Tevo's being included in their plans. But he still seemed to think that his master had been beyond desperate, to recruit this female juvenile delinquent as his sole hope for a return to full god status.

Leila grinned at him. The bird's constant carping brought out her mischievous streak, and though she knew they truly needed him for his unique abilities, she couldn't resist twisting his beak. "It's quite simple, Yeil," she said, "and you will have a major part in it. Tonight the Mysterion, acolyte Ademji, the sacred black leopard cat and our equally sacred and also quite sagacious *djimdjim* bird, are going for supper and an audience with the High Archon – head of the Gaspari church, in case you're not aware."

The bird looked at her with an unreadable glance, as if her pronouncement had not been worthy of a reply. Finally he spoke. "I know that our master said you must do so, but why? Isn't he in league with Lucia, Betsalel's sworn enemy?"

The girl got serious. "Not necessarily, Yeil. He's supposed to be the top priest in the Gaspari religion, but that's not just worship of Lucia. Most people think of her as chiefest among the deities, I know – and from what Betsalel told me that means that she probably is. But the High Archon is supposed to honor *all* of the gods, equally. He had a pretty good idea that I was contacting him on behalf of the Shadow God, and he went ahead and invited us to dine with him anyway. It's been two hundred years, and people have short memories. Most people I've talked with see Betsalel as a sort of bogey-man – an abstract personification of evil. They don't even think of him as a real god anymore, and he isn't. Not completely, not like the others."

"So you're going to try to talk him into letting our master back into the pantheon?" Yeil asked.

"Pretty much," Leila acknowledged. "I'm going to tell him how it really is, how what happened two centuries ago was a power play by Lucia and how Betsalel is no worse than any of the other gods. And I need you to provide some supernatural backup. I don't want the High Archon dismissing me as a con artist, just because I *am* a con artist. You talk to him just as you talk to me, as the god's envoy, and we'll see what he says."

Chapter 73

The cabs came in various sizes, and the sun was still well above the western horizon when they piled into one meant to seat four. The trip to the Temple of the Seven was not that far, a few minutes away; but certainly too far for them to walk. At the Temple they were met by an acolyte, the same boy who had come to their door the night before, and escorted past the main sanctuary to the High Archon's private quarters on the floor below.

The high priestess Laleihala was doing a great job of appearing aloof, walking along with her head held high while the sacred black leopard cat stalked at her heel and the equally sacred black bird rode on her shoulder. Covered in black cloth except for her eyes, it was an easy pose to maintain. But slight movements of her head betrayed her surprise at seeing the idols in the sanctuary of Parat's Temple of the Seven for the first time.

Each stood on a broad circular platform of gray stone, making them seem even taller, and each of idols had been carved from stone colored appropriately for them. They must surely have been dyed, somehow, she assumed – and the idols stood nearly twenty feet high! Some colors of stone might be found in that size, but certainly not all of them – unless, perhaps, the idols had been created by the gods themselves? Leila realized that, for a supposed high priestess, her grasp of theology was pretty nebulous.

As they passed down the broad stone steps to the lower level, Leila saw that this place was configured similarly to the Treasure House on the hill above –spacious public areas on the ground floor, with hidden rooms beneath. From the number of priests and acolytes moving about, this level must be where most of the temple's personnel had their residences.

Shortly they were ushered into a cool, dimly-lit apartment that seemed to be constructed entirely of the same pale marble that made up most of Parat's public buildings. They came into a receiving room, and found Gabriel Sforza, the High Archon himself, seated in a comfortable chair at the back of it. Lamps cast a golden glow around the room, and he rose to greet them.

Leila was amazed. She had heard that the High Archon was in his mid-nineties. His hair was silver, his face lined; but he stood straight and strong, seeming a hale man in his sixties or early seventies. This man must indeed have the gods' favor! Ademji and Laleihala made their curious Palamban genuflections, and introduced themselves. He smiled at them, a look of anticipation on his face as if he thought he was really going to enjoy this evening, and beckoned them to sit. Similar comfortable chairs ringed the room, offering seating for perhaps a dozen.

"My acolyte must maintain the *kad'r* as a sign of respect," Laleihala declared, but I would remove mine now that we are private – also as a sign of respect, that you may see me as I am." The High Archon nodded, and the high priestess undid the frogs down the front of her all-encompassing black garment and took it off, handing it to her acolyte. He solemnly folded it and tucked it away about his person. Beside him, he had set the case in which the Palamban figurines resided.

Gabriel Sforza's eyes traveled over the high priestess with appreciation. The Gaspari church made no demands of celibacy on its priesthood, did not even require those who served to remain in their posts forever if other aspects of life called them away. In his time he had married, and their two children had gone on to produce a small army of descendants. But his wife was long gone, his children dead of old age as well. It had been a long time since he had seen anything like this "Mysterion" of the Palamban church.

Leila had really put some effort into this costume. It needed to be exotic enough to ring true to someone who'd never laid eyes on a Palamban, dignified enough to fit the role of a high priestess; and sexy enough to melt the mind of any straight man within her range. Tevo, also surreptitiously checking her out from within his black hood, thought she'd pulled it off nicely.

The color scheme was all black, of course – cropped black top cut low in front to expose her dark brown cleavage, black skirt riding her hips while above them a bright red ruby glowed in her navel. She had another red "jewel" glued to her forehead, a heavy application of black makeup around her eyes, and enough "gold" bangles around her arms to finance a small independent country – had they been real.

"Your Holiness," Laleihala said in vibrant tones, "I am so very glad that you have agreed to meet with me." She looked into his somewhat watery blue eyes with her deep green ones, and saw a spark there that told her the old man was, most definitely, not dead yet.

"We have much to discuss," she went on smoothly, "But first I would like to present you with the gift that we have brought to your Temple of the Seven from our own temple in Palambo. These figurines, while not religious in nature, represent a great treasure of our people, which we are bringing to you as a token of our desire to establish a friendship, an accord, between the churches of the Gaspari Dominion and Palambo."

At the Mysterion's gesture, her black-clad acolyte rose from his chair and brought the bloodwood box forward to set ceremoniously on the small table that occupied the center of the room. He unfastened the clasps and opened out the wings, so that the twenty-three figurines were on display. Swaddled as they were in their protective wool, the High Archon could not really see them; and he rose from his chair, lips apart in an expression of awe, and came to stand beside the table.

Sforza called his own acolyte, who was on duty and had returned to the chambers' entryway, to help unwrap the treasures. Each was more exquisite than the last, the details of the carving beyond belief, the cunningly faceted and inlaid gems turning each figurine into a priceless treasure. Actually of course they'd all *had* prices – and Count Wilhelm had paid them.

The Church also had a museum, but one not open to the public. Only those who took religious orders were allowed to see the treasures they'd amassed. Leila fervently hoped they would stay hidden away from the general public until she was long, long gone from Parat.

The High Archon took in the whole collection, lovingly lingering on each little statuette in turn. Clearly, whatever else he might be, Gabriel Sforza was a man who appreciated beauty – and the skill required to create it. "Thank you, Mysterion, for this truly priceless gift," he said. "The Church of the Dominion of Gaspar will treasure it always, as well as the sentiment that inspired its giving."

Oh yeah, and a politician – Leila mentally added that to her list of the High Archon's attributes. It made sense. If the gods had been molded by humanity, they were as susceptible as anybody to the attributes that let men rise to power among men. Or, rarely, women. History marked half a dozen times when the High Archon had been of the "weaker sex."

Despite her cynical attitude, Leila found that she quite liked the High Archon. There was something about him that inspired a feeling of warmth, of trust – he seemed like a good man. She hoped her feeling was right. It wouldn't be the first time in her short life that she'd erred in that regard.

"Gaban, please pack the figurines up in their protective wrappings and have them delivered to whoever is on duty in the Treasury this evening," the High Archon directed his acolyte. The boy, who looked to be no older than Leila, jumped to do his master's bidding. It must be a high honor, indeed, for one so young to be the personal servant of the Church's highest official. Leila wondered if the boy might be one of Sforza's own descendants. What she'd read suggested that he had dozens of them.

"We'll go in to dinner now," the old priest said with a twinkle. He led the way through a door to left of his chair and they found themselves in a long dining chamber. The table could have sat a dozen, but there were only three chairs. While they'd been talking, it seemed, servants had laid a feast of sorts near one end. Presumably the High Archon was to sit at the head, with his guests at either side. The animals had most likely not been expected, but neither had either Sforza or his acolyte looked askance at them.

The old priest held out a chair for Laleihala to be seated, his hand brushing her bare shoulder as she sat down. Ademji seated himself, nodding as if this were all as he had expected. Leila thought it surprising that her acolyte, theoretically a servant, was being granted a seat equal to her own. Perhaps the Archon was uncertain of the Palamban customs, and figured that it was better to err on the side of more rather than less respect. Had it been unseemly for the black-clad underling to share a table with his mistress, she could easily have ordered him away.

Gabriel Sforza seated himself, and looked around at the dishes on the table. Though the man was slim, looking as if he had not gained an ounce of body fat since he was in his twenties, he had clearly not lost his enthusiasm for the pleasures of the table. Nor for looking at attractive young women, it seemed.

The High Archon lifted the cover from one of the dishes, and smiled. "Oh, you must try some of this!" he said with enthusiasm, spooning some of its contents first onto Laleihala's plate and then onto the plate of the black-clad acolyte. Tevo ceremoniously unfastened the hood of his *kad'r* so that he could eat, and made a slight bow to Sforza and another to his mistress.

Leila was dumfounded. She felt as if she were dining at the home of a family friend, or perhaps some distant relative only rarely seen. Or rather, as she *imagined* that would be – in her life, she had never known either situation. This was *not* what she'd expected! But she needed to keep her cool. She still needed to be the mysterious foreign hierarch by the time she began her pitch.

But the High Archon's human warmth beckoned to her, and she couldn't help responding. The overall effect was of a woman delighted by the hospitality but maintaining a slight natural reserve, as the three of them worked their way through half a dozen dishes. Marcelina's cooking was excellent, but seemingly whoever the priesthood had cooking for them at the Temple of the Seven was… divine.

Kathal had not eaten in the past few hours, and the smells from the table were beginning to drive her crazy. She'd remained seated like a statue since they had entered the dining room, but when the High Archon removed the cover from a dish of braised beef with mushrooms and currants, she came padding over and nudged Leila's knee. "Mirao?" she asked.

The high priestess stiffened. "Kathal, go and wait!" she commanded, and the cat cast a resentful glance over her shoulder as she returned to her station.

"My goodness!" the High Archon exclaimed with a chuckle, "I've never seen a cat so obedient. I suppose the Nima pards can be trained thus, though. Are the species related?"

Laleihala blotted her mouth with a napkin and a slight smile appeared on her lips. "The leopard cats of the Palamban jungle are similar, I believe, to the desert ancestors of what your Nima call 'pards.' But the leopard cats are more wild, not usually domesticated. Kathal is a member of that species' rare black morph, and she was taken from the wild as a kitten to be raised by our cult. All creatures of that color are sacred to our god," she added, in case the Archon needed to be hit over the head with a cudgel to get his attention.

The meal concluded with some candied fruits, washed down with a sweet wine. Then the party returned to the room they'd first entered on arriving here. Finally, Leila thought with an internal sigh of relief. She'd kept a tight rein on how much wine she was drinking, wanting to maintain a clear head. Now, at last, it was time to sell her cause to the religious leader of the entire bloody Gaspari Dominion.

Gabriel Sforza settled himself once again in his comfortable chair, seeming replete and in a mellow mood but not in the least the worse for drink. "Ah," he said with a sigh, smiling broadly, "that was most delicious. And your company, Mysterion, most pleasant. How is it that one so young as you has risen to the rank of high priestess, might I ask?"

Looking dignified beyond her years, the high priestess replied "I was born to it, Your Holiness. In my cult it's believed that the soul of the departed High One, whether male or female, flees to the body of the nearest child not yet possessed of a soul. So the next child to be born is examined by the elders of the Church, and if the signs are there the child is declared to be the reincarnation of the high priest. Or priestess. In my case, the prior High One had been inhabiting a male body."

The High Archon looked astounded. After digesting her utterly ad-libbed claim for a moment, he remarked, "Can't say you look very much like a former man..." Laleihala dimpled at him.

"Nor do I feel like a man, I assure you! But before him, there was a woman... Who can say what the gender of a disembodied soul might be?"

Sforza chuckled, and she joined him in his laughter. Tevo, greatly amused at all this behind the hood he'd once again fastened around his face, grinned broadly but remained silent. "So then," the

Archon said, thinking through what the Mysterion had said, "you were trained in the mysteries of your religion from earliest childhood?"

"That is correct," she replied shortly.

"Perhaps," he said thoughtfully, "it is time for you to tell me what you came here to tell me, then." Laleihala nodded solemnly.

"Holiness," she began, "what do you know of Betsalel?" There was no sign of surprise. Clearly, the High Archon had already known what the subject of their discussion was to be.

"A little more than two hundred years ago," he said, "the Emperor of the Dominion of that time, Fernand IV, was given divine guidance by Lucia. He had been drawn to her worship as a young man, had been a member of her cult, and after he was crowned emperor it was announced that she had given him a revelation."

Leila cocked an eyebrow, a gesture she'd spent hours practicing in front of a mirror. "A revelation?" she asked. The High Archon nodded and continued.

"She had revealed to him that the worshipers of Betsalel, her opposite number and supposedly her consort under our understanding of theology, had turned to evil. That Betsalel himself had turned to evil. And Fernand, as Emperor of the entire Dominion, had the power to stamp that worship out."

"Was this not obvious to the average citizen?" Laleihala asked casually. "I would think that if one of the cults had turned to human sacrifice or some such, people would not need a bulletin from a competing deity to know that it was true." Her wording was specifically designed to remind Sforza that Lucia was not an uninterested party. The High Archon sighed. He had studied the histories long and hard, and had been unable to draw any conclusions. Whatever had really happened two hundred years ago, it was a done thing – and there were no living witnesses.

"Fernand was convinced," he explained half-apologetically, "and that was enough for everyone else. The Shadow God's rituals had always, by their very nature, been shrouded in darkness. It was not hard to convince people that horrible things were being done in his name, in secret. And the denials of his believers went unheeded. There was mob violence, and slaughter, and within five years the worship of Betsalel had been wiped from the Dominion forever. These days, I think, few even view him as a god. Just a scary tale to keep children in line, or a mythological demon perhaps."

Laleihala's eyes widened, and she stared at Sforza with an intensity that soon made him uncomfortable. He went on, "But you are here, and clearly the mysteries of the Shadow God continue in Palambo. His worship here is still against the law, a law that's been on the books for more than two hundred years. But I doubt anyone is enforcing it. Certainly not against foreign nationals. So tell me, Mysterion, why are you really here?"

More than an hour later the high priestess, accompanied by her acolyte and sacred animals, were shown out of the Temple of the Seven and found another cab to carry them back to their home less than two miles away. They left behind them an old man who was deeply troubled. Could it all really be true?

Divine Lucia had been honored as the highest, purest, and most holy of all the gods throughout his life – and that was a long, long time. The Palamban priestess' tale of gods who required human worship to retain their powers, of eight siblings who vied with each other for supremacy, had turned everything he had been taught, everything he had believed, on its ear. It was madness! But somehow it had a ring of truth.

The bird who spoke as a human did (in two languages, no less!) had been the kicker. After listening to this Yeil speak, he knew he was in the presence of a creature who was in direct communication with a god. A god wronged, cast aside, unable to die but deprived of what he needed to live. Laleihala's demonstration of the Shadow power granted her by Betsalel had been just the icing on the cake.

It was long past the hour he usually went to bed. Gabriel Sforza, High Archon of the Dominion of Gaspar, might be hale and hearty beyond anyone else his age; but he was still an old man. Yet his mental turmoil would not let him rest. "Gaban," he called, and the boy was at his side. He never faltered, was always there when needed. "We're going to the sanctuary," the Archon explained. "I need to have words with the gods."

Chapter 74

Laleihala and Ademji, clad in their *kad'r*, were breakfasting in their dining room at home when Gaban arrived at their door with a message from the High Archon. They had seen him coming up the walk and Marcelina was in the kitchen cleaning up after the meal; so Ademji got to his feet and fastened the hood across his face as he went to answer the door.

He opened it before the lad had knocked, and executed a slight bow. "We meet again, acolyte," he said. "You have a message for us?" Gaban started. Just what arcane powers did these exotic visitors have, he wondered? Certainly they had impressed his master. He held the message out to the black-clad figure, stammering

"Y-yes, uh, your…?"

"Acolyte, the same as you," Ademji said, and took the folded and sealed paper. "Thank you for delivering this. I will give it to my mistress at once. Will you wait for a reply?"

This time Tevo didn't let the kid inside, but left him standing on the other side of the closed front door. He wasn't sure what the High Archon's message would be, and he wanted his discussion with Leila to remain private. He returned to the dining room and handed the message to her, as she had hastily finished the meal and was wiping her mouth on a napkin. She looked up at him inquiringly, and he shrugged.

The message, once again sealed with the High Archon's elaborate signet, looked to have been hastily scrawled in Gabriel Sforza's own hand, and was much less formal than his prior communication. It read simply, "High Priestess, I have considered all that we discussed and I believe that what you told me is the truth. Please come to the Temple of the Seven immediately, as I must speak with you."

This looked like the start of another busy day, so Laleihala began fastening the hood of her *kad'r* as she walked through to the kitchen. "Marcelina," she said, "we have been called to the Temple of the Seven again and are leaving immediately. I think it likely we will not be here for lunch, but in case we are delayed this evening please prepare some supper for us and put it in the ice box."

The housekeeper eyed her, but nodded. "Yes, High Priestess. I will do that. Thank you for letting me know." Laleihala nodded briskly and turned on her heel, returning to the dining room.

"You have money?" she asked her acolyte, and he jingled the coins in the pocket of the trousers he wore beneath the *kad'r* by way of answer. "Let's go then," she said, a hint of excitement in her voice.

They hailed a cab to speed the short journey to the temple, sending it on its way when they arrived. Gaban accompanied them as they went in through the main entrance. They found the High Archon not in the sanctuary, which at this hour was full of worshipers doing homage to their gods, but in his ground floor office. While much of his job involved being a ceremonial figurehead, the leader of the largest organized church in the world had many more mundane responsibilities. He looked up anxiously as Gaban led them in, his face pale.

"Ah, thank you for coming so quickly!" he said, beckoning them to chairs. "Gaban, thank you as well. You may go to your post now." The boy left the room and closed the door behind him. He took a chair in the hallway and slumped into it. He'd had less sleep than he needed last night, and had started the morning with a mad dash across the Temple District.

The High Archon noticed that neither the cat nor the talking bird had accompanied the two emissaries from the Palamban church this morning. Perhaps they had not had time to bring them along, having responded so rapidly to his request. "Mysterion," he said solemnly, addressing Laleihala, "what you told me last night shook me greatly. I have been in the church for a very long time, and some of what you said is contrary to everything I have been taught."

The High Priestess nodded at him. She reached up and unfastened the hood of her *kad'r* so that he could see her face, now that they were in private. He hadn't learned all the details of this custom of remaining covered from head to foot while in public, but assumed it was an overlay of Palamban cultural practices on the religion that they both, to some extent, practiced.

Laleihala gave the old priest a look that said, "Please go on" and he continued. "After you had departed I went seeking comfort from the gods, hoping to ease my troubled mind. As it is they who put me on my high seat, I alone of all in the Gaspari church can be sure of an audience if I come requesting one within the sanctuary of Parat's Temple of the Seven."

"Only here?" the Palamban priestess asked, curious. Betsalel had said that this temple was the foremost seat of the gods' power on earth. The old man nodded. "Here, our traditions say, is where the gods first appeared to mankind in the days when we dressed in furs and planted no crops. Where now this temple stands, there was a broad circle of stone, naturally formed. And upon that circle of stone, eight stone idols appeared. Each was no taller than a small child, roughly formed as male or female – but with no further details, and not by the hand of man. As our remote ancestors came to know these gods, so the idols grew and took shape until they became as they are now, standing within the sanctuary that was built atop the circle of stone."

Laleihala's eyes widened. The ancients thought they were "learning" about their gods, when they were really shaping them. This was powerful magic, indeed, magic from the bones of the earth. "So you have spoken with the gods, then?" she asked. What had they told him? Given Lucia's history, it was clear that the gods were human enough to tell lies. Only having a fragment of Betsalel embedded within her body had let her know for certain that he spoke the truth.

"As Lucia was accused, I first polled the others," the High Archon said. "One by one I approached to speak with them. And one by one, they admitted that what you said was true. Betsalel was no more inherently evil than any being, but had been unjustly attacked by his sister Lucia – yes, they confirmed that the eight are siblings, not mated pairs as we had always thought – and his divine powers bled away as his worshipers were killed and his temples destroyed." Laleihala nodded, a glint of triumph in her eyes. At least the others had been willing to confirm what she knew to be true.

Sforza looked older this morning, old and tired and sorrowful. It could not be easy for one his age to accept that beliefs he'd held for many decades were wrong, and Leila admired him for doing so – and at such cost. "Finally," he went on, "I approached divine Lucia. And she was furious! She denied everything, accused the others of conspiring against her. I feared she would come down off her pedestal and smash me to a paste!"

He laid his hands on the desk, and Leila could see that they were trembling. What a shock to the poor old man's system! "High Archon," the Mysterion said, "my mission here has been more than just to relay these facts to you. I was tasked by Betsalel himself to restore his idol to the Temple of the Seven, opening a pathway for his return to the power he once held."

The old priest blinked at her in astonishment. "But surely that idol was destroyed more than two centuries ago!" he said. "Its removal from the Temple of the Eight, as it was then, and the destruction of the Shadow God's own temple in the northeastern part of the city, were the first acts in Fernand's campaign against him." Laleihala shook her head. "It was not destroyed," she replied serenely. "My god revealed to me that he and his loyal followers had rendered it impregnable. So Fernand's guards took it away and hid it, encased in brick, in a forgotten corner of the Imperial Treasure House."

As the old man was digesting that, the high priestess went on. "My acolyte and I have located the idol, and we will soon be seeking to free it so that my god can manifest within it and return to his place in the Temple – which will be the Temple of the Eight once more, the Balance restored. But he needs more than this to regain his former powers. The minds of believers must be opened to him again. They must not fear him, but instead come to him in worship and supplication so that he can give them the gifts of rest, of sleep, of surcease from pain that the shadows bring to all – nightly, or at the end of life."

The High Archon seemed transfixed by her speech. Then, startled from his reverie, he said "Er, ah... I suppose I can issue a statement of some kind. I *am* the head of the church, after all, and I can command the church hierarchs to tell their flocks that Betsalel is once more an accepted member of the pantheon. But I have no true temporal power. I could encourage the Grand Assembly to pass a bill rescinding the old law forbidding the worship of the Shadow God, but it would be up to them to decide whether or not to heed me."

"When you talked to the gods, did any of them offer to step in and support Betsalel's return?" Laleihala asked. The old man shook his head sadly.

"While each confirmed the truth of what you and the bird had told me, none indicated a willingness to take up your cause. Lucia is now so much more powerful than any other of the gods, that unless all of them join together it is likely she could bring down any one – or even two – who rose up against her."

Silence fell for a few moments, as those in the room considered their quandary. Then the High Archon spoke. "Mysterion, you are a very powerful and persuasive young woman. Perhaps if you can talk to the gods, each of them alone, you might convince them to back me up? Many worshipers, especially those within the mysteries at the gods' own temples, will want confirmation from their chosen deity that my pronouncement is true."

Leila pondered this. How had she *known* today was going to be another busy day? She hoped she'd be able to squeeze in a good night's sleep, soon. "Can I speak with them here in the Temple of the Seven as you do, Holy One?" the Palamban priestess asked.

"Not a good idea," the Archon responded. "Lucia could easily eavesdrop on what was said, and I fear it would constrain the gods from offering you their assistance. You will need to go to each of the deities' own temples, which are scattered around the city. I'll mark them on a map for you."

"Will they speak with me when I call them there?" Laleihala asked. Deep down inside she was just a teenage thief and con artist, not a high priestess. No gods other than Betsalel had ever had a word to say to her.

"As you set out, I will speak to each of them here and request that they give you a hearing. I think they will listen to me."

The Palamban religious officials, once again covered from head to foot, left the Temple of the Seven and hailed another cab – even as Gabriel Sforza was down on his knees again in the sanctuary behind them. In the cab, Leila squeezed Tevo's hand and kissed him through the two layers of cloth separating their faces. "Looks like it's going to be a long one, Ademji." He nodded, grinning beneath his hood.

Chapter 75

Leila had no idea how long it was going to take to talk with each of the six gods, and hoped she was going to be able to get it all done in one day. Just traveling to each of the temples by cab, through the busy streets of Parat, was going to take long enough. They planned a route that took them to the temple of Belantos, nearest to the Temple of the Seven, and then looped around the city to each of the other five.

Ademji pulled two florins out of an inner pocket and handed them to the cab driver. "You will please wait for us here, and take us to the other places we need to go after we return. I trust this is enough to hire your services for the day?" The cabbie gawked at him. Two florins was more than he usually made in a week!

"That'll be fine, uh, honored sir," he said, having no idea how these exotic foreigners should be addressed. After the two had proceeded through the door of the Temple of Belantos, he pulled a pulp novel out of the storage area beneath the driver's bench and resumed reading it.

They found the temple staff in an uproar. The god (manifesting in the idol that occupied the sanctuary here) had made a general announcement that they were soon to have important visitors, and that all was to be made ready for them. Wow, Leila thought, as they were ushered inside and provided with comfortable seats before the idol, the old Archon has definitely got some clout!

The idol, a smaller version but identical in every other way to the one they had recently left behind, represented a very muscular man in his prime. His long hair was bound in a queue behind his head, he had a full beard, and instead of a loincloth he was dressed in full, antique armor. A long sword was hung at his side, and the entire idol – flesh, hair, clothing, and weapon – was a uniform blood red.

Here, at least, Leila figured she could expect some kind of favorable reception. She hoped. Belantos was awfully scary-looking. "O Mighty Belantos, I am Betsalel's chosen representative. I beg that you will speak with me." Leila figured that the whole "Palamban high priestess" rigmarole might be offensive to divine beings – who could presumably see right through her lies.

As they watched, a ripple passed across the idol and it came alive. The red color remained in the skin, but the hair and beard became darker and the armor and weapons took on the appearance of real ones – save that they were so outsized. Before them stood the living war god, and he looked down on them with an expression of… amusement?

The god waved a hand and an enormous throne-like chair appeared on the dais behind him. He sat on it with a clank. Oh good, Leila thought. Sitting down seemed like a good sign. "My brother Betsalel has long been gone from among us," Belantos said in a deep and resonant voice. It reminded her of the Shadow God's own. "How is it that he now troubles the Dominion, after such an absence?"

Getting a grip on her nerve, Leila rose to her feet. She was so small, and the god was so enormous! Beside her, she could feel Tevo sending her encouragement. "The Balance was broken when your sister Lucia brought down her other half," she pointed out. "Since then, Betsalel's worshipers in Palambo have begun worshipping an imaginary demon in his name, and have lost their connection to their god. This has fractured the Balance further."

The god nodded, acknowledging the truth of her words – though he hadn't known about the Palamban situation. The gods rarely communicated with each other, meeting only within temples where all were represented. "You and your fellows confirmed to the High Archon that Lucia's campaign two hundred years ago was based on lies," Leila went on. "And when he then spoke with Lucia, she flew into a rage and insisted that the rest of you were conspiring against her."

Belantos looked troubled. None of them were happy at what their sister had done, but they didn't want her coming after *them*, either. The bitch had reaped way too much personal power thanks to that coup. "You yourself, Belantos, have fallen far from your former power here within the Dominion," Leila said – stating the obvious.

She went on, "It seems likely that Lucia might seek to increase her power still more, especially if she believes the rest of you are conspiring against her. Probably it'll be you, or maybe Dionos, she goes after next. It wouldn't be hard to sell the idea that you are the representation of strife and destruction, harmful to our land – and that the worship of Dionos is an affront to social mores."

Belantos clutched the arms of his throne. Damn, the girl was absolutely right. But what could he do about it? Lucia could destroy him, reduce him to a spirit wailing in the wilderness with a flick of her finger. Especially if peace were to break out in Palambo or the realms of the Hando…"

"The High Archon intends to issue a proclamation refuting the claim that Betsalel is evil, and petition the Grand Assembly for the laws banning his worship to be rescinded. Nor will he stand in our way when we restore the Shadow God's idol to the Temple – not of the Seven, but of the Eight once again. Only if you and your siblings conspire against Lucia in fact can the Balance be restored. Will you stand with us, tell what worshipers remain to you the truth?"

He was the God of War! Belantos thought. What was he doing, cowering before the very idea of getting in trouble with his sister? She might be powerful, but she was in the wrong. And this young woman, last priestess of Betsalel (or was it first?) spoke wisdom. Only if they united could they defeat Lucia and rein her in. And how her power and prestige would tumble, when worshipers learned that she had lied – and that all the other gods had censured her!

Belantos rose to his feet, the stone floor vibrating slightly as he stood. Leila managed not to flinch. She'd expected to be having a dialogue, not delivering an oration. "Priestess," he boomed, "I will stand with you. My cultists among the Dominion's church, and my many worshipers elsewhere in the world, will learn the truth of my brother's downfall."

Leila couldn't help smiling, though she still felt overwhelmed. "Thank you, Great Belantos," she said formally. "I go now to speak to each of your siblings in turn (Lucia excepted, did not need to be mentioned). Are you able to communicate with them and inform them of your support for Betsalel's return?

"My siblings and I can converse only when we are manifest in our idols," the god replied. "You mortals, who molded us and made us what we are, have seen fit to constrict us in this manner. And if I manifest in the Temple of the Seven to impart this news, I fear that

Lucia will learn of our plot before it is fully formed. But I will give you this token."

Drawing that enormous sword, the god leaned forward and held his left hand high, Then he drew the blade across, scoring the red flesh. A single enormous drop of blood fell, and Leila convulsively put out her hands to catch it. It felt hot in her hands, but had become a crystalline teardrop, deep blood-red – a smooth gem the size, and roughly the shape, of a fig.

As Leila gazed at it in wonder Belantos sheathed his sword. The chair behind him vanished, and as he resumed the posture the idol was always portrayed in, motion ceased. They were once again looking at a hard idol formed of red stone. She shivered in reaction, then placed the gem in a pocket of the clothes she wore beneath the *kad'r*. One down, five to go.

Chapter 76

And so it went through the day, as they made their way from temple to temple around the loop. They stopped near midday for a hasty lunch at a café, and when they neared Pleasance Street Leila stopped to call on Yeil. The raven had been hopping around the back yard looking for grubs.

"You're here!" he croaked in surprise. "I had begun to imagine that you'd bought this place just so you could spend all your time elsewhere."

"Busy, busy," she replied, refusing to rise to the bait. "I've been thinking about the problem with the Treasure House," Leila went on, "and I can imagine only one possible way to get into that room."

Yeil cocked his head at her. For all his bad-tempered carping, he was beginning to think his master had not been wrong in choosing this young firebrand for his agent. The things she had accomplished! The girl sure had a mouth on her, though.

"Through the roof," Leila continued after letting the bird's suspense build. The raven looked thoughtful. "It stands to reason," she said. "The building's roof is fifty feet off the ground – atop smooth, windowless stone walls around three of its four sides. There are openings only in the front area where the museum is, and that area's well lit and no doubt heavily guarded at night. But nobody would expect a burglar to break in from above, I think. I need you to go do some aerial reconnaissance while we're running around asking the gods for favors."

Ravens are big, heavy birds and not fond of flying long distances. But Yeil had been getting bored hanging around the back yard. "Excellent idea," he replied. "Is there anything in particular I should be looking for?" Leila pulled out a map of the Treasure House's top floor. It captured the building's footprint as seen from the air. "Here is where our master's idol is hidden," she pointed. "Can you sense it if you get close?"

After consulting his inner being Yeil said "Yes, if I am within a few dozen feet I should be able to sense the idol, even encased in brick and removed from its nexus of power."

"That will be great," Leila said, getting ready to hurry off. "Check the roof for loose tiles, projections we can use to climb up by, and anything else that might help us. We'll try to go out there tonight and break in, if you find what we're looking for. See you later!" She returned to the cab waiting in the street outside the house, and the raven took to the air. The sky was partly cloudy with a light breeze, and it seemed like a nice day to fly up the hill to the palace.

Belantos had been the easiest of the lot to sway, by far. He was both vulnerable to Lucia's attacks and bold enough to step up anyway. Mira, the goddess who was his opposite number, wanted nothing to do with a conflict. But she was finally convinced to agree that, if asked, she would tell the truth rather than refusing to answer. She would confirm that Betsalel was blameless and had been wronged. Before vacating her idol she produced a live dove out of the air, which launched itself from her hand only to become a tiny jade carving of a dove – Mira's token.

Mulia, her attention taken up with domestic things and in no danger of losing her worshipers as long as womankind still relied on her for help with making a home and bearing children, could not be convinced to speak out against Lucia. But she, too, promised that she would answer truthfully if asked. Her token was a single head of golden wheat.

By the time she got to Andros, god of the manly arts like smithing, tanning, and hunting – not to mention the highly popular virility – Leila was beginning to tire. During their lunch stop they'd picked up a bag of hard candies at a sweet shop, and she sucked on one to ease her throat as they approached the Temple of Andros.

His idol was muscular (though not as much as Belantos had been), with long hair hanging down to his shoulders and a full beard. He was nut-brown all over, and except for the beard and his obvious maturity he reminded Leila a little bit of Tevo. Andros was jolly in a bluff sort of way, friendly enough. But it took some talking to convince him to join with them and actively let his worshipers (who were legion) know that Betsalel had been wronged. His token was a little brown cylindrical object that, when Leila examined it closely after the god's departure, caused her to flush crimson beneath her dye. Virility, huh?

So far the goddesses had all agreed to passive support but refused to pledge any active assistance. As Betsalel's departure had left the goddesses with a numerical advantage over their male counterparts, Leila wondered if they were practicing some kind of sisterly solidarity. But Deline, the goddess whose domain was learning, reason, and the arts, examined the tokens Leila had brought with her and immediately stated, "Of course I will support your cause, priestess. It is clear that my sister Lucia is now well outnumbered, so that is the logical course of action. I will inform all who reach out to me of the truth."

Wow, Leila thought as she went on her way. Power in numbers. The afternoon was wearing on, and she wondered how Yeil was doing with his mission. Oh! That reminded her. As they passed a smithy while approaching the last temple on her list, Leila asked the cab driver to halt. "Ademji," she said quietly lest they be overheard, "We are in need of some items from yon smithy." Pulling a piece of paper from within her *kad'r*, she hastily sketched a crowbar and a grabbling hook. "Two of those, one of the other," she said, pointing. Then added a coil of rope to the picture. "A hundred feet of that, strong and not too thick. Got it?"

"Yes, mistress," Ademji said, climbing down. He didn't need her picture to know what was on his shopping list. "I will bring these items to the cab and wait for you outside the temple, unless I am unable to obtain them before you are finished talking with the god. In that case, return and meet me here." Leila nodded, and the cab drove on. In a few minutes she was inside the temple and petitioning the god Dionos, personification of lechery and debauchery, to come forth and talk with her. She was beginning to wish she'd thought of that hardware purchase earlier. This was one god she wasn't sure she wanted to be alone with.

Dionos' temple was quite unlike any of the others Leila had visited today. Instead of small altars, ceremonial urns, or other such religious objects the room was lined with couches – evidently for the drunken orgies that constituted Dionos' favorite form of worship. Pornographic murals decorated the walls.

The god's idol was a rather horrendous shade of orange. Leila mused that perhaps all the good colors had already been taken while he was off getting drunk somewhere, and he'd been stuck with whatever was left over. It depicted a young man, beardless so perhaps a youth, with a wreath of flowers surmounting a crown of ringlets on his head. He had a bit of a pot belly but was otherwise clean of limb, and wearing nothing but a very skimpy wrap around his loins that did nothing to hide the large erection he was sporting. Good grief! He had a bottle of wine in one hand, and a chalice in the other.

Might as well get it over with Leila thought, biting her lip as she stepped forward and stood before the idol. There was a comfortable-looking couch immediately behind her but she declined to sit on it. "O Dionos," she called "I have come to speak with you on behalf of my master Betsalel." In an eyeblink the idol was transformed into the incarnation of the god himself. The orange color had been picked up only in the loincloth, Leila noticed, though the curls had a coppery glint.

Weaving slightly, the ten-foot god leered at her. "Saving the best for last, eh?" he said with a wink. Leila half expected him to hop down off his dais and grab her ass. But he did something worse. With a lazy wave of his hand her *kad'r* vanished and she found herself wearing a costume she assumed would be at home in a Palamban harem dancer's wardrobe. Her bald scalp was now covered with flowing black locks reaching down past her waist. And in her hand was a large chalice full of a deep amber fluid that smelled like brandy.

Leila blinked, then glared at the god in outrage. "Hey!" she snapped, "Show some class, will you? This is a serious discussion." Dionos took a big swig of the liquid in his own chalice.

"Relax, sweetheart," he slurred, "don't be so uptight. I'm just trying to lighten the mood a bit. I mean, *seriously*? Was that black thing my brother's idea of appropriate garb for a priestess? Give me a break." He drank again, emptying the cup, and poured some more from the bottle.

Oooooh… It was probably a good thing that all of Leila's daggers, as well as everything else about her person, had vanished with her clothes. She doubted that knifing a god, however richly this particular god deserved it, would be considered diplomatic. "Come on, honey," Dionos went on – seemingly getting more drunk by the minute. Did gods get hangovers? "Drink up!" He tapped his own chalice, then pointed at hers.

"No thank you," she said coolly. "I prefer to remain clear-headed."

The god's cup and bottle abruptly vanished into thin air as he bent over, hands on his knees, and roared with laughter. "Clear-headed!" he wheezed, tears coming to his eyes. "I'll bet my sister Deline ate *that* up with a spoon!" He burst into fresh gales of laughter, then stood gasping and hiccupped. The bottle and chalice reappeared.

Leila noticed that Dionos' erection had not ebbed in the slightest, though there'd certainly been nothing sexual about their encounter… so far. Had she been clad like this in front of Tevo, she would have had to keep him at bay with a stick – their agreement notwithstanding. But surely, Dionos must have willing women coming to him all the time. Huh, maybe it was her non-availability that turned him on?

Enough was enough. Drawing herself up to her full height of slightly more than half that of the god, she said sternly, "Dionos, you more than any of your siblings are vulnerable to Lucia's attacks. As she feels her position threatened by Betsalel's return, you know that she will seek to consolidate her power. And the easiest way to do that is to get all the prudish, judgmental matrons convinced that your worship is an abomination that should be stamped out. How many of your drunken revelers will stand by you, do you think, if the penalty for doing so is death?"

The bottle and cup vanished again, and instantly the reeling god appeared to have become stone cold sober. "That bitch!" he said mournfully. "She's never had a proper appreciation of fun. So, what did my brothers and sisters say? Is it all for one and one for all?"

Leila felt around, and discovered that while everything else she was carrying had vanished, the gods' tokens had remained. They were in a pocket at the rear of the lower half of her costume, which she would not have believed could have room for such a thing. It barely covered her butt.

She displayed the five tokens for Dionos, and he looked at them with interest. "Ooh, collect the whole set!" he exclaimed, smiling delightedly. The bottle had appeared once again, but without its cup, and he raised it to his lips to down what seemed like more liquid than was plausible for a vessel of that size to contain. Lowering the bottle again, he let out an enormous belch – then grinned in self-satisfaction.

"Aaah," the god said, in obvious pleasure. "The good thing about being a god is I can do this whenever I want and never suffer any consequences. Who could want anything more?" He took another impossibly large swig of whatever was in the bottle, and appeared to have gotten rip-roaring drunk again in little more time than it had taken for him to get sober, a minute before. He gave Leila a crooked grin that made her quiver inside, it reminded her of Tevo so much. "Tell you what, love... I'll throw my support your way, give you my token, if you'll do one little thing for me first." Uh oh. Leila was starting to ask herself what good it was having support from Dionos in the first place. Would his drunken worshipers even care one way or the other about Betsalel's return?

Still, it would be nice to "collect the whole set."

"Uh," Leila asked uneasily, "what is it you want me to do for you?" The god appeared to be drunk as a lord once more, floating on a wave of power and ecstasy.

"Why, give me a kiss, sweet thing. Just one, chaste little kiss. No hanky-panky, I swear." He held the thumb and forefinger of his left hand in an "O" and pantomimed with his right index finger what he meant by "hanky-panky."

Leila's eyes went wide, and she hastily stuffed the gods' tokens back into their unlikely resting place. "That's absurd!" she cried, "You're twice my size!" In an instant the god shrank where he stood, until he was now only a little taller than Tevo.

"How about now?" he asked pleadingly, with a ludicrous puppy-dog look that made her want to burst out laughing.

"Oh, all right!" she said. "But no hanky-panky!" Eyes alight with triumph, Dionos stepped down from his dais and swept Leila into his arms. He pressed his mouth on hers, his tongue halfway down her throat. He tasted faintly of honey. Meanwhile his hands roamed her body, pulling her tight against him (that ever-present erection throbbing as it pressed against her belly), squeezing her buttocks.

"Mmmph!" Leila squealed, running out of breath and patience both. She squirmed away, and in an instant Dionos was back on his dais and had resumed his former size. The erection appeared to have gotten proportionately bigger still.

"Oh, that was sweet!" he declared, as Leila stood gasping for breath and staring at him in shock. Girls who have sworn a vow of eternal chastity might we well warned to stay away from church, if *this* guy was the god being worshipped!

"Hold out your hands, dear," the god said almost gently. Leila did as commanded, but she quailed. Considering Andros' token, might that of Dionos be the same thing but on a much grander scale? But no, what appeared in her hands was a little glass vial. She grasped it between thumb and forefinger, and held it up to the light. The amber liquid within seemed to shimmer, even when the vial was held motionless.

"Be of good cheer, Child of Shadows," Dionos said kindly. His drunkenness seemed to have vanished like the mists of morning once again. "When life is bleak and you can't find a smile, sip from this bottle. It will replenish your spirits, and its own contents as well. Just as the human spirit is forever renewable." With those words he became once again the bright orange idol, standing motionless before her. Leila found that her *kad'r* and her other clothing, along with all she carried with her, had been restored.

Chapter 77

Tevo had been able to find two crowbars and a hundred-foot coil of thin, strong rope ready-made, but it had taken the smith time to fabricate the grappling hook. "Going mountain climbing" as an explanation for needing such an item had seemed no better for the forbidding-looking Palamban acolyte than "Going to break into the Imperial Treasure House"; so he'd reverted to his standard inscrutable glare and proffered far more money than the item was worth.

Leila and the cabbie found him there, waiting while the hook cooled. They loaded the rest of the items, wrapped in a burlap sack, into the cab. The cab driver and his horse had quite enjoyed the day, really. They'd traveled a fair distance around the city, but had also had hours of time in which to sit and do nothing strenuous. It was like having a well-paid vacation, and neither of them had any complaints.

The hook went into a second sack, and in due course Leila and Tevo, in their *kad'r*, were dropped off at the Pleasance Street house and went in by the front door. The sun was almost down, and the house was quiet and empty. After they'd dropped their sacks of burglar tools Leila threw herself back onto one of the cushions in the living room with a "pumph."

"Oh, Betsalel!" she declared, "what a day!" She'd decided not to give Tevo any details about her interview with the God of Debauchery. It didn't seem politic, even if the two of them were not technically lovers as yet. For Tevo's part, he'd spent most of the day with little to occupy him and was looking forward to their night raid on the Treasure House – assuming Yeil's report was favorable.

"You relax, Leila," he said. "I'm going to see if Yeil's around." A couple of minutes later Tevo reappeared in the living room with a bottle of wine and two glasses, and some sharp cheese on a plate with a knife beside it. He held open the back door, and the raven flew inside to perch on the table.

He eyed the cheese with interest, and Tevo cut off a sliver and tossed it to the bird. He caught it easily in midair and swallowed it down, just as Leila sat up on her cushion and began to take interest.

Lunch had been hours ago. Soon she and Tevo were both eating chunks of cheese washed down with the delicious red wine, and Yeil was making the report of his afternoon's visit to the Imperial Treasure House.

"There's no sign of any guard activity up there at all," he said, foregoing sarcasm for once. "The roof is slate, and it's certainly been replaced a few times over the centuries but not recently, I'd say. There are some tiles cracked and a few that have fallen out and slid down, exposing older, even more deteriorated slates beneath. Once you're up there, it shouldn't be a problem to dig down through the slates to the wood beneath, and then cut through that with an axe or a saw."

"You were able to find the spot on the roof above where our master's idol is being held?" Leila asked, washing down a bit of the savory cheese with a swallow of wine.

"It called to me like a beacon," the raven replied. "I marked the spot for you." She looked blank.

"Marked? How?" The bird's expressionless, hard-beaked face somehow managed to convey disgust.

"How do you *think*?" he asked, waggling his tail feathers suggestively. Oh!

"Anything up there that would give us good purchase for climbing up, using a grappling hook and a rope?" was Leila's next question. The bird considered. He had absolutely no experience of climbing, grappling hooks, or rope for that matter.

"There are quite a few short, sturdy pipes piercing the roof," he answered.

"You said they have modern plumbing there?" Tevo asked. Leila nodded. She'd told him all about her excursion yesterday. "Those are probably vent pipes, then," he explained. "For water to run down, air must come in from above." She nodded sagely, willing to take his word for it since she had no idea what he was talking about.

The Treasure House had been built before the concept of gutters and drainpipes had been developed; nor had those been added during any of its renovations. Snow and ice could be problematic with gutters, and as the walls of the building were stone there was no fear of runoff rotting the siding. Leila sighed. Drainpipes were one of her favorite methods for scaling buildings, and if gutters were strong enough they might have provided an anchor point for the grappling hook that could support her own slight weight.

"I don't suppose you have strength far beyond that of a normal raven, Yeil?" Leila asked hopefully. Bringing the bird along to carry the hook up onto the roof and wrap it around one of those vent pipes would be nice. But the hook, with the rope attached, probably weighed ten pounds. And Yeil looked like he weighed less than that.

"Sorry," he said a little testily, "what you see is what you get. I can speak two languages fluently, three if you count Raven, but I lack any special powers beyond that."

"Just thought I'd ask," Leila said defensively. They let Yeil go back outside, where he was soon settling down to roost for the night in one of the tall evergreens.

"I think we ought to have something more substantial than cheese," Leila said. "We need to get up in a few hours and go to the Treasure House. Did Marcelina leave anything for us in the icebox?"

"She did!" Tevo grinned. "In fact, I put it out on the dining table for us. Shall we adjourn, my dear?" He offered her his arm. They'd already shed their *kad'r* and were comfortable enough in the clothes they'd been wearing beneath them.

They dined on cold sliced meats, fresh bread, and a sort of salad of cold pickled vegetables with a sweet/sour dressing for dipping. It was all delicious. Then they stripped to their underwear and fell into their respective beds. Both of them had spent years as thieves, and had a good innate sense of time that would let them awaken when the hour was right.

Chapter 78

Cyryl Kubasz was feeling burned out. He'd returned to his day shift harbor duty, watching all of the river traffic docking on this side as well as pedestrians crossing from the far side on the bridge; and he had seen no one remotely like Rosa Estares, her chestnut gelding, or her golden cat. It was if the girl had vanished from the face of the earth.

Standing at the bar in a dockside tavern, he sank his teeth into the greasy but hot and filling sausage sandwich that was, tonight, doing duty for his supper. His shift was over, and he felt fairly starved. As he chewed, a thought occurred to him. Perhaps Rosa Estares *had* vanished from the face of the earth.

She was just a young girl, a sneak thief and perhaps a bit of a con artist. But other than the cat, which could certainly be dispatched with a crossbow or even with a cudgel, she had no personal protection. She might easily have been relieved of her valuables by the first people she tried to sell them to, her body sunk to the bottom of the Vizha and even now drifting out to sea. He shuddered a bit at the thought, and had another bite of his sandwich.

A hand grasped Cyryl's elbow, and he turned with annoyance to see a familiar figure clad in priest's robes standing beside him. The man could not have looked more out of place in this sailors' dive if he'd painted himself purple and begun flying around the room. "What do you want, Radan?" he hissed with annoyance.

"Got something for you, Ran Kubasz," the acolyte said eagerly. The man liked his vices, and his lowly position within the Gaspari church didn't pay enough to cover them; so it had been easy enough for Cyryl to acquire an informant, somebody within the Temple of the Seven who could feed him information. Brother Radan Czersky had proven useful a time or two, but Cyryl found him personally distasteful.

Hastily stuffing the remainder of his sandwich into his mouth and chewing furiously, he grabbed the acolyte by the hand and dragged him through the press of seamen and lowlifes to the door. When his mouth was free again he said, "You need to *think*, Radan! You don't just walk up to me in a crowded bar and started talking about something. You know where my office is. Leave a message there, and I'll get back in touch with you in the usual way."

"Office is closed," Radan replied sullenly. It wasn't bad enough his fellow members of the religious orders at the Temple treated him like something they'd scraped off their shoes – he had to endure it from Ran Kubasz as well.

"It'll open again in the morning," Cyryl pointed out. By now they'd reached the building where Cyryl's team had set up its harbor observation post, and the thief taker led the informant up the stairs to where the night man, Janosz, sat watching the waterfront through binoculars. The room was darkened to prevent anyone seeing him up there, only a faint illumination creeping up the stairs from the ground floor.

"But this is *important!*" Radan whined. Cyryl looked at him in the dim light, waiting for more. The acolyte pulled a much-folded piece of paper out of his monk's robes, and smoothed it out on the table. Not that they could read it without lighting a candle… "You remember you gave me this list of stolen items, told me to keep an eye out and let you know if I saw any of them?"

Cyryl had given copies of the list to everyone he knew, hoping that by blanketing the city with the information he might bring the thief to justice before the treasure had been sold off. Likely she would need money, and it would have been the most logical course of action to simply sell one piece here, another there, to raise a little cash. No fence would suspect she had a hoard worth more than five thousand florins. Except for this list…

Cyryl's mood had soared from tired annoyance to excitement. "You saw one?" he cried, seizing Radan by the front of the robe, "Which one? Where?" The acolyte drew himself up and brushed the thief taker's hands from his robe.

"I expect full payment for the information, and a share of the reward, as well," he said stiffly.

"Of course!" Cyryl said, "No problem – whatever you want! But tell me what you found!" Radan looked at him with a smug expression, barely detectible in this light.

"I didn't see one piece, I saw two dozen of 'em," he said. The thief taker was practically quivering with anticipation. "It was those

Palambo statuettes, they were all on the list and described in detail. And right now, they're on display in the private church museum we've got on the lower floor of the Temple, just for Temple personnel to enjoy."

"What? How…?" Radan's smile deepened. He was really enjoying punching a hole in the thief taker's superior attitude, watching him get all excited about something he, Radan, had found out.

"They were donated to the church just last night," he went on, "by the Palamban high priestess who came into town a few days ago with her acolyte. Her all dressed in black, with the black cat and the black bird and all."

To the acolyte's utter astonishment the dour thief taker seized him by the ears and planted a kiss on his mouth, then pulled every coin he possessed out of his pockets, and dumped them into his lap. "There'll be more, when we collect the reward!" he promised. Then he turned to his associate. "Janosz, put down your binoculars and come with me. We have to go and get the constables to help us with a raid!"

Chapter 79

Leila awoke and looked at her watch, where she'd set it on the nightstand. She'd left a candle burning, not wanting to let her tiredness lead her into too many hours of sleep. She heard Tevo stirring in the bedroom across the hall and put her feet on the floor. Ugh! The night was just getting started and she was already tired.

She dressed in her dark gray burglar gear, and went next door to see how her accomplice was doing. He, too, was already dressed. It seemed as if they lived most of their lives without seeing each other's faces, these days. But soon, perhaps, this would all be over.

Downstairs they used the toilet and gathered their equipment: crowbars, wrecking hammers, goggles for eye protection, a saw, the grappling hook and the rope, among other items. Soon they were ready to set off for the palace complex's hilltop, a goodly hike. But they could scarcely take a cab, this time. They went out the back door and Leila took Tevo by the hand, calling down the shadows around them before they moved to the sidewalk at the front. The two, invisible in the darkness, turned left at the next corner and began climbing upward.

The exercise felt good, Leila found. There had been far too much of riding around in cabs and talking with people since they'd arrived in Parat. Getting her heart rate up and breathing faster left her feeling more clear-headed, less exhausted by her trying conferences with the gods. A secret smile crept over her face behind her hood as she recalled the interview with Dionos. What a scurrilous character, but it had been fun!

Breathing easily but perspiring beneath their snug-fitting "night work" clothing, the two thieves reached the summit and crept into the grounds. The gates to the compound were kept open day and night, as there were members of the Imperial staff on duty at all hours. Armed guards stood on either side of the gates now, at close to midnight; but they didn't notice the shadowy figures as they crept past.

Streetlamps burned through the night hours, illuminating the paved roads that linked the various buildings within the complex. Leila and Tevo left the road and walked into the gardens, hugging the shadows as they made their way around toward the left side of the Treasure House. The front of the building, where all the doors and windows were, was well lit and well-guarded. But the building's sides and back were deep in shadow.

They went back quite a way, wanting to get far enough away from the front that the sound of the grappling hook hitting the slate roof would not be heard by the guards. Here was where the crunch came. If Tevo could not throw the hook up onto the roof, or if it could not find purchase, they'd have to slink back to Pleasance Street with their tails between their legs and go to work on Plan B.

Tevo was strong, and he was able to whirl the hook around on its rope and then hurl it up, up, up. It cleared the edge of the roof, they could barely see in the darkness, and clattered on the slate tiles. There was a faint cracking sound, and a little cascade of broken slate slid down the roof to fall to the ground near where they stood.

The eaves were deep, three feet at least, and the stone bits landed on soft leaf debris from the surrounding shrubs without making a sound. Leila and Tevo, frozen with ears pricked for any indication the guards had noticed the noise, finally moved again. Tevo gave a gentle tug, and the hook slid down off the roof and followed the broken tiles to the ground. Shit!

Half a dozen more tries, and many more bits of broken slate, but still the hook refused to get a purchase on the roof. At least there'd been no sign that the guards had heard anything. "Crap, I was hoping that if I just kept hitting the same spot I'd dig right through the tiles and into the wood beneath," Tevo murmured.

"Even if it did, it probably wouldn't dig in enough to hold my weight," Leila replied softly. "We need to get the rope wrapped around one of those vent pipes, but how are we supposed to know where to aim?"

She looked around in the darkness. An enormous oak tree, more than seventy feet high and in full leaf at this season, grew some fifty feet out from the wall a little further down toward the rear of the building. Its spread was such that its longest limbs strong enough to climb out on would still be twenty feet away – too far to climb and then jump to the building. But maybe they could use it to see where the pipes were!

Leila nudged Tevo and pointed to the tree. "Climb up there and see what you can see," she suggested. He grinned at her, unseen in the darkness, and coiled the rope over his shoulder and around his body, the hook hanging behind him, so that his hands were free. Leila had let slip her shadows as soon as they'd come into this dark area beside the Treasure House.

Tevo was a good climber. Despite his greater weight, he was probably as good at it as Leila was – strong and agile. The ancient oak's bark was rough, and it offered plenty of thick limbs and good handholds all the way from six feet above the ground to near its top. He stopped climbing when he'd gotten to a point a little higher than the eaves of the building, and peered out through the branches. If only it wasn't so damned dark!

He could barely even see the building through the thick branches. But the one he was standing on was strong enough to support his weight, even several feet out from the massive trunk. He began walking along it like a tightrope walker, ducking the upper branches and stepping carefully over water shoots, until he had a good view of the building sprawling before him. The place was huge, and Leila had said that the part you could see was only the top third!

The stone of the walls was pale in the starlight, with some light from the streetlamps more than a hundred feet away on the road reaching him as well. The gently peaked, complicated slate roof was a darkness against the greater darkness of the sky, with here and there paler colored vent pipes poking up from it. They had painted the iron pipes to retard rust, and they looked like a few pale blades of unmown wheat remaining after the field was harvested.

Now, if he could just manage to throw the hook without snagging any of the tree's branches or falling off his perch… Tevo carefully removed the rope from around his shoulder and rested the coil on the branch ahead of him. If it snagged, the hook would be pulled up short. Damn, too bad the raven wasn't one of those mythical rocs, that could just drop them off atop the roof before flying home.

Moving a little further out along the branch, wanting the best possible shot, Tevo felt it start to flex and give beneath his weight. Don't break, don't break! He whirled the hook around on a short length of the rope in his hand, and took aim on the nearest of the vent pipes. It was no more than ten feet in from the edge of the roof.

Tevo released the rope, and the hook flew straight and true. It overshot the pipe, but passed near it at an angle and then, with good momentum, looped back around and went twice around the pipe before one of its tines caught on the rope trailing behind it and it stopped. He'd done it! Tevo took the last bit of rope, now strung across the gap between the tree and the roof, and hurled it off into the darkness so that Leila could get it and start climbing.

As he did so, the branch beneath his feet gave way – not with a crack, thank Betsalel, but by bending so sharply that he lost his footing and fell off of it, hitting the branch below with a sharp release of breath – then slipping, clawing, continued on down toward the ground. Leila's heart was in her throat as she watched him fall.

But in seconds, Tevo recovered his wits and was able to grab a passing smaller branch firmly with both gloved hands. The branch bent and whipped, not strong enough to support his weight; but it slowed his fall, and as he came to the next large branch on that side he landed gracefully and bent his knees. Then he came the rest of the way down to the ground like an acrobat, as if the entire thing had been a planned trick.

Leila's hands were clutched together, her dark eyes glinting in the starlight. He gave a jaunty little bow, and she rushed to throw her arms around him and hug him hard. "Don't *do* that!" she murmured. "You nearly gave me a heart attack."

"All part of the show, ma'am," Tevo murmured back.

With the boy now the anxious one, Leila soon began climbing the rope that was hanging down over the eaves. Another ten feet of it dangled on the ground, and once she'd gotten a few feet up Tevo held the bottom of it to make it easier for her to climb. She soon hauled herself up onto the roof and ran a few extra turns of the rope around the pipe, securing it to the hook to make sure it would take his greater weight. In another minute he was beside her, and they gathered up the hook and rope and headed off toward the part of the building where they hoped Betsalel's idol would be found.

It was very dark up here, and they went carefully. Their earlier attempts with the hook had only added to the damage, and it seemed as though there were loose slates everywhere. Clearly, it had been quite a few years since anybody had performed roof maintenance. Leila wondered how many ancient treasures were being ruined by rainwater and snow melt, leaking in from above.

Suddenly Leila's dark-adapted eyes picked up a white splash in the darkness ahead. Yeil's mark, beyond a doubt! She pulled out a glowstone and checked their location against the map. Shit marks the spot, she thought, and set down her bag of tools. There was another vent pipe a dozen feet back toward the edge of the roof, and Tevo tied the rope firmly to it. They were on a slope here, though not a horribly steep one, and they had to be careful that their bag of tools didn't slip off. That would be almost as much of a disaster as dropping roof tiles on the heads of the guards!

With the bag temporarily secured to the vent pipe for safekeeping, they brought out their crowbars and began quietly removing the besmirched slate tiles from the area that had been marked. They planned to make a hole approximately two feet square, just enough to allow them to slip down into the room with the barred door. In a pinch they could climb back out the hole using the rope, but they hoped that the god himself would be opening their exit path for them once they got him free.

Anxious about making noise, they carefully carried the removed slates down to where two sections of the roof joined, making a valley between them, and stacked them there. A second layer of slates, much deteriorated, lay beneath the first. And beneath that was ancient wood, planks of it – two inches thick, Leila would be willing to bet.

They'd brought an axe, but realized now that the noise it would make chopping through the roof planks would be sure to bring guards back here wondering what the hell was going on. They wouldn't be able to spot them up here in the darkness, unless maybe they climbed that oak tree – but it wouldn't take much imagination to guess that thieves were trying to break in. Fifty feet was awfully long for a ladder, but the Imperial maintenance corps must own such a thing. How else would they get up here to fix those roof leaks?

So, they needed to break through the roof using something that was quieter. Leila used the blunt side of the hand axe to tap quietly in the area of board they'd exposed, locating the rafters. They didn't want to saw through a rafter, and have half this section of the roof collapse under them.

There was a little bit of space between the boards, not a lot but enough to let the wood expand and contract without buckling. Tevo got the tip of his crowbar into a gap and wrenched on it with all his strength, splitting the ancient wood. Bit by bit they enlarged the opening, got the saw blade in there, then began sawing away at it. This was not silent, but the sound was less penetrating and obvious than pounding on the boards with an axe would have been.

The night was cool, but soon both of them were sweating heavily beneath their garments. "Ugh," Leila said, dropping out of her crouch to flop on her butt beside the growing hole. "I'm tired, and we haven't even gotten started on the bricks. If Betsalel's idol is as indestructible as he said, we should have just stolen some of those explosive devices the miners and road builders use."

Tevo kept sawing. While they might have located such a thing here in the largest city in the Dominion, neither of them had any idea how such things were used. They might have freed the Shadow God, but blown themselves to bits in the process. Yet he, too, was starting to wish they'd gotten more sleep.

Finally, with a slight tearing sound, the second of the board sections came loose and plummeted into the cavernous darkness below. Faintly they heard it strike the floor of what they really, really hoped was the room containing Betsalel's entombed idol. They peered down into the opening, but could see nothing at all.

Chapter 80

The Dominion had had more than a thousand years to develop its system of laws, and each succeeding generation of Assembly members had seen fit to add more. So after rounding up two more members of his crew, Cyryl Kubasz took them across the city in a late-running cab to the Central Office of the Parat Constabulary.

The city's police, under the aegis of a separate governmental agency from the Imperial government, operated twenty-four hours a day. But at this hour, forces were reduced and the many branch offices would not have enough staff – or an officer on duty with the authority needed to issue a warrant.

Had a professional thief taker engaged by a private citizen located the thief who was sought, the laws permitted him (rarely her) to take that thief into custody. But the person arrested, and any evidence of their crimes, must then be delivered into the hands of the legal authorities. Nor did Cyryl and his crew have the right to break into a private residence, or even a rented hotel room, in search of thieves or the goods they had stolen.

They brought along the priest, who testified to the lieutenant on night duty regarding evidence that the woman known as the Palamban priestess Laleihala, resident at 320 Pleasance Street, Parat, had delivered to the Temple of the Seven goods identified as having been stolen from Count Wilhelm of Oester.

By the time all of the paperwork had been processed and two constables drafted to accompany them on the raid and verify that the laws were being obeyed, it was past midnight. But Cyryl didn't mind. He'd have been happy to wait another hour or two, if needed. Breaking in on miscreants in the middle of the night, when they were asleep in their beds and were slow to react, was his preferred approach.

The man with Rosa particularly concerned him. So the young girl had not been killed and robbed of the treasure she'd stolen – she'd acquired a protector. The man wasn't particularly large, but he looked competent enough. Surely she wouldn't have bothered hiring his services (with what coin, Cyryl could speculate) unless he was armed and dangerous. Much better if he and his men came upon the pair locked in each other's arms and fast asleep.

They took one of the constabulary's wagons with them – a long box capable of holding a dozen, drawn by four horses. The thing was noisy, so they parked it two blocks away and Cyryl, along with his three crew members and the two constables, crept silently toward the house. Radan had been told to return to the Temple.

They climbed the steps at the front of the house and stood on the front stoop, staring at the hanging on the front door. In the dim light from the streetlamps, many yards away, the red of the painted symbols seemed to jump out at them. All six men stood shuffling, hesitant to try the door as a creeping feeling of unease grew within them.

Cyryl was impatient, eager to get to work. But he didn't want to lose his prey, and kicking the door in might well alert them. At the very least, they might find themselves in a bloody fight. All of them were armed, and all experienced in fighting; but he didn't want anybody hurt, and he wanted the thief and her bodyguard alive and able to testify in court.

"Let's try around back," the thief taker suggested. Though the constables were the ones with the legal authority here, it was he who had instigated this raid and he who was in command of it. They went back down the stairs and around to the rear of the house, shrouded in darkness. The ground sloped up from front to back, and the back door was closer to the ground. But it bore the same symbols as the front.

Once again there was hesitation, each man waiting for somebody *else* to be brave enough to go through the door. Cyryl's impatience and ire were rising. But when he stood before it himself, his sense of unease was so sharp even he had to turn away. There must be magic of some kind in the symbols, he realized. Was it possible that Rosa's disguise as a Palamban priestess had some basis in truth?

Probably she just paid a mage to work up some wards, he guessed. There was nothing to fear, really. Worst-case scenario, six armed men had to fight off a teenage girl, her slightly-built protector, and maybe the cat and the bird. Absolutely nothing to fear! The ominous door was locked, unsurprisingly, but Cyryl produced a set of lockpicks from his pocket and soon had it open.

Yet, as he tried to lead his party in through the door, the fear rose up and threatened to overwhelm him. He stepped backward involuntarily, to the sound of a sharp "crack!" nearby. Turning in the darkness to his left, Cyryl dimly made out the form of Janosz standing near a window with crowbar. The window was open.

"This way!" his fellow thief taker hissed, and profound relief flooded him as he turned away from that dreaded door. Cyryl was the first one to scramble into the house's living room, nearly tripping over a large cushion that was set below the window. As he got his feet on the floor, a feeling of dread washed over him – those hangings were here, as well!

He nearly jumped out of his skin, then, as the air was rent with a demonic "Reeyowl!" and he saw two disembodied, lambent golden eyes staring at him out of the darkness. Cyryl kept a tight grip on his sphincters, as he realized it was only the cat. It was way bigger than your average pussycat, but certainly no catamount or tiger. His men were starting to come in the window behind him, and he turned to warn them "Watch out for that cushion. And the cat's here. Don't kill it – I want it alive as evidence."

He stepped to one side as the rest of the crew came inside, fumbling as they trod on the cushion and spreading out around the darkened room. They weren't afraid of the cat, but one and all felt the nameless dread return as they stood in the living room between the hangings marked with the Shadow God's symbols.

Cyryl was afraid that the thieves would already have been alerted by the cat. That was what Nima pards were used for, he recalled. They stood guard on their masters' caravans and yowled if intruders were spotted. At forty to fifty pounds, the animals surely couldn't be much use for anything besides sounding an alarm – the mastiffs used as guard animals on the estates of the rich weighed four times that much.

Two of the thief takers put their fear aside, concentrating on the animal that had sat silently staring at them from the rear of the room since they'd come in through the window. When they had closed the distance to five feet and the animal hadn't moved, Oddard hissed "Get it!" and they pounced.

With another ear-splitting screech, the cat moved with lightning speed. It raked both men with its claws on the way past, and in another second had scrambled out the open window and was lost in the night. "Shit!" Cyryl exclaimed, keeping his voice down despite his fury. "How hard is it to catch a damn cat?" Oddard displayed his blood-dripping forearms by way of demonstration, and his boss turned his fury elsewhere.

Overcoming the dread by sheer force of anger, Cyryl ripped the two hangings down off the living room walls and flung them out the window after the cat. Immediately everyone in the room felt a flood of relief, all of their fears washed away in an instant.

Cyryl stood panting, enjoying the sensation for a moment as his ears were tuned for the sounds of any reaction to the commotion. The house was dark and silent. Was it possible all that racket had gone unheard? Nobody was stirring upstairs, and he thought he would have heard it if upstairs windows had been opened and the thieves crawled out over the roof to escape.

Or perhaps the house's occupants, alerted by the noise, had armed themselves and were now waiting in ambush for the intruders? Either the thieves were here or they were not, but the thief taker realized that there was no longer any need to operate in darkness. "Get some lamps lit!" he told his men, and in moments light blazed up as they went around with Lucifers lighting the oil lamps in their wall sconces.

The décor in the living room was odd, certainly, but the rest of the ground floor looked ordinary enough. There was no one to be found in the kitchen, dining room, parlor, or bathroom; and the master bedroom looked as if it had never been used. A massive bed was its only furnishing, neatly made up with what looked like new bedding. Were Rosa and her bodyguard even really living here?

The cat's presence certainly suggested they were. Maybe upstairs? There had still been no sounds, and Cyryl was disappointed but not surprised to find the two upstairs bedrooms empty of occupants. The windows were closed and locked from the inside, and the beds showed signs of recent use.

Two beds. In separate rooms. Perhaps he'd wronged Rosa in assuming she'd used her feminine wiles to bind a protector to herself. From the look of things, the two had been here earlier but had gone out. Performing another robbery, perhaps? If they returned and found all the lights ablaze, they would undoubtedly flee. But what could he and his party do? Sit silent in the dark for the rest of the night, hoping their quarry would fall into their arms? "Come on men," Cyryl growled, "let's find the rest of that treasure."

Chapter 81

Leila descended the rope in utter darkness, the feel of a musty but cavernous space around her. She needed both hands to climb down, and felt as if she had been struck blind. Her feet hit something that felt like wood, echoing hollowly, and after getting her balance she pulled out a glowstone.

It made a wan pool of blue light perhaps twenty feet in diameter, not far enough to see the walls of the room around her. But in moments she had taken off her pack and dug out the two small lanterns she'd brought with her. Stepping down off the crate she'd been standing on, Leila set one lantern atop a much smaller crate around ten feet away and lit it. The other she set on the opposite side, and called up through the hole nearly fifty feet above her head, "All right, you can come down."

When Tevo had joined her they looked around in the warm glow of the lanterns at where they'd landed. They had found what they were looking for, all right. The crate they had come down on could only be the one containing Betsalel's idol. It was more than twenty feet long, and perhaps five feet on a side. It must have taken dozens of men to carry it in here!

Four of them, or what was left of them, lay sprawled in a half circle around the room's door. The door was enormous, yet they must barely have been able to get the crate into the room through it. Heavy steel brackets had been fitted into the door's frame, and an even heavier steel bar laid across them. It was probably as much as the four guardsmen (Leila assumed that's what they were, by the tattered remains of the uniforms clothing the skeletons) could lift into place. Then they must have immediately swallowed poison. Such dedication!

Not every item in the Imperial Treasure House was a treasure, apparently. This room, while far from full, contained many items in wooden crates. The Imperial Lumber Room, perhaps. Obviously anything of any great value had been removed from here before the room was sealed.

"It looks like Yeil's sense of his master's location was pretty accurate," Leila remarked quietly. Tevo nodded, then peeled off his mask. That was followed by the jacket that formed the upper part of his burglar costume, leaving him standing with arms and chest bare. She removed her hood as well and grinned at him. "Thinking of a little hanky-panky before we get started freeing the Dark One?" she asked casually.

Tevo blinked at her in surprise, then grinned and shook his head. "I have the feeling this is going to be sweaty work," he replied. The tool bag had come down with him, loaded with their crowbars as well as the saw and the hammers. "You might want to strip off a little yourself," he suggested. "We'd better get started."

The boards of the crate were nearly as thick as those in the roof had been, but this time they could use the axe. The sound of it striking wasn't likely to penetrate to the ears of the guards, up through the hole fifty feet above their heads and all the way to the front of the building. That the noise of their demolition work would alert the guards patrolling the corridors inside the building was a certainty – but then *those* guys were on the other side of a heavily barred door.

Leila was thankful they'd thought to bring along several skins of water – this was thirsty work. As they broke through the crate and began prying up its boards and flinging them aside to expose the brick beneath, she found herself wishing that dear old Oliphant from the Night Guild were here. That man-mountain could have knocked his way through into the idol's tomb with his bare hands, probably. Or at least he'd have been a lot more effective with a hammer than the pair of wiry teenage thieves.

They didn't try to completely dismantle the crate before beginning work on the bricks. The crate had been laid on its side, but there was nothing to say which end was which. So they had picked the end nearest where they'd come down. Leila didn't know how the bird's ability to sense the presence of Betsalel's idol worked, nor was she sure whether the god would be able to manifest inside it if he could not see her. She hoped all it would take was exposing the idol to her own sight and touch, and then the god would free himself the rest of the way and she and Tevo could go off the clock. It had been a *long* twenty-four hours.

Tevo's advice seemed good, and Leila removed the top of her burglar suit to work in her camisole and pants. They each donned protective goggles of the type used by stonemasons, leather with brass frames holding panes of heavy tempered glass. Then, having removed the crating from an area of the brick pillar some four feet long and open on three sides (the side next to the floor being of course unreachable), they each picked up a long-handled sledge hammer and began flailing away at the bricks.

In the dimly lit corridor outside the room, Dzurgo Velisch had completed another lap of his nightly round, his feet moving while his mind drifted. This must surely be the most boring duty on the planet, he thought idly. He'd only joined the Imperial Guard Corps less than a year ago, and he was eagerly looking forward to being promoted. Grunts got the night shift, and if they endured this duty for a year they could work their way up to day shift – and gradually more important and useful tasks.

He'd been told by his sympathetic fellows when he first got this assignment that there hadn't actually been anybody caught breaking into the ground floor of the Treasure House in more than twenty years – longer than Dzurgo had been alive. The warren of underground storage areas, with its many small and portable treasures, was a more frequent target of thieves.

But the ground floor night guards couldn't just find a soft corner and sit down to nap away their shifts – at irregular intervals, an officer on duty out front would make a pass through the corridors, checking up on the grunts. Dzurgo sighed and did an about-face, trudging south again. There was nothing to hear but the sound of his boots on the stone floor.

Or was there? What was that? It was muffled and far-off, but it had sounded a little like the shriek of nails being pried out of wood. He thought it had come from ahead, far down the corridor. Dzurgo broke into a trot, ruefully wishing he had not just been offering a silent prayer to the Seven for something to alleviate his boredom.

He stopped as he neared the second cross-corridor, ears tuned. There, again, and much louder now: the sound of steel striking something hard – like masonry. Were thieves trying to batter their way through the walls of the Treasure House? Absurd, but what else could it be?

Far down the corridor he spotted Alfdan Brugovitz, a fellow night shift grunt. When they could, the night guards tried to time their rounds so that, just by chance, they met each other at the crossing corridors and could stop to chat – ears pricked all the while for the approach of Lieutenant Drovski. "Alfdan!" Dzurgo shouted, "Get up here!"

The two night guards, eyes glinting with excitement, hurried toward the sound. It had become steady now, "Bam! Bam! Bam!" and from the rhythm more than one implement was being wielded. They stopped and stared at the door behind which the noise seemed to be originating.

"Somebody must be trying to break in from outside into this room!" Dzurgo said.

"You nit," Alfdan replied, "There's no outside wall on the other side of this room. Unless somebody's broken into the one behind it, and is now coming through the back wall, they have to be inside the room trying to break out."

The two turned and looked at each other. Neither explanation made any sense, but sure as shit somebody inside this room was pounding on masonry with what sounded like a big wrecking hammer. Or two. "Try the door!" Dzurgo said. Alfdan was his senior in the Corps by some two months and a bit brighter as well, and he was eager to pass this whole quandary over to someone else.

The night guards carried no keys to the storage rooms, but Alfdan knew what Dzurgo meant. He gave the heavy door a shove, and it wiggled a little. More than it should have, if it were locked. Yet it wouldn't open more than a quarter of an inch – certainly not far enough to clear the inside sill.

"Dzurgo, run around the other side and see if the door to…" he calculated in his head, looking up at the number posted above the door, "room M326 is still locked, and see if you can hear any sounds coming through the door if it is. If it's not, don't go in until I get back. I'm going to go get the looey and some reinforcements!" The two dashed down to the crossing corridor together, Dzurgo turning left while Alfdan went right.

Inside room M227, Leila rested the ten-pound head of her hammer on the floor at her feet and writhed, trying to ease the aching in her shoulders. By all the Eight, this was hard work! The hammer head had weighed ten pounds when she first picked it up, but now seemed to weigh fifty – yet its effect on the bricks was no greater. If she gave it all she had, they shattered when the head came down – but each blow removed only one or two bricks. And there were a *lot* of bricks.

Tevo kept swinging, glancing over at her in concern. His little Leila was one of the strongest people he had ever met as well as one of the smartest, but she *was* just a slip of a girl. For all her wiry strength, she was not cut out for demolition work. "Go ahead and rest for a while," he panted. "Have some water!"

She grinned at him thankfully and stooped to get a drink from one of their water skins. While she was at it, she dug a hunk of bread out of her pack and ate a few bites. This was thirsty, *and* hungry, work. Putting the skin back Leila pulled out her watch. Holy crap, past three in the morning. Not that they had a deadline, exactly… But once morning came on, how long would it be before the Guards thought to bring out their fifty-foot ladder and check the roof? Trying to free the Shadow God while neck deep in armed guards seemed like a *bad* idea. Back to work!

They labored for almost another hour, and then cleared the rubble away. The idol was there all right. But it was upside-down! They had opened the wrong end of the crate, and were looking at Betsalel's feet – pointing down toward the floor.

Leila crouched beside them, brushing off brick dust. The stone was black as night, smooth and cold and hard. Inanimate. She put her left hand over her heart, pressing hard as she sought the fragment of the god within her. With her other hand she grasped the idol's foot, calling out to him in her mind. Betsalel! Come to me!

She thought she felt a ripple, a faint tugging as if the god had tried to come through their link. But it faded, and the stone remained cold. Damn! "We have to open the other end, Tevo!" she said – distress and rising panic clear in her voice. "I can't bring him in unless I can see his face!"

Tevo drew an arm across his brow, wiping sweat out of his eyes. He had much greater upper-body strength than Leila did, but he too was tired and aching. And now they had to start all over again. After taking a drink from a water skin the boy swung hard with his hammer, smashing the far corner of the crate to splinters. From the other side of the door, they could hear a rising commotion. They both ignored it.

When Lieutenant Drovski had first been alerted to Cadet Brugovitz rushing out the front door of the Treasure House calling for him, he'd been annoyed. It had been a quiet night in a long stretch of quiet nights, so what on earth was the kid so worked up about? The cadet's story was incoherent. Detailing a couple of the Guard squad from the front to accompany them, Drovski let Brugovitz lead him down the corridor.

From the other direction, they spotted Cadet Velisch running toward them. Not the sharpest knife in the drawer, that one, the lieutenant thought. He joined them just as they were reaching the corridor down which room M227 lay, panting. "Room M326 is locked up tight!" he reported to the group in general, forgetting to salute. The Imperial Guard was the closest thing the Dominion had to an army in this era of the long peace, and it was run like one.

"I told him to check the room on the other side of 227's back wall, sir," Brugovitz explained, "In case for some insane reason somebody had gotten in there so they could break into 227 from behind. It seems like 227 is barred, or maybe something's fallen down inside and blocked the door."

The region around Parat was geologically stable, and there had been no earthquakes here within living memory. But the building was hundreds of years old. Who knew what might have happened before anyone here had been born? That the door could be barred from the inside made no sense.

The party gathered before the door of M227. "It's not locked, sir," Brugovitz said, demonstrating. They could all quite clearly hear the sound of hammers hitting masonry, the sound of shards flying around and striking the bronze door. They were not superstitious men. The gods of their world were real, and approachable, and capable of refuting any unfounded beliefs that might arise regarding the world of the supernatural. But it still gave them all a shiver as they tried to imagine what...*thing* might have awakened inside this sealed room and be trying to hammer its way out.

"Let's all push and see if we can open the door further," Drovski commanded. With five of them throwing all their strength at it, virtually anything small enough to have been locked inside this room in the first place should have been shoved out of the way. But the door wouldn't budge by so much as another eighth of an inch.

"I think it *is* barred," Brugovitz said with a shudder. "What's inside here, anyway?" Drovski didn't know. He was older than the cadets, but not by a hell of a lot.

"Corporal Dietz," he commanded, "Get over to HQ and find somebody who knows what's in this room, or can find someone who does. Come back here as soon as you've got someone."

As the corporal ran off, Drovski addressed the rest of his troops, "Whoever's in there could have just picked the lock and then barred the door behind them." Not that he could imagine why or how one of these rooms should be equipped with a bar. He pulled out his set of keys and handed them to the other guard he'd brought with him from the front. "Mroczkowski, check all the adjoining rooms to make sure somebody's not inside them trying to batter down the walls. And Brugovitz, go out front and see if you can come up with some kind of a battering ram."

Tevo and Leila were quivering on the edge of exhaustion, yet they had only just finished removing enough of the crate's other end so they could start to attack the bricks surrounding the idol's head. Wish I'd thought of those explosives, Leila considered with a sigh. Dying in the explosion would be easier than this...

As they struggled onward, swinging their hammers until their arms felt like lead, the commotion outside the barred door had increased. Soon they heard a loud pounding, as of a battering ram hitting the bronze door. It rang like a bell, but the heavy steel bar and its fittings held. Those had been both bolted and welded to the frame, Leila realized.

Well, the ram might be heavy but it certainly couldn't be all that long. The corridor was no more than fifteen feet wide, so they wouldn't be able to get up much momentum. She was far more concerned about the roof, and in between swings she kept glancing up anxiously at the hole above their heads. All was dark and quiet in that direction.

Drovski and the squad of men he'd drafted from the Treasure House front guard had been battering futilely at the barred door for quite some time, with little effect. What they needed was a proper ram, of the sort he had read about when he was a boy. Back when war was common in the area now covered by the Dominion, there had been mighty castles with stone walls and massive gates. Then, whole tree trunks fitted with handles and heavy iron beaks at the business end had been used against those gates with devastating effect.

Admittedly, according to those same books, the men wielding the ram would have been subject to boiling oil being poured on their heads as they worked. The lack of boiling oil was slight compensation for the fact that he and five others were trying to knock down a heavily barred, solid bronze door set in stone – with an eight-foot balk of timber borrowed from a construction project on the far side of the Palace complex.

They had downed the roughly-hewn log and were taking a break, easing their sore hands, when Corporal Dietz returned. He was not running, but hurrying along – accompanying a bent figure nearly a foot shorter than he was. As they came close enough for Lieutenant Drovski to see who it was in the dim light, he swallowed hard. How much trouble had he just gotten himself into?

General Kurtzin must be eighty if he was a day, but he had seen real military service along the border with Palambo when he was young. Even after a thousand years of peace the Dominion still had to guard its borders, and there were occasional raids along those borders by Palamban tribesmen. The kingdom of Palambo was made up of dozens of different racial and ethnic groups, and its government had its people under much less control than was the case in the Dominion. Only guardsmen who'd seen real military action ever made it to the very highest ranks.

This was whom Dietz had found, to answer the question of what was behind the seemingly impenetrable door of room M227? The most senior member of the Guard Corps (if technically retired from active duty)? Shit. He'd been expecting Dietz to roust some old scholar from over at the Archives out of bed, somebody who wasn't in a position to have the man who'd given those orders busted back to cadet. Shit.

But when the corporal and the elderly general came up, the general didn't look annoyed at having his sleep disturbed. He looked terrified. "You've been banging on the door?" he quavered.

"Yes, sir!" Drovski said, saluting smartly.

"Well, stop! We do *not* want that door opened!"

General Kurtzin peered at the lieutenant, who was looking at him in incomprehension. "What is behind that door has been a state secret of the Dominion for two hundred years!" the old man thundered. "I am the only person living who knows it, the secret to be passed on to my successor by sealed orders – opened only upon my death. Don't just stand there – get more guards, now!" Eyes wide, face pale, Lieutenant Drovski bolted like a hare for the front of the building.

"Can't... lift... my arms..." Leila gasped, the hammer dropping of its own weight to the floor at her feet. So tired!

"Drink some more water," Tevo urged. "We're nearly there!" The top and back of the idol's head and most of its shoulders and back had been exposed, but the face was still buried in brick and rubble.

He swung the hammer again, hitting the edge of the opening in the bricks, and an entire large chunk broke off. There must have been a flaw in the mortar along the fracture line! The section he had freed was enormous. The idol's pose had its arms forward of the body, which meant that there was a good-sized pocket of air within the brick column in front of its face. If they could just pull this massive chunk of masonry away from it!

Tevo tugged, but he weighed no more than a hundred and fifty pounds and he just didn't have enough mass to pull it away by himself. "Leila! Help me!" he cried, "We've almost got him free!" She had been gazing up at the hole in the ceiling, clearly visible now. It was growing light outside.

Leila whipped her head around and realized what Tevo was doing. She picked up one of the crowbars, thrown aside what seemed like ages ago and now half buried in dust and broken masonry. "Let's try to pry it away!" she said eagerly, joining Tevo on the side where the major chunk had broken loose. She inserted the crowbar in between the broken slab and the still-intact main body of the pillar, and pulled on it with all her might.

With a grinding sound, the slab began to come away. A foot or so of it was on the bottom, scraping against the tattered remnants of the crate. The two heaved, and the slab overturned and almost fell on top of them. They jumped out of the way, and it broke into several smaller pieces as it hit the floor.

Tearing off her dusty goggles, Leila ignored the aching of her muscles and slipped beneath the column, under the idol's face. Betsalel, she thought, gazing up at the closed eyes and the enormous but unlit ruby in the forehead, if this doesn't work I'm going to tell Lucia she can have you.

Once again putting her left hand on her heart and reaching up to touch the idol's jeweled third eye, Leila spoke. "Betsalel, I am here. Come to me, please!" She felt it coming, like thunder from a long way off, like a pressure wave in her mind. Light spilled out through her camisole and she felt a searing warmness in her chest as the ruby under her right hand burst into flame. The god's eyes opened.

Chapter 82

"Leila," Betsalel's voice purred in her mind. "You have saved me." She lay back on the bricks, gazing up at him. A transcendent joy was flooding her heart, but it wasn't long before practical considerations intervened.

"My lord," she said weakly, "I think there might be just a few Imperial Guards outside that door. And you're still mostly encased in bricks, I'm afraid..."

The pounding had ceased some time ago, but it sounded as if there was a crowd gathering in the hallway. "Get out of the way, please," came the god's voice. Leila wriggled out from under him and grabbed Tevo by the arm, pulling him back.

"I heard," he told her softly, transfixed with wonder. Though he had supported her whole-heartedly, Leila realized that until this moment he had not, perhaps, fully believed in the truth of their quest.

They stood well off and Betsalel, twenty feet long and in the near presence of two who believed in him wholly, flexed his arms and legs within their sheathing of brick and wood. With a tremendous crash the bricks shattered, the remaining wood of the crate blown to splinters, and the Shadow God got to his feet. He threw his arms back like a man tasting freedom after years of imprisonment, opened his mouth, and roared, "I have returned!" The walls shook, and on the other side of the door General Kurtzin fell into a dead faint.

Betsalel's glistening black flesh was covered in masonry dust, which he banished with a thought. Then he beheld his rescuers. So fully had Tevo given himself over to his task that the god knew him, though they had never met. He stepped toward them, tiny as toddlers in comparison with his height, and touched each of them on the shoulder.

Leila's eyes widened as all her pain, all her exhaustion, vanished in an instant. Dionos had needed no touch to make things happen, and through her astonished delight she wondered if Betsalel just used a different technique, or if he was rusty after not having any powers to use for all these years. Each of the gods had their own unique powers, conveyed to them by the worship and belief of humans – and surcease from pain and restoration of strength were among the powers attributed to the Dark One through his gift of sleep.

Betsalel stood upright again and turned from them, saying "I must go to the Temple of the Seven, and quickly! Come with me!" He stepped to the door and ripped the heavy bar from it, flinging it to one side. Then he heaved on the massive door handle, pulling the door itself from its hinges. The doorway was tall, but even so he had to bend his head as he came through it.

A horde of terrified guards were massed in the corridor outside, and he brushed them aside with sweeps of his arms before turning toward the exit. The Temple of the Seven, his birthplace and the greatest nexus of power on the planet, was calling to him and he needed no map to guide him there.

Leila seized Tevo's arm and cloaked them both in shadows. "Quick, while the guards are still out of commission!" she cried, and they ran through the doors after their departing god. Lieutenant Drovski had been knocked from his feet but not injured or rendered unconscious by the monstrous apparition's assault, and with General Kurtzin still out he was the ranking officer present.

Nobody had bothered to inform Drovski of the dark god's imperviousness to attack, and he rallied his men. That creature must not be unleashed on the helpless citizens of Parat! Even now, the streets would be filling with throngs of them – going about their daily business.

"After it! Shoot!" he commanded the men who were getting to their feet, cocked crossbows in their hands. Half a dozen bolts whizzed out toward the god's retreating back as he marched down to the corridor to the doors at the front. Five of them bounced off harmlessly. At Leila's side, Tevo suddenly collapsed to the ground and she was dragged to a halt. Gasping, she released his arm. Then realizing her own danger in the crossfire, she dispelled her shadows and fell to her knees beside him.

"Tevo, no!" Leila sobbed. This could not be happening, after everything they done, just as they were about to triumph! Still shirtless, Tevo had a small hole halfway down his back on the left side. A widening pool of red was spreading around him on the floor.

The astonished Guards skidded to a halt. Their quarry was already long gone, scattering more of their fellows as he crashed out through the front of the building and made his way down the hill toward the Temple of the Seven. But where had this strangely-dressed, dark-skinned, bald-headed girl and her half-naked companion come from? There had been nothing in front of them but the walking idol when they had fired their weapons.

Lieutenant Drovski came up on them. "Who are you, girl? And how did you get in here?" he demanded. She looked up at him in anguish, tears pouring down her cheeks, then seemed to gather herself. Rising shakily to her feet, Leila banished her sobs.

"I am Laleihala, Mysterion of the Palamban Cult of the True Shadow," she said coldly, her voice hardly quavering at all. "My acolyte and I have accomplished the purpose given to us by our god, Betsalel. He will now resume his rightful place in the pantheon of the church of the Dominion."

Betsalel! The troops pulled back a little. The general had identified the room's occupant only to Drovski, and he had not relayed the information to his troops. Laleihala was hardly an impressive sight, clad in baggy pants and a camisole top, covered in masonry dust. But the fact that she and the shirtless man by her side had appeared out of thin air did add some weight to her words.

"The High Archon and the Seven will deal with your god!" Drovski said, wishing he felt as confident as he sounded.

"The High Archon supports us!" Laleihala replied, "He should be issuing a proclamation declaring that Fernand's destruction of Betsalel's church was a wrongful act, even as we speak! My master goes now to the Temple of the Seven, where he will be received in welcome by his brother and sister gods."

"We'll see about that," the Lieutenant declared. "Seize her! We're going to the Temple of the Seven!" Rough hands grabbed Leila by the shoulders, nearly lifting her off her feet. "Not without my acolyte!" she insisted. One of the Guards looked down at the figure bleeding all over the stone floor. "Sorry, uh, miss, but he's dead."

"No! No, he's not!" Leila shrieked. "I won't let him be dead! Carry him with us, or I'll bring down the power of Shadow on your heads!" Shrugging, Drovski gestured to two of the guards and they scooped the man up off the floor. One of them heaved the body, which didn't weigh all that much, over his shoulder and they came along as the troop, Leila in custody, began following in the god's footsteps.

Chapter 83

It was no use. They'd been here for hours, tearing the house apart. They had ripped up floorboards and searched through the ashes in the boiler, moved the entire pile of coal in the cellar – and the Count's treasures were not here. Could Rosa have sold them all off already, somehow, Cyryl wondered? Or, worse thought, had the thieves somehow learned of the forthcoming raid in advance and made off with them, on the run again?

They had certainly found plenty of other evidence, though, if not the treasures they so desperately wanted to find. Under that unused master bed was a black sack, in size and shape like a sailor's sea bag. Cyryl recalled having seen it, looking quite full, on the back of the black-clad man leading the horse that first day the strangers had come to Parat.

The bag was half-empty now, but it had contained clothing for four or five disguises, makeup, a wig, dye. Some of that clothing had been described in the bulletins as belonging to Rosa Estares. As daylight was coming on one of his men had gone into the garden, warning the servants away and trying to examine the horse more closely to see if it might not really be black. It had nearly killed him.

And hidden in a secret compartment in the floor under the bed in one of the rooms upstairs had been nearly two hundred florins in gold and silver. Not nearly enough to be the proceeds from selling the Oester treasure, but a suspiciously large amount of money anyhow.

The "priestess" and her companion had not returned to the house, and it was now morning. Cursing his luck, Cyryl ordered his men to gather up the evidence they'd found. It would be taken into custody by the constables, including the cash – leaving the thief takers with nothing to show for their night's work. Damn that elusive woman!

The tired and discouraged group of men trudged out the front door, and Cyryl angrily ripped the last of the evil wall hangings from it and threw the thing into the bushes. As they emerged on the street, they realized something exciting was going on. The street was full of people crying out, babbling, gesticulating as they shared the news.

Some were screaming and running for shelter, others (the majority, it seemed) surging south in the direction of the Temple of the Seven little more than a mile away.

One of the constables seized a man by the arm, plucking him out of the river of people flowing south. The citizen was angry, but seeing the uniform and badge he didn't raise a fuss. "What in all the hells is going *on*, man?" the constable demanded angrily. He had been up all night and had no arrest to show for it.

"It's the Shadow God, officer!" the man said, "He's come back, and he's goin' to the Temple. There's going to be a showdown, and I don't want to miss it! Let me go!" The constable, staggered, released the man's arm and in moments he'd rejoined the flow moving toward the Temple.

"Betsalel?" Cyryl asked in disbelief. Like many men of his generation, he had thought the "Evil One" to be nothing but a tale told to frighten children into good behavior. Everyone knew demons weren't real. But all these people seemed to believe that the Shadow God, in the flesh, was here in Parat and heading for the Temple. It made no sense. It was a well-known fact that gods could manifest physically only through their idols – and assuming Betsalel *was* more than a fairy tale, all his idols had been smashed during the reign of Fernand IV centuries ago.

Well, they weren't going to be able to get through this crowd to return to Cyryl's offices – or his home, the thought of which beckoned to him like cool water to a man dying of thirst. Nor were the constables going to be able to carry the evidence with them back to the Central Office. They sat down on the curb, and watched the passing parade.

Only a couple of minutes had elapsed when they began to see Imperial Guards – a lot of them – joining the crowd. Had they been called up as riot police to contain the turmoil that was sweeping the streets? Then Cyryl's head went up as he saw an armed troop marching fast. One of them had what looked like a dead man thrown over his shoulder, naked to the waist. And two others had a small figure held between them: a girl, dark brown of skin, with a shaven head. It was the Palamban priestess – Rosa!

The thief taker bolted to his feet. The guards had the woman he had spent the past weeks of his life searching for – the woman whose capture would have given him a reward that, even shared among his associates, would have set him up with a comfortable life for years to come. No, it wasn't fair! They couldn't have her!

"Come on!" he shouted to his men, "We have to catch them – they've got the girl!" The thief takers all knew what girl their leader meant, and they plunged with him into the street – into a crowd that was filling it from curb to curb and spilling over onto the sidewalks as latecomers sought to gain an edge on those who had come before them. The two constables backed up through the gate onto the property at 320 Pleasance Street and closed it, then peered through the bars at the scene on the other side. The world had gone mad!

Chapter 84

The Shadow God, mindful of the political repercussions of hurting people during his return to power, was very careful not to kill anybody as he hurried toward the Temple of the Seven. What *were* he and his siblings, really, but political creatures – molded and shaped by the masses of humanity, and obtaining their power through them? The spell of indestructibility that scores of his faithful worshipers had given their lives to create still protected his physical form from all harm, so what need had he to take life?

Death was his realm, as were sleep and night. But he did not drag people screaming into death, rather welcoming them in when their time had come. Their souls soon moved onward, finding new bodies or joining The One, and the pain of their mortal bodies was left behind. He was the kindliest of gods, not a creature to be feared!

His goal was at hand, the Temple of the Seven. With his long strides, though he could not run fast without shattering the pavement under his feet, Betsalel had outstripped all his pursuers. There was only the usual crowd you might see here at this hour on any ordinary morning.

People screamed and ran as the Dark God mounted the steps of the temple and went inside. Its portals were tall, as befitted the gods who resided there. Fernand's people had tried to dig up the pedestal, the spot where Betsalel's idol had grown from a formless lump of rock to its current size and shape over many thousands of years. No more able to do that than to destroy the idol, they had built a sort of decorative stone housing over the top, on which rested an ornamental vase. Few who visited the temple knew what lay beneath it.

As some people ran and others cowered in shock, the black god swept the stone structure away. The vase toppled and shattered, slabs of marble fell to the floor as he pushed them to the side and stepped onto the spot where he had been born. With an unbelievable jolt of energy, power surged up in him. As it did, and his mind became clearer, he realized that he had left Leila and Tevo far behind. How was it that he had been able to remain manifested in his idol? It usually required the presence of at least one believer, one worshiper, to provide the conduit.

Then he saw him, the old man. While others of the priesthood ran around like ants from a kicked anthill, this tiny figure remained standing in the center of the Temple – in the spot where the golden urn would have stood to collect the gods' tokens when he was voted into office. He was just an old man, a frail mortal. But he blazed with power, with belief, with love. Betsalel had had no part in this man's choosing, this Gabriel Sforza he learned – as he reached out and knew him. But his siblings had chosen well.

As the Shadow God stood in his place of power, and people realized that he had not come here seeking revenge, members of the priesthood began to drift back into the sanctuary. Many others were crowding in from outside, all of them come to witness what happened here today. That it might be dangerous, to be a close spectator at a battle of the gods, had evidently not occurred to them.

The vast room began to fill, and the High Archon spoke to his underlings. "Open wide the doors!" he cried in a voice with surprising power. "Let all witness the righting of a wrong!" The high priestess Laleihala had not had a chance to inform him of the results of her day-long quest to win the other deities' support – but he had other ways of finding out.

The old priest looked around. Clearly, the high priestess had somehow managed to pull off what he would have thought was impossible to do, given the fact that she had been unable to call on her lord's powers to assist her. So where was she? Why was she not here to witness his moment of triumph?

The sanctuary had eight broad doors, each more than twenty feet tall, and all had now been flung wide so that the building was open to the air around most of its circumference. "Make way," a voice could be dimly heard over the babble of excited voices, coming from the north, "Make way!"

When Lieutenant Drovski had seen Leila's confidence grow as they approached the Temple of the Seven – and realized that the dark god was not in fact wreaking destruction on the city, but rather making a beeline for the place he'd occupied since the dawn of mankind – he ordered his men to escort her without manhandling her.

When they reached the Temple the squad was tasked with pushing through the crowd surrounding it, creating a path so that the priestess of Betsalel could join with her god. The burly guard carrying the limp body of Tevo followed behind. The High Archon smiled as he saw her and her escort approaching, the crowd parting before them. But his expression darkened as he beheld the young man being carried by the guard walking in her wake. Could that be Ademji? The face was hidden. What tragedy was this?

For that matter, the Mysterion's garb was strange indeed. That camisole was a sort of cream color, not black – and while the pants were close to black, their cut didn't seem like anything Gabriel Sforza imagined the Palamban high priestess would be wearing.

Leila broke away from her escort and reached out a hand to the old man, pulling herself into the circle of clear space that surrounded him. "Your Holiness!" she panted, exhausted all over again from their hurried trip. "Call the gods!" she urged, "Now is the time for the world to know that my master is not evil!"

The High Archon looked at her mildly. "I can do that, certainly, my dear," he said. "But I suspect you may be able to do it as well." Leila nodded, realizing the truth of what he said. She pulled the gods' tokens, six of them, out of one of the many pockets hidden in her "night work" pants. Picking one at random, she found it was the one for Belantos. Were divine powers guiding her to repeat the order in which she had spoken with them originally… was it only yesterday? Leila had managed scarcely four hours' sleep in the past thirty-six, and were it not for Betsalel's boost she'd have been collapsing. Anxiety drove her on – she had to do this right, and she had to do it fast!

Approaching the war god's idol, she knelt before it. "Belantos, I beg you to come to me!" she said. "I, Leila, request it!" Leila? The High Archon thought. Maybe it was a nickname? One by one the gods manifested in their idols, coming to the call of this tiny, dark woman few in the massed audience had ever seen. Who was she, that had such power? Only the High Archon was supposed to be able to call the gods at will.

Once again, Dionos was the last. Yet he seemed almost… respectable, by comparison with his comportment the day before. He stood straighter, he was apparently not drunk, and he had an expression of… seriousness, almost, on his finely sculpted features. He gazed out at the crowd as if he were about to do something portentous. Then he looked down at Leila. His lips curved in a slight smile but did not move as his voice spoke in her mind. "Good work, kiddo," he said. And winked.

Now the High Archon took over. Lucia was still conspicuous by her absence, nor was her presence yet required. "Two hundred years ago," he said, his voice somehow carrying to every person in the throng, "our Emperor Fernand IV declared that the worship of the Shadow God, Betsalel, was abomination. He leveled many accusations against the dark god's worshipers, and the people accepted his authority. They rose up and slaughtered all who would not renounce their god, and his idol was removed. The Temple of the Eight became the Temple of the Seven, and all traces of Betsalel's worship were expunged from the land."

The old priest paused, looking around him. The throng was waiting for him to tell them something they didn't know. All right, here we go then… It had occurred to the High Archon that even *he* was not immune to being ripped limb from limb by a mob, if they rejected what he had to say.

"I have recently learned that our late Emperor was led astray by lies told to him by Lucia, the goddess of light." There was a collective gasp. "Yes," the High Archon went on, "we have shaped our gods in our image. And it is well within the power of humankind to lie, to deceive in order to further our own advantage. The gods derive their power from our worship, and Lucia sought to steal the worshipers of her brother and take them for herself."

The crowd broke out into a babble of voices, exclaiming on what the head of the church had said or arguing about it. It was no easier for the average citizen of Parat to accept than it had been for the High Archon himself. The old priest spoke again, and as if by magic the throng went silent.

"Here before you," he said, "stands the Shadow God – returned to his rightful place in the pantheon of our church. His attributes are dark, but they are not unwelcome. The Balance requires that there be darkness and death as there is light and life, male and female, peace and war, seriousness and gaiety. We must honor all of these things, as they are all a part of life. None of these deities is evil, and none without flaw. They belong to us, they are the expression of our humanity. And by our worship, they become more."

There was an awed silence as those assembled considered the High Archon's words. Every listener knew that he spoke the truth. "The Eight came into being as brothers and sisters, all equal and without form," the old priest declared. "Our worship, our needs, have made them as they are. Six of Betsalel's siblings also stand before you. Let them tell you whether I speak truth."

"My brother Betsalel is not evil," Belantos said. "Our sister Lucia sought to steal his power, and succeeded. She is no more pure, and no worse, than any of us. But she deserves censure for what she has done." Everyone there, gods included, paused for a moment. They were all half-expecting the Goddess of Light to manifest and fry them where they stood. But nothing happened.

There was a slight murmuring in the crowd, then Mira spoke. "I confirm what my brother Belantos had told you," she said simply. "It is the truth." Leila stood, face shining with triumph, as each of the manifested gods and goddesses declared the truth of what the High Archon had spoken. The fact that the whole business had started with lies from one of their number was problematic – suddenly the deities of the pantheon were not such unimpeachable witnesses – but the consensus seemed to be carrying the day.

The seven deities standing in the Temple, Betsalel included, were swelling with the power conferred on them by the assembled masses. They felt ready, at last, to face she who had betrayed them all. "High Archon," the Shadow God spoke at last, "I thank you for accepting the truth. It is time for all of us to stand in judgment on she who caused this all by destroying the Balance two hundred years ago. Will you call my sister Lucia?"

Gabriel Sforza steeled himself. Things seemed to be going their way, but the goddess surely had the power to obliterate him on the spot. And ninety-four or not, he was not eager to die. The old man walked over to where the idol of Lucia stood. Gleaming white, spotless, shining in the rays of the sun coming in through the open doors of the sanctuary. Transfixed, the crowd seemed oblivious to danger as they watched him go.

His knees far less stiff than you might expect for one of his years, the High Archon knelt before the gleaming idol. "Lucia," he said, his voice resonating around the room, "I, Gabriel Sforza, High Archon of the Gaspari Church, call you. Come to me." There was no beseeching in his tone. It was more like a command.

The crowd gasped in awe as Lucia's idol flared incandescent white, fading in a moment to its normal color as the goddess manifested within it. She moved her arms and looked down at him, but did not step down off the pedestal that was her conduit to power. Last time they had spoken, he had asked her for the truth about the events of two centuries before. How had he learned of that? Her coup had been a huge success, and she had been basking in the power brought to her by millions ever since. Having only just now manifested in this place, she was quite unaware of what had transpired in the sanctuary in her absence.

"Yes, High Archon," Lucia said haughtily. "You called, and I have answered. Have you reconsidered your ridiculous accusations?" He had asked, not accused, but she wanted to take the upper hand. Then her focus broadened, and she realized in horror that the temple was thronged with people as far as the eye could see.

And standing to her immediate left, beside her as her consort, stood Betsalel. No! It could not be! "You!" she hissed (in a voice that rocked the human observers back on their heels) "It cannot be! I destroyed you!" Betsalel smiled at her, his three red eyes glinting.

"Sister dear," he said sadly. "Surely you must realize that we cannot be destroyed? We are eternal, created to serve the people of this world, living forever until the end of time."

"You know what I meant," she replied frostily. "You are evil, wrong, a blackness! You dim my light by your very presence, and nobody loves you! Who could love death and darkness?"

Lucia looked around the room: at the people standing in awe at the spectacle of two deities having a family spat; at the old High Archon standing firm in the center of the room; at her siblings, all of them manifest in their idols, standing on their centers of power and looking at her with disapproval.

"So that's it?" she said, her voice rising toward a shriek, "You're all against me? I should have *known* you would all conspire against me in the end! I am the Goddess of Light! All goodness flows through me. Me! Without me, all of you are nothing!" Leila stood entranced, mouth open in wonder. The Goddess of Light appeared to have gone off the deep end.

"That's it!" Lucia snapped, still not moving off her power nexus. Had the worshipers a better understanding of the importance of the exact spot where the idol stood, they might have been less worried about their gods stepping down and going on a murderous rampage.

"I will withdraw my light!" the goddess averred. "If this black beast" – she gestured at Betsalel – "is not cast back into the darkness where he belongs, I will blot out the sun! Do not doubt that I can do it!" Lucia concentrated her energy, and the crowd cried out in consternation as a shadow fell across the temple. The sun seemed to be ebbing, fading moment by moment.

"*I* doubt it!" Leila cried out, her voice ringing loudly and somehow managing to drown out the frightened murmurs of the crowd. Everyone stared at her. "You seek to shadow the sun, Lucia," the dark girl said. "But the sun is a natural part of our universe, not a gift from you! And shadow is your brother's domain, not yours – you have *no power* to withdraw the light!"

The crowd's murmur rose to a roar as the sun's light increased. The Goddess of Light seemed to shrivel before them, and as the people's belief in her collapsed like a sodden tent her power left her in a rush. "You!" she shrieked, "You will pay…" With that the idol's surface dimmed, less white than it had been before. The goddess was gone.

Chapter 85

The murmur became a roar as the observers reacted to what they had seen. Lucia, chiefest of the Seven, had proven false! She did not have the power she claimed, and she was losing more of it by the second as the news spread. And if there is a loser in the contest, must there not also be a winner?

"Betsalel! Betsalel!" the crowd chanted, and the Shadow God was astounded. All he had wanted from this was to be returned to his rightful place, to be acknowledged as part of the Balance. The acclaim made no sense. It was all due to Leila, he realized – the little thief who had literally taken him into her heart.

Swelling with power, Betsalel stepped down from his pedestal. He had no need of the nexus, while waves of human belief were pouring into him. "Leila," he said gently, "this moment is yours. Whatever thing you want, I shall grant it to you." Freedom, she thought, I want my freedom. To be who I am – no more hiding, no more impossible quests.

"Tevo!" Leila cried. The guard holding the boy's limp form came forward and laid him, face up, on the temple floor. His face was ashen below the dark dye, his chest covered in blood where the crossbow bolt had passed through him. "Heal him, Betsalel, heal him!" the girl demanded. Tears were starting in her eyes, running down her cheeks. She knew.

The Shadow God lowered his head, looking down on them with sadness. "I'm sorry, little one," he said in his deep, dark voice. "He is dead."

"I don't *care*!" she screamed, the tears streaming freely now. "You are a god, you can do anything! Bring him back! It's the only thing I ask!"

With that the girl fell to her knees, throwing herself across the body of the boy, sobbing. Betsalel looked down at her, his heart rent with grief. She had done everything for him, everything! And the boy had helped her whole-heartedly, questioning nothing. Could he not do the one thing she asked?

He looked up at the crowd, and the power of their belief, their hope, came rushing at him like an avalanche. Raise him, raise him, they seemed to be saying from their hearts. Prove your goodness with this act of mercy, release the boy from your realm of death, and we will cleave to you! It is the price of our worship!

Twenty feet tall was far too much for interacting with mortals. Betsalel shrank himself to a more manageable six feet and knelt, putting his hand on Leila's shoulder gently. "Leila," he murmured for her ears alone, "let me in." She rose up in wonder, scarcely daring to hope, tears drying in her wide eyes as he put his hands on Tevo's body.

The wound in the boy's torso closed, the skin unblemished. Slowly, a flush rose to replace the pallor in his dye-darkened cheeks. Then with a surprising flash of light, his chest rose. And fell, and rose again. Tevo opened his eyes, and struggled into a sitting position. The crowd broke into a scream of adulation.

Chapter 86

The drama was over, and the crowd (still higher than kites on the morning's incredible happenings) was starting to disperse. Cyryl and his men, after struggling impotently – unable to move an inch for close to half an hour – were at last able to push their way into the sanctuary.

They found the girl they were convinced was Rosa Estares, her arm around the waist of an equally dark young man, standing in the center of the Temple of the Seven. Or was it now eight? They were in conference with an old man Cyryl recognized as the High Archon – and with the Shadow God, currently looking like a tall, muscular, three-eyed, and very black man.

Cyryl had long since passed the point of owning any good sense. It had been a long night; and so far, a very frustrating morning. "Rosa Estares!" he shouted, marching up and seizing the girl's arm. "As a duly licensed thief taker within the municipality of Parat, I hereby arrest you on the charge of stealing certain treasures from the collections of the Count of Oester!"

Leila looked at him in astonishment. Really? After all that? The dark god grew half a foot taller. "You shall not have her," he said quietly. "She is my high priestess, the first and foremost of my new church, and she stands above your laws." Cyryl sputtered. As Betsalel grew another foot, he suddenly realized he was standing on shaky ground. No! It simply wasn't *fair*!

"But she's a thief! Uh, your… darkness?" he stammered lamely. What am I doing, he asked himself in shock. Arguing with a *god*?

"Oh, I know," Betsalel replied smoothly. Growing another foot. "She has stolen a part of me, and I hope that she never lets it go."

Leila looked up at him. She'd been hoping that she might still sneak in that wish for freedom, after the god had granted her the most important one. She sighed. "Sir," she began, addressing the thief taker, "uh, I don't believe we've been introduced?" Cyryl nodded to her. Whatever else he felt about this young woman, he had to grant her his respect.

"Cyryl Kubasz," he said, presenting his warrant for her inspection.

"Leila," she responded with a slight curtsy. "No surname, at this time. I freely admit that I, under the name of Rosa Estares and in the employ of Count Wilhelm of Oester, did take some things that didn't belong to me." He stared at her slack-jawed.

"What can I say?" Leila dimpled at him (an effect that might have worked better if she'd had some hair and not been covered in dirt, sweat, and masonry dust), "I had a troubled childhood. But I am truly repentant for my crime, and I would like to return to Count Oester all that I have stolen from him."

Cyryl still hadn't formulated a reply, and Leila continued, "I regret that the Palamban statuettes have been donated to the Temple of the Eight. Your Holiness," she went on, addressing the old man beside them. "I must apologize for presenting the Temple with goods that were not really mine to bestow. Would you consider returning them to their rightful owner?"

Gabriel Sforza looked at her fondly. The little imp, she had had him completely fooled! But Palamban or not, she truly was Betsalel's priestess. As the boy was his acolyte. He had literally given his life for his god – and had it given back again!

He eyed the thief taker with reproach. "Perhaps, this Count Wilhelm would be satisfied with the temple's thanks for a truly precious gift?" he suggested. "The pieces are really lovely, and his generosity would of course be greatly appreciated."

Cyryl shuffled uncomfortably from foot to foot. He had been so close to winning everything, and now he was beginning to get the idea he'd be lucky to escape with his skin. "I'm confident the count would be delighted with the church's gratitude," he mumbled. He wasn't confident at all, had not even met the count; but surely the man could be reasoned with?

"So," he said to the girl thief/priestess. "Please tell me where I can find the rest of the count's treasures, and I will be on my way. My claim on you appears to have been superseded." Leila smiled sweetly at him.

"Thank you, Cyryl," she addressed him familiarly. "Do you happen to have a shovel on you? And perhaps, some gloves?"

Epilogue

Darkness was falling on Parat, and the High Priestess Leila and her acolyte Tevo were finishing a delicious meal in the dining room at 320 Pleasance Street. Marcelina had been distraught at the destruction the search party had wrought, and she and Maks had spent most of the day putting the place to rights. Then she'd outdone herself with this meal, and Leila (now bathed, able to dress as she pleased, and hoping her hair would soon be growing out) had given her a two-florin bonus and sent her off for the evening.

Lacking any evidence to prove that the money confiscated from the house was illegally gained, the constables had returned it – and the rest of their possessions – earlier this afternoon. Count Oester's treasures, cleaned and deodorized, were now on their way back to their owner.

Leila and Tevo were sitting close together at one end of the table, finishing their wine and toying with the last morsels of rare beef on their plates. They were holding hands. "I still can't believe I was really dead," he said. "One second I was running down that corridor with you, and the next I was looking up at the ceiling of the sanctuary with you and the High Archon and Betsalel looking down at me. And I felt fine."

She smiled and kissed him. "You were my one big wish, sweetie," Leila said softly. "If I never get another one, it was worth it." He clasped her hand tighter and looked into her eyes.

"But what about freedom?" He asked, "Wasn't Betsalel supposed to take back his gem and release you from his service, after you restored him to his place in the pantheon?"

Leila nodded a little sadly. "But he still needs me," she said thoughtfully. And he loves me, Tevo. I can feel it inside me." She set down her wine glass, which was empty anyway, and rested a hand over her heart." With a sigh she added, "I know I'm going to absolutely hate it here when winter comes."

"Maybe the Temple of the Shadow needs to have a winter retreat," Tevo suggested, pulling her hand from her breast and kissing the fingers. "We could set up a branch temple in, say, Jena?"

She gave him a brilliant smile and threw an arm around his neck, drawing him close for a deep kiss. "I love you, Tevo," she said simply. They rose from their chairs and embraced, kissing each other with greater concentration now.

"Leila," Tevo breathed as they pulled apart, coming up for air. "How long have you been drinking your 'special tea'?"

"Long enough," she murmured, and fell back into his arms.

The End (for now)